Dreams Held Fast

A novel by Frances Anne Cooney

&

Caryn H. Shaw

Dreams

By Langston Hughes

Hold fast to dreams

For if dreams die

Life is a broken-winged bird

That cannot fly.

Hold fast to dreams

For when dreams go

Life is a barren field

Frozen with snow.

Prologue

Dreams are bizarre phenomena. Everyone has them. We don't always remember them upon waking. They keep us going and give us hope; that is, most of the time. Often though, they are insights delving into our psyche' and could be as harmless as wish-fulfillment for a sexual tete' a tete' or inspiration for a creative ambition. They could be a struggle to rescue a beloved friend or revenge filled with violent thoughts of murdering one's enemy. We are not responsible for what we dream. Her dreams kept her going and evened out her uneven coping skills during the day. Many times they were attributed to her basic desires and her striving for the fame and success she craved. However, some of her dreamscapes were formed out of loneliness and the longing for sexual gratification from her latest conquest.

> *"They agree to play games. "Here are my rules. You can do anything to me but you cannot kiss me on the mouth, she says provocatively. Kissing my mouth is forbidden." "*

Some dreams were whimsical and a wonderful release to her fantasies and freedom.

> *"Off in the distance was a young man with a blond curl poking out of a top hat. He was wearing tap shoes. She thought it was comical since they were on a beach. Just then he reached out his hand and said, "Let's hit it, Ginger.""*

Some dreams were sad, yearning to bring a loved one back to life, even though she knew she couldn't save him.

> *"She sees the sallow skin of the man in the bed turn a baby pink color as the sides of his mouth curve upwards. She gravitates towards the body. Her warm lips touch his stone-cold lips."*

Some dreams were humorous, seeking her own form of comical revenge.

> *"She raised one of her fingers and put a deep gash across his lips, with her bright, red fingernail, dragging the rest of her hand along for the ride."*

Once in a while her "night frights" took her to the dark side. They were filled with vengeance and the need to "get even" when she felt desperate or scared. What she could not manage in her waking life, she resolved to take care of in her darkest "reves la noir." "She had erased him from her forever; rubbed him away; rubbed him out. She then walked around the side of the pool table where he was, kicked him in the leg to ensure there was no movement, and proceeded to slowly walk home."

We invite you to read on and learn the secrets and mystery; the inspiration and gratification; the innocence and the expectation of her deepest desires. The other characters you will meet will bring their perspective too. They will lead you on a journey full of honesty, intrigue, and humor with surprises on nearly every page.

Nonetheless, the ultimate interpretation of all of the dreams will be left solely up to you!

1

Contents

PART ONE
CHAPTER 1
Revenge

Patsy Mahoney sat at the makeshift vanity in her tiny bedroom, staring forlornly at her 32AA breasts. She squeezed them together, wondering if her latest heartthrob Fred Astaire would find her cleavage acceptable, then stuffed tissues into the cups of her bra to make them Bs—or at least full As.

Most 13-year-old girls ogled over David Cassidy, Donny Osmond, or John Travolta, but not Patsy. Her mother's passion for old-time movies really rubbed off on her. She was infatuated with the stars from the 1930s and 40s. Today, she danced around her room in her underwear, pretending to sway along with Fred in his top hat.

Not to say she didn't like the stars of her generation. She loved to turn up her transistor radio when Andy Gibb came on singing, *I Just Want to Be Your Everything*. She'd blurt out in full Bee Gee falsetto, *"Open up the heaven in your heart and let me be, the things you mean to me, and not a puppet on a string."*

Shouts and the rumbling of floorboards outside her door upstaged the music, interrupting her perfect dreamscape. She let out a fierce "Shut up!" to her bratty siblings running up and down the narrow hallway outside her room.

Her younger brothers—Michael, Patrick, and Brian—were chasing their poor little sister, Cathleen, yelling in unison, "Duck, Duck, Goose!"

Then, Michael shouted, "Run, run, fat moose!"

Cathleen pleaded as she called downstairs, "Mom, make them stop!"

Her mother Bridget spoke up from the bottom step in a monotonous voice, "You boys get down here and leave that child alone."

The boys didn't stop, and Patsy, enraged, tasted bitter bile in the back of her throat. She quickly pulled on a robe, picked up laughter when her brothers mocked her about stuffing her bra. She wanted to embarrass him the same way he shamed her. She was seething inside and getting ready for her big one-liner a la Betty Davis or Katherine Hepburn.

As the kids tried their best to grab their coats and hats, the men began to shuffle in and took their regular seats at the bar.

Roney yelled out again, "Dammit, Bridget, can't you move these kids out any faster? The guys are lining up to get in. Next time no cake and ice cream. Do you hear me?"

That did it. Before her mom could say a word, Patsy shouted, so the kids and adults could hear, "Leave my mother alone! Don't be so damned impatient."

Roney, already half-drunk and in a fury, jumped out from behind the bar and stood in front of Patsy. His hot whiskey breath spread like a bitter stench as he raised his right arm to backhand her. Patsy didn't flinch. "You little bitch. You shut your pie hole and mind your own goddamn business."

Bridget intervened, but Roney pushed her aside just as the last few kids began to whimper and run to the exit. "Stop it, Roney, you're scaring the children."

The last of the patrons shuffled in, astounded at the scene. Some made a move to break up the altercation, but most stayed back. No one wanted to mess with a drunk Roney.

Patsy didn't move an inch or say a word.

Everyone was staring at Roney now. He walked back behind the bar and poured a large whiskey, muttering under his breath, "I'll be stoppin' this kiddie show if me wife can't keep to me own schedule. I tell you, I will." He downed a half bottle of Southern Comfort before disappearing for the rest of the night. His brothers told everyone he was sick, but the crowd buzzed about the incident far into the night.

Patsy basked in the sweetness of her long-awaited revenge. She exposed her rotten father for the major asshole he'd always been. It was a perfect part to play and she, at long last, was both leading lady and heroine. She gave herself three curtain calls and a standing ovation.

CHAPTER 2
Dance

Patsy and her mom spent most evenings together. Roney usually didn't come home until past midnight. Patsy's favorite time was when her father was out, Cathleen was asleep, and the boys were watching TV in the basement. Often, Bridget put on a show just for Patsy, or they danced together. Tonight, they would be Irish dancing.

"Are you ready?" Bridget asked after they pushed the couch against the wall.

"Ready!" Patsy sat on the loveseat to watch.

Bridget held her arms down by her sides as she rhythmically clicked her heels and tapped her toes. There was a lightness to her step, despite the drama of the metal striking the hardwood. Her long blond hair flowed with each movement and there was a gleam in her blue-green eyes as her smile radiated throughout the room. Bridget looked young, like she did in old pictures Patsy thought, even with the crow's feet by her eyes and the gray hairs around her scalp.

"Bravo! Bravo!" Pasty leapt up, cheering on her mom.

"Thank you, thank you," Bridget said as she took a graceful curtsey and plopped down on the well-worn loveseat. Patsy sat again too, and cuddled up next to her mom.

"You're as good as Ginger Rogers, Mom. Even better I think. Remember that scene in *Swing Time* when Ginger and Fred are in dance class together? That was one of my favorites. They were made for each other," Patsy said, longing to be in love herself.

"And don't forget Gene Kelly and Leslie Caron in *An American in Paris,*" Bridget added.

Patsy envisioned dancing with a man who sweeps her up in his arms and dips her deep before holding her close again.

"And I just love *Daddy Long Legs*!" Bridget remembered. "Leslie Caron was such a beauty. She made every

10

move and every motion look so very graceful and natural." They sat in silence for a moment, drifting off into their own fantasies.

Bridget rose and started tapping on the wood floor as if the Greek muse of dance Terpsichore summoned her. Her shoes clicked melodically on the wood. When the front door flew open, Patsy's body tensed up, and her heart began to pound. Her drunken father stood at the entranceway. He took one thunderous step into the house and the whole floor vibrated. Bridget stopped and lost her beautiful posture.

What was he doing home so early? They were having so much fun.

Patsy was so strong at the bar a few months before. Her dad seemed more cautious with her since then, so she didn't understand the fear overtaking her right now. She opened her mouth, but nothing came out. She looked over to the kitchen, thinking about the drawer full of knives and wishing she held one right now. But she did not want to leave her mother alone in the room, even for a minute.

Roney's bloodshot eyes glared at Bridget. He stared at the stacks of laundry, and the many different-sized coats and shoes strewn around the room. Bridget wilted as she raced to the piles, collecting coats, hats, and gloves. Patsy glared at Roney as he took shaky steps towards Bridget, his face red, a vein pulsing on the side of his neck. Bridget kept her head bowed, refusing to look up at her husband.

"Why is this house so goddamn messy? What's the use of having women around that don't clean?" Roney slurred. He moved closer to Bridget, and Patsy's heart pounded harder with each step.

"I'm hungry. I hope someone left me some food."

"Yes, it's in the kitchen. I'll get it right away," Bridget said as she stood with a bundle of clothing in her arms. Unbalanced, she leaned on the loveseat behind her, now face-to-face with Roney with just inches between them.

11

As Roney stepped forward and lunged towards Bridget, Patsy jumped in front of Bridget, "Don't touch my mother!"

"I'm just going to sit down, you stupid bitch," he sneered as he pushed Patsy out of the way and fell onto the couch.

Her fear, and a new surge of hatred she knew she would feel for the rest of her life, lay on her like an ugly stain that wouldn't wash off. She turned and sprinted up the dark, narrow stairway to her room. She thought she heard her mom call "Patsy" after her, but it was drowned out by Roney's barking. "Get me some food, woman. I'm hungry."

Patsy entered her dark bedroom and quietly clicked the door shut so as not to draw her father's anger upstairs. She pressed her back up against the door and slowly slid down it, each vertebra pressed into the hard wood until she collapsed on the floor. A chill came over her, yet she was sweating. Her mouth watered as a lump formed in her throat. Her mantra, *I hate him, I hate him,* played over and over in her mind as a dark gloom settled within her.

She feared an impending attack. Her eyes darted back and forth in the darkness as she clenched her jaw to stop the chaos in her brain. Her head felt like it was exploding, and she could hear her heart pounding as her body shook uncontrollably. It happened before—this sensation—and she was terrified. Sometimes, she feared she'd die. She shook her head wildly again and again until finally, thankfully, it passed. She began to cry.

CHAPTER 3
Smells

School was Patsy's escape, her excuse to be away from her horrible father and obnoxious brothers, who seemed to be turning into replicas of Roney and his critical *I'm-the-man-so-you-do-what-I say* ways. Patsy worked hard to do well in school. It made her feel good about herself and it proved that females were just as smart as males, despite what her father thought.

She joined a few after-school clubs to stay away from home longer, but not too long. She knew if they interfered with her home chores, work at the family bar, or the dreaded babysitting, she wouldn't be allowed to continue.

She also went to the first tryout for the class play. As she walked into the crowded auditorium, she noticed a cute boy rehearsing. She stared at him—he was so animated and cheerful as he headed for the stage, almost dancing up the steps. For a split second, she imagined herself as his leading lady. Just as swiftly, her confidence waned, and she walked towards the group laughing and having fun on the side of the stage. When she saw the competition up close, she hurried out, feeling not good enough. She convinced herself she couldn't stay anyway because chores, waiting tables, and dirty noses were waiting for her.

All the way home she fantasized about the cute boy. He was in her French and math classes. His name was Henry, and he was so different from the other boys. He for sure wasn't a jock, which was the last type of guy she'd ever want to be around. He wasn't a chess-club guy, and he wasn't a loser. He was, well, he was Henry—her Henry as she secretly began to think of him, making up scenes in her head of how they would become friends, then eventually lovers.

One day, early for French class and strolling the hall, Patsy felt pretty, wearing a new pink pastel V-neck blouse she thought was quite feminine. She stopped abruptly though, overcome by a foul odor. She barely heard the janitor, Mr. Hopkins call out, "Careful girlie, clean-up ahead, walk the other way."

Patsy nearly choked as the acrid smell of Lysol and vomit invaded her nostrils, reminding her of an ugly scene from her childhood. Her face grew red, and her head started to spin. She couldn't figure out what was causing her body to react so severely. "Sorry, Mr. Hopkins," she said, almost losing her balance and nearly slipping on the wet floor.

"You okay, Dear?" he asked.

"I'm okay," Patsy cried as she ran to the ladies room, her eyes stinging and her heart pounding. She entered the bathroom stall and collapsed on the toilet seat, shaking. Transported to the past by the memory of that awful smell, she swayed back and forth, covering her nose with a wad of toilet paper. She couldn't stop trembling as her mind drifted to thoughts of her mother.

Bridget, very pregnant, holds her nose while mopping the floor of their family bar as her father, drunk and smiling, just sat there pouring himself another glass of Jack Daniels. He raised his glass, "To my wife, the cleaner of floors, the maker of babies, and the dancer that never was." Her mother glared at her father, then continued mopping.

Patsy recalled the pity she felt for her poor mother as she strained to listen to the rest of the conversation. She wanted to attack her father, but knew she was helpless. Her whole body shook as she clenched her fists to control the tremors.

Under her breath, Patsy's mother mumbled, "Shut up, you rotten bastard," but her dad didn't hear while banging his way through whiskey bottles in search of another drink. Only Patsy heard as she crouched behind the piled-up empty beer crates beside the door, her eyes tearing up again.

Fighting the disinfectant smell and burying her nose in her sleeve, she willed herself to stay quiet. That combination of disgust and despair on her mother's face remained engrained in

Patsy's memory, and so did the anger and fear. But, she buried it for so long....

Why did this awful memory come to haunt her now she thought as she snapped back to reality? She was alone in the bathroom, but when she heard several girls enter she jumped up. She washed her hands, feigning normalcy, and said a quick hello to the girls.

Anxiety turned to worry as she was late for class. She ran down the hall, shoving a wad of toilet tissue into her jacket pocket, trying to compose herself. She stopped briefly to remove her jacket to show off her V-neck blouse, and calmly walked into French class. The scent that awaited her there was almost magical. Like a miracle, an aromatic cologne wafted through the air and transformed her.

Patsy took her seat. Henry's fragrance made her body tingle as she took several deep breaths in and out, feeling his essence permeate her lungs. Gathering all her courage, she murmured a pleasant, "Bonjour." She almost added, *"You smell tres bien,"* but couldn't.

He whispered back, "Bonjour," and his bright white smile nearly melted her heart.

It was 1980, and they were both fourteen. Henry was dressed like Michael Jackson, with an open button-down deep red shirt over a tight white t-shirt, white socks with black Capezio shoes, and of course, the sparkling white glove. Patsy watched him remove his glove and pick up a pen, opening his textbook and thumbing through to a clean page in his notebook.

She laughed to herself, thinking his blond ringlets and ocean blue eyes were quite a contrast to Michael Jackson's dark hair and dark eyes. She knew most of her friends thought Henry was flamboyant and funny in a weird sort of way, not like the football jocks they drooled over, but Patsy couldn't take her eyes off him.

She opened her textbook and dreamed of a joyous French tete-a-tete with Henry as the class discussed the south of France.

15

She inhaled his cologne again as she fantasized about romance on a Saint Tropez beach. Just as the dream was about to intensify, the teacher ended class with, "Adieu, mes amis."

Patsy, quickly brought back to reality, gathered her belongings. As she walked by Henry's desk, she took another deep breath. That would have to do for now.

She hurried off to her next class, avoiding any unpleasant odors in the hall, trying to lose herself in a utopia of Henry's lovely scent. She breathed in deeply as she imagined waves breaking on a secluded beach, with both their sun-warmed bodies moving toward each other to share a first kiss. For the rest of the day, she held that image in her heart.

CHAPTER 4
Henry

As she walked up the path to the Klein house, Patsy was still shocked her mother let her go to a friend's house on a Friday afternoon. Fridays were a hectic night at Mahoney's Bar, and Patsy usually waited tables while keeping an eye on her younger siblings. Thanks to her mom, she was relieved of the strict schedule for today.

Patsy took a deep breath as her index finger pressed the doorbell. She patted down the wrinkles in her acid-washed jeans and fluffed up her teased and sprayed strawberry blond hair. The door opened and she was startled to see Henry.

"Bonjour," he said.

Patsy nervously mumbled back a tongue-tied, "Bonjour." Henry acknowledging their *bonjours* from French class made her heart skip a beat.

She took him in completely. He wore tight jeans and a bright blue plaid button-down shirt. The blue in his shirt made his crystal-clear eyes stand out even more. Although he usually wore the same type of clothes, his shoes changed often— Capezios, snakeskin boots, green suede moccasins, soft brown loafers. He seemed to own them all. He also had on his cute round rimless glasses. Patsy was fascinated with the way he set the glasses low on his nose, even though she was sure they were only an accessory and could see perfectly well without them.

"What are you doing here?" Patsy asked sweetly.

"I hang out here pretty much every Friday. Anything is better than being home." Patsy nodded in agreement. She understood well. "Do you want a drink?" he asked.

"Sure!" Patsy followed him, looking at the outline of his calves through his jeans. His soft brown loafers gracefully touched every step up to the kitchen area. She got a whiff of his sweet floral scent and took several deep breaths. It made her dizzy…in a good way.

17

"Susan does this every Friday after school. Her parents don't get home 'til seven. They assume her older brother Larry is watching us, but Larry's never home, or he's locked in his bedroom with his girlfriend."

"So where are Susan and the others now?" Patsy asked, sitting at the kitchen table.

"They went to fool around." Henry said, as he took a couple of beers out of the fridge.

"Oh, okay," she said, a bit surprised, but didn't want to show it.

During eighth grade, Patsy couldn't believe how some of her classmates, Susan Klein, Denise O'Malley, and Laura Romano—girls who were never much to look at—sprouted breasts and curves as if they were eighteen, not fourteen. The boys couldn't stop staring at them.

"Make some room for those Double Ds," Anthony Giannotti would exclaim as Susan walked into French class. Anthony would then pull a desk chair away, motioning for Susan to sit down next to him.

"Oh, shut up," Susan always said, wearing her painted-on GUESS jeans, glaring at him with a flirtatious grin.

Patsy wondered if Henry noticed how developed these other girls were. He usually seemed to be in a fantasy world all his own when Patsy saw him—like herself, she thought. He was so unlike the other boys who practically salivated every time one of the girls with big boobs walked into a room.

Patsy felt a tinge of guilt. She knew her mother would disapprove of her being in a house with all these kids, especially boys. Plus, if her mother knew Susan's parents weren't home, Patsy would be grounded and never allowed out of the house again except for work and school. Even worse, if her dad found out where she was and who she was with, it would be a disaster. She swallowed hard thinking what Roney might do, but those thoughts vanished as she focused on Henry.

Henry found a bottle opener and easily opened both beers. He set one in front of Patsy. "Cheers!" he said as he raised his bottle and chugged half of it down in record time. Patsy did the same.

"Are you and Susan good friends?" Henry asked.

"Well, I knew her in elementary school, but we really got to know each other this year in French. I borrowed a pencil from her because I forgot my mine since I had to help my brothers and sister pack their lunch, check their homework, button their coats, and even tie their shoes." Henry listened politely, but Patsy finally realized that she was sharing too much information and ended the story.

"I was just wondering because I've never seen you here before." They simultaneously banged their empties on the table and Henry got up to get them each another beer. "How did you learn to drink like that? Most girls I know take a sip at a time, and it takes them all night to finish one beer."

"I've spent many days sneaking beers at Mahoney's, although I don't even need to sneak them. My father believes the drinking age laws in the United States are ridiculous and that we should follow the wisdom of other countries like Ireland, which has no drinking age. Of course, most normal parents have causes like women's rights, animal activism, or cancer research, but my father wants to eliminate the drinking age in the US." Only an alcoholic could believe in such a cause, Patsy wanted to say but didn't. She'd already said enough about her awful father and changed the conversation, "So, what's your favorite thing to do?" She watched Henry's face intently. His fair skin was so smooth, she wanted to reach over and caress his cheek.

Henry tilted his head and looked up as if he was dreaming. "Going to a Broadway show."

Patsy's eyes almost popped out of her head. That was the last thing she thought any teenage boy would say. "No way, me too!" she exclaimed.

19

Henry's face lit up. "I do odd jobs all year to save up enough money to take Metro North into New York City to visit my sister. I usually go in once or twice a year to see a show, depending on how much money I can save up."

"I usually go in once a year. My mom is infatuated with Broadway. She wanted to be a professional dancer. She should have been too. She's amazing."

"So why didn't she?"

"She met my father when she was young, got married, had kids and that's the end of the story." Pasty lowered her head as her voice filled with sadness. "Although every summer around the time of my mom's birthday, my dad pays for tickets for my mom and me to see a show. It's the highlight of our year. He takes my brothers to a sporting event. He doesn't want to go to any 'stupid show,' as he calls them, and my little sister, Cathleen, stays with our cousins. My mom always makes such a big deal about how nice this is of my dad, but I think his motivation is more guilt for not allowing my mom to follow her dreams rather than out of the goodness of his heart."

Patsy couldn't believe she said this to Henry. The words just flew out of her mouth. "I'm so sorry. I shouldn't have shared this with you. I don't know what I was thinking."

"Please don't apologize. Believe me, my parents aren't rock stars."

The conversation turned to lighter topics. They talked about their favorite shows, the scenery and costumes of *Cats*, the storyline of *Les Misérables*, the music and dancing in *A Chorus Line*. Henry told Patsy all about *La Cage Aux Folles*, which was one show Patsy hadn't seen yet. "You have to see it one day. It's one of my favorites," he said.

Finally, the others staggered into the kitchen, one couple at a time, with messed-up hair and disheveled clothing. They looked like they just woke up. The kitchen got crowded and loud as they grabbed beers from the fridge. Patsy checked her Swatch and realized it was six o'clock and she needed to get home. She

20

promised her mom she'd be home before dark. Even though Bridget wouldn't be home—she'd be at Mahoney's—Patsy didn't like to disobey her, especially after Bridget agreed to let her go. She said goodbye to Susan and thanked her.

"Au Revoir," she sang out to Henry in what she hoped was an appealing tone.

"Au revoir, mon ami," he replied, flashing a movie star smile that sent chills up her spine.

Patsy ran all the way home with the innocent beginnings of romance in her heart.

CHAPTER 5
Manslaughter

That evening, after everyone was tucked in, Patsy recalled the afternoon with Henry. She laid down on her white lace comforter and closed her eyes. As she breathed in, she pictured Henry's beautiful face smiling at her. The creaking of the bedroom door brought her back to reality. As the light from the hallway illuminated the room, Patsy saw Bridget eyeing her.

"Mom, what's wrong?" she asked, raising her head from the pillow.

"Oh, nothing. I just wanted to check with you to see how your afternoon was," Bridget whispered as she laid down.

"It was good," Patsy replied cautiously.

"How many other girls were there?"

"Five," said Patsy, keeping her answers as succinct as possible.

"That's nice. What did you do?"

"Not much. You know how girls can just pass the time gabbing away." Patsy was getting nervous with all the questions. She didn't want to have to lie to her mother.

"Patsy, are you okay? Do you have your period? You know you can talk to me."

From the time Patsy first got her period, Bridget often asked her how she was feeling, if she needed thicker pads or was suffering cramps, and reminded her she was a woman now. Patsy hated those horrid embarrassing talks and never told her mom Susan and Laura had been giving her tampons for the last year. Sometimes, her mother didn't have a clue about modern life.

"No, I do not have my period," Patsy answered, then changed the subject, "How did you know you were in love with Dad?" Bridget perked up. She loved to talk about the first time she laid eyes on the handsome and funny Roney Mahoney.

22

Bridget cuddled up closer to Patsy. "Well, as you know, your father was born into a carnival family, and although the Mahoney's were of Irish heritage, there were rumors and tales of gypsies way back in their lineage." Patsy heard this all before, but figured she was on safe ground now. Bridget continued, "The Mahoney's were from a small town in Maryland, but lived a trailer park existence. They brought their home wherever they roamed, from Virginia to New York each spring and summer. They were a part of a large carnival group, but their small caravan included your father, his three brothers, and their grandfather. Their parents stayed behind. The boys loved the summertime, that's for sure.

"The boys performed juggling acts, operated Ferris wheels, tended to freak show acts, and mastered every amusement game. Your great-grandpa Mahoney took care of the scheduling and finances and was a famous carnival barker." After each telling of part of the story, Bridget paused. Patsy watched her mom recall the story she'd told her a thousand times.

"Every town the carnival stopped in, the Mahoney's were greeted with enthusiasm and excitement. They became famous, traveling to the same towns year after year. Your father told me that the cheers of 'Ma-ho-neys! Ma-ho-neys!' could be heard for blocks away, and he hung out the window of their gold Winnebago waving and throwing kisses to his fans.

"Your father just loved the attention. He competed with all his brothers, but he was always the favorite. He told me your great-granddad only allowed your father to stand with him at the carnival entrance and take the microphone." Bridget sat up, pretending to speak into a mic, "Hurry, hurry, step right up, only one dollar to see the marvelous freaks—the boy with three feet, and the fire-eating man. He was a gifted carnival barker," she sighed as she sat back down.

Cathleen interrupted her story with a loud snore, reminding them both she was in the bedroom too.

Bridget leaned into Patsy and whispered, "You know, your father was quite a hit with all the young girls."

"Ewww," Patsy squealed softly and scrunched up her face. The thought of that nauseated her.

"Really, he was so handsome, tall and strong, and he possessed the Irish gift of gab. He kept everyone laughing with his made-up stories and jokes," Bridget got even quieter, "I was 18, just finished high school, and as a graduation present my Aunt Bea took me on a vacation for the whole summer to celebrate. Aunt Bea, with her fondness for carnivals because of her past in Vaudeville, saw to it that our first stop was lovely Atlantic City.

"When we reached the entrance, your father was standing there at the microphone. Aunt Bea noticed me staring at him and encouraged me to talk to him, but I said, 'I can't!' I was so nervous. She told me, 'Of course, you can. You only live once, girl. He's staring right at you. Now is your time to shine.'

"I remember my knees were so weak I could barely walk, and my hands were shaking as I moved closer to your father. The minute I finally said hello, and he said hello back, my whole body melted. I saw the sparkle in his eyes and that movie-star smile, and I knew. I never felt like that before. We talked for hours as I followed your dad around while he worked. We were there until every light was turned off that night and closed the carnival down."

Bridget stared into space for a moment. "Not only did I like your dad, but Aunt Bea played up to your great-granddad, who was a widower, even though he was quite her senior. She and I returned to the carnival every night for two weeks, then followed them from destination to destination to the end of August.

"On the last day of vacation, your dad told me he was going to join the Marines. He said he wanted to be a hero and he loved the tough Marines and their uniforms. He was so excited, and sure he'd be a big hit in the military, just like he was in the

24

carnival. I remember I was devastated my summer romance was ending, but we promised each other we would stay in touch." Bridget stared at the ceiling with her hand over her heart and quietly added, "We were so in love and so happy then.

"I went back to Edison, and your dad joined the Marines. He tried telling his stories to his Marine buddies, but they weren't impressed. He actually cried to me one time when he said the guys dubbed him 'Roney the Phony.'"

Bridget looked sad as she continued, "His confident and braggadocious nature began to suffer, but it only made me love him more. Being a Marine was a lot of hard work—not what your dad conjured up in his unrealistic mind. Although he never showed them how upset these jokes and their chiding made him, it truly hurt him. I know his only saving grace was our long-distance relationship.

"We stayed in touch and wrote long love letters," Bridget said. "Would you like to see them sometime?"

"Sure," Patsy agreed, though she didn't really want to see them. She just knew it would make her mom happy.

"After months of writing back and forth, one spring morning your father surprised me by showing up on my doorstep holding a bouquet of gorgeous red roses. He got down on one knee and asked me to marry him." Bridget looked down at her ring finger and twirled the tiny diamond and matching gold band round and round.

"We had a brief ceremony at St. Matthew's church in Edison, then moved to Camp Lejeune the next week. One year after we were married, you were born." Bridget smiled at Patsy, sighing as her voice trailed off.

Patsy noticed the look in her mother's eyes—nostalgia mixed with sadness—and realized their current situation dominated her mother's life. She vowed to not end up like her mother, then patiently let her continue. "The constant anger, exhausting work, and disappointment in the service changed him, and he started to drink too much. He showed up one too

25

many times late to an assignment after a night of drinking. He came home to you, a little toddler, and me, pregnant with another baby soon on the way," There was a bit of anger and spite in her words, "It wasn't an easy time for me, Patsy, but I tried my best to keep the peace.

"Your father was discharged after only two years in the service. I remember that horrible night when Roney never came home. I called my sweet neighbor, Lucille, a Marine wife for 20 years, who was always so good to me. I remember her calming words, 'Don't worry, I'll send Tom and his buddies, and they'll find Roney. Stay calm and take care of yourself and that darling baby of yours.' Hours later they found him outside a local bar curled up in a ball, reeking of whiskey and snoring so loudly he wasn't even aware the sun was up, or that life was going on around him," Bridget said sadly.

"Now that's the man I know," Patsy said.

"I know you must think of him that way now, but you have to believe me, it wasn't always so. He was funny, handsome, and charming…," Bridget trailed off, smiling.

"Okay, Mom," Patsy said, rolling her eyes.

"No, really, I mean it," Bridget said, trying to convince her daughter, "You know he has a lot of stress with the bar and all."

"It doesn't matter. He doesn't have to be so mean."

"You'll understand one day," Bridget sighed. Patsy gave Bridget's hand a compassionate squeeze, feigning understanding. Bridget kissed Patsy's forehead. "I love you," she said softly.

"I love you too," Patsy said, feeling sorry for Bridget and resentful of her drunken father as she drifted off to sleep.

She is walking in the darkness down a long, narrow tunnel. She finally sees a door with a light surrounding the frame of the door. She walks faster. As she opens the door, she is standing in a familiar place.

She is in the Pub, and no one is there except a man with a little boy. She cannot make out their faces, but she can hear the man call the boy "son." She quietly steps forward and catches a glimpse of the man giving the young boy sips from his bottle of beer, forcing him to swallow until the boy practically chokes.

She rushes to the sink behind the bar and smashes a whiskey bottle. Shards of glass fall around her. Her fury overtakes all reasoning. She holds the bottleneck in her right hand and waves it above her head. As she approaches the man and the boy, their images become hauntingly familiar. The little boy jumps from his chair. She orders him to go home and not say a word to his mother that he was drinking beer. Terrified, the boy runs out the back door.

When the door slams shut, she lunges at the man, clutching the broken bottle in her hand. She chases him around the pool table as he laughs with a loud drunken screech, like a wild hyena. "Catch me if you can, you little bitch," he taunts. His unsteady steps nearly cause him to fall as he winds his way around the table. She reverses her position and turns the other way, where she confronts him.

For a split second, she sees Satan in his eyes. He raises his hand to punch her, but she is too quick. She leaps towards him and pushes the jagged edge of the bottle deep into his throat. She watches as bright crimson streaks run down his neck onto his shoulder. He falls over the pool table, then slowly slithers to the floor. He collapses in a puddle of his blood as a gurgling sound escapes his throat.

She glances down to see two tiny red droplets staining her favorite white chinos and she becomes livid. These are her favorite white chinos. She runs to the bar to get a cloth and soaks it in club soda, just like her mother taught her, rubbing frantically, trying to get the stain out.

When it's gone, she feels power rush back into her soul. She has erased him from her forever. Rubbed him away. Rubbed him out. She walks around the side of the pool table where he lays, kicks him in the leg to ensure he's dead. She walks back towards

27

the door she came through to leave, but it is no longer there. She frantically tries to find any exit, but there is no escape. There is no way out.

Patsy awakens with a sudden jerk, but cannot move. Paralyzed in a tangle of sheets, her body is wet with sweat as she tries to fight her way to a conscious state, struggling through the layers of the troubling nightmare.

Finally, with pins and needles giving way to movement, she sits up, a streak of sunshine peeking through her window. She feels grateful to be alive, and so relieved not to have committed bloody murder.

CHAPTER 6
Acting

Whether it was her hatred for her father, her mundane existence, the life-altering experience at Susan's house, or just her teenage hormones, Patsy knew she needed to get away from her family. She needed time with others her age, or at least private time alone. One evening, Patsy waited until her siblings were asleep before she approached Bridget, who was busy picking up shoes and clothes strewn around the family room. She took a deep breath, "Do I have to work at Mahoney's so much? Can I please stay home—at least on Thursday nights?"

Bridget started without missing a beat in her cleaning, "You already have Friday afternoons off and Thursday is our corned beef and cabbage night. How can I keep an eye on your brothers and sister when Mahoney's gets so busy?"

"Please?" Pasty begged. "I'll do all the laundry and scrub the toilets." Patsy didn't care how desperate she sounded. She just knew she needed some time alone. After all, she was 15 now. Tears burned Patsy's eyes. One escaped, but she quickly wiped it away. She couldn't breathe as she waited for her mother to reply.

Softly, Bridget turned to face Patsy, "Okay, you can stay home."

Patsy ran to her mom and tightly wrapped her arms around her with the biggest smile on her face. Patsy promised, "I will do all the chores you want this weekend and forever!" Then darted up the stairs to her bedroom.

When Thursday night came around, Patsy helped everyone get ready to leave for Mahoney's. She scurried around the house to ensure all jackets, shoes, and other belongings were found. Cathleen asked, "Why isn't Pasty coming?"

Winking at Patsy, Bridget said, "She has to study tonight."

29

Cathleen pouted, "I don't like to go to the Pub without Patsy."

"Patsy will come with us another time," Bridget said as she helped Cathleen button her ill-fitting grey wool coat, grabbed her little chubby hand, and led her outside into the cold wind. Patsy could see that her hoodlum brothers were already halfway down the street, not even waiting for their mother and baby sister.

Patsy felt it in her stomach. The guilt. She knew Cathleen needed her at the Pub, but as soon as the door shut, Patsy sprinted straight upstairs to take a bath. Her mother's often repeated words played like a song in her head, *"Every woman should pamper herself once in a while."*

The closest thing to bubble bath Pasty could find in the bathroom cabinet was Prell. To her utter delight, the shampoo made fabulous suds. As the water filled the tub, Patsy made up commercials, another thing she loved doing. She felt so free being alone in the house. It was nothing short of divine.

She found a can of AJAX cleanser by the commode and an old pair of her mother's rubber gloves. She decided to do a commercial using an empty toilet paper roll as a microphone and the improv began. She gazed into the tiny mirror over the sink and in her most pleasant voice, began," Hello folks, it's me, Madam Patrice, with a friendly reminder to scrub it clean with AJAX, then sit back down and RE-LAX." She sang the jingle at the top of her lungs. She held up the AJAX cleanser and gave a final farewell to her loyal TV patrons saying, "Don't let your hands do all the work, let AJAX, the foaming cleanser, do it for you! See ya next time, folks!" She turned, tossed her hair, and walked towards the white porcelain tub, acting as her audience, clapping for the performance, and taking several bows.

When the bubbles touched the top of the tub, Patsy shut off the water. She removed her nude-colored push-up bra and white cotton panties and stepped in. The warmth of the water enveloped her body. She wanted to stay there for hours, but knew she didn't have much time before her annoying family would return.

Sometimes Patsy's darker thoughts emerged from her subconscious when she was having fun, but not this time. She was determined to have this private time with her fantasies without any negative thoughts of her dull life as a Mahoney. She hated her last name anyway and decided she should change it.

She imagined herself as a sexy woman, *Bubbles Lamour*—for the beloved tub bubbles that floated all around her, but also because it evoked a temptress with large breasts and a fun attitude. The last name *Lamour* was a product of her French class. It denoted love in the French style. So seductive.

She leaned back, touching the porcelain faucet with her right toe. If she had a cigarette, she would place it—and glass of champagne—right next to the tub. Patsy envisioned herself having it all.

As the weeks went on, she added props to her Thursday night soiree in the suds. One night, when her father passed out on the couch, Patsy managed to steal a few Marlboros from his pack. She already snatched a plastic champagne glass from Mahoney's backroom.

Each Thursday, she filled the plastic glass with cold water and put an unlit cigarette to her lips while in her bubble-bath sanctuary. She sang like Marlene Dietrich in a low gravelly voice, *"Black Market, laces for the misses, chewing gum for kisses...."* She was in heaven.

Before the last of the bubbles dissolved, she scooped up enough of them to cover her bud-like breasts. She wished they were bigger and fuller, but all she could do was pretend they were, holding onto the fantasy as long as she could. Sometimes Henry crept into her fantasies, but mostly they were about her—alone in her perfect world.

This became her favorite routine, whether she was in a warm bubble bath or just in the private world of Bubbles

Lamour, her alter ego and best friend, always there whenever Patsy needed her.

CHAPTER 7
Kisses

Patsy dutifully did her chores as promised, went to school, and looked forward to the gatherings at Susan's on Fridays. Henry and Patsy drank and talked while the others disappeared into various rooms. Patsy always wondered why Henry never went into a room to "fool around" with someone and one day mustered up the courage to ask him.

Henry shrugged, "It's not my thing."

Patsy felt embarrassed she opened her mouth and thought maybe he wasn't attracted to her. She tried to think of ways to make him want to fool around or at least go in for a tender kiss.

A few weeks later after they had a few beers, she leaned over to Henry and gently placed her lips on his. It wasn't quite like the long passionate kisses she saw in the movies, but it was long enough for Patsy's body to tingle with excitement. It was a bit awkward because Henry seemed stiff, but he didn't resist. To her delight, when their lips touched again, Henry loosened up and kissed her back. Suddenly, loud footsteps approached. They quickly unlocked their lips and jumped back as the crew started filing into the kitchen.

Patsy and Henry stared at each other like children who just stole from the cookie jar. Patsy leapt up and mumbled a quick goodbye, stating she didn't want to get home late. She sprinted out the front door and floated on air all the way home. She kissed him, and it was wonderful. She would never forget it—the way his soft blond curls gently touched her face, the way his baby soft skin felt, and his cologne, the one that made her melt every time she caught a whiff of it.

One Friday, she got up the nerve to ask him the cologne's name. *British Sterling.* Two days later, Patsy carefully counted out her allowance and bought a bottle from the neighborhood variety store. She sprinkled it on a pretty hankie and went to bed, breathing in the fragrance as she thought of his sweet kisses.

She woke up in the middle of the night, startled to see her mother standing over her. "Why are you sleeping in your clothes?"

Patsy mumbled, "Um…it was a long day and um…I drifted off."

"And, what's that smell?" she asked as she spied the bottle. "Why do you have men's cologne? I can lend you my Tabu perfume. You don't need to buy men's cologne, for God's sake."

Patsy lied, "Oh, it's for Dad. I'm putting it away for his birthday."

"You are the sweetest girl ever," Bridget smiled, "I'll keep your secret, don't worry."

Roney would never get a drop of her precious Henry's scent Patsy thought, but it would suffice as an excuse for now.

Serious again, Bridget continued, "Is something going on with you?"

"Nothing, really. I'm just waking up." Patsy thought sometimes the lies came too easily, but then she justified her falsehoods—Henry was her secret, after all.

"I'll let it go for now, but tell me if you need to talk, okay? I know teenage life can be confusing. Get some more sleep , we have to get up early for Michael's Little League game."

Pulled back to the harsh Mahoney-family reality, Patsy wished for the thousandth time she was an only child.

CHAPTER 8
Hats

The first few years of high school seemed to fly by. Patsy and Henry moved on to "fooling around" at Susan's house every Friday through their freshman, sophomore, and junior years. Henry also started visiting Patsy at her house on Thursday nights, when the other Mahoney's were at the Pub.

Patsy dreaded the day when her siblings wouldn't want to go to Mahoney's anymore. She feared losing her precious alone time. But right now, even her oldest brother Michael didn't mind going. His friends often met him there to shoot pool and sneak beers. Roney always favored his sons anyway and bragged about them to his regulars.

Patsy had the routine down pat—helping her mother get everyone out of the house then rush to the back door to give the "all clear" to Henry, who was hiding behind a big oak tree five houses down. They'd run upstairs to her parent's bedroom and unload her mother's tap shoes and hats onto the bed—all kinds of hats in all colors. Some had veils and ostrich feathers, others featured delicate silk flowers and golden buckles. There were also a few bowlers and jaunty caps. Henry tried on all the hats, even the most flamboyant ones. His favorite was a hot pink fedora with a veil and a huge feather.

The first time Henry came over, he squeezed his feet into Bridget's size 8 tap shoes. "They're a little tight, but they'll do for today," he said. "Next time, I'll bring my own." Even with his squished feet, Henry managed to tap around the room like Gene Kelly in *Singin' in the Rain.*

"How on earth did you learn to dance like that?" Patsy asked, amazed at his skills.

"My mom was determined that my sister become a famous ballerina. We spent endless hours at the ballet studio. When I was five, my mom decided to sign me up for tap classes. Instead of running around playgrounds like most five-year-old's,

35

I was tap dancing and even doing some ballet three or four days a week. My father was not thrilled having a ballerina for a son, however."

The pair danced around the small bedroom as if they were Ginger Rogers and Fred Astaire. Patsy's heart beat out of her chest as she worked hard to keep up with Henry. It was so beautiful how their bodies moved in sync, as if they were indeed the characters in their own fantastic musical. Henry's ocean-blue eyes sparkled when he danced. Patsy never felt as alive as she did when she was dancing with him.

At the end of each performance, Henry grabbed her close with his muscular arms, spun and dipped her, and then leaned in for a long-drawn-out kiss, just like the movie stars did. Then he'd sweep her up, carry her across the hallway and into her bedroom, where he placed her on the twin bed, and they'd kiss some more. They fooled around a bit, not unlike their Friday night encounters, but it was never more than fully clothed pelvic grinding. Patsy wanted more. She was ready and willing. She moved faster and pushed harder, but nothing seemed to work. Henry never went any further.

CHAPTER 9
Gone

The summer before senior year, Patsy's life changed. It was 10 p.m. on a Wednesday night when Patsy answered Henry's usual goodnight call. His voice sounded different, "Patsy, I have some exciting news. My sister worked some magic and I've been accepted into Julliard. It's an elite summer program and they only take a chosen few!"

Patsy listened silently. She knew what this meant to Henry and could hear the pride in his voice. But she also knew this meant they wouldn't be together—for the whole summer. She was devastated. The summer was supposed to be "their time." She even dreamed they would finally go all the way.

The day Henry left for New York; Patsy waited with him on the train platform. It was a chilly June morning, and they stood holding each other tightly. Patsy was choking back tears, but Henry was so excited he didn't seem to notice.

As the train rolled up, Henry leaned over and softly kissed Patsy on the lips. Then he gave her a big hug and stared directly into her eyes," Au Revoir, my love."

"Au Revoir," Patsy replied as a tear rolled down her face. Henry gently kissed it away and was gone.

Just like that.

Patsy walked around like a zombie that summer. She continued working at Mahoney's, switching from waitressing to bookkeeping. Her dad was supposed to oversee the bookkeeping, but his drinking was getting progressively worse. Most nights, he could barely tell you what one plus one equaled by 8 p.m. Whenever she wasn't at Mahoney's, Patsy was at Susan's house—drinking.

At first, Henry called about once a week, but the calls became less frequent as the summer went on. She feared she might never see him again. One afternoon in August, Henry called. Patsy was elated. She hoped he called to tell her when he was coming home.

"Bonjour, mon ami!" Patsy sang.

"Bonjour," Henry replied, not so enthusiastically.

"Are you ready to come home?" she asked, ignoring an inkling that something was wrong.

"Well, not quite. I'm happy to report that I've been accepted into the school for fall! I...um...won't be coming back to Yonkers."

Patsy felt like a knife was just plunged deep into her heart. "Oh."

"I'm so sorry, Patsy. I miss you so much, but this is such a great experience for me, a once-in-a-lifetime chance. It's everything I've...we've dreamed about. You can come to visit all the time and move here after you graduate!"

Patsy knew Henry believed that could happen, and she knew how much he cared about her. Still.

"Please, Patsy, say something."

"I'm happy for you."

"Thanks, Patsy. I know it's hard now, but it will be great once we're together again. I hafta go, but I'll be in touch soon. Adieu, mon ami!"

"Adieu," Patsy managed to say. She put the phone back in the receiver, lowered her head into her palms, and cried.

She was sick with grief and threw up twice, even though there was nothing in her stomach. She took an Alka Seltzer and went to bed early. She felt like her life was over and hated herself for not trying to keep Henry with her. He chose something over their relationship, something more exciting and glamorous. She was just a plain girl from Yonkers and now Henry was a part of The Big Apple. She loved him and hated him at the same time. She fell asleep, exhausted.

She saw a small boy with a large man looming over him. The man was dressed as a carnival barker and told the boy they

38

were off to the circus. The man pushed the boy into a colorful wooden box, telling him to stay put, but the boy kept popping out of the box. Every time the boy popped out; the man pushed him back in. Finally, a rusty old blue pickup truck drove up and the man loaded the box onto the back with the boy still inside. "Okay, this one's ready. Take him away," he said.

Patsy's last year of high school was difficult without Henry. She still hung out with Susan and her group, but since she spent so much time with Henry, she never really got to know any of the others very well.

One Friday afternoon, the usual crowd gathered, except for Laura Romano, who was sick with the flu all week. After grabbing their beers, the couples scattered into their "rooms," and Patsy found herself sitting at Susan's kitchen table with Laura Romano's boyfriend, James Peterson. James was six-feet-three inches tall, thin but muscular, with dark hair and brown eyes. He was one of the star players on the Yonkers High basketball team, and there were rumors several college teams were scouting him.

James was always friendly to Patsy, but they never said more than a few words to each other over the years. He popped open a beer and asked, "Do you miss your '*boyfriend*?'"

"Yes," Patsy answered honestly, noting the sarcasm in his voice.

"You were a great sport to help him cover up his…um…tendencies," James laughed, taking a long pull of his drink.

Patsy had no idea what he meant. "His what?"

"You know, his…gay tendencies. I mean, you knew, right?" As her face grew hot, Patsy did all she could to hold back tears. She knew no such thing. "Come on, Patsy, I'll show you what a real man can do," James crooned as he leaned closer.

Patsy pulled away, mortified, her thoughts racing. True, she and Henry never got past kissing. He did usually choose the

39

most feminine hats. He *was* obsessed with Broadway and avoided anything macho. No! She refused to believe this about her wonderful Henry. James was wrong and even jealous. She despised him.

Patsy jumped up and stormed out of Susan's house, gasping for air. How could Henry be gay? It was absurd. They kissed all the time—though he stopped easily, as she longed for more. No! Didn't James know Henry was better than all of them? Just because he was refined and sophisticated didn't mean he was gay.

When Patsy was with Henry, all her worries melted away. He wasn't gay. He couldn't be! She sprinted home, her heart pounding. She fumbled with the key to unlock the front door and as soon as it opened, ran to the phone to call Henry. She picked up the receiver, then put it down. What would she say? *'Hi Henry, are you attracted to me? Did you feel what I felt when we kissed?'* She ran to her room, burying herself in her covers as the tears streamed down her face.

The next morning, sitting cross-legged on her bed and holding her pen over a pad of paper, she thought about what she could write: *Henry, mon ami, please come home. Do you love me like I love you? I need to ask you, could it be you are gay?*

Patsy never actually wrote a letter to Henry or called him, and he didn't call her either. As much as she craved to see him and wondered if he might be gay, she didn't want to be the one to ruin his dreams. She didn't want to do to him what her father did to her mother and guilt him into coming home to a life that wasn't fulfilling. Most of all, she didn't want to ruin the image of her first love. She assured herself that James was just a jealous prick who tried to cause problems. She convinced herself Henry was not gay—not her perfect Henry.

CHAPTER 10
Employment

Stuck in Yonkers—without Henry—Patsy found herself feeling more miserable by the day. To remind herself she was still alive, she found a steel nail file and stabbed it into her thigh, just to feel something. She felt the pain and watched the blood begin to bead up. "I hate you, Henry Johnson. Damn you to hell! Why did you leave me in this awful house?" she said aloud.

The wound began to burn. She reached into the medicine cabinet for a bandage and the Bayer® chewable Aspirin. *How is hurting myself gonna bring Henry back? Why am I bleeding over that jerk?*

She limped downstairs to put on the kettle for a cup of tea. When it whistled, the shrill sound pierced her ears and she felt salty tears sting her eyes. Her anger melted into despair as self-doubt rushed in, and questions plagued her again. W*hat could she have done differently to keep Henry here? Would she end up forever in Yonkers? Would she have a life of boredom like her poor mother?*

"No, I won't!" she exclaimed. This was it. No more blaming herself. No more inflicting pain on her body. She couldn't deny the anger losing Henry caused, but she vowed to make a conscious effort to push away the gravity of her hurt and feelings of abandonment. *I Will Survive* became her mantra. At first, the process was challenging and tinged with self-pity, but it became second nature over time. She buried her emotions deeper and deeper. She wasn't living, only existing now day-to-day.

A week before graduation, Bridget bounded into Patsy's bedroom, wearing a grin from ear-to-ear. "I have such good news for you!"

Patsy barely looked up from her bureau, where she was rearranging her underwear neatly by color. It was the fourth time

41

she folded the same sets. "What's Up?" she replied, disinterested.

"Me and your aunts are throwing you a graduation party at the bar! I put some money away for you to buy a new dress too!"

Patsy nearly screamed, "No! I don't want that. I really don't."

"Sure you do, Patsy. It'll be fun."

"I really don't want any party," Patsy felt sick at the thought. Even after all these months without Henry, Patsy couldn't bear the idea of him not being at graduation. She didn't have a date for the prom, but she didn't care. She just wanted to get on with her life after high school, whatever that meant.

"Nonsense. You can even invite your friend Susan and any other friends too. Dad said we can have all of Saturday afternoon at the bar if we clean up after. I'll clean so you don't ruin your pretty new dress."

Patsy sighed. She was too defeated to even argue about a stupid party, so she gave in. "Okay, but please, just our family. I don't want a crowd. Anyway, Susan is with her brother Larry in the city, so I won't even see her," she lied. Patsy forced a smile so her mother wouldn't think she was the most ungrateful daughter in the world, but she knew a dumb party at the Pub would be humiliating. There was no way she'd let Susan and her friends witness her drunken father, subservient mother, and out-of-control siblings running wild. She would never invite them—she didn't even want to be there herself.

Instead of graduation being the beginning of the rest of her life, if her father got his way, graduation would be the dead-end of her dreams, with a boring job in Yonkers, and she'd end up just like her mother, even after she vowed not to. That was all he talked about for the last few months—what kind of job Patsy would get so she could start contributing to her room and board.

Patsy went back to methodically folding her underwear and wished she could crawl into the drawer and smother herself

42

in the pastel bras and panties. At that moment, she truly wished she were dead. "When do you want this party to happen, Mom?"

"Well, graduation is next week, so why not the following Saturday?"

Her mother's enthusiasm made Patsy want to scream, but instead she just nodded, "Fine. Whatever."

"Don't be so glum, Honey. We're going to have so much fun." Bridget gave Patsy an unwelcome big hug.

The party went on as scheduled, with Bridget in all her glory. She wore a new purple floral silk chiffon dress that accentuated her gorgeous figure. Patsy hoped she'd inherit her mother's beautiful shape and was in awe that Bridget looked so good after five kids.

Patsy wore a simple Gunne Sax white dress with pink lace. The dress was not something she would have picked for herself, but Bridget insisted. Since this indeed was Bridget's party, Pasty decided not to put up a fuss and be grateful her mother finally gave up nagging her about inviting friends.

Bridget bopped from guest to guest, filling people's glasses, urging them to eat more. But Patsy was already sick of all the "Oh, Patsy, you're so grown up and so gorgeous. You look so much like your mother" comments. About forty kids were running wild. Luckily, a drunken Roney left early and went to the track, which was fine with Patsy. Everyone was having a great time—except her. Patsy made her way into the tiny ladies' room and cried. After a few minutes, Bridget came in.

"Patsy, what's wrong, Dear? It's such a nice party, don't you think? Why are you crying? Please, tell me."

"I'm fine, Mom. Just overwhelmed at how nice you tried to make everything. You're the greatest." Patsy knew she must shut Bridget down from any more questions about the real reason for her sadness. They hugged, and Bridget began dancing with Patsy, swaying and twirling like so many times before.

A few days later, Patsy overheard her father pressuring Bridget to get Patsy out into the working world. "The party is over! Listen, I'm sick and tired of Patsy moping around. She's yours to handle, and you need to get that girl a job," Roney spat out in an uglier-than-usual voice. Bridget stared at the floor during his tirade. "She can't be leeching off us forever. She needs to contribute her share now that she's finished with school. It's not enough for her to just help out at Mahoney's." Roney was waving his finger at his wife. When he ended, she just nodded.

Patsy was sitting at the kitchen table that night, meticulously folding a black t-shirt, when Roney came home. Stacks of laundry filled the table. When she looked up, she saw this strange, intense look on her father's face. He scared her, and Patsy stood up and backed away. Roney hardly ever spoke to her one-on-one except to put her down for being, as he put it, "just like your mother." Looking into his eyes now, trying to figure out how drunk he was, she realized he was sober. She breathed a sigh of relief.

"Patsy girl, you are sure going to thank your old man once you hear about the great deal I made for you today," Roney said, as he pulled up a chair right next to hers. "Come on, sit back down." She sat, unsure what to expect.

"Buddy Crenshaw has a great job for you as a bookkeeper at his insurance firm. Plus, he's offered to pay for you to take some bookkeeping classes. And to top it off, you will be working with his son, Max, so you won't be lonely." He said the word lonely with a lascivious look on his face and a wink that made Patsy cringe.

Patsy was speechless. She didn't know if she should laugh or cry. Max, from what Patsy knew of him, was a nerdy kid with glasses and freckles, a year or two older than her. She remembered seeing him accompany Buddy to the bar. He was nothing to be excited about.

Roney continued, "I told Buddy that you'd give one hundred percent effort, so I don't want you to let this family down. You are a Mahoney, and Mahoney's work hard. Half the money you make goes to me for room and board, but the rest is yours to spend on whatever you gals spend money on."

That was the end of the conversation. Roney left the room without even waiting for a reply. Patsy's body tensed as blood rushed to her head, and her ears felt like they were stuffed with cotton. She stifled the panic surging to the surface until it finally dissipated, but she knew she was trapped.

All the kids in the neighborhood were doing the same thing after graduating high school. It was like that in the Irish section of Yonkers. Very few were destined to have prestigious or exciting career paths, or even to attend college. They were kids from the 'hood. Many of the guys were cops, firemen, or construction workers. The girls, if fortunate, went into nursing or worked in offices. She just never dreamed that would happen to her.

Bridget came running in, throwing her arms around Patsy, "Dad just told me the good news about the new job. I'm so excited for you!"

"Why is life so unfair?" Patsy whined.

"What's wrong, Baby? This is such a great opportunity."

"Mom, you know what's wrong. I don't want to be working in an office or a bar my whole life. I want a better life, a more exciting life. I want out of Yonkers!"

Bridget grabbed Patsy and stared her straight in her eyes. When she spoke, her voice was sympathetic, "I know. I know exactly how you feel. But this doesn't have to be forever. You can save some money until you have enough to be on your own."

Bridget tried to lighten the mood, "We can make this fun. Dad gave me money so we can go shopping and buy you some new outfits. Don't worry. I know you'll make it out one day. I'm on your side." Patsy looked on sadly as Bridget lowered her head. "You won't end up like me," she whispered. "I promise."

"Thank you, Mom," Patsy whispered, choking back tears.

CHAPTER 11
Max

While Patsy lacked the energy to even think about the new job, Bridget was always talking about what kind of clothes Patsy needed for her new job and reminding her Roney gave them money for a new wardrobe. "That in itself is a miracle!" Bridget enthused as they set out on their first shopping spree. She gave Patsy a big hug, "C'mon, smile! This is the beginning of something new and exciting. Don't look like it's the end of the world."

It felt like the end of the world to Patsy. She tried not to cry as her mother brought what looked like old-lady dresses into the dressing room, tidy sheaths and pleated skirts, a crisp white blouse with a Peter Pan collar, and dull brown and blue sweater sets.

Patsy was so exhausted from trying on all those stupid clothes, she didn't even want to think about shoes. But on they shopped, to Baker Shoes, where she knew her opinion wouldn't matter anyway, so she stood like a mannequin and waited.

"Looky Hon, these are perfect!"

Patsy was livid as she gazed at navy blue patent leather slip-ons with a tiny French heel and the biggest gold buckle she'd ever seen. "Mom, please stop. I'm not a Pilgrim!"

The whole store turned and laughed. To Patsy's surprise, she burst out laughing too. At first, Bridget didn't get the humor. She stared from Patsy to the shoes, then a smile slowly spread across her face. Soon she was laughing too, making Patsy laugh even harder.

"Well, they were good enough for Betsy Ross!" Bridget joked on the bus on their way home, and the guffaws began anew. "I still say those shoes were sharp as hell, and I know Max would like them," she added as they calmed down.

Patsy was grateful at that moment for her Irish sense of humor and the relief of a good laugh with her mom. "Max is no great catch. He's the biggest nerd. Really. And kinda gross looking too."

"Okay, I'll stop with the Max comments. At least you'll look professional and beautiful," Bridget smiled. Patsy elbowed her, and they both laughed again.

Patsy started work two days later. Mr. Crenshaw was very kind to her, but just as she expected, Max was a grade-A nerd with his red hair, freckles, and slight overbite. He was Patsy's height and didn't weigh much more than her either. Still, the first few weeks working with Max were surprisingly tolerable. Patsy was thrilled that she was well-prepared because of her school studies and bookkeeping at Mahoney's. Her abilities kicked right in.

Max, however, was as nervous as a cat. He seemed in awe of her and acted like an anxious teenager. Her bookkeeping was miles ahead of his, and he complimented her on her skills for the simplest of tasks. His lack of confidence gave her more confidence for some reason. At the end of the first week, in a barely audible voice, Max said, "I think we'll make a good team, Patrice."

Patsy quickly responded, "Oh please, call me Patsy, and know that I'm eager to learn." She grinned at him.

Max melted. "I'm eager to teach you all I know, Dear."

Patsy shot back, feeling annoyed, "Hey Max, I said call me Patsy!" All his knowledge could fit into a thimble, she thought.

Max turned pink through his freckles, and Patsy laughed. He looked like the Howdy Doody puppet she played with as a child.

Max recovered quickly, and like the nerd he was, didn't realize how exasperating he could be. He snapped his fingers, "Gotcha—Patsy, it is!"

After that, they worked easily together. They made small talk, and Max seemed excited to familiarize Patsy with the accounts. She was responsible for completing customer invoices, making journal entries, and reconciling the accounts. It wasn't much different than what she did at Mahoney's, so she was on top of things.

As the weeks went on, the work became a boring. Max however, was starting to get physically closer to her while they worked. One day Max was so close to her, she could smell tuna fish on his breath. She pulled her chair in closer and closer to the table until it became impossible to type or even use the rickety old adding machine. He stood so close, his stiff member pressed against the lower part of her back. Patsy was virtually trapped.

Luckily, Buddy Crenshaw saw how uncomfortably close Max was perched near her and shouted, "Get off that poor girl!" Max jumped back, coward that he was, and didn't try anything like that again.

Patsy only told her mom what happened that day. Bridget just laughed, "That's the price you pay for being beautiful!" She never told her dad, who was just happy Patsy was making money and contributing to the household. She knew better than to rock the boat with Roney. She muddled through most of the summer doing what she was told, putting her feelings and dreams aside. She worked five days a week, went to school two nights a week, and waitressed every other weekend. She was in a routine and existing, but not really living—except during the alternate weekends when she wasn't waitressing.

On one of her free Saturdays, Patsy took a stroll to a construction site a few blocks away, just because she felt the urge for a little excitement and, maybe a little danger. She wore new capri pants and a halter top, feeling sexy. As she neared the site, she slowed her stride down a little, but cowered slightly as the catcalls began. "Hey, Beautiful, I've been waiting for you all my life!" a curly-headed blonde guy yelled out, trying to impress his buddies. All the guys chimed in, whistling, and making woo-hoo noises and kissing sounds.

A large, burly guy stepped up in front of the first guy and shouted, "Hey Sweetness, how would you like a date with a real man?" Patsy burst out laughing when she saw him tear his shirt off. Nervous, but feeling bold, she went into what she hoped would sound like a comedy skit.

"Ooooh, sure, I would love it! Do you know one?"

"Holy shit, we have a feisty one today!" the guy chuckled with his friends, as Patsy continued quickly, leaving the catcalls behind. As she turned the corner, she heard someone yell out, "Hey Dougherty, that chick shot you down good." All the guys howled, and for a minute, Patsy felt gratified, having a little female power, and getting the last word in.

She was also secretly happy that they found her attractive. She needed the boost badly and decided she would make her looks a new priority, now that she experienced exhilaration she remembered feeling when she was with Henry. So much of what she craved was lost to her when he left. Now, Patsy felt she was coming alive again.

At home that night, Patsy danced around her room trying out new steps and singing to herself so loudly Michael yelled from the hallway, "Shut the hell up, Patsy, you can't sing anyway!"

"Stuff it, Moron. I sing, dance, and look twice as good as you!" Patsy went right on singing, even louder now. The Lambada was the new dance craze and she loved it. It was sexy and sensual. Patsy pretended she was in the arms of a hot Latino lover as she glided around her room. She willed herself happy as she belted out, *"C'mon baby, C'mon baby, do the samba. I know you can't control yourself any longer…."*

She fell exhausted onto her bed as her make-believe Latin lover fell next to her. Immersed in the fantasy, she began kissing her pillow and murmuring, "Ronaldo, my darling, I can't control myself any longer!"

CHAPTER 12
Monique

Patsy sometimes thought she would fall into a pit of despair so big she'd never be able to climb out of it. She continually searched out new venues, as going to the same place too often was boring. One afternoon she saw a full-page ad in the Yonkers newspaper about a new club opening in the area.

Club Indigo:
A cool, chill place
to get your groove on.

Her heart skipped a beat. The dark intrigue of it all fascinated her with its promised atmosphere. She remembered now hearing about it one night at Mahoney's, that it was going to feature great music and cater to the underground in-crowd. She was happy to learn it was close to home and determined to do everything possible to be a part of that in-crowd.

She decided to buy a new outfit first, so she was ready to get her "groove" on before the weekend came. Patsy's style was now a little bit Goth and a little bit Boho. When she wasn't at work, her physical presence and dress were becoming more and more daring as she yearned for diversion from her mundane existence. She particularly loved jewelry and wore several rings and bracelets of turquoise and silver, and large hoop earrings. She added some subtle brown streaks in her long blond hair for a pretty contrast. She wasn't an overtly sexy type, but she dressed a little provocatively, with a glimpse of the cleavage she finally had showing, favoring tight leather pants and crop jackets over softer camisoles of silk and lace. She thought the look was just sexy enough—with a bit of mystery.

She shopped in a tiny store called "Monique's Chic Boutique." The owner's daughter, who was also the store manager, was just a few years older than Patsy. Her name was

50

Monique Basilique. She was French Creole and spoke with the prettiest accent. The two of them became fast friends.

Patsy noticed Monique was always staring at her. Patsy didn't mind at all. She liked the attention. "Hi Beautiful," Monique murmured one evening while Patsy was shopping. "I just got this silver lamè crop top in, and I haven't even priced it yet, so go ahead, strip down and try it on, but hush, don't let Papa know. He is the official owner. I only bear the store's name."

Patsy laughed, "Your secret's safe with me." God forbid Patsy's own father ever saw how she dressed. She never left the house in her new clothes. She carried them in a bag and changed in ladies' rooms.

Patsy emerged from the dressing room and began to walk through the store, back and forth like she was on a catwalk. She turned at the end of the aisle and jutted her hip out, looking over her shoulder and blowing a kiss in Monique's direction.

Monique whispered in her soft accent, "You are a natural. Pick any outfit you want, and I'll reduce the price."

Patsy squealed with joy, "You're so good to me!" She noticed Monique glowed when she said those words. Patsy enjoyed this exclusive, clandestine relationship with her friend. She knew deep down Monique may have other intentions, but for now it was a time when she felt young and beautiful, and enjoyed this more glamorous aspect of her life. Patsy felt tingles of excitement when she was with Monique.

The first time Patsy came home with a few new outfits, she was excited to show her mom. She held up each item and then laid it out on the bedspread. She was careful to only show Bridget the feminine choices, not the leatherette or flimsy camisoles. She showed Bridget navy pinstripe culottes, a white eyelet blouse with puffy sleeves, her usual silver and turquoise bracelets, and several dainty silver necklaces, but not the high platform shoes with ankle straps. They would be too much for Bridget's Pilgrim-shoe taste. A second outfit featured black gabardine gaucho pants with a bold print off-the-shoulders bolero top. To complete the look, she chose soft, black leather shoes that laced up her leg to the knee.

"Oh, Lordy me," Bridget sighed. "Look at all these lovely things."

"Quiet, Mom!" Patsy admonished. "This is just between you and me, remember? I have to swear you to secrecy. Dad can never know I'm spending my meager salary on clothes. Promise me, okay?"

"Okay," her mom said quietly, "but wow, look at those pretty bracelets."

Patsy laughed out loud. "They aren't bracelets. They're earrings. That's the style now—they're called hoops."

"These clothes are so fancy. How did you afford these and the jewelry too?"

"I got everything on sale. I became friends with the owner of a great boutique, and she lets me know when a sale is coming up, sometimes as much as fifty percent off. Plus, she puts certain pieces aside for me on a layaway plan," Patsy lied. "Maybe you could come with me one day, spiff up your own style?"

"Okay, maybe one day," Bridget said, not very convincingly. Patsy believed deep down her mother wanted to, but knew it was unlikely with drunken Roney lurking around.

"We could be shopping buddies like before, only this time, no Pilgrim shoes." They both laughed as Bridget hung the huge hoops from her ears and danced around the room.

On her next visit to the shop, Monique rushed over to Patsy and gave her a great big hug. "I have some new makeup for you to try. It's a loose powder. I even have this wonderful rich sable brush. Do you want me to apply it for you?"

"Sure, I'll try anything you want." Patsy sat in the dressing room.

"Okay, look up at me, Girlfriend, right into my eyes." Monique smiled and began the application with shaky hands.

52

Monique urged Patsy to remove her blouse to not get makeup on it. Patsy obliged. She sat there in her bra while Monique brushed the powder onto her cheeks and forehead, then the bottom of her chin with soft, slow strokes.

Monique very seductively let the brush slide down Patsy's neck to the tiny space in between her breasts. They looked at each other, and Patsy quite impulsively kissed her softly but fully on her beautiful French Creole lips. Monique put her hand on Patsy's breast and rubbed tenderly as she put her tongue inside Patsy's mouth.

Patsy, mesmerized by the feeling down below, couldn't stop. But then, in a rational moment pulled away, a mixture of emotions going through her head—and her body—ranging from embarrassment to desire. Did she really just make the first move? "I'm sorry, Monie, it just felt so good, and I'm so lonely, please forgive me, you must think I'm crazy."

"Not at all, Girlfriend, I love it! It's your primal instincts guiding you. It happens to me all the time," Monique exclaimed with a wink.

"No, really, I'm sorry. I won't let it happen again." Flustered, Patsy grabbed her blouse and turned her back towards Monique.

Monique stepped closer and kissed Patsy on the back of her neck. "So sorry, I couldn't help myself. You're just so damn beautiful." Her words were apologetic, but the tone was not.

They laughed awkwardly. However, neither said a word after that encounter, and it didn't happen again. Patsy couldn't risk their incredible friendship. She needed Monique in her life, and she knew it.

Later that night, Patsy fell into a semi-sleep as her mind drifted to a hazy dreamscape.

A tall woman moves towards her. Off to the woman's right is a tall man. She tries to reach out and touch him, but her hand goes right through him, and he disappears instantly into a cloud. The woman says to her, "I'm still here for you. If you want me, come closer to me," and the woman walks towards her, but feeling frightened, Patsy turns away, her heart beating fast. She begs the man to come back. He is close to reappearing when she feels the stirrings of desire consume her. She doesn't know if it's the woman or the man causing her passion, but she doesn't care. She only knows she likes the feeling.

Cathleen burst into Patsy's bedroom and jumped on her bed, yelling, "Get up, Patsy, it's time for Patrick's baseball game. Mom wants you to take me."

Startled, Patsy yelled back, "That's a lie, get away from me. It's my one day off! Leave me alone." Her anxiety and frustration brought her back to the harsh reality of her life as it was.

Patsy walked into the boutique and Monique's eyes lit up. "Patsy, so great to see you," Monique said with a shaky voice. She didn't run over like she typically did, but Patsy went to her and gave her a big hug. When they disengaged, Patsy locked eyes with Monique and smiled. From that moment on, there was an unspoken agreement they would just be friends.

On a whim, Patsy asked, "Do you want to come to Club Indigo on Friday night? We could pick up some guys 'cause we are happenin' chicks."

"I'd love to! I'll close early."

"We will be *Two Hot Girls on a Hot Summer Night* just like Carly Simon sings," Patsy replied with a chuckle.

"Right on, Sista! Why don't you come back this week to pick outfits?" Monique exclaimed.

"Perfect!" Patsy replied.

Patsy, at last, could look forward to sharing excitement and happiness with her new friend. She started to sing, *"I have to admit it's getting better. It's getting better all the time."* The Beatles always came through. She thumbed through the racks of pastel camisoles at Monique's Chic Boutique and giggled with delight as she picked out a soft, lacy beige one.

CHAPTER 13
Richie

On Wednesday, Patsy and Monique sat in the boutique sifting through piles of tube tops, trying to get just the right look for their debut at Club Indigo. Intrigue and suspense hung in the air as they discussed the strategy for their Friday night adventure.

"I have to work, but will close up early, hopefully without Papa noticing," said Monique.

"Me too, but my mom is covering for me, so I'll take a cab and meet you there."

"You got it Girlfriend," Monique said, throwing her a kiss along with a beautiful camisole she pulled from the pile of tops. "This will get you a bunch of attention."

"Oh my, it's beautiful. Thank you, I'll see you Friday. I can't wait," said Patsy throwing back a kiss.

Club Indigo doors opened just a few weeks ago. Patsy wasn't sure how crowded it would get, but it was still early for a Friday evening, even for Yonkers, where Friday nights usually started with happy hour at 4 p.m. This club wouldn't start filling up until closer to 10 p.m. Patsy couldn't wait to get out of work, away from her family, and have a good time.

She was all set with fake ID cards compliments of Monique. "Here ya go, Sweet Thing, the only change is your year of birth, in case they ask. We made you twenty-two, and Honey you can pass for that. I'll bet they won't even ask for it. They will be too busy checking out your tatas!"

"Thanks, Monie, you're the greatest!"

As Patsy walked up to the doors of the Club Indigo for the first time, she called on her alter ego of *Bubbles Lamour,* putting on all her charm for the bouncer.

"How ya doin' beautiful?" the bouncer said, looking her up and down.

Patsy responded quickly, "Better if I could touch those big muscles of yours," she said, touching his enormous bicep.

He winked at her then held the door wide open. Patsy was in rare form, full of anticipation—flirty, and exuding a great deal of confidence. All it took was some cleavage, her natural beauty, and her charisma. They let her right in. She said to herself, *thanks, Bubbles. You're always around when I need you.*

Patsy noticed Monique, already at a high table towards the back of the bar three steps up from the main floor. It was dark, so Patsy carefully ran up the steps and gave Monique a big hug. She was so glad her friend was there ahead of her. "Oh, Patsy, forgive me. I was hiding up here because I was alone."

"I would do the same thing, Monie. Hope you weren't waiting too long."

"No, isn't this place fabulous?" She pointed out the beautiful décor, "I love the red lanterns on each table. It's so very sexy!"

"And look at that chandelier in the middle. It lends just the right class," Patsy added, "and that Club Indigo sign behind the bandstand is epic!"

The drummer began to play, and the lights flickered on and off, signaling the start of the music. The two made their way to a table a little closer to the stage. "Let's get up front before a crowd comes in," said Patsy grabbing Monique's hand.

A handsome waiter rushed up to escort them to a table up front. "Right this way, pretty ladies. I'll return for your drink order in a minute."

"Wow," Monique said, "that was service. We are certainly two hot girls on a hot summer night like the Carly Simon song goes!"

Patsy's eyes flashed to the bandstand and there was a vision that made her heart skip a beat. He was standing in the corner of the stage, talking to a tall, thin guy who was jamming on a Fender Rhodes keyboard. Patsy immediately heard his laugh and saw his dark sex appeal and black curls from across the room. She was so glad they moved up to a much better view.

When 10 p.m. hit, the musicians cued up. The gorgeous guy grabbed his saxophone and strung it around his neck. To Patsy's delight, she observed that Mr. Eye Candy was the leader of the band. In a deep but melodious voice, he said, "Welcome to Club Indigo. I'm Richie DiOrio, and this is my band, *Agents of Soul*. Hit it boys, one, two, one, two, three." He began to play Kenny G's tune, *Songbird*.

Patsy was lost in the music as it whaled through the room. Richie exuded sex with each smooth action, and she couldn't help but feel the vibration of the drums right through her body. She closed her eyes briefly, but then opened them to capture the movement of Richie's hips as he held the instrument close to his body. His eyes were closed too while he gently swayed to the melody. Patsy couldn't believe the sound of his saxophone made her feel so full of desire. She looked up and Richie gave her a flirty wink. She wondered if it was all a dream.

Patsy made a promise to herself that she would come back to Club Indigo every Friday night until he talked to her. She was determined to know Richie DiOrio and hoped to get closer to a private concert—just the two of them.

These were high aspirations for sure, but she felt she must do it. She thought, *it's my destiny. I just know it.*

Richie then played the song, *I Want to Know What Love Is*, by Foreigner and stared right at Patsy as he said, in his deep, sexy voice, "Dedicated to the pretty girl in leather and lace." She wasn't imagining it. He was gesturing right toward her.

Monique shrieked and clapped. "Patsy, that was for you. Throw him a kiss."

Patsy mouthed the words, "Thank you." She was both mesmerized and ecstatic. She threw him a kiss when he finished holding that last, long note. This magical night could only be a gift that finally came her way after the months of agonizing loneliness and boredom. The music lit a fuse in her soul, and she thought of the lyrics to the song that played in her head, *I wanna know what love is. I want you to show me. I wanna feel what love is, I know you can show me.* When Patsy saw his hips swaying back and forth, something inside her from her stomach to her thighs started to pulsate. She whispered to Monique, "It's almost like he is making love to that instrument. I wish I was a saxophone right now."

"I'll bet he's hiding a big boner for you under that sax right now!"

"You are a naughty girl!" Patsy laughed. Deep inside, she was excited, and she knew Richie DiOrio would be her first real lover. All she could think about was getting Richie to make love to her, with Foreigner singing in the background.

Later, Patsy and Monique went to the ladies' room, and Patsy applied her new lipstick, *Passionate Rose,* and Monique spritzed on *Opium* perfume. They were having a ball. Monique teasingly said, "Girl, that sax player has the hots for you."

"Do you think so? I wouldn't even know what to do. I'm not exactly experienced."

"Oh Honey, trust me, it will all come naturally."

Patsy was embarrassed she never went all the way. She desperately wanted Henry to be her first, but it never happened. Now her body was so hot and so ripe, the fruit was about to fall off the vine.

She was obsessed with sex and thought about it all the time. She read everything she could find in trashy novels and Cosmopolitan magazines on the newsstand. Patsy was able, ready, and willing to have Mr. Gorgeous be the one. The ad she read about Club Indigo in the Yonkers Gazette was so right. Patsy Mahoney was indeed ready to get her groove on.

And Monie was probably right too. It would come naturally. Her instincts, her mind, and her body were ready to make it happen.

So every Friday night, Patsy visited Club Indigo. It was the place to see and be seen. Patsy quickly made friends with the bar staff, the waiters, and patrons and even managed a quick hello and welcome back from the band members. As she got to know the crowd at Club Indigo, her eyes always strayed to Richie. The keyboard player noticed Patsy and Ritchie checking each other out. "Hey, Sweetie, proceed with caution," he whispered. "This guy is known for his rep as a smooth operator."

"I can take care of myself. Don't you worry." Patsy didn't care what people said about Richie. She made up her mind. She wanted to have him.

Monique even tried cautioning Patsy, "Mr. Slick is known as a bit of a Playboy."

"Don't worry about me. I just want to have some fun. I'll be his Playgirl," Patsy chuckled.

Monique also laughed, "I'm just trying to help a girlfriend avoid some heartbreak."

"Don't worry. My heart won't be in it. It's pure lust." The girls both laughed.

During the week, Patsy spent long days in the office and continued waitressing, but begged her mom to convince her father for more time off. Bridget finally admitted she was tired of Patsy's pleas and promised she would speak to Roney. "But listen," said Bridget, "your father doesn't care about anyone's happiness except his own. So don't get your hopes up."

One day Patsy overheard an argument from the hallway when she was on her way to the tiny bathroom to get ready for her job at Mahoney's. She listened as best she could to the muffled voices as they grew louder and louder. The surprisingly high-pitched sounds were coming from her mother. "Roney, give the girl a break. She's older now and needs a social life besides the office and Mahoney's."

"I don't give a shit about her happiness. She's gotta work, and I have a business to run."

"Oh yeah Mr. Big Shot, we'll see how it is running your big fat business without your other kids and me. I could leave in a minute. Aunt Bea wants me to come back to Jersey anyway."

Patsy inched down a few steps until she could see Roney's face through a slit in the door, beet-red color, poking a finger right in her mother's face. Patsy almost panicked for a minute, getting set to rescue her mom if he got violent.

She heard him yell, "Get the hell out of me face, woman! Let your precious Patsy have her social life. I could care less. It's just gonna mean more work for you, and don't you ever threaten to take my boys away from me. Do you hear me, Bridget, NEVER AGAIN, or you'll pay!"

Patsy ran back upstairs as she heard Roney crash the screen door storming out of the house. Then her mother yelled out after him, "Fine with me!" and she added in a final expletive, "Mr. Eff'ing Big Shot!"

Patsy stifled a laugh when she heard her mother say "eff-ing." Her mother was by herself, but still wouldn't really swear out loud. Patsy thought what a good Catholic woman her mother always was and valued that about her. God's name in vain or even dropping the F word was not her style.

She felt the deepest love for her mother and was so proud of her for standing up to her bullying father. She would cherish this special day, when her mother stuck up for her and even fought and sacrificed for her. She was also ecstatic that she gained more time to get back to the hot new club and her pursuit of Richie DiOrio.

It wasn't until the seventh time Patsy was at Club Indigo that her fantasy finally came true. Monique left early, which was all right with Patsy. She sat alone through Richie's last set. His music and the seductive way he moved was driving her wild.

After Richie's final song of the night, he walked off stage and motioned for Patsy to come towards him with his long slender finger. She felt the blood rush to her face. She knew this was her chance to give herself to the romance she was craving.

She rose unsteadily, but was determined as she made her way through the rowdy, smoky crowd. The only light was the massive chandelier in the middle with dim red bulbs and a tiny red candle at each table.

Patsy took a deep breath and whispered to herself, *"It's showtime. Please, God, don't let me trip."* When Patsy finally stood face to face with Richie, goosebumps ran up and down her body. There was a sensual and almost decadent atmosphere in the room. Patsy caught a whiff of Richie's cologne as he came close to her, and her heart skipped a beat. She put her hand out to shake his, but he instead turned it over, and gently kissed her wrist.

"Hello Beautiful Angel," he leaned over and whispered in her ear, "would you join me outside for a cigarette?" Patsy, too entranced to speak, nodded her head and followed Richie to the deserted back alley of the building. He led her past a dumpster to a darker, more isolated part of the alley where they were totally alone.

At first, he tenderly lingered, holding her face in his hands. Then, he continued methodically kissing her neck and then her lips. She felt the scruff of his beard on her cheek, but it made her even hotter as she let him put his tongue in her ear. She was moaning now, losing control, and not sure if her legs would give out. His lips were soft and wet. Her senses became so acute as she smelled Ivory soap and a hint of cologne, mixed with Marlboro cigarettes. She breathed him in.

He then gently pinned her shoulders against the cold brick wall. She eagerly responded to the movement of his hips, pushing in and out in a swaying motion. She felt him grow stiff against her thigh and caved to the desire rushing through her body. Positioning herself on his hardness, she let herself go as she rubbed against him.

"Oh my God," she moaned as her body tightened and then exploded. She lost all sense of the world. There was only Richie and this first real orgasm of her life. It began way down in the lower part of her belly and trembled to the top of her thighs, nearly rendering her helpless as her legs turned to jelly. She held on tight to him and even fully clothed, an uncontrollable moan escaped her half-opened lips. All the while, she was singing to herself the words, *"I wanna know what love is...."*

There wasn't much talking. But she did hear him call her baby girl. At that instance, a raw passion enveloped her like nothing she felt before. "Girl, you are hot. Come on, let's get out of here," Richie said impatiently. He grabbed her hand and led her to his beat-up blue Mustang convertible.

Patsy didn't think twice about where he was taking her or that her parents might wonder where she was. Often on Friday nights, Patsy crashed at a friend's house, so she felt free to do whatever she pleased on this most memorable Friday night. Nothing, or no one could spoil this ecstasy she felt. Patsy didn't care about anyone except Richie and what he wanted. It was what she wanted too.

Prince's Purple Rain album was blasting from the cassette player, while Richie very deliberately held her hand, guiding it to his already rigid manhood. At each red light, Richie leaned over to gently kiss her. They couldn't keep their hands off each other, and Patsy would have done anything he wanted. She was so into this beautiful man. Oozing sexuality from every pore of her body, Patsy sighed as Richie pressed her hand down firmly on his crotch. She heard him let out a moan, and it made her even hotter. She realized triumphantly she was turning him on, and it was the most natural instinctive thing in the world.

During the drive to his tiny apartment in New York City, they were mostly quiet, lost in the awareness of each other. For most of the ride there, she kept her eyes closed to savor the experience.

"Home, sweet, home," Richie exclaimed as he parallel-parked his blue Mustang up against the trash-filled curb of the city street. For a minute, Patsy felt a pit in her stomach and realized the precarious situation she was putting herself in, but she didn't care. She could only see him, and her mind and body yearned to be closer, feeling the surge of anticipation for what would come next.

Patsy looked up at his building. It was a little run-down, but among other similar brownstones. She wondered what part of the city she was in, but she felt safe with him. Patsy desperately wanted to feel the sensation of another orgasm too.

"After you, my angel," Richie proclaimed as he held the car door open for Patsy.

"Thank you, my prince," she replied as she stepped out of the car.

They bolted up the outside steps and into the building. They ran up the stairs leading to an apartment on the second floor. The number was 213, and the door was left slightly open.

As Patsy walked in, she noticed Richie shared his place with others. It was messy, and there was a half-eaten pizza on the coffee table next to an empty bottle of Dewar's scotch. There was even a guy sleeping on the couch which Richie ignored as he led Patsy quietly into his bedroom. Inside Patsy noticed nothing except the mattress on the floor a foot away from the entrance.

Still standing, Richie slowly and methodically opened her jacket and moved to her lace camisole, kissing her breasts, and reaching down her leather pants.

Before he could go further, Patsy stripped down to her bra and panties as she laid on the mattress, eager to feel him on top of her. He took his clothes off so fast—pants, shoes, and socks littered the room in a frenzy. They were both giggling as they lay in each other's arms, impatient to begin the ritual of lovemaking.

His body was so beautiful to her, and his olive complexion was such a contrast to her lily-white Irish skin. As Richie playfully jumped on her, a loud squeak came from the mattress, and they both burst out laughing. That slight interruption ended any nervousness Patsy had as they laid together completely naked. Each time Richie touched her, Patsy's desire grew greater. She was so wet by the time he entered her that she didn't feel any of the discomfort she was expecting. He put his cock halfway in her and then pulled out, gently asking if he was hurting her. She murmured a faint "no" as she welcomed him back inside. She deeply felt one orgasm, then instantly another, and without realizing it, she was scraping her nails into his back as her body shuttered with unbridled passion.

"Oh Angel, you're so tight," Richie said, then cried out, "Oh baby, I'm coming…I'm coming." At the last second, he pulled out and came on her stomach.

Finally catching his breath, he turned to her, "Are you OK, Angel, are you OK? I couldn't wait another minute. You are so beautiful. I was ready to explode."

"I'm better than OK, I'm fabulous," Patsy purred.

Richie ran for a rumpled towel from the bathroom. He noticed the small bloodstain on the mattress and started to ask sheepishly, "Is this your first time?"

Embarrassed, Patsy answered, "Yes, did I do OK?"

"You were the best ever, beautiful angel."

They caressed and held each other all night. Patsy hardly slept a wink. She watched Richie as he snored ever so softly. It wasn't until the morning sun peeked through the dilapidated blinds that hung by one cord that she saw how crooked they were. It made her laugh.

Richie awoke at the sound of her laughter and propped himself up with his elbow. The contrast of his dark hair and dark eyes against the bright light made him look even more striking "What's so funny?" Richie asked with a groggy voice and half-opened eyes.

"The blinds."

"Oh, I thought you were laughing at me!" Richie chided. Patsy realized he was more vulnerable than she thought.

"I would never!" Patsy exclaimed as she moved in closer for their first sunrise kiss, which lasted more than a few minutes and, as naturally as breathing, turned into deep caresses and tender morning sex.

"Good morning, beautiful," Richie whispered in her ear.

"Good morning, handsome," Patsy murmured back.

CHAPTER 14
Lust

In no time at all, Patsy became what Richie called his main squeeze. Patsy thought it was cliché, but she didn't care. On the contrary, she was proud of it. Patsy ignored all the others who warned her that Richie D., aka Mr. Slick, was a smooth operator. As she got to know the crowd at Indigo, all the regulars gave her subtle, but firm speeches about Richie's reputation. Even Richie's keyboard player said something.

Monique too tried to warn Patsy of Richie's playboy ways. "Hey, Patsy, we'll have to fix you up with some birth control girl. You can't be taking chances," Monique stated adamantly. Patsy nodded her head and followed Monique's lead. She knew it was dangerous to be so careless. Patsy laughed when Monique added, "And you better make him wrap it up too. That boy's been around!"

Patsy was grateful to Monique, but still didn't want to hear any negativity about her man. No one could convince Patsy that Richie would break her heart. Patsy often retorted, "I don't give a rat's ass if he breaks my heart. I'm having the time of my life, and nothing is going to stop me!"

Patsy Mahoney and Richie were inseparable. He introduced her to scotch whiskey and marijuana on their many trips to the city, but she wasn't really interested in either. She just wanted to be in the same room with Richie no matter what was going on. Patsy noticed he hung with some crazy friends, including other band members and dopers who were into jazz and seemed to idolize him. A lot of girls rushed to surround him, and his entourage consisted of groupies and other musicians. Richie managed to be charming to all of them. He craved the attention and signed autographs and tape cassettes with delight.

"Sorry Denise, come back next time. We're all sold out of the latest tape," Richie quipped to an admirer. I'll surely save one for my girl, free of charge too!" Patsy watched from the sidelines, feeling so proud of her new man. Strangely though, Patsy felt they posed no threat to her. She knew the chemistry between them was unmatched.

They strolled down Canal Street together on weekends. Once when they were at a sidewalk stand, they stopped simultaneously and admired the Andy Warhol prints. "Andy Warhol is one of my favorites, so much uniqueness. I just love the simple imagery of pop culture. It's so real and so today," Richie reflected.

"I love him too! His Marilyn is my favorite!" exclaimed Patsy while she grabbed the print of Marilyn and hugged it to her chest.

"You do?" Richie was surprised. "Then I'll buy them for you! Pick out your favorites." Patsy grabbed a few prints, and Richie handed the man a wad of cash.

"Thank you!" Patsy exclaimed and passionately kissed Richie.

"For a kiss like that, I'd buy you a few more." Richie laughed.

"You don't need to buy me anything for a kiss."

They visited galleries in SoHo and explored Washington Square Park, often witnessing drugs being bought and sold. Men of all ages, races, and appearances approached them, asking, "Want some crack? Want some blow? Some nose candy for your sweet suga' here?" Whether it was a homeless, toothless man, a young skinhead druggy, or a clean-cut businessman, these dealers' patrons came from all walks of life.

There were even drugged-out, large breasted, high-heeled, bright pink lipstick-wearing prostitutes, calling and smiling at Richie, even though Patsy was on his arm, "Want a little fun? Two for the price of one."

They grabbed cabs and went to second-hand and vintage stores where they tried on platform boots and jaunting caps, but Richie always kept his style intact with his leather jacket, chains, and chunky rings. Patsy was more feminine but not afraid now to be sexy with her clothing, even wearing a garter belt and thigh-high stockings with skimpy bikini panties, a far cry from her day of the week underwear she wore in high school. Richie went wild when he saw her, and they kissed passionately on the subway, copped a feel under the table at a café in the Village, and in the evenings when Richie wasn't playing his sax, they went to the Palladium or the Metropole and danced until they closed the place.

Patsy and Richie were in lust and enjoyed every precious moment with the canvas of New York City as the perfect backdrop for their romance.

As much as their physical yearnings created the basis for their relationship, Patsy wanted to know more about Richie's background. She asked him about his family life, and learned Riccardo Antonio DiOrio came from a strict Italian family who made him practice his musical craft every day and take lessons every Tuesday and Thursday.

In the first conversation about his childhood, he shared, "Doll Baby, there was constant studying and constant rehearsal. It was a grueling hell at the time, but I thank my parents now."

"They must be so proud of you, but not as proud as I am."

He explained his whole family was musically inclined. Patsy began kissing his hands and fingertips as he spoke to her. "My dad played the Stradivarius in an orchestra, and my mother was an a capella singer. I was low man on the totem pole as far as talent was concerned, although I mastered the clarinet, the sax, and the piano pretty quickly. I even made a go of it on the drums at a couple of gigs when a band member didn't show."

When Patsy heard his list of talents, her brain went wild with enthusiasm. Not only was he the sexiest guy she'd ever known, his abilities bordered on genius.

She couldn't help herself as she brazenly grabbed him, reaching for his crotch. She kissed him, yelling out loud, "Come here, my great big drummer, get over here and bang on me." Patsy jumped on him like a female dog in heat, "C'mon Big Guy

69

and bring that beautiful instrument with you to beat my drum hard." She moaned as she wrapped her legs around him and pumped away, thinking to herself, *I have Richie DiOrio, who is the most talented guy who ever lived.*

It was not only great sex, but also great romance and excitement. She longed for Henry so many times and dreamed of ways to make him want her too. But it never worked, and she blamed herself and her inexperience. With Richie, she knew returned sexual gratification was so much more fulfilling. She realized everything about her was looking and working just fine and she stopped putting herself down. Henry dissolved into a fading wisp of memories.

Thanks to her mom, Patsy's schedule at Mahoney's and her babysitting days were now limited. Bridget allowed Patsy to come and go, and would cover for her. She hardly even saw Roney, and when she was home, he was either smashed on the sofa, sleeping it off, or at the pub getting loaded. For Patsy, life was good, and Richie occupied her mind every waking hour.

Things were winding down with Monique too. The *Agents of Soul* played at the Yonkers club less and less, so Patsy decided to pay her a surprise visit at the store. "Hey Monie, I used the back door key. Where are you, girlfriend?" That's when Patsy caught Monique sneaking out of a dressing room half-naked.

"Oh, Patsy, I wasn't expecting you. How ya doing, beautiful?"

"Just thought I would say hello. Am I bothering you?"

Just then, a gorgeous dark-skinned girl with long black hair and beautiful brown eyes poked her head out of the dressing room and spoke provocatively, holding out her hand. "You must be the famous Patsy that Monique talks about. Why not join us?"

Monique spoke up, "Our girl is straight and lovin' on a cute sax player, so don't even think of it, Renee."

70

It was an awkward scene as Monique introduced the two. Finally, Monique slipped on her blouse and walked Patsy to the door. "Sorry about that, she said. Renee is very outspoken."

Patsy laughed nervously and as she walked out, grabbed Monique's hand, "I miss you. Call me sometime. Now go back and have fun."

Monique kissed Patsy on her cheek, "Now you go and have fun with your Smooth Operator." They both laughed and hugged.

Patsy walked away knowing her Monie found another gal pal, and even though she felt a tinge of jealousy, deep down she was happy for her. Everyone deserves a little romance and she hoped her dear friend finally found hers. She surely would miss Monique, but her life was taking a different turn now, and the change was inevitable. It was all about Richie and passion, and fabulous New York.

Patsy loved the wild scenes with Richie, but she sometimes thought besides their time alone, she liked best the evenings they spent with two of his good friends, Mandi and Carla. They were the quintessential party girls, and often the four of them met up at the same clubs. Mandi was tall and eccentric with a bit of a grunge look. She came from money, and her wealthy parents covered the bill for all her whims and desires, including the rent on a Greenwich Village apartment. Mandi was at NYU, majoring in photography and minoring in music.

"I'm goin' on my fifth year at NYU," Mandi told Patsy when they first met.

"Fifth year?"

Mandi replied nonchalantly, "Yeah, well, the parental units want me to stay in school and they don't seem to care how long it takes as long as I come out with a degree at the end. I figure it's an easy life for me to take one or two classes a semester, party all night, and have all my expenses paid. What could be better?" Patsy nodded, but deep down she felt a bit jealous, thinking to herself, *if only I got a full ride to attend NYU and all expenses paid to live in New York City, my life would be amazing.*

Carla was Mandi's partner in crime. Carla was petite, cute, and a great dancer, but not as fortunate money-wise. However, she was an excellent companion and the yin to Mandi's yang.

Both were free spirits who loved music and wanted to have fun. Much to Patsy's surprise, they accepted her right away, which was cool. Mandi and Carla loved Richie, and unlike most groupies, they were educated and more intelligent than the typical hangers-on. They loved to sit around and smoke pot, talk music, movies, and what it took to make it in the arts. Carla said she would graduate and be serious about making a living as a photographer, which was her natural talent. She placed her achievements all over the apartment, and her black and whites were particularly original and thought-provoking. She was a natural and captured street scenes and everyday life making them authentic yet with artistic charm.

Mandi and Carla's place in the Village was unkempt, but comfortable. They each had their own bedroom, Mandi of course with the larger room since her dad was footing the bill. She enjoyed a queen bed, which was so soft it felt like sleeping on a cloud. She also owned an antique white six-drawer dresser. Glass bottles of perfumes and nail polish filled the top of the dresser, and all six drawers were stuffed with clothes practically bursting out of them. Unlike Mandi's room, Carla's was half the size, but it was neat and orderly with a pull-out bed that folded up to a comfy sofa. Patsy preferred it mainly because it was the tidiest room in the whole place and an inviting space to lay her head. Also, Carla bought Patsy her own quilt, and the two girls slept peacefully together.

There was a six by eight-foot kitchen where dirty plates, silverware, and glasses often lined the limited counter space and filled the sink. Patsy was constantly tidying up. Despite this, the apartment was unusually cozy, with hardwood floors covered with a plush fuchsia area rug and a worn-out white leather sofa. There were pink and teal sheets hanging from the ceiling and from the window frames, which gave an Arabian look to the room. There was also an electric keyboard with a microphone in the corner of the small living area.

Richie crashed at Mandi and Carla's place occasionally when he didn't want to go back to his own shared pad. Mandi and Carla shared the larger bedroom and gave the other to Richie when he stayed over.

Often Richie talked Patsy into staying in the city instead of going home to Yonkers. "Please Baby Doll, can you just stay the night? I want to be one with you all night long, fall asleep with you and wake up to your adorable smile," Richie pleaded.

"How can I resist that offer?" Patsy flashed him a big smile then planted a kiss on his inviting lips.

As time went on, Patsy knew there were big decisions to make about the direction of her life. She knew she must escape Yonkers. Patsy also realized she needed to hide her magnificent Richie from her crazy father. It was hard to keep a coherent storyline to her web of lies. Her mom was constantly questioning if she liked a special guy. Patsy laughed it off and said there were a few she liked, but no one special, and she was merely having a good time with her girlfriends and their sleepovers.

Patsy wanted so badly to absorb all the precious talents that she could take in from Richie, and he, in turn, loved her attention. She watched him practice, write, and rehearse and even joined in. They would spend hours together and she hung on his every word. She was learning so much. He taught her how to harmonize, and even read and write music. The lyrics came easily to her, being a sort of a backstreet poet herself.

Richie caught Patsy one day strumming on Mandi's guitar and singing, "My heart pumps love, love in my veins, it keeps me real, it makes me feel again."

"Baby, that's awesome!" Richie exclaimed.

Patsy jumped up, "I—I didn't know you were there."

"I didn't mean to scare you. You are good."

"I don't know. I'm just fooling around," she said quietly.

"No, Baby, for real. I've seen many musicians, some good and many not so good, but you are a natural."

"Really?" Patsy was surprised and thrilled at the same time. "You don't know how much that means to me!" She ran to him, jumping into his arms and wrapping her legs around him.

Richie even invited Patsy to join him on stage at some of the local haunts a few times. He said he couldn't allow it on his big gigs but claimed he saw the underlying talent and was proud to be her mentor. Patsy was eager to please Richie, and he gave her confidence as he basked in the adoration. They were a dynamic duo.

One night, in a local club where the *Agents of Soul* were playing, Patsy decided to surprise Richie and sat up front in the dimly lit, smoke-filled room. Richie spotted her right away and when he took his twenty-minute break for intermission, he motioned to her to join him in the hall. Richie was all sweaty from his set, and for some reason, that turned Patsy on. She grabbed his silk shirt and pulled him into a tiny nearby broom closet, where she aggressively pushed him down on a stack of paper towels.

He unzipped his fly and sat down on an overturned bucket, then hungrily pulled her jeans down past her hips. He gently pushed her silk panties to one side and slowly sneaked his fingers in to caress her wetness. Patsy was more than ready as she commanded him, "Put it in. I need to feel you fill me up right now."

Richie could not resist, "Oh yeah, Baby," as he slipped his rock-hard cock inside her.

Their moans were heard down the narrow hall as they moved up and down in the confined area. Still facing each other, they kept pumping up and down and came almost immediately in a burst of noisy passion that ended up as uncontrollable laughter.

They were startled when a knock came on the door. Luckily, it was the keyboard man yelling, "It's time, Richie. We're on in five." Richie and Patsy checked the hall to see if the coast was clear as they ran off to their respective restrooms. They were disheveled and wrinkled but so much in love.

They would frequently laugh about their time in the tiny closet. It was their favorite story, and although fast and furious, it would be a shared memory that would last a long time.

As the weeks went on, Richie was getting more and more gigs in New York City and playing the Yonkers club reduced to once a month instead of once a week. The real money was in the city. Even worse, Richie was complaining it was making him nuts too, trying to balance seeing Patsy and playing his music. It wasn't easy. He kept urging her to come to the city more often to see him, and she desperately wanted to. She couldn't figure out how to make it work until Richie came up with what he thought was a perfect plan.

"You can move in with Mandi and Carla. I know they wouldn't mind. They love you, and you'd be in a great location, and their couch is pretty comfy until you find a place of your own. You can pursue your dreams. You don't want to be stuck in Yonkers your whole life, do you?"

The minute Richie said it, she knew he was right, and someday, somehow, she was going to make it happen. "You're right," she sighed, "and it'll happen soon. But I just can't up and leave my mom and Cathleen. They need me." What she couldn't admit to, and a more profound truth, was her fear of her father. He'd be furious if she left the clan-like neighborhood, no longer providing room and board to him, and enraged if he thought she was pursuing her dreams. She knew Roney never wanted her to be happy.

75

CHAPTER 15
Trifecta

It was only a few weeks later that Patsy's father won big at Yonkers Raceway. At home and at the bar, it's all she heard about. She felt like her head was going to explode. As she went about wiping tables in Mahoney's bar and filling salt and pepper shakers, he was ranting about what a remarkable streak of luck and what a smart system he boasted of picking the winners. And now, to top it off, he was planning to go to yet another track, the "Big A," as he put it.

She chuckled to herself, *the Big A-Hole is going to the Big A. That's where he belongs.*

Roney caught her laughing, "What the hell are you laughing at, Patsy?

"Oh nothing, I just never heard of the Big A is all."

With that, Roney stated with his vast wisdom and a shot of whiskey at the ready, "At the Big A—Aqueduct, they have some of the most famous jockeys in the world, and the track is huge! Did you know it's the biggest racetrack in New York City - two hundred and twenty-five-splendid acres?"

He ensured that all of Yonkers knew he was now a major player, and that the Yonkers track was for amateurs. He and Buddy Crenshaw started to travel a little further away to Aqueduct Raceway and try their luck at a bigger, better track. On their first excursion, they both won double what they bet. Aqueduct soon became their new place of play.

"Heaven help us all," Patsy moaned to herself as he repeated the same story for the umpteenth time.

"I'm teaching Patsy's boss, Buddy Crenshaw, how to play the odds and study the bloodlines. I got me-self a system, and it's foolproof," Roney yelled out to anyone who would listen.

Patsy disgustedly watched her dad read the paper, incessantly studying the stats of the horses. Then, when she went to work, her boss was doing the same thing. It was never-ending.

Roney often included "his boys," in the racetrack fun, but rarely invited Patsy or Cathleen to join along. Then one morning, Roney came into her room to announce, "Patsy, I want you to come to the track with us. I have a good feeling about today with my lucky horse, *Shamrock Kelly*. Now that you are an adult, you need to do more adult things and this is one of them, and I'll show you how smart your ol' father really is!"

Pasty, sleepy-eyed, looked up at Roney, "But—"

"No buts about it. You *are* coming with us," he said with that ugly, domineering tone of voice that told Patsy she held no options. As soon as Roney left the room, she rose from her cozy bed and pulled on jeans, an oversized yellow sweatshirt, and white Keds sneakers. She glanced over at Cathleen, who was sound asleep, and whispered, "Lucky her, she doesn't have to go to the track."

Patsy walked out of her room and saw Patrick, Michael, and Brian heading down the stairs, each waving their $10 allowances. "I'm goin' for the long shot today. I have a good feeling about this," Brian exclaimed, barreling down the stairs.

Patrick and Michael followed him, almost pushing him aside, "That's what you said last time, and your stupid horse came in dead last!" Patrick chuckled, and Michael joined in as they made fun of their younger brother.

"I don't want my boys growing up to be racetrack bums," Bridget stated half-jokingly. She was hugging them each as they made it to the bottom of the stairs.

"Oh Mom, what would be so bad about that. All we'd have to do is hit it big one day, and we're set for life. We won't have to work a day in our lives. A dream come true!" Michael said as Patrick and Brian nodded in agreement.

Bridget smiled, "You know there's more to life than just money. Money doesn't always bring happiness." The boys shuffled past her, barely listening to her sound advice.

Patsy followed her brothers down the stairs sulking. "It won't be that bad, and maybe you'll win big!" Bridget exclaimed, kissing her on the cheek and slipping her a twenty.

Although Patsy was miserable about spending the day with "the boys," she knew it gave her mother a break. When Roney was preoccupied, it meant a reprieve from the daily acrid smell of booze and a bad temper she suffered through because of his drinking.

When they reached the Big A, Roney and Buddy and the boys sat in one row, filling out their racetrack forms with their little yellow pencils in hand. Patsy sat two rows behind, but she could hear every word. She was relieved that Buddy left Max minding the office, or he would be breathing down her neck.

"Ok, Buddy, it's the trifecta race in fifth that we need to focus on the horse Shamrock Kelly." Roney was confident, "It's an Irish horse, and I just know he's going to win. It's a sign from my dearly departed granddad in heaven,"

"You know the trifecta is the hardest to win," said Buddy uncertainly.

"Between you winning the daily double last week and my winning streak, I am feeling lucky!" Roney boasted, "And the horse's name is Shamrock Kelly—it's an omen!"

"But, it's a long shot."

"Ah, come on, trust me on this one. But hey, you do what you want. I'm putting all my winnings on Shamrock Kelly." And he played his Irish named horse across the board.

Patsy played a horse called King Richard. She didn't care if the horse won or not. She'd save the ticket and show Richie she was always thinking of him.

When it was time for the race, Roney and Buddy toasted, each with a Guinness they sneaked in from home, then glued their eyes to the track. Patsy grew excited as the horses lined up at the gate. The announcer called each by name and number as the jockeys, with a whip in hand, led them to their stalls, ready to run with anticipation to the same finish line. Then the trumpet sounded, and came the magic words, "They're off!" Of course, this was just the beginning, but Patsy was cheering as the excitement mounted.

Now everyone was ready to cheer Shamrock Kelly on. "Go, go, go," Patsy shouted, "C'mon, Shamrock, Get up there boy, Go faster!" She couldn't believe she was screaming just as loud as her brothers and her dad. Shamrock Kelly must have heard them all as he came from the number four position up to third place and gaining on the outside. They were all jumping up and down now. And go he did, far past the others now gaining from third to second place.

As the horses were getting to the final stretch, it looked like the chances of Roney's horse winning were getting greater and greater. "Go, go, go!" screamed Roney and Buddy.

"Yes, yes, yes! Hurry, hurry, hurry!" Roney yelled out, just like his Granddad did at the carnival. "C'mon, C'mon, Lucky Shamrock, you can do it, you can do it! Holy shit, holy shit, here he comes, he's in the lead, Go!" Roney screamed at the top of his lungs.

Michael, Patrick, and Brian were jumping up and down, and all of them ran to the rail as they watched the long shot take first place by more than a length. The race announcer called, "We have a winner, and it was a long shot. First place goes to Shamrock Kelly!"

Roney screamed at the top of his lungs, "I won! I won! I'm a lucky son of a bitch. It was me granddad in heaven, I tell ya!" Roney threw his arms around Buddy, and a few tears even rolled down his face. He raised his beer to the sky, "Cheers, Granddad."

Patsy's horse came in next to last, but she held onto the ticket anyway and wished she was with Richie instead of her brothers and Mr. Crenshaw. Still, she couldn't help running down to congratulate her dad. The excitement was contagious, and in a brief, special moment, they were all hugging and jumping.

Roney and the boys ran to the cashier's cage with a stack of winning tickets. As the boys were all underage, Roney took charge of all the tickets. And, it was even better than just Roney's horse winning. His two other favorites made up the rest of the trifecta, which meant even more money for him.

Patsy and her brothers watched on the side as the cashier counted green bill after green bill creating a large stack of hundred-dollar bills. It looked like so much and then Roney cashed in another ticket. Finally, the cashier discretely motioned the guard to come over and for Roney to step aside.

Patsy and the others watched, awestruck. A guard appeared and escorted Roney to a secret side door. An official-looking man in a business suit and the security guard ushered Roney into a private room where Patsy saw her dad disappear, leaving them all to wonder what was going on.

Patsy scolded her brothers, who were starting to act up. "Shut up you guys. Dad has this under control, so don't draw attention to yourselves. For God's sake, try to keep a low profile."

Michael shot back, "My dad is rich, I know it, I know it."

"Shush, Michael!"

They all hovered together patiently for about twenty minutes. When Roney emerged, there was a look of complete delight on his face strutting like a mummer in that Philadelphia parade. He gathered his family and Buddy in a huddle and said in a whisper, "I got me-self a cashier's check for 90,000 dollars. I'm rich, your daddy is rich and don't worry Buddy, there's a thousand in here for you and plenty for all of you. I'm a rich man, a goddamn rich man!"

Patsy never saw her father even remotely happy as he was at that moment. He ran to the nearest payphone and didn't even bother to close the door. As Patsy, Buddy, and the boys huddled around, Patsy saw Roney with a giant smile on his face shouting into the phone, "I won big! I won big, me darlin' wife! Meet me at the bar in an hour and invite everyone we know for free beer and champagne all day!"

The security guard stayed with them until they were safely in their family station wagon.

Roney then took a swallow of whiskey from a silver flask he was carrying before he entered the car and threw the car keys to Buddy. Roney could hardly talk on the way home. Patsy never saw him quite like that, and she was grateful he wasn't ranting—not yet anyway.

When they made it to the bar, it was packed full of patrons. The day just got crazier and more chaotic as it went on. At one point, Roney cried real tears as he said prayers of thankfulness to his granddad, whom he said smiled down on him from heaven.

The story got more embellished with each new telling and each double shot of Canadian Club whiskey. At least he was kind to Mom in all of this, Pasty thought. She could hardly believe it when she saw Roney hugging Bridget, which was a rare sight. He even threw hundred-dollar bills to show off. Bridget, thinking quickly, scooped them up and put them down her bra.

Patsy was amused at the fuss but still not as happy as the rest of the crew. She wondered to herself why she couldn't feel excited for him. Deep inside, she was only hoping he would give her a few of the hundred-dollar bills, but other than that, she was anxious to get home and wondering if the *Agents of Soul* band were rehearsing right now.

Finally, Patsy got fed up, "Mom, I can't take any more of this bragging. I want to go out with my friends."

Bridget gave a flat reply, "No, you're not. The town is buzzing with the news, and the Mayor might stop by. Patsy, your dad is a hero, and we need you here to help. Anyway, he's already given me a bundle of cash, and there's money for you too. Try for once in your life to be happy and grateful for your dad."

Patsy sighed, "OK, I'll do my best."

"That's my girl!" Bridget grabbed her by the hand and, before Patsy knew it, she was on the dance floor. Dancing with her mom felt like the old days. Her father brought her a glass of his best Canadian club and Ginger Ale, and for a few minutes, Patsy, her mom, and her father danced together. It all felt good, like they were a real family.

When the Mayor of Yonkers appeared, he downed a few and soon was dancing the Hustle with Bridget. It was a blast for a while, but the buzz soon passed, and Patsy found herself alienated from the celebration. She was sure she could come up with a plan to get out of Yonkers to be with Richie and become a real New Yorker.

The party continued throughout the weekend, and Patsy watched as Roney became the star of his show. Finally, he was at long last getting all the attention, adoration, and respect he so wanted. He was renowned in the neighborhood by everyone. Bridget and Roney's relatives and friends decided to plan a small parade for the following week on their adjoining streets, where Roney would ride in a red convertible amid streamers and confetti.

"Your dad is making a big contribution to the Yonkers Recreation Club, and the Mayor wants to give Roney a parade and a plaque," Bridget told Patsy. "It's going to happen next weekend, so don't make any plans. And you know what else? Your dad is buying me a brand-new stage at Mahoney's with velvet drawstring curtains too, and maybe a new washer/dryer combination. I won't have to use the wringer washer!" Hugging Patsy, she went on, "Oh my, he's back to being the boy I met at the carnival."

Patsy wanted to barf and thought to herself, *Money really makes people act differently.* She wasn't impressed or fooled by her father. She knew the other dark side would emerge eventually—the drunken, nasty side.

The Mahoney Big Shot Party seemed to go on forever. The only thing that made it the least bit bearable was that Richie was away on several gigs and wasn't reachable. So she called Mandi. The answering machine picked up and Patsy left a message, "Hey girl, it's Patsy, I miss you so much, but I've been stuck in this lifeless town for too long. Call my office if you get a chance. Would love to hear what's been going on with all of you. Bye!"

When she hung up, she realized how much she missed the city and especially Richie. She was so craving his kisses and his arms around her. She began to cry. Her dreams, too, were full of anxiety about getting away and finding Richie.

She ran through the bushes in the dark wet forest. Her hair got mangled in the thorny vines as she hurried to the cave where the music was coming from. It was getting louder and louder, and she started to sprint, losing her shoes, and nearly flying towards the cave. The sign read: Love Inside, and she knew he was waiting.

As she stepped barefoot inside the cave, she couldn't contain the desire that enveloped her body. She turned the corner, and there was a shadow with his back to her. She saw the figure and heard him playing a sultry tune on the saxophone.

She inched closer, and as the figure turned around, she gasped in horror. What she saw was a Howdy Doody wooden puppet playing a plastic saxophone. The wooden mouth moved up and down, saying, 'Hello Dear. Hello Dear,' in a robotic sing-song way. She reached out, trying to rip apart his tangled marionette strings. Her feet were muddy and sticky, and her hands were tied together with strings now. She was stuck in the cave with the puppet as the loud music stopped playing. She heard instead the children's theme song, "It's Howdy Doody Time, It's Howdy Doody Time…."

She freed her hands to put them over her ears and tried to scream, but no sound came out.

The dream felt like a nightmare. Instantly, Patsy understood its mystery. She knew she must act soon, or she would lose her mind. When she walked into work the following Monday, they were still celebrating. A cake shaped like a shamrock and boxes of expensive chocolates and green carnations were on every desk. She fought her way down the aisles with green balloons and streamers hanging from the ceiling. Patsy wanted to puke, but smiled when the office applauded as she sat at her desk. It was compliments of Buddy, who now was throwing money around like a sailor on leave. Patsy wondered when the celebrating would stop.

Then, as if some magical powers sent Richie a message, he called her at the office that afternoon. He never called her at work before, so when she answered the phone, she said, "Good afternoon, Crenshaw Insurance. How may I direct your call?" When she heard his voice, her whole body began to melt.

His voice was low, and the words came as slow and sweet, "Hey, I'd like to find out where my baby has been. Can you help me?" Then he started singing the opening lines of the Hall and Oats song, *"Baby, come back, any kind of fool could see, there was something in everything about you...."*

Patsy's eyes were hot with tears, and she bent her head in case snoopy Max was around. Then, clutching the phone close, she whispered, "I'll be there this weekend and maybe even for good. I can't live like this anymore."

"I'm counting on it."

"Me, too. I'll make it work, I swear, and this time I'm not returning home."

"I love you, Baby Girl."

"Who was that?" Max asked when she hung up. He smiled at Patsy, and when he did, his yellow teeth and lips were full of dark brown chocolate. She realized then he was the scary puppet in her dream.

Patsy stifled a laugh. This little creep was soon to be out of her life. Turning back to her desk, she said, "Just the bank. I called earlier to make sure a check cleared. Here ya go, Max, take my chocolates. I'm allergic to nuts."

"Thanks, Patsy, mine are gone already!"

Patsy watched him as he walked away with the chocolates. Then, she began humming to herself, "It's Howdy Doody Time. it's Howdy Doody time...."

Her escape to New York City was finally in the works, and she knew she would do anything to make it happen. She wrote her step-by-step strategy in a steno notebook.

1. Go to the clinic for birth control.
2. Pack my best outfits, but not too many.
3. Study and memorize the train schedule.
4. Hoard the money Mom gave me and my savings.
5. Get out of Yonkers while everyone is still on the *Shamrock Kelly* high.

It would be a piece of cake, but she needed Bridget in on the plan. She devised a scheme of a made-up job interview in the city. She just had to convince her mom this was the only thing that could make her dreams a reality. It must work, she told herself. It was now or never.

CHAPTER 16
Manhattan

Bridget was beyond excited about getting a new stage. But to Patsy's dismay, it was all she talked about. Patsy listened politely, but her thoughts were never far from seizing on the moment she could coax her mom into helping her escape. There was no other reason for her to listen so politely to the same dull stories.

"Patsy, with this new stage, I can expand my tap-dancing classes and teach more students. And your dad bought Patrick, Michael, and Brian season tickets to the Yankee's games, and the latest gear too for their sports, and oh so generous was he with donations to the baseball and football teams." Patsy smiled a fake smile and nodded her head.

Bridget continued her rant, "The uniforms will all have Mahoney's logo on the back. Your dad is so kind, Patsy. He's even buying all the kids on the team new Air Jordan sneakers. There isn't anything he wouldn't do for his boys and their friends. And, for his girls too. Cathleen picked out a new ten-speed bike in her favorite color—bright purple!" Bridget reached into her pocket, drew out two crisp one-hundred-dollar bills, and handed them to Patsy, "For some new outfits, Honey! And there's more where that came from. Your dad said go and have fun and do whatever you women do. What do you say? You and me get a manicure and get our toes done too. We'll become real glamour girls!"

"Sure, that'd be nice. And Mom, you are looking so happy lately." Patsy meant the compliment. She also knew this outing would put her mom in a positive frame of mind. Patsy was anxious to share her escape plans with her.

The next day, Bridget and Patsy visited the only full-service beauty salon in Yonkers. Bridget got her first facial, a vibrant new golden blonde hair color, and bright red nails. Patsy loved seeing her mom pampering herself, and she noticed that she was acting more like a girlfriend than her old housewife mom.

The following day was also a good one. Roney complimented Bridget's new hairdo and even danced her around the kitchen. Bridget enjoyed herself, and Patsy caught her singing *Happy Days are Here Again*, followed by *I Feel Pretty*.

When her dad left the kitchen, Patsy thought this would be a great time to divulge her plan. "Mom, can you come up to my room please? I need to talk to you, and I need some privacy." Patsy had rehearsed her little speech and went over the details of what she would say, even though she fabricated most of the story. Pacing back and forth, she turned, and her mom was standing there.

"OK, what's so private, Girlie?"

Feeling very nervous, Patsy spoke fast, "Well, you won't believe this, but I applied for a job in a great upscale restaurant in the city and never thought they would get back to me so quickly. It was an ad I saw, and I went in on a whim, and when I met the owner, she said I would be perfect as a day hostess, and they even want me to start right away. The best thing is that I have a place to stay with two of my girlfriends. It's like a dream come true for me."

Bridget, still on Cloud Nine from Roney's windfall, wasn't at all surprised. Her only retort was, "Don't you want to stay to see your dad get his plaque from the Yonkers Humanitarian Society?"

"No, Mom, I have my orientation today and must go. I promise I'll call you every chance I get. Please wish me well. I didn't want to tell you until I was sure."

Bridget pulled out a large wad of cash, "Here's a little something from me. New York is a very expensive place," Bridget clasped Patsy's hands, holding the money inside.

Bridget stared at Patsy for a long time. Her eyes got watery, and her smile tinged with sadness. She reached out and hugged Patsy tightly. "Oh Honey, you're all grown up now, and I think it's the right thing to do."

"You do? Just like that, no pushback. No saying Dad will blow his top?"

Bridget shook her head and laughed. "I'll take care of your father. And you couldn't have picked a better time. He's so wrapped up in his good fortune. But I suspect you figured that out!"

They both giggled and hugged. "I love you, Mom!"

"I love you, Patsy, with all my heart. And I want you to have all the happiness in the world. I want you to do it for you and for me. I mean it. Your breaking free and going for what you really want is the best gift you could give me." Bridget belted out a song while doing a tap dance routine. *"I'll Take Manhattan, the Bronx, and Staten Island too."*

"You're a trip Mom, you really are. You always crack me up." laughed Patsy.

When Patsy arrived outside of Mandi and Carla's apartment door with her meager belongings, her stomach dropped, and a feeling of panic started to take over. She'd left home in such haste she didn't consider the enormity of this move or even have a chance to think about what she was doing. She left life as she knew it behind. It was not a beautiful life, but there was security and comfort in a home with family. Before she allowed the scared voice in her head to change her mind, she was able to disconnect from her thoughts and knock feverishly on the apartment door.

Mandi flung open the door, "We've been waiting for you!" Mandi and Carla embraced Patsy, and they all jumped up and down like schoolgirls.

Patsy's fears slipped away. "I can't thank you enough for letting me stay here until I find a place of my own."

"We're happy to have you. You can crash here for as long as you want," Mandi replied.

Carla chimed in, "You'll share my room. We squeezed another twin bed in our room for now." Carla picked up Patsy's worn-out Samsonite suitcase and walked into her room.

That night Mandi danced into the room, saying, "Let's celebrate, Amigos, and get on our best rags. We're hittin' the clubs, and here's a little somethin' to help you get in the mood." Sometimes Mandi used Quaaludes, sometimes even Ecstasy, but this time, she handed Carla and Patsy small black capsules that she called Black Beauties.

Carla shouted out, "Right on, girlfriend!" as she grabbed one and washed it down with a Fresca. Patsy took one and shoved it in her military jacket pocket. She said she would save it for later, but knew she wouldn't take it. It didn't bother her if others did drugs, but she liked to always keep a clear head.

A few days later, Patsy called her mom to thank her for all the money and the support. She was anxious to know how Roney reacted to her move. Bridget repeated the whole story to Patsy with the lilt of laughter in her voice. She was ecstatic, telling the latest tale of her Big Shot hubby, "Patsy, I told him three times that you left, but he was so into himself and all his new friends, of which there are many now. Then the other night, when he was at the height of his Big Shot routine, he took a break. He didn't even take a drink, and he called me over. "OK, woman, I just want to tell you I heard what you said about Patsy moving out and getting a new job and all. Tell her it's OK with her old man. And if you didn't give her a few hundred from her fabulous father, tell her it's coming!"

"Does he know about the money you already gave me from the stage builder? Do you still have enough to get the new stage?"

Her mother laughingly shot back, "Oh, Patsy, I'm not so dumb. Listen to this, Shamus O'Hara came in saying he wanted to congratulate Roney M. Rockefeller. As soon as that happened, your dad was off and running and in his glory. He roared, 'Come have a drink, my friend, it's Open Bar all day!'

Well, I saw my chance and quickly called the contractor and yelled out to your father, making it loud enough for all his new-found friends to hear, 'Hey, Roney, the contractor needs a bit more money to do the stage in real style.'

"Your dad being a Big Shot took out a huge wad of hundred-dollar bills and handed them to me shouting like the carnival barker he is, 'Here, Bridget, get the new stage, new velvet curtains and have them throw in a spinning Disco Ball while they're at it!'"

Bridget was laughing as she went on, "Everyone cheered and slapped him on the back, but, my dear, I laughed hardest of all! I always know how to get around your dad. You can count on me, Patsy."

"Thanks, Mom, you are the coolest ever."

Patsy became more and more acclimated to city life and the pace of New York. Her days and nights were full of endless excitement. She held down two waitressing jobs and kept up with Mandi and Carla and their constant partying. As time went on, the three of them frequented every popular club in the city, even the renowned Studio 54. Their nicknames around town were Bad Mandi, Crazy Carla, and Pretty Patsy. They were getting reputations around New York clubs as the Three Amigos.

Richie was another story. He played gigs every night, and the few nights Patsy spent with him were not as wild and intoxicating as they used to be. Their former crazy sex life was dwindling, and with it her interest in his music. Rather than obsessing over everything Richie, she was back to concentrating on her dreams and ambitions.

When they were alone, Patsy ignored Richie while he was playing a new harmony on his sax, and instead was scanning the Village Voice for auditions. They hardly said a word to each other, which was becoming the norm lately.

Richie, finally putting the sax down, spoke in a low, pleading voice showing sad puppy dog eyes, "Make me happy, Baby."

"No can do, I'm running late for an acting workshop," Patsy lied, just wanting to get out of sex altogether. She stared at his pouty bottom lip, which looked pathetic to her. Patsy was sure now that her priorities would be her career.

Richie looked perplexed and muttered under his breath, "Go then, knock yourself out." He grabbed his already emerging erection and added, "Say goodbye to my little friend!" He was trying to be funny, but Patsy didn't laugh like she used to. His jokes were becoming stale.

As the days turned into weeks, there was less and less sex with Richie and more and more partying with the girls. Although happy with her newfound freedom, her dream of performing on stage was not coming to fruition as quickly as she hoped, and auditions were few and far between and filled with others in search of their dreams. The reality was setting in, and the small-town girl felt just a little insecure as she pondered her life. She wasn't meant for this competition that existed in the city, and who knew if she would ever get a break and have someone notice her.

There were so many who she imagined were better than her with training in the performing arts. The negativity filled her head. She tried to shake it off with the realization she would just have to fight harder for her goal. One thing was for sure—she couldn't go home, and her negative thoughts couldn't get the best of her.

Even though she knew she would never go back, she missed her mother at times, especially their memorable mother-daughter moments. Patsy kept in touch with her mom, but the phone calls were all about Moneybags Roney. She told the same stories over and over about how he was spending the winnings. There was little talk of their shared days together.

Patsy only listened to bits and pieces of the one-way conversation, "Dad just bought a new TV if you can believe it. I got that new Jordache purse I've dreamed about, and I just bought Cathleen one of those nameplate necklaces in 14-karat gold." Patsy listened and feigned enthusiasm, but she didn't care that much.

"Let me get Cathleen. She wants to talk to you, too!" Bridget exclaimed.

"Hi, Patsy! You won't believe how great our room looks now. Mommy helped me redo it, so it's just my room now. I love it, thank you for leaving, and I hope you don't come home anytime soon 'cause I have cool posters up now on all the walls, and you might not like them."

Patsy laughed, "Don't worry little sis, I promise I won't. The room is all yours. You deserve it!"

"Thanks, and I really do miss you, but don't come back! Here's Mommy again."

"We all miss you so much, Patsy. Even Buddy and Max Crenshaw miss you, but they understand you want to better yourself. How are you doing? I worry about you. Do you need any money?"

"I don't need any more money. I'm doing great and working hard and have so many opportunities here. I'm happy you are doing well. Give everyone my love. Gotta go, I'm late for an audition," she lied again, and hung up the phone. In the back of her mind, she only wished it were true. One audition, any audition, but her mother could never know that.

Every morning Patsy scanned the *Village Voice, Variety,* and the local papers for auditions and try-outs for anything. Mandi encouraged Patsy to take a few classes at NYU to learn more about music and acting.

Patsy smiled when Mandi said, "Hey girl, I believe in you, and I'm going to get you into some studies that will look good on your resume. You gotta impress these theatre types. They go for all that BS."

"Grateful Amigo, this helps so much and means the world to me."

92

Thanks to Mandi's help, Patsy signed up for improv and film classes and anything to do with music and even joined a comedy sketch group. She started going to as many local plays and workshops as she could. Patsy was happier than she'd ever been. Even more than when she first met Richie. She didn't need a guy right now. She was lucky to have great friends, and because of their support, her musical side began to flourish. She was also meeting the most interesting people, the kind she would never meet if she stayed in Yonkers. They were talented people in musical theatre, screenwriting, composing, and acting. She began to make new friends fast. They were so lovely to her and so cool and modern. She was a bit intimidated, but her confidence grew each time she ventured onto something new. She absorbed each experience like a sponge.

Patsy sat in on a practice session after music class with her new buddy Bernard. He was a prodigy and lived his music 24/7. He was eccentric and always wore a bow tie and horn-rimmed glasses even though his vision was perfect. There was a rumor his IQ was a whopping 165.

"Hey there, Bernard, show me more of that jazz sound you composed on the keyboard. I'm lovin' the beat and the scatting parts," Patsy said, "It's way mellow, man. Your tempo is so groovy!"

"Solid, pretty lady. Just for you. I'll play all night."

With new connections, Patsy did a few walk-ons in off-Broadway plays and tryouts for low-budget movies shot in Tribeca and SoHo. But she was happy hanging out with Mandi and other 'up and comers' in the Biz. She felt she was in with the in-crowd.

One day, after getting off a little early from her waitressing shift, Patsy felt a little lonely and thought maybe she would give Richie another try and perhaps even rekindle their sex life. She decided to surprise him and show up at one of his gigs. His crew knew her and waved to her as she walked backstage.

She heard the keyboard player say, "Uh oh, maybe she should wait just a minute or knock before she enters to see if he's decent."

Patsy heard them laugh and suddenly there was a queasy feeling in her stomach. As she walked into the back room, she got a whiff of cigarettes and Ivory soap, but a robust floral fragrance was also there. As she scanned the room, she saw his dark curls, and cuddled next to him was a woman with long, straight hair. They were both hunched over a table. She couldn't figure out what they were doing, but as she approached, Richie swiftly raised his head after sniffing in the white line of powder. He caught a glimpse of Patsy and turned to her. His beautiful dark eyes were bulging and bloodshot, and he said, "Hey girl, what are you doing here? Want to join us?" He looked like a puppy that got caught peeing on the rug. He added quickly, "This is Rachel, our new singer."

With that, Richie made a gesture for Rachel to leave the room. Patsy felt it was an unspoken signal between them as Rachel scurried out giggling and saying, "OK, catch you later, Richie." Patsy glared at her when she saw the white powder still smudged on Rachel's nose.

"I see you're busy," Patsy said to Richie, "and I'm sorry to disturb you, but I'm glad I saw this." She started to leave, then turned and continued, "It makes it easier to end this craziness and get on with my life. It's over, Richie. There's no way forward for us anymore. I feel bad, but I'm relieved. Have a good life."

Richie grinned and said, "Baby, don't you know I have to have attention, and you've turned cold. A man has his needs and listen, they come on to me, I don't go after them. You changed Patsy, and I need to have some fun—"

Patsy cut him off, "Have at it, Richie. You're just another sorry, coked-up musician, and I'm way beyond that lifestyle now." Saying those words, a lump formed in her throat, and she

94

was afraid she would cry. She fought the urge with all her might. She would leave strong and sure of herself.

Richie looked up at her with bloodshot eyes smirking, and defiantly bent down to finish another line of coke. Patsy walked out the backstage door as angry tears started to flow. She wasn't quite sure why she was so upset since she was the one who distanced herself from him these past months. And, she realized it wasn't that he was doing coke, it was a norm around the music scene. Instead, it was seeing him with another woman. She couldn't help wondering if he'd been sleeping around the whole time they were together.

Patsy ran home to Mandi and Carla and shared the brief, shocking encounter she witnessed with Richie. Mandi said tenderly, "Hey girlie girl, just remember, we're the three amigos, and we stick together. Screw Richie, you come first with Carla and me!" Patsy felt so relieved that they chose her over Richie. She knew Mandi and Carla loved her as a fellow clubber, but she realized they loved her as a friend too.

After that night, Patsy was more determined than ever to get on with her ambitions and career goals. It wasn't easy in New York, but the independence she felt now gave her the strength to concentrate without distractions. She was on a mission, and her whole attitude focused on doing everything to achieve each goal she set for herself. New energy encompassed her entire being.

Patsy was still waiting tables when she obtained her SAG card, and went on every audition, curtain call, and even did poetry recitations in reading rooms and coffee houses. Fitting all of this in was exhausting, but also satisfying.

Patsy enjoyed her social life and went along when Mandi and Carla christened a new club or attended, by invitation only, the latest smoky lounge. Always though, her ambition took precedence over everything else as she begged off the late hours, opting for auditions or try-outs instead of new club openings.

The dating scene was getting complicated too. The musical and artsy crowd sure liked to party, and Patsy became enamored with them to a certain extent. Along the way, she met many guys who were into her and engaged in a few one-night stands since the excitement was feeding her sexual urges. There was nothing serious with any of them, and Patsy felt no guilt. It was the cliched atmosphere of sex, drugs, and rock and roll, but it soon ceased to thrill her. After a conversation with Carla, she put the brakes on. "No more, Carla, I'm just not interested in the social scene, and clubbing is wearing me out!"

"Hey, girlfriend, we understand. Just know Mandi and I will be here for you always!"

"I know, and I so appreciate your support. I love you both so much!" Patsy gestured dramatically. "I'm determined to be famous one day. That will always be my first love, and nothing can transcend that dream."

Mandi and Carla both clapped at this performance and egged her on. "Bravo, Bravo," they shouted together as they applauded, and Patsy took a bow and threw kisses.

She tried her luck at everything that looked the slightest promising, even volunteering to read to children at the local library, where she acted out the parts of the characters in the stories. It didn't pay anything, but she decided to do everything possible to utilize her talents and hone her craft.

Other gigs weren't as easy as she thought they would be. Some of the casting calls were routine and boring as she waited her turn in crowded rooms. Then when she went on stage, half the time the casting directors looked bored and yawning from hearing so many others ahead of her. She knew what to do instantly, making her intro brief and smiling all the while.

She was cautious, never knowing if a guy who looked like a hobo could be the director. She was polite to everyone. She also was given impromptu scripts and was always ready to put her spin on things. Little by little, she was learning and growing with every experience—good or bad. She was determined.

She heard the assistant yell out, "Next," and then the casting director, "Go" or "Action," and she was off. It was becoming second nature.

On her one day off from waitressing, she sipped her tea and glanced at the want ads in a Pennysaver newspaper. It read simply, *Pleasant looking Actress wanted for a cable cooking commercial, Having Fun with Desserts. No experience necessary.*

Hmm, this might be something, she thought and quickly scribbled down the address.

The audition was in Brooklyn and was easy to find, but the neighborhood wasn't the best. She walked in the door of the run-down building and was greeted in the dingy hallway by a short, stocky man. She knew not to make first impressions based on looks, but he was unattractive to her, sporting a receding hairline with shiny bald spots that stood out against his dark oily hair. He was wearing a bright blue button-down shirt with four buttons undone to expose his hairy chest. A large cross hung from his neck and his beer belly flopped over his too-tight pants. For a split second, she thought of ditching the whole thing, but then convinced herself that any audition was worth a try.

With a big cigar dangling from his mouth, he said, "Honey, you are just what I have been lookin' for. Step right in and let's get started."

"I'm Patsy Mahoney, and I'm here for the cooking audition."

"Perfect, I can tell you'll be great. I just can tell. Follow me!" Patsy smiled and felt better that the man was so friendly. He led her to a mostly empty, dark room.

She walked into the room where there was only a dilapidated folding table in the middle. There was no kitchen or chef. It was just Patsy and this rube of a director.

97

Apprehensively, Patsy asked, "Excuse me Sir, where are the other actors?"

"I already auditioned them. I want your unique spin on it and see how you can improvise on your own. See, there is no script. Come on, Sweetie. Let's get started and show me your stuff." The way he talked and the lascivious way he looked at her made her feel a little uneasy, but she did his bidding and considered it a creative challenge.

He then said, "Walk around and ad-lib as if you were passing out bowls and spoons to the pastry chef."

She thought it odd but did it anyway and walked around, making up little blurbs like, "Here ya go, Chef," and, "Can I help you with that, Chef?"

He seemed delighted and handed Patsy an apron to put on. He said it would create just the right effect. Patsy did as he asked, and then the sleazeball said, "Just to be a little more provocative, Honey, could you lose the tee shirt and just wear the apron?"

As the creep edged closer to her and touched the seam of the tee-shirt, Patsy began to calculate her next move. She sweetly smiled, "Oh sure, just give me a second and let me put some fresh lipstick on."

"That's not necessary, Sweetie, just lose the top," he sort of snarled the command.

"No, I want to look just right for you," she said in her best breathy voice.

By this time, he was practically salivating. Patsy pulled out the tube of pepper spray disguised as lipstick that Mandi gave to her. She shot him directly in his left eye.

The old sleazeball dropped to his knees and screamed. "You little bitch, I'm calling the cops on you," he yelled, rubbing his one eye frantically.

"Go ahead, you dirty bastard, and I'll tell them what kind of a scam you're running here!" When he tried to get on his feet, she gave one last squirt, hitting him in his other eye. Laughing now, she asked, "Is this provocative enough for you, you old pervert?"

As she rushed out into the hall, she heard him moaning, "I'm blind, I'm blind, you little bitch, I'm blind."

Once out on the street, Patsy felt exhilarated. Realizing she was still wearing the apron, she tossed it in a dumpster nearby and slammed the top down hard. She was triumphant and felt like a real New Yorker now, unafraid and fighting back. Patsy was learning the ropes and becoming empowered. She was determined to make it now, and nothing was going to stop her.

She quickly flagged a cab and jumped in. "Please go—go fast!" she yelled at the cab driver.

"Ok, girl, I'm goin'," he said in his thick Jamaican accent, "You, OK?"

"Yes, yes, please, just go." Once the car started moving, Patsy couldn't contain herself and told the cab driver the story about the sleazeball so-called casting director.

The cabbie said, "Hey, ya want I should go back dare and punch dem lights out?" Patsy and the cabbie ended up laughing until the end of the trip.

Patsy told her story of bravery to everyone. She got advice and sympathy from all her friends, but Mandi was the one who affected her the most when she said, "Right on, girl! You are fierce. I'm so proud of you. You are one bad-ass broad. You're a real New Yorker now!"

Some said to report the guy, but not Mandi. She said, "I'll bet that guy is scared shitless now. We are gonna change your name from Pretty Patsy to Pitiless Patsy." Patsy laughed and declared her love for her friend, who always told the truth and made her feel good about herself.

CHAPTER 17
Bubbles

This same routine lasted for about a month, one mediocre audition after another until an advertisement changed her life. Again, it was Mandi who came to the rescue. "Patsy, my girlie girl, look at this! It could work for you, especially with your looks!" Mandi shoved the paper in Patsy's face.

Patsy read aloud, "Contest for the most original rendition of a one-minute commercial for Calgon bubble bath." Patsy's face lit up with a smile from ear to ear.

"Is this perfect for you or what?" Mandi flopped next to her onto the couch. "Go on, keep reading."

Patsy read the contest rules, "The applicant has to write, sing, and star in the commercial. The prize for originality is $1,000 and a year's contract with Calgon."

As Patsy read, a phenomenal idea was forming. She decided to take the humorous angle instead of the beauty angle she felt sure others would pursue. The ideas flowed like sweet honey. She didn't have to memorize anything. Instead, her ad-lib talents kicked in. This was her moment—her commercial, and she knew it.

Once she performed her act in front of her friends, Mandi introduced her to a classmate at NYU who was studying videography. With her photography experience, Carla was also thrilled to help. Another of Mandi's friends owned an old clawfoot tub and lived only a few streets away. They all got together in a group effort to shoot the production.

The rest of the props were easy. Patsy used one of her mother's fancy hats she took when she left home and she found some outrageous dangling earrings and granny glasses at a thrift store. She channeled her glamorous teenage tub-time alter ego Bubbles Lamour, but decided this time Bubbles would be a more humorous character and less provocative siren. It was as though the stars were aligning for her.

The one-minute time limit was challenging—to make everything come together in sixty seconds. Patsy carried a stopwatch with her and practiced until it became sheer perfection down to the second. She put on a command performance for everyone who helped. Mandi, who owned the expensive video camera, worked with the other videographer as Carla shouted out, "Action!"

Looking coyly into the camera, Patsy began, "Bonjour, I'm Bubbles Lamour, and I say Goodbye troubles. Here comes Bubbles. And I'm here to let you know…." Then, in her best Marlene Dietrich voice, she belted out in the tune of *Life is just a bowl of cherries*, "Life is just a tub of bubbles, so live and laugh at it all." At the end, she added, "And blow all your troubles away with Calgon," as she blew bubbles off into the air.

It was excellent, and the girls hysterically laughed and cheered when they saw the final film. They thought her performance was comedic genius.

Patsy's appointment for her audition was Thursday at 2 p.m. Promptly at that time, the production assistant called her onto the set. There were three judges. The older grey-haired man showed little emotion as he said, "State your name and contact info and then proceed."

Patsy almost froze up for a moment when she spotted the tub in the middle of the room. She was so terrified, she nearly shouted Patrice Mahoney, but at the last second decided on Patsy. After that, her mind went blank, and she stumbled, trying to remember her full address, finally just saying Greenwich Village and mumbling an inaudible phone number.

The grey-haired gent said, "Calm down honey, let's see what you got."

Patsy thought to herself, *what the hell, I'm here, I'm rehearsed, I'm going for it.* Patsy said, "I have a few props." All three of the judges laughed at that. Patsy laughed too, and suddenly confidence flooded her being, and she felt ready to become Bubbles Lamour.

Patsy grabbed her hat and granny glasses, hopped in the empty tub on the set, and started her one-minute audition. The bolero top she was wearing was pulled down over her shoulders, showing them bare, and she quickly put her granny glasses on the end of her nose. Next, she plopped the ornate hat on her head and grinning, began her carefully timed sixty-second performance. She sang out in a clear, French-accented voice and finally made the gesture to blow bubbles in the air. She said to herself, *I did it, I did it, just as I dreamed it would be.* At that moment, no matter the outcome, she knew she was the best she could be.

When she finished the skit in person, and the judges viewed and timed her one-minute VHS tape, the same grey-haired gentleman said, "Thank you. If you are chosen you will be notified within the week." She thought she heard a slight giggle from one of the judges, but didn't know if that was good or bad. And just like that, it was over.

Even though the audition was nearly perfect, after seeing the stoic faces of the three judges, Patsy couldn't determine whether they liked it or not. They barely said more than two sentences to her. As she passed the remaining contestants in the waiting room, Patsy saw at least five more beautiful girls and even one guy waiting to audition. Her previous self-assurance took a big, fat nosedive. Her stomach churned as she felt defeated. Yet, in her heart of hearts, she gave it her all and honestly felt her audition would be beyond the others in originality. With a lump in her throat, she calmed herself, *Don't worry, Bubbles, our day will come. We're not giving up, not yet anyway.* Tears stung her eyes as she bravely hailed a cab to return home.

The following day, at 10 a.m., the phone rang. It startled Patsy, who was already on edge and suffering from a nervous stomach from the audition. She took a swig of Pepto Bismol and answered the phone, not recognizing the deep nasally voice on the other end, "My name is Madge Stein. I am calling for Patsy Mahoney on behalf of Calgon."

"I'm Patsy," she said anxiously.

"First, I'd like to ask your permission to be your agent related to this Calgon commercial. Second, congratulations, kid. You were the fastest decision ever made for the funniest commercial that the Calgon executives ever saw!"

Pasty couldn't believe what she just heard, "Excuse me?"

"So what, *Schatzi*, are you hard of hearing? I said you—" Madge began again, sounding slightly annoyed.

Patsy cut Madge off as she stuttered, "I'm sorry, I understand. I think I'm just in shock!"

"You should be. It's a big deal. Honey, this is 'bashert' for sure."

"Bashert?"

"It's Yiddish. It means it's meant to be. Now, what do you think of my offer?"

"Yes, yes, of course you can be my agent!"

"Come to my office tomorrow and sign some papers, and we'll be all set. My secretary will call you later with a time and address." Madge hung up.

Patsy shouted out to Mandi and Carla, "Oh my God, thank you my friends. I got it! I can't believe it. I got the commercial!" Tears rolled down her face as she thought to herself, *Thank you, Bubbles Lamour. We're on our way to making our dreams come true.*

Bubbles Lamour – Calgon Commercial

CHAPTER 18
Madge

When Patsy walked into Madge Stein's thirty-fourth street office two days later, she shook all over. Her palms were sweaty, but her heart was singing, *zip a dee doo-dah, zip a dee ay, my oh my what a wonderful day!*

There was no one at the desk outside of the glass door marked Madge Stein. Patsy peeked through the glass, and although the office was small, Patsy was impressed by the unusual antique furnishings. Red velvet curtains framed a cushy, tufted sofa. In one corner was an old roll-top desk. An elegant, highly polished coffee table was between two leatherette chairs. Off to the side was a beautiful, huge cherry wood desk. She was sure Madge loved antiquity by the look of her office.

Patsy knocked softly on the door. "Hello," she called quietly, feeling her knees tremble to match her trembling voice.

A large head shot up from under the desk, "Come in, come in. Don't be shy. Get your *tuchus* in here. My dumb secretary Rhonda must be on her thirty-minute break. That *meshuganah* broad smokes like a chimney, and dammit, hold up a minute, I can't find my fancy-schmancy shoes."

Patsy walked in timidly, and noticed Madge was huge, probably six feet tall. Her shoulders were broad. A pencil was stuck behind each ear, and she wore large square Sally Jessie Raphael red glasses low on her nose. She also had on a vintage-style tent blouse which housed two gigantic breasts that bounced underneath. Patsy wondered if she wore a bra. She donned tie-dyed denim bell-bottom pants and leopard mules that were at least a size 12. Peeking out were red toenails with yellow daisies artfully painted on top. All of this was capped with curly, dark black hair that stuck to her forehead in sweaty ringlets.

Patsy shakily reached out her hand to shake, "How do you do?"

Madge wanted no handshake, and she waved it away as if it were an annoyance. She forged ahead with a big hug, "How the hell are ya, *Shayna Punim*?" Patsy didn't understand what she was saying, but Madge grabbed Patsy's chin sweetly and affectionately, so Patsy knew it must be good. She immediately took to this big, honey bear of a woman and relaxed.

Patsy's eyes glanced down at Madge's leopard mules and noticed her own feet were half the size. "I like your shoes," was all she could think to say

Madge proudly answered, "Yeah, half price at Filene's basement." Patsy could feel in her bones this was the beginning of a beautiful friendship. "Calgon wants to keep your identity on the down-low and exclusive to them. So, they want you to sign a one-year contract and a non-disclosure agreement," Madge said, getting down to business.

"Is this routine?"

"Sure is. Don't you worry, I'll never steer you wrong."

Something about Madge made Patsy trust her, so she signed the paperwork, gave Madge a big hug, and professed, "You have no idea how much it means to me having you as my agent."

Madge waved her away, "Capisce, now get your cute ass outta here Tootsie, or I might cry."

The following week, Madge and Patsy met to pour over newspapers and connections Madge set up for auditions. They included TV spots, parts for stand-ins, and any other gig that would bring in a little extra money apart from the Calgon job. "OK, Sweetness, show me some of your dance moves and sing a favorite song too. We got to get you some greenbacks while you wait for your big break."

Patsy danced, sang, and acted as if she was already star quality. Madge gave her motivation to run lines and do improv. They fed off each other, and their humor and laughter were contagious.

106

Madge took Patsy aside one afternoon and asked point-blank, "How would you feel about a change for the better in your living arrangements? A place of your own? I could help with that, you know."

Patsy listened to Madge's suggestions and carefully weighed her words before she answered, "Madge, why are you so good to me? I could never repay you."

Madge spoke sincerely, "I see something in you, kid. One look at you in that Calgon commercial and I knew. You and me working together can go places. We just must go at it hard. You got it, girlie, you're special!"

"Thank you, Madge. I'll always do my very best for you."

The next several weeks changed Patsy's life. With a steady paycheck in her future, she only stayed close with Mandi and Carla, who proved to be true friends. Madge sent her on at least one audition a week for bit parts, improv skits, or even walk-ons. It was much easier when she presented her SAG card and mentioned Madge's name as her agent. Things were starting to pop all around, and Patsy basked in the glow.

Madge was her friend and mentor now. She even put Patsy in touch with a realtor who helped Patsy find a small apartment in Tribeca. The apartment was on the first floor in a sweet, historic Brownstone, and even came with blooming red roses climbing up a wrought iron trellis in a small garden in the rear. The privacy fence made it her haven. Calgon even gifted her with a claw foot tub and a year's supply of Lavender Honey Bath Crystals so she could enjoy her beloved tub time.

Although she enjoyed living with Mandi and Carla, this was luxurious to her, and it was hers alone. "Oh, my Lord, Madge, I cannot believe this little piece of heaven will be mine to live in. I feel like crying with joy!"

"Save it for the stage, kiddo. We got work to do! Old Madge is gonna hook you up with my vendors. Get ready for some bargaining tips when you shop and learn from the very best."

Patsy smiled as she jumped up and down, "I can't believe it—it's so beautiful, I can't believe it's gonna be mine!"

"Believe it, Baby. Now let's go shopping!"

Patsy, in a constant state of euphoria, asked Madge's advice on everything, "What do you think if I keep with the theme of white on white like Donna Karen features in the decorating magazines. It looks so clean, and with these hardwood floors, it'd be spectacular, don't you think? Donna says it gives the illusion of rooms appearing larger too!" Patsy just couldn't contain her happiness.

Madge grinned, "Whatever your heart desires, *motek*."

Patsy laughed, "OK, another Yiddish word that I don't know. I hope it's good."

"The best, my *motek*. It just means sweetie. So, what do you say we schlepp over to a discount warehouse I know and pick out a few things wholesale—cheap at half the price, my darling girl, that's what old Madge does best: bargain!"

Madge had connections with wholesalers and shabby chic stores everywhere and walked into the places as if she owned them. She yelled at the storekeepers in Yiddish when she couldn't get a good enough deal. If nothing else, Madge made Patsy laugh so hard she would almost pee her pants. Patsy would beg her to stop as Madge shouted out in the middle of a showroom, "Sol Mendelbaum, you better be good to my girl here, or I'll shove this roll of wallpaper up your tiny sphincter."

Patsy continued to decorate her humble abode. She poured over countless books and Country French and Cottage Style decorator magazines. She took Madge's advice and frequented shabby chic stores and made friends with the wholesalers Madge knew. Patsy acquired a white Chifforobe with a full-length mirror on the front. It was finished in a distressed look and beautiful embossed roses on the periphery. It was gorgeous, and she built the rest of her place around it. She was preoccupied with making her tiny space all her own and developing a unique style—she never experienced having anything in her life that was all hers.

It was hard to believe Madge was not only her fabulous agent, but becoming her best friend too. Whenever they were together or even on the phone, they bounced off ideas for her career and her apartment, and when Madge suggested they go to estate sales and flea markets in Jersey, Patsy jumped at the chance.

Madge drove her VW Beetle, and they sang all the way, *"Start spreading the news, I'm leaving today, I want to be a part of it, New Joisey, New Joisey."* They became hysterical at themselves singing New York songs, but adding New Jersey towns. They finally arrived at the Golden Nugget Flea Market and began to sing *Golden Nugget* to the theme of the movie *Goldfinger*. They ran to the entrance like heaven's gates were waiting for them.

After several trips to Jersey, her apartment was perfect. They found curtains of Battenberg lace and ruffles, and several decorative pillows to place wherever she wanted on the bed, chairs, and couch. It didn't matter since everything in the small space was white. Her authentic feather bed with a white chenille bedspread did though hide black silk sheets—a sexy little touch. A white faux fur throw topped off the look elegantly.

The floors were the original pinewood and quite beautiful and rich-looking. She loved the gentle creak as she walked across them in her bare feet. Two wrought-iron filigree chairs surrounded a subtly flowered, comfy sofa patterned with white-on-white roses. The small kitchen housed just a sink and stove, along with two stools under a counter where she grabbed quick meals. The cabinet had opaque glass doors that she loved. She couldn't wait to fill them with beautiful items.

On the counter were always fresh flowers Patsy picked up from an outdoor stall she passed every day. The blooms added a smidgen of color to the whole place, and it was quite beautiful as the sun poured in through the half windows providing just the right amount of privacy.

An ancient tea kettle graced the stove and whistled loudly when the water boiled. Patsy usually drank her tea from the pretty porcelain cups she picked up at an estate sale, but occasionally she formally served herself in the silver teaware Madge gave her as a housewarming gift.

"Madge, you really shouldn't do all this. It's just too much," she told Madge when receiving the gift.

"Bullshit," Madge replied. "I'm happy to, Beautiful *Punim*. It's a *mitzvah*, don't you know?"

Patsy's walk-in bathroom held an old-fashioned sink, but Patsy installed gold-like fancy fixtures and made a little skirt for the bottom hiding the rickety chrome legs. Even the commode's gold flusher made a statement, and the clawfoot tub set off the room with an aristocratic air. Several thick terry towels lay stacked on a little wooden table with an engraved label that read, "Made in France." Patsy smiled each time she reached for a towel. Several hooks hung over the tub for instant access after her bubble time. There was a tiny window which opened to a charming garden. Patsy often kept the window open as a sweet-smelling breeze wafted in, mixed with her bath beads and toiletries. Patsy was living in a fairyland meant just for her.

When most of the touches were complete, Madge made a toast with a tiny airplane bottle of scotch, saying, "Here's to a job well done, if I do say so myself. *L'Chaim!*"

Patsy replied, "*L'Chaim*," as she swallowed the scotch whiskey, "or as the Irish say, may you be in heaven a half-hour before the devil knows you're dead."

They both laughed and hugged each other.

Once the decorating was nearly finished, Patsy invited Mandi and Carla over to see her pad. Patsy admitted that it wasn't totally complete, but to them, it was the most luxurious little abode they ever saw. Patsy excitedly told them all the plans

110

she dreamed of for her new "little piece of heaven," as she phrased it.

"Wow, this place is fabulous, and you have your own bed. You go, girlfriend," said Mandi as she flopped on the soft feather bed. Carla jumped on it too, and they rolled around in the softness laughing like schoolgirls.

"Oh yeah, well, just take a look at this, my friends," said Patsy as she ran from the bedroom to the bathroom and jumped in the clawfoot tub. She yelled out, "How you like me now? I'm the real Bubbles Lamour, and here is the proof!" They were laughing and crying at the same time.

Suddenly serious, Patsy said, "I could never have done all this without you guys. You made my dreams come true." They huddled together as they celebrated with cake and champagne, and hugs and kisses too. They toasted each other and vowed to meet often and keep their famous names forever of Bad Mandi, Crazy Carla, and Pretty Pitiless Patsy.

"Here's to the Three Amigos!" they said in unison as they clinked their glasses.

Patsy opened their housewarming gift, a beautiful ceramic figurine of three Mexicans in sombreros sitting together and engraved with the words, *The Three Amigos*. Patsy started to cry. "I love you guys and thank you for taking me in and sticking by me. I'll never forget you."

Some interesting-looking people lived in the building, but Patsy never got further than a simple greeting of "Good Morning" or "Lovely Day Isn't It?" That was fine with her. She was happy maintaining her low profile. There was however, one very attractive man who occupied the basement studio. She surmised he was some sort of artist or photographer. He carried colored pencils and charcoal in his pockets.

She could see his place as she walked down the few steps from hers. She noticed a gold nameplate on his door. Curious to find out who he was, she tiptoed down the outside stairs to his basement apartment and read the name above the buzzer. It simply read, *Cristo*. Sometimes she noticed good-looking men and women entering or leaving his place. It began to make sense when she saw flyers in neighborhood coffee shops and the tiny bookshop on the corner that announced an upcoming gallery showing in Soho for Cristo.

One day she checked out the Soho gallery, and there was a poster of the beautiful Cristo. Beside the poster was one of his paintings. It was a provocative piece of two images done in a shadow effect. The male figure held the female in his arms, but bent her back as her hair flowed down with her face turned away. It was haunting and mysterious. With a fleeting fantasy, Patsy thought of putting those black silk sheets of hers to good use one day.

She couldn't stop thinking of the mysterious artist who lived in the basement apartment. On one occasion, as the artist was walking out of their building and Patsy was going in, he stopped and put a hand up to frame her face and said in an authoritative voice and sounding quite serious, "I will paint you one day—so get ready!" It wasn't a question or a request of any sort. It was a declaration. Patsy didn't answer back, but watched him as he walked away, shaking his head, and pulling the rubber band out of his ponytail in one swift motion.

Over the next few weeks, Patsy saw Cristo off and on. He was always flirtatious as he threw her a kiss and declared, "I'm coming for you, so get ready."

Patsy giggled and replied, "Oh yeah, Van Gogh, catch me if you can. I'm no one's easy muse!"

"Just watch! I will make you my special subject de art. You will see!" Patsy laughed at the gesture, and she felt very flattered.

One morning while taking her ritual bubble bath in her sweet little "Salle de Bain," she opened her tiny bathroom window to let the sounds of nature come in. She turned on the water and got in the tub to let the water fill in around her. She began thinking of Cristo and fantasizing about their next meeting. She would let him paint her, but what if he requested a nude? She giggled, knowing she would never let that happen, but allowed it in her delicious thoughts as she relaxed in the hot lavender-scented water.

The open window allowed some breezes and sounds of birds singing to accompany her perfect little euphoria. "Ahhh, this is heavenly," she sighed. She soon felt blissful and began fantasizing about her handsome neighbor, the mysterious artist.

It began with a knock at Patsy's front door. When she opened the door, Cristo was standing barefoot and shirtless, with tight ripped jeans and a red handkerchief around his right forearm. His bronzed skin glistened over his well-defined muscles. Without a word, he grabbed Patsy firmly and her hips molded against his. Their eyes locked. He tilted his head and their lips touched.

Patsy began to slowly pleasure herself, touching ever so lightly until the motion became faster and faster in time with the warm wetness streaming in. Reaching ecstasy, she let out a moan so loud it drowned out the sound of the rushing water.

The shock of excitement through her whole body startled Patsy back to reality. The beautiful illusion of Cristo would have to do, she thought, until the real thing came along. Shutting off the faucet, she sank back into the bath. One last time, she brought herself to climax as the bubbles slowly began to vanish around her.

As she rose to dry herself, a rustling sound came from the tiny backyard. She stood perfectly still for a few seconds with her back away from the window. She heard a distinct sound. Click, click, click. Wrapping a towel around her, she turned and peeked out her tiny window. She saw nothing stirring in her private little garden, but noticed a few broken branches snapped off near the gate.

The hairs on the back of her neck rose and she felt suddenly uneasy. Trying to convince herself it was a woodpecker or a frisky squirrel, she closed the window and made herself a pot of tea.

PART TWO
CHAPTER 19
Stalker

The Calgon offices were in a steel and glass building so tall, the top was beyond Patsy's view. As she walked in, a little intimidated, but chin held high, she smiled at everyone she passed. She might only have done one commercial—so far—but she felt like the star of her own show. It was surreal. Patsy finally felt a part of the New York hustle-bustle.

Calgon was on the tenth floor. The elevator ascended so quickly Patsy's ears popped. It was her third week at work, but the first time she was on her own without the comfort and security of Madge beside her. Patsy felt a twinge of insecurity with her absence, but saying hello to everyone from the maintenance men washing windows to the cleaning crew wheeling supplies, helped calm her. As she walked down the hall, she took in the pungent aroma of the coffee and the smell calmed her jitters.

***

The camera was strapped around his neck as his fingers stroked the imported leather casing. He thought of his father, a multi-millionaire who secured him the low-level job at the National Enquirer. Deep down he despised him, but was grateful for the career break, although right now, he was a mere copy boy. He would show him, though. He would show all those who bullied and made fun of him. He would be promoted to ace photographer in no time. He stroked his camera again and looked up. Suddenly, he spotted the most beautiful woman he'd ever seen. Who was this girl? She ran by and he heard her say, "Good Morning!" Tongue-tied, he couldn't answer. Then poof, just like that, she disappeared into the building. He felt the familiar twitching in his pants and knew this beautiful vision would become his muse. Maybe she was a model, and he could practice his camera skills on her. Maybe she'd be his big break.

He followed her into the building, catching a glimpse of her as she vanished into the elevator. He decided to skip work and wait in the lobby of the Calgon building until she came back down. He paced back and forth thirty, forty, fifty times—'round and round' the huge lobby.

Finally, around 4 p.m., she appeared. He followed her out of the building, down the street toward the subway. Careful, he warned himself as she turned around. What if she sensed him shadowing her? Once in the station, he walked a few feet in a different direction so she couldn't see him, then turned back, frantic not to lose her. He rushed through the turnstile, pushing off a slow-walking older man with a cane. "Watch it, old man," he barked as he elbowed the guy.

It was thrilling to be on her trail. He spotted her standing on the platform now as he hid behind a large pole. CLICK, CLICK, CLICK. He took several shots of her body and even a close-up of her profile with a swish of his zoom lens.

She boarded the train and he very craftily slid into an empty seat adjacent to her. She was still standing. She grabbed the center pole and hung on tight. Once more, he pointed the lens at her surreptitiously. CLICK, CLICK, CLICK. As the train passed through a dark underground tunnel, the lights flickered precisely in time with his shutter to disguise the noise. Perfect.

She got off the train in Tribeca and he knew he must follow her home. When she disappeared into a well-kept Brownstone, he hid behind a row of neatly planted evergreens and spied on her through a tiny window on the first floor. He was salivating now, but could not see much through the narrow window until a first-floor light switched on. Off to the left, he noticed a gate that led to a small yard. He scurried around the bushes, to the back of her apartment.

There he saw a tiny window past the locked gate, an opening into her secret life. His body shook at the endless possibilities, and he knew what he wanted to do, but that would

116

have to be for another day. For now, he couldn't wait to get to his make-shift darkroom to develop his subway photos.

At home, he paced up and down anxiously. The clicking sound of the camera in his brain radiated through his body as he clipped the wet photos in a neat row along the rope. He knew all along what his favorite photo would be the one he took with her eyes closed. Was she dreaming of him? Yes, yes…of course she was. He couldn't wait as he unzipped his pants and masturbated right there, standing in the dark space. As he howled in climax, he was sure she wanted him too.

He decided to return to her house the following Sunday. He snuck around the side to unlock the gate but couldn't manage it. He needed to climb over the chain-link fence. It wasn't easy, but the adrenaline he felt coursing through his veins helped. When he got to the back of the building, he spotted the tiny window opened halfway. He smiled. And waited.

About half an hour later, he watched as she opened the bathroom window wider. Was that lavender he smelled? Sweet, just like her. He moved closer as the clicking in his brain grew louder. He tensed up and then became so annoyed at the hard-on beginning to push through his khaki pants, he almost lost his balance, rustling the bushes around.

Righting himself, he nearly gasped out loud as he watched her step out of the bath and reach for a towel. His mouth watered as he felt his cock grow stiff and his lens found just the right angle of her shapely derriere. His hands shook as the light meter spoke to him, *Go ahead, go ahead, do it!* He acted quickly. CLICK, CLICK, CLICK. His camera went wild, taking shot after shot, zooming in closer and closer.

Oh no, oh shit, he realized she heard him. He saw her walk closer to look out the window. Think, think, don't let her see you. He crouched low behind the thorny rose bush until she shut the window and moved away.

His heart was beating fast as he ran through the bushes, scraping his hand on the thorns protruding from a long rosebud

117

stem. Quiet, quiet, he scolded himself even though the cut ripped his skin. He sucked the red blood before it dripped, careful not to get it on his expensive camera. He clambered over the chain-link fence and disappeared from the tiny yard, feeling exhilarated and triumphant. He sped down the walkway and down the street to the subway. His adrenaline and excitement carried him home.

He burst into his darkroom to develop the photos with shaking hands and watched them come to life. He would make her famous, and he knew what he would do next.

The National Enquirer was always asking for exclusives, tips, photos, and general leaks from the public. So, he strategically stationed the brown envelope of his best shot of her in the in-box of the assistant editor with a note that said, PRINT, ASAP. And they did, with a blurb asking readers who belonged to this beautiful derriere. He was triumphant, but knew not to reveal his identity just yet. He was on a journey to make this beautiful muse his and his alone. Every night, a wet dream awakened him as he plotted his next move. He was sure now. She was the one. His beloved had finally arrived.

***

Three weeks later, Patsy Mahoney was relaxing in her clawfoot tub with her lavender Calgon bubble bath. As an extra treat she applied a soothing mint facial mask, so when the phone rang, she let the answering machine take the call.

"*Bubala*, have you seen the National Enquirer rag? A racy photo on page three bears a striking resemblance to your cute *tushie*, my dear, and your bathroom décor too. Were you a naughty girl?" Madge chuckled, adding in a more serious tone, "I'm not jumping to conclusions, but this might affect your spotless image. Call me kiddo, and make it quick."

Patsy washed off the facial mask, got out of the tub and was just about to call Madge when the phone rang again. This time, it was a frantic Carla. "Patsy! Did you see the National

118

Enquirer? I swear it's you girl…and your tub…and definitely your fine ass."

"I just heard from my agent saying the same thing. I don't know what's going on."

"Sit tight girl," Carla said, "I'm coming over to show you what I'm talking about."

"Hurry, Carla, please. I can't call Madge back until I see what you're talking about." Patsy put the phone in the receiver and willed herself not to panic.

She paced back and forth on the creaky hardwood floors, saying the same thing over and over, *It's a mistake…it's a mistake…it must be a mistake!*

Carla arrived in record time. She showed Patsy the photo, and immediately Patsy's heart began to pound. She felt sick. The shot was a little blurry and nude. Patsy examined it closely and noticed the Calgon boxes on the shelf, the blond hair in an upsweep, the towels, and the bare bottom. *Oh no, oh no, please, God.* But God couldn't save her. Patsy was staring at a photo of herself. With shaking hands, she read the caption. *Who possesses this gorgeous derriere? Is it someone everyone knows, or is it some lovely stranger yet to be discovered?*

National Enquirer Photo – by Anonymous

119

Patsy's face turned red and then white, and she gagged as she bolted to the bathroom. Carla followed and gently patted Patsy's forehead with a cold compress. She tried to make Patsy laugh, "Hey, you do have a great ass, be happy at least for that. You could have a flat bum like me."

Patsy laid on the couch and sobbed. She was livid, panicked, but mostly overwhelmed by a dark sadness. She had been exposed. She was sure people would soon realize it was her. They would see the boxes of Calgon on the shelf. They would recognize her blonde hair, and even a few would be able to identify her backside.

With a suddenness that shook her, she realized her job could be compromised. *What would Calgon do? Would Madge drop her? What if they didn't believe her? Would she be reduced to just another girl who posed nude to get ahead? Would she lose the new home that she loved?*

The media would also have a field day and might even think of it as a publicity stunt or a gimmick to sell more Calgon. *Would this make her into a desperate, attention-grabbing sensationalist? Would anyone believe her? Would her discreet persona of good taste and comic innocence be vanquished forever?*

Worst of all, she felt dizzy from the horrible invasion of privacy, the shame she would endure with her family. *What if her father found out?* Patsy was horrified. The same insecurity and frustration she'd felt living with Roney and his bullying came back. She didn't deserve happiness, and this was the universe's way of telling her just that. Her world seemed to be crumbling around her. *Who could have done this?*

A thought came to her, and she rushed to the bathroom and peeked out the small window. Slowly, the realization that some pervert took the photo from the yard caused a shiver to run down her spine. She turned to Carla, "Oh my God, someone was

120

watching me through the open window, and I didn't even know it, Carla. I didn't even know."

"Call Madge right now. Maybe this is a matter for the cops?"

Patsy dialed Madge who was there in less than twenty minutes. Before even hugging Patsy, she said, "Whatever you do, do not get the cops involved. It would be deadly for your career and for Calgon. We have ways of managing these situations, and I have just the man who will help you. Leave it to old Madge."

Madge and Carla helped Patsy board up the small window that led to her tiny yard, making her feel a little better. They sat down for some tea while Carla and Madge urged Patsy to relax. When it was finally time for them to leave, Patsy hugged them both tightly. After she shut the door behind them, she quickly double-locked the door. She thought of home and Yonkers and felt like crying, feeling once again like a helpless child. The stalker's attack and her father's verbal abuse brought on the same despair: an ugly besmirch on an already heavy heart. She fell into a fitful sleep that turned into a horrible nightmare.

She felt the rush of adrenaline escape through her core and move down her arms to her hands. She paused for a second to look at her hands and quickly admired her new, blood-red manicure. The polish was appropriately named Cardinal Sin.

Standing over her was a stranger, looking lasciviously at her naked behind. She turned around and glanced up quickly to see his face before her. She jumped up to grab her terry robe to cover herself.

Feeling fierce and full of power, she methodically placed her long fingers around his thick neck. Her thumbs pressed on his Adam's apple. She squeezed with every ounce of her might, all the while still admiring her crimson-red polish.

121

He was short, so she looked right into his popped-out eyes, delighting in her power. Then he smiled. She was infuriated that he was enjoying this painful treatment. She squeezed harder, raised a finger, and slashed her bright red fingernail across his lips. He bit her finger. Reflexively, she raised her leg and kneed him in his groin. Once, twice—her dominance was exhilarating.

Suddenly the scene changed to her tiny yard. She watched him collapse in pain in the grassy garden and fall into a hedge of prickly roses. His smile became a grimace.

She saw a decorative rock near flowers that were beginning to bloom. The word PEACE was written on it. She picked it up with an urge to smash it into his mouth, the very mouth that bit her finger. She quickly abandoned the thought as she stood triumphantly over his diminished form. She'd done enough.

His body looked so disheveled now, like a raggedy teenager, but she felt no pity. And suddenly, anger for what he did came back. She lifted her leg high and brought her foot down on his balls. Finally, a feeling of calmness enveloped her.

She placed the PEACE rock carefully back in the garden. She was at peace. As she walked away, she hurried inside to make a call to the salon as she spied one jagged, red nail.

Patsy woke with clenched fists, but she also felt a strange sense of relief as she dragged herself out of bed to make some chamomile tea. She tried to hold on to the dream and make some sense of it. She was in the middle of writing down the dream when Madge called. "Hello, my sweet *Shayna Punim*, it is I, your *Bubula*, and I want you to get that sweet *tuchus* over to see my guy, and I'm not taking 'no' for an answer. So gear up baby, we're going to my Yogi Shantar. And yes, *Schatzi*, we're going to Namaste you."

Patsy was exhausted, but Madge's words made her laugh. In less than an hour, Madge was at her door wearing a striped

122

sports band around her head and a black leotard showing every bulge and crevice on her misshapen body. Patsy never saw such large thighs. She carried two mats and was sucking on a tasty freeze. "I've got yoga mats for both of us. Let's go."

Patsy was at the mercy of this huge Jewish Wonder Woman and was soon at the bidding of another Jew who claimed he was from India, the renowned Yogi Shantar.

The studio was more like a 10 x 10 windowless box. There was a giant Buddha in the corner, candles lit all over, and the smell of sandalwood incense enveloped the room. Yogi Shantar sat in the middle of the room, cross-legged on his mat, and just nodded his head, first to Madge and then to Patsy.

Madge rolled out her mat and whispered, "Just follow his lead and let him bring you back to life. He's a strange one, but he will make you surrender to your inner self, and you will have peace of mind, just like me."

Patsy laughed, but with a wave of his hand, Yogi Shantar motioned for the two of them to sit quietly. She watched Madge close her eyes, then did the same. He didn't utter a sound for a full five minutes except to chant "OHM" three times. He then asked in a sing-song voice, "Are you ready to glide into nirvana? Imagine a beautiful scene and go deep, deep, deep into your soul to find a place of peace."

Patsy surprisingly let go of herself and found an image instantly. She was dancing and swaying with Fred Astaire in an ethereal trance, gliding on air with her feet barely touching the floor. It was a strange fantasy but very pleasing.

Yogi Shantar's voice brought on a hypnotic state as he chanted, "Go deeper, deeper, deeper. You're almost there." Patsy opened her eyes slightly and saw him effortlessly standing on his head. He returned to a sitting position and said, "Open your eyes slowly and come to stand."

Patsy followed every move closely. Being an agile dancer, she conquered every pose with ease, except when he put his leg around his neck. In the end, Patsy was serene, lying flat in a semi-conscience state.

Yogi said, "When I ring this chime three times, you will feel nothing but serenity as you emerge from your peaceful place, bringing with you that same peace filling up your soul."

Patsy sat in awe as she heard the chimes ring and a soft voice say, "Namaste." She felt euphoric and wanted to thank Yogi Shantar, but he disappeared from the room.

Patsy glanced over to Madge, who had not yet come out of her dream state and was lying flat like a beached whale, snoring like a drunken sailor. Patsy gently patted her on the arm. Madge woke smiling, in blissful euphoria. "Well, *Schatzi*, how are you feeling now?"

"Oh, Madge, I am filled with calm. I didn't think it was possible. When can we come back?"

"Oh honey-bunny, Yogi Shantar is booked solid. I had to promise him a donation to his Ashram in the Himalayas before he saw us. I'll see what I can do, but I can't make any promises."

"I understand, and thank you Madge. You always know how to make things better."

"No problem. Anything for my girl. But have I lost any weight from my ass?" Madge joked, bending over, and sticking out her enormous rear-end.

"Absolutely, Madge, absolutely!"

Patsy started doing yoga daily at home, and even though it was helpful, the next few days were challenging as fear and loneliness returned. Patsy locked doors over and over and constantly peeked out her windows. She continually asked herself, *who would do such an invasive thing…and who had been watching her?*

Madge was by her side every day, offering sage advice and humor, "Promise you will call if you need Mother Madge."

One day, Madge visited twice, the second time surprising Patsy with a loud knock at the door. Patsy panicked and jumped at the sound. "Who's there? Who are you? What do you want? I have a gun."

The voice was familiar. "Don't shoot, Annie Oakley. It's just me. Earlier you sounded like you're coming down with a cold so I brought chicken soup. Let me in!" Madge demanded.

Patsy rushed to the door and hugged Madge crying out, "Thank God."

"No, God's busy, it's just me, and I got soup, Jewish penicillin, what's with the *fakakta* gun story?"

Feeling embarrassed, Patsy just laughed and hugged Madge tight.

CHAPTER 20
Dearheart

Over time, Patsy's fears diminished, though she was still worried about what Calgon might say and waited patiently for the call that finally came. "Hello, *Schatzi*, I have some news that's gonna make you happy again. Calgon is taking care of the situation. Don't you worry one bit, you're not going to lose your job. A meeting is set for tomorrow at the Calgon offices. Be ready at 9 a.m. and dress very conservatively, and don't wear high heels. The mediator is short. We don't want to intimidate him," Madge said.

Patsy was relieved, but now nervous about the instructions to look conservative. "Do the Calgon people think I purposely posed nude?"

"Now, my sweet love, don't fret. Old Madge will take care of you. You and me—we're the best team ever."

Patsy paced up and down after the call. The creaking of the floorboards kept time with the wringing of her hands. "Pull yourself together. You got this," she said aloud. Now if she could only believe it.

Madge arrived early the following morning and gave her a great big bear hug. "Don't worry, just follow my lead. I have my man, Mr. S, sitting in as representation, and he will make everything kosher."

Madge flagged down a cab, and they hopped in. As Madge chatted with the driver, Patsy was overwhelmed with self-doubt. She began to shake and had to fight off an impending panic attack. She couldn't stop the negative thoughts swirling through her mind. *Am I doomed? Is this the end? Will I have to go back to Yonkers?* As her old enemy despair started to take over, she decided to distract herself, "Tell me about this Mr. S. What does the 'S' stand for? Who is he? How is he going to help us?"

126

"Honey, we have the best negotiator in the business. He's an expert and is legendary in the industry. His name is Sidney Sabsowitz, but he's known to all of us as Mr. S. He'll set the Calgon and the National Enquirer people back on their heels, don't you worry." Madge patted Patsy's knee and went on, "Me and Mr. S have been friends and colleagues for years. He gave me my first big break as an agent, and I'll be eternally grateful. I tried several times to repay him for his kindness, if you know what I mean, but he wasn't interested. As you see, I am a big woman. In Jewish terms, I am considered quite 'zaftig.' Mr. S is five and a half feet tall on his best day, even in his fancy-schmancy two-inch Stuart Weitzman's. With these double Ds, I could smother the little guy!"

Patsy burst out laughing, picturing Madge smothering a little man with her gigantic boobs. Madge continued, "We became and still are best of buddies, and I knew that only Mr. S could clear up this National Enquirer mess. He is a wizard in entertainment law and possesses what could best be described as 'moxie.' I told him what happened to you, he was appalled, and promised to protect you. His exact words were that he will 'make it all go away!'"

"I can't wait to meet him, and I'm so grateful for your help, Madge." Patsy's bottom lip began to quiver and right on cue, she teared up.

"Stop it. You'll spoil your mascara," Madge grabbed Patsy's hand and pressed tenderly. "We got this," she whispered as they stepped out of the cab. She folded her fingers in prayer, placed them under her chin, and said an intense, "Namaste, Baby!" Squeezing Patsy's hand again, she added, "If you get scared, squeeze back."

They approached the building off Park Avenue. Patsy needed Madge to help her open the heavy glass door. They stepped into the large marble foyer and walked towards the rows of elevators. They rode to the fifteenth floor and walked into the offices of Mr. S.

127

"Right this way," the receptionist said as she led Madge and Patsy into a large conference room. As Patsy cautiously entered the meeting room, she saw six people sitting around a huge oak conference table. She immediately noticed the man at the head of the table. He was a stranger, but Patsy felt his importance right away.

Madge leaned over and whispered, "See, I told you. It's already a done deal. All those papers are signed. It's a legal document each one has in front of them."

Patsy shook her head. "I don't understand," she whispered.

"Trust me. I've seen it lots of times. A nondisclosure agreement that says that everything discussed has to stay in this room only." Madge introduced Patsy to the room.

Mr. S jumped up immediately and ran to her. "Everything is going to be okay, and you have nothing to worry about. I will take care of making all the misery disappear like this," he said, then snapped his fingers. He gave her a big hug, and she felt so relieved she nearly fell into his arms. "Somebody get her some water!" he yelled, and three people jumped up.

Most of the meeting went over Patsy's head. Mr. S knew the editor-in-chief at the National Enquirer, and he was somehow going to make him promise there would be no follow-up on the photo. He would have the editor sign a waiver to squash anything having to do with this debacle. She wasn't sure how Mr. S would get him to sign the release, but it sounded like he would threaten to close the paper down if Patsy suffered any mental or medical repercussions.

Mr. S spoke directly to Patsy, "It was mentioned you were only twenty at the time you signed the Calgon agreement, and even though it might not be entirely true, it should do the trick. You see, any editor would fear these accusations and would sign the agreement, no problem. Also, I promise you all this will happen without any mention of your name or having your identity exposed."

The meeting ended and everyone shook hands. Mr. S embraced Patsy again. "Invasion of privacy is my pet peeve. I was born to handle stuff like this," he said softly. Madge grabbed him and gave him one of her huge signature bear hugs.

A few days later, Mr. S called Patsy and confirmed. "Like I told you, the deal is done. Don't worry another minute, Dear."

Patsy felt tears come to her eyes as she said, "I don't know how to thank you. I owe you everything."

"Ack, you owe me nothing. It was my pleasure. But we can meet for lunch someday. I have ideas for some great parts for you. Madge tells me you are one talented lady."

"Of course! You name the place and time Mr. S, and I'll be there." It felt like the weight of the world was lifted off her shoulders.

"Perfect! I'll be in touch."

After that, Mr. S and Patsy made lunch plans often. Patsy was eager for each meeting as they went to a different restaurant every time and engaged in fascinating conversations about Broadway. Patsy felt her confidence begin to flourish as he seemed to bring out the best in her. She often shared stories of her past and her struggles, along with her dreams and desires. It was just so comfortable talking with Mr. S. The two developed a close and playful rapport.

At their fifth luncheon, Patsy danced toward him as she spotted him in a back booth at Sardi's. *"One singular sensation, every little step she takes,"* she sang.

Mr. S howled with laughter and stood up. *"Chorus Line,* one of the best," he said as pulled out Patsy's chair.

She usually bubbled over talking about herself, her passion for show business, and her desire to make it her career, but today she asked him about his past and how he achieved his dreams. "I don't mean to pry or anything, but I always feel like I'm bombarding you with my past and I still don't know much about you. I mean, you don't need to share with me if you don't want to, but I would love to hear how you became so famous."

129

"Dearheart," Mr. S started, "as a young man at Solomon Shechter Jewish Day School, they called me 'Little Sid Caesar' because I was extremely witty. Although with you, I think I met my match." Patsy leaned in for more. "From the time I was young, I wrote plays and even dreamed of getting to Broadway someday. I was not attractive enough for a leading man since I was very short, thin, and needed bottle-bottom glasses to see. It didn't bother me much though because people were drawn to me. I attribute much of this inherited charm to my father who got me my first gig in the Catskills and constantly spurred me on. In no time, I became the summer social director and that made me the most popular kid around," Mr. S stated proudly.

"Tell me some of the things your dad did for you," Patsy urged. She was feeling the need to hear a positive story of a loving father.

"I remember one summer I told him I wrote two skits, and I asked if he wanted to hear one. Right off the bat, he said, 'No. Do them both. The Rosenbaum's are coming, and Moishe's brother is a booking agent. Now's your chance.' So, I did both skits for the Rosenbaum's and was dubbed from that time on as *Baby Sid*, and as they say in *Dirty Dancing*, nobody puts baby in a corner!"

"I love this," Patsy said, laughing out loud.

"I performed some magic tricks and even did little skits I wrote. I had a pal named Jose who worked as a waiter. He helped me do an act where we improvised a scene from 'The Lucy Show' at the Copacabana nightclub. He played Ricky Ricardo, and guess who I played?

"Oh no!" Patsy gasped, "I can't believe you were Lucy!"

"Yes I was, and my Lucille Ball became a standing theme. The crowd would yell 'Hey, Lucy!' and I would rush out on stage crying out, 'Hey Ricky' as Jose appeared, and we'd go into our routine. It was great, and we ad-libbed a different scene each time for each new show." Patsy excitedly egged him on. "Well, with my dad's prodding and a few connections, I went on to work stand-up in local comedy clubs in Brooklyn and a few times in Times Square dives. Patsy, it was the best time of my life." His voice trailed off as he tenderly put his hand on hers. "Now it's time for me to learn a little more about your childhood," he said.

Patsy hesitated. "Parts of my childhood are not as encouraging as yours. My mom was a good influence with her dancing and love of films, but my dad is another story. I feel a little reluctant to share that with you and perhaps a little humiliated too."

"You want to hear humiliation? Listen to this tale of woe." He continued very softly now. "About twenty years ago, I attended Hamilton College. There was a petite little girl by the name of Sarah Handelmann. She was so damn cute and shorter than me too. To top it off, she was quite taken with me and my talent and sense of humor. We became inseparable," he said, lowering his head.

"I even wrote a play for her—and paid for expensive acting lessons—and tutored her in creative writing. I called her my superstar, even though she couldn't act at all. I loved her that much and thought I was the luckiest guy in the world. Looking back, I should have realized Sarah had no real physical attraction to me, but she gave in to my advances and we began a sort of romance that went beyond casual. We never went all the way because she said she wasn't quite ready.

I took her home to meet my folks and told my dad I wanted to buy her the biggest diamond I could afford. I was ready to pop the question. My dad was thrilled and got in touch with his friends on Jewelers Row in Manhattan. However, my mom—the proverbial Jewish mother—sensed a sort of, well, shall I say a casual frivolity when it came to Sarah Handelmann being in love with her only son. My mother thought Sarah lacked the devotion that went along with a real and meaningful relationship.

131

"I remember she said, 'Sidney, you're the only one who is smitten and has blinders on.' My dad was all for the union and thought Sarah was ideal. Of course, I sided with my dad and thought my possessive mother was just jealous. It turns out she was the one who was smartest of all, God rest her soul. Still, I told my dad, 'Put one of those big marquise diamonds aside for me.'"

A look of sadness took over his face, "Then, one night my world was blown apart. Sarah told me she could not attend rehearsal 'cause she was going out in the city with her friends, Stella and Brenda. She seemed excited, so I said, 'Go already, have fun.' Those were my last words to her. Long story short, she met a Navy man at a bar in Times Square, had sex in the backseat of his car, ran off with him, and became pregnant with twins in just three months. She never returned to school, and I never saw her again. I had to learn through her girlfriends, who were just as shocked as I was. The thing that bothered me the most was when they described him as tall—six-foot-two! Dearheart, I tell you, I was crushed, and not because of losing her. It was the degradation I suffered with growing whispers among of my college buddies, the shame of being played and not feeling good enough or tall enough. I felt worthless without her."

He paused a few seconds and shrugged, "I hear she is miserable and living in Kansas on a farm, and now that I'm wealthy and successful, she wants me back. Ha! Karma's a bitch, ain't it?" Mr. S laughed, but there were tears in his eyes. "I retreated into myself, and from that time on, I poured all my energies into my work, and my sole salvation for complete privacy began. I never wanted to be vulnerable again."

Mr. S took Patsy's hand and spoke sincerely, "That's why I'm so taken with you, sweet girl. You were hurt and embarrassed like I was, and both of us were unsuspecting. I think we were meant to meet."

132

Patsy felt her eyes fill up with tears. She was stunned that this powerful man had just shown her such a pure, honest side of himself. Patsy felt love for this little man with the big heart and their relationship evolved into something they both cherished. It would never be physical, but every other aspect of their bond was sacred and brought them immense happiness.

Their lunches became fancy dinners in the city. She delighted in putting together new outfits for their nights out, with Madge's help of course. Madge knew all the best thrift and secondhand shops, and her opinion always influenced Patsy.

One night, Mr. S phoned and announced, "I'm taking you to a premiere of a new Rock Opera tonight, so be ready at 6 p.m."

"I think you should wear the purple off-the-shoulder sheath and your floral print platforms with the silver hoop earrings. I love a big hoop, as you know," said Madge, sitting on the bed as she watched Patsy's fashion show and judged the outfits.

Patsy laughed, "That's what I thought, too, or should I be more mod with the black and white mini and spectator pumps? I have these great black and white hoops to match."

Madge was firm, "No way girlie, you look like you're seventeen with plastic earrings."

Patsy wore the purple dress Madge recommended and was so happy she did. Her hair was in a French twist with curly tendrils on the side, and her earrings were dangling cluster seed pearls. And respectful of Mr. S's height, she wore flats. "You look so beautiful," he said when he saw her, "as if you could look any other way." Patsy was elated.

This was the start of her days filled with openings, premieres, shows on—and off Broadway, Lincoln Center, the Met, Carnegie Hall, shopping at Bergdorf's, and workouts at the New York City Health Club. They enjoyed a certain amount of celebrity around the circuit and relished every minute of it. Most people thought Mr. S showed up with a new starlet on the horizon and didn't pay too much attention to their spending time together. It was a normal thing to see producers out with up-and-comers. As for Patsy, she felt protected and cherished.

One day, Mr. S made her an offer that astounded her. "Hey Sweetie, how would you like to move on up to one of my penthouses? There's one available right now on Park Avenue," he said matter-of-factly. "Not to worry, sweet thing, no strings attached…just trying to keep you safe from this *meshugana* asshole stalker, and my buildings have security 'round the clock."

"Oh no, I'm so happy in my little apartment, and I feel quite safe now," Patsy replied, careful not to sound ungrateful. "I am so secure, thanks to you. You made the Calgon Peeping Tom debacle completely dissolve like bubbles down the drain."

Mr. S said, "Don't you worry, sweet angel girl, you won't be bothered anymore. I'll see to it."

Patsy replied coyly in a British accent, "What can I ever do to repay you for your generosity, kind sir?"

Mr. S joked back, sounding like Groucho Marx, "Well, I can think of a few hundred positions—I mean *things*—I might consider…."

Patsy countered right on cue, "My dear man, I'm in no position to accept your positions.

Laughter ensued.

She often accompanied him to his "tryouts" for auditions, happily giving her opinion, and what was even more exciting, he was paying attention to her advice and critiques. As a result, Mr. S managed to secure a minor part for her in one of his Broadway productions. She was featured in one of his plays, but only as a backline dancer. It wasn't exactly what she wanted, but he explained his rationale one night over a lobster dinner at Fulton Landing Seafood Company restaurant.

"Tread lightly, my dear, all good things come in time," he said, "I don't want you to get too popular because the National Enquirer incident is still fresh. Exercise caution. Too much exposure could be dangerous. Things are to be for safety's sake for now. Fame will come later."

CHAPTER 21
Panties

One quiet Sunday evening, Patsy was feeling incredibly lonely. She needed a male companion. She longed for touch. Cristo came to mind. She thought about how nice it would be to feel his arms around her. Deciding she had nothing to lose, she made her way down to the basement apartment.

She listened for any voices or movements and when she heard nothing, she knocked on his door. There was no response. She started to walk away, feeling disappointed. Then she heard the door creak open, and Cristo confidently declared, "My subject is finally here," as if he had been expecting her all along. She turned around, and he motioned for her to come inside. She felt suddenly frozen with fear and stammered, "I'm sorry to bother you," she stammered, "I just thought—"

"Please come in," he said softly.

She took a deep yoga breath and followed him inside. She was surprised to see sweet little gingham plaid curtains, and sunflowers in a vase placed on the edge of a breakfast nook. The décor showed a women's touch, yet it held an artistic charm. There were paintbrushes in jars lining shelves in neat rows and supplies everywhere. She was excited to be in a real artist's studio.

Cristo took her hand, walked her over to a lone wooden stool in the center of the room, and lightly touched her shoulders, guiding her to sit. Every time she tried to speak, he put his finger to her lips. So, they sat in silence as he stared her up and down. She felt like his dark blue eyes could see right through her clothes and body, and straight into her soul. Finally, he spoke, "Come back next Sunday at seven." He reached for her as if to escort her out.

Although nervous, Patsy boldly stared into his eyes, "Is that a request or an order?"

Cristo laughed, "It's a plea, my lovely one, a plea."

"In that case, I'll give it careful consideration." She made her exit, knowing it was her decision, not his.

This first meeting with the handsome artist had not exactly been what she anticipated. She was used to more attention, men wanting her, but Cristo was different. He wasn't trying to win her over with any affection. As odd as that sounded, it was refreshing and enticing to Patsy, an unfamiliar challenge. Deep inside, she was craving more. He was someone to be reckoned with, and she admitted to herself, she liked the feeling.

Returning to her apartment to do yoga, she fell asleep on her mat during the *savasana* resting pose, still dreaming of this first encounter with the artist with the laser blue eyes.

She sees him in the dark of night. All-consuming thoughts of holding him close to her naked body take over. They agree to play games. Here are my rules, she tells him. You can do anything to me, but you cannot kiss me on the mouth. Kissing my mouth is forbidden. He agrees and counters with his own rules: you can do anything, but you cannot make a sound, not even a murmur or a whimper. Sounds are forbidden.

They begin the game, each determined to win, but not too reluctant to lose. Desire fills her body as she quietly and cautiously approaches him. He takes her jeans and silk panties down past her hips in one swift motion. He runs his tongue along her bikini line and kisses her soft stomach, stopping only to flick his tongue into her belly button. She feels a tingling sensation and must put her hand over her mouth to subdue a moan. He nearly stops then, believing he has won the challenge already. He is wrong.

She purses her red, ripe lips, which begs him to move up and kiss them. He looks up, but continues kissing her belly. He spreads her legs apart and she jerks forward as he buries his head into her softness. It takes all her strength when she feels his

137

tongue inside her not to moan, but her desire to win is great, so she wills herself to remain silent.

She places her hands under his arms to pull his head up to meet her face. He enters her as he begins ravenously sucking on her mouth, her lips, her tongue.

She wins the game and is triumphant. She then experiences a deep orgasm, as every fiber of her being silently screams in unbridled rapture.

Her eyes pop open. She is still in the yoga resting position, but the eroticism of the dream crept into her conscious mind and for a moment, she doesn't know where she is. She hopes in her heart of hearts that the fantasy will come true. Her body and mind need it. She yearns for Cristo's healing touch, even though she hardly knows him.

As the week went by, she did not see Cristo, but thought about him every day. He was the first thing she thought of when she woke up in the morning and the last when she went to bed. She thought of him for all the hours in between as well and dreamt of him more than once.

On Sunday at 7 p.m., she nervously stood at his door. Her heart beating fast, she knocked lightly, but there was no answer. She waited, then knocked harder and louder. Finally, her excitement started to change to disappointment. Patsy put her ear to the door and tried to hear any footsteps or noise inside, but heard nothing. She breathed a sigh of pity and turned to leave. She was embarrassed, thinking she was making more of their previous encounter than he was. He would have to make the next move now she decided. It would be better that way.

Her days became routine. She spent hours at her favorite coffee shop, Java Joe's, sipping coffee or tea and reading the *Village Voice*, or scouring the news for want ads. She sometimes saw Cristo there but stayed out of his sight and never engaged him. She was trying to stay focused on her career, but more than that, she was more than a little miffed that he wasn't there for their planned evening.

One Friday morning, she heard a knock at her door. Outside stood Cristo. "It is time!" he declared. Patsy was annoyed and reluctant to follow him, but those bare shoulders were calling to her. As much as she was trying to conjure up feelings of anger, she couldn't. *Damn him.*

Once inside his apartment, he shut the big metal door and locked it. Then, he marched Patsy to the wooden stool in the center of the room, where she sat the last time she was there.

He smiled, "I'm so happy you are here so I can begin my masterpiece with my lovely muse." Patsy felt herself blush and was about to question him about standing her up, but she wanted to word it exactly right to show she was not a pushover for a quirky artist. Cristo spoke instead, "I must apologize for the Sunday mishap. My mentor called me to the city, and I had to obey. I had no way of letting you know…please forgive me."

"I forgive you," Patsy said sweetly.

"Thank you," Cristo flashed his million-dollar smile.

Patsy watched in awe as Cristo blended colors and began to paint on a big white canvas. His strokes were dramatic, but it was his intense concentration and smile that fascinated Patsy. He was so intriguing in his state of utter enjoyment. He was tall, almost six feet, very lean, and muscular. She assumed his fit physique came from moving sets, props, and easels. She could never imagine him at a gym or jogging. He tied back his long golden-brown wavy hair into a ponytail, and wore a manicured beard Patsy could imagine stroking so tenderly.

As much as she enjoyed taking in Cristo's beauty, over an hour passed, and Patsy was growing tired of sitting. She was also thirsty and hungry. Finally, after wiping paint from his hands, Cristo approached her. He threw her a kiss as he thanked her, but before he could escort her out, she hopped off the stool and headed to the door. Her rear end was numb. Modeling was not as glamorous as she thought.

"Thank you so much. You will be my newest work of art. Please come back next week," were his last words. The steel door closed behind her.

Patsy's fantasies of Cristo seducing her began to fade. This had not been the rendezvous she dreamed of. Nor were the next sessions. For three weeks, she sat while Cristo painted. Conversation was limited to him telling her to turn or sit in a certain way. Clearly, her fantasies were all in her mind, and not shared by him. He was consumed by his work. Patsy had to admit she was his subject, nothing more.

She used her imagination as she watched him paint and daydreamed to pass the time. Once, when he wore sandals and shorts and a tight black undershirt, Patsy imagined him as a mad Picasso who craved her like Pablo craved Francoise Gilot. On another occasion, he wore a white artist's blouse and a cute, black beret. She imagined him as Michelangelo.

Patsy had reluctantly given up on the possibility of romance when early one Sunday morning she heard a knock at the door. She was groggy from a long, dream-filled night so just called out, "Who's there?"

"It is I, come to fetch my muse," Cristo said. He was likely expecting her to obey and follow as the obedient puppy she'd been, but she decided today would be different.

"It's not a good time. I'm really tired," she said, her eye against the peephole. Cristo looked perplexed. He nodded his head and walked away, looking defeated and Patsy felt her first victory.

Later that day, he knocked again. This time, she opened the door. Cristo stood there, looking vulnerable, with a bouquet in his hands. Handing the flowers to her, he said, "For you. Please can you come and let me paint you today?"

She'd never seen this softer side of him. He looked a little pitiful. She reluctantly agreed and followed him to his apartment—his robot muse once again.

140

This time though, Cristo didn't point her to the wooden stool. He led her to the much-worn leather couch in the corner of the room. He asked her if she would like a glass of wine, and she nodded yes. He disappeared and came back with two glasses of red and made a toast, "To my lovely subject."

They clinked glasses and Patsy took a long sip, feeling all her senses tingle and anxious to see what his next move might be. Cristo barely touched the edge of the glass to his lips when he set it down and settled in next to her. She could smell his Paco Rabanne, a hint of charcoal, and paint. He reached out and gently caressed her thigh. She didn't even mind his calloused skin. It aroused her.

Cristo touched her chin, then outlined all the features of her face: her ears, her eyes, her nose, and finally her lips. He pulled back her hair, lightly at first, but then tugged it to make her head fall back and took a long hard look at her face.

She wasn't sure if he was preparing to sketch her or kiss her. Either way, she felt a surge of excitement. As his thumb lingered on her bottom lip, her desires grew. His fingers left her lips and traveled down her throat, reaching for her left breast, then her right breast, and then teasing her by rubbing her inner thighs and cupping her vagina through her clothes. His hand fit perfectly, and she felt herself grow hot and begin to throb. He made a soft, but firm circular motion with his palm, and she was instantly wet—then remembered she didn't have on her silk panties. Since she expected to spend the day alone, she had on her old cotton ones. Wednesday, she believed. Oy Vey, as Madge would say.

She started to wiggle out of his embrace, but her desire for Cristo was so strong that even her old cotton panties couldn't deter her. She was too far gone. In the grips of passion, she hoped he would rip those cotton panties right off.

When his lips finally met hers, they were warm and wet, and his beard was unusually soft. His tongue explored her mouth. Patsy kissed him back with an intense passion that was

141

building for weeks. She often stared at his well-defined muscles during their painting sessions, but now, as he took off his shirt, she couldn't believe how beautiful his body truly was. He was his own work of art, with paint stains on his skin and a small tattoo of a heart under his collarbone with *Babcia* written across it. She didn't understand the word and wondered if it could be the name of another woman, but the thought quickly faded as Cristo moved on.

He took off Patsy's old white T-shirt and bra and started to caress her breasts with his strong fingers. It was just like him to savor every touch so precisely, she thought. Every tiny lick of his tongue made her nipples erect as she fought for control. But she started to quiver and moan, quiet sounds that came from somewhere deep inside her, a primal response from the world where only the two of them existed.

He stood up, swooped her into his arms, and carried her over to his large wooden worktable. He laid her down among the sketches, charcoal, brushes, and paints. The glass holder of an unlit candle crashed and shattered as paintbrushes fell to the floor.

The thought of making love on Cristo's workspace was thrilling, but Patsy wondered if he always did this with his models. He was in complete control and never uttered a word. It did not seem like his first time, but Patsy realized she really didn't care. It was her turn, and she was going to enjoy it.

As he straddled her on the old table, the wood was hard on her back, but that was nothing compared to the hardness she felt against her thigh. He kissed her breasts and then made his way down her stomach as he teased her, running his finger along her waistline. Before she knew it, he removed her old sweatpants and cotton panties and she was grateful he didn't seem to notice them.

His long fingers knew exactly where to touch her to make her moan, and when she couldn't take it anymore, she turned and took a more assertive position. Now they were facing each other sideways, their arms and legs intertwined. Papers and paintbrushes fell to the floor as wet paint splattered everywhere.

Cristo again took control. As he entered her, Patsy groaned with delight. He was inside her at last. His movements were smooth, rhythmic, and strong, until neither of them could hold on any longer and they came to orgasm together. Cristo pulled out, his sperm spewing on her stomach as he uttered a throaty howl.

Perhaps it was the pure animal passion that took over, or maybe it was the built-up stress from everything that happened, but for whatever reason, Patsy began to cry. Cristo very softly wiped away her tears as he took her chin in his hand. He murmured low in her ear, "Don't cry, beautiful one. Don't you know you're my work of art?" Patsy looked down at her paint-stained body and laughingly replied, "Yes—literally!"

Cristo continued to hold her close until Patsy finally spoke again, "May I use your bathroom? I'm a mess!"

"Of course," he replied. Then like a naughty child, he yelled out, "Don't forget these," as he tossed the cotton panties her way.

Patsy thought she heard him laugh as she walked off, but she wasn't embarrassed. Not anymore. On the contrary, she was thrilled. She felt like she was starring in a movie, and Cristo was the leading man she didn't have to fantasize about. He was very, very real.

"Would you like another glass of wine?" he asked when she returned.

"No thank you," Patsy politely refused, giving him a wink and a wave.

"I'll miss you, beautiful lady," he said, holding up his glass. "Until next time."

Patsy's artfully staged tryst with Cristo gave her pleasure for days. She thought about it constantly, even when she filled her sink to wash all of her lingerie, that is of course everything except her cotton panties because she could still smell him on them, and was sure she would cherish those old white bloomers forever.

She turned up the volume on the radio when a Donna Summer song came on, and belted out the lyrics, *I need some hot stuff, baby, tonight. I want some hot stuff, baby, this evenin,'* and danced around happily as she washed her lingerie in the hot soapy water.

CHAPTER 22
Valentine

***

He was furious. Oh, how he hated the people at the National Enquirer—hated the whole staff of losers. There hadn't been an ounce of response from the perfect photo of his beloved. Not one! He was fuming as he hurled two cameras across the room in a fit of rage. Grabbing a framing knife, he stabbed his favorite picture of her repeatedly and then cried tears of deep sorrow as he picked up the slashed photo and kissed it. "I'm sorry, my darling. I tried so hard to make you and me famous so you would love me and be mine. I'll make the fucking pigs pay. I promise."

His only good fortune came when his father was on a cruise with his latest big-bosomed, filthy harlot when he dropped dead of a massive heart attack. He hated his father since his mother's death, mainly because his father never dealt with or understood his mother's struggle with mental illness, so his father's demise was no loss to him. At the reading of the Will he was - shocked to learn his father left him five million dollars. His heart raced and he knew immediately his next course of action. Now he could devote his every moment to her pursuit. He knew he must quit his job immediately and set out to find her again with newfound freedom and determination.

The day he submitted his resignation to the newspaper, he brought in tainted overstuffed chocolate cookies. That morning he scraped out the frosting and stuffed every other one with dog poop he collected from around Central Park, then covered it with the extra icing. He arranged the cookies on a beautiful platter and left them in the break room without anyone noticing, left his resignation letter at the front desk, and walked out the revolving door.

He wanted to make things right in his mind for those who thwarted his brilliant plan. They meant nothing, and now he could continue without their interference and with an enormous amount of money. He laughed as he thought they could eat shit and die for all he cared.

It was going to be so easy now to capture the heart of his beloved. He grabbed a cab and got out a block from her place. Coming up to the fence in her yard, he couldn't believe it—wood boarded up the window. His head began to spin as the tormenting CLICK, CLICK, CLICK blared in his ears. Like a scared rabbit, he ran down the street to the subway and went home seething with rage.

They were keeping her from him, he knew it. It wasn't her fault. He felt sure she was waiting for him and longing for him as much as he was for her. He was ready, ready to strike again. And this time, he wouldn't fail. They couldn't take possession of her. She was his and his alone.

He carefully composed a note on his best, imported card stock from France—embossed with roses, smooth to the touch. He stroked it softly, then wrote, *My heart bleeds for you.* He pulled up his shirt and cut into his chest with the blade of his framing knife. With his finger, he drew a perfect image of a heart with the tiny droplets on the notepaper, let it dry and then snapped a photo of it to develop later. Excitement consumed him. He was ready to send his first real Valentine. He sucked on his bloody finger as his engorged cock throbbed. Grabbing it, he pumped hard, yelping uncontrollably as he came.

He changed his blood-stained shirt and put a bandage on his wound. He was off now to place his declaration of love in the mailbox of his precious one. He was sure he would defeat the enemy. She would fall in love with her hero. His heart beat wildly as he emerged from the subway train at the Tribeca stop. The victory was his.

***

Patsy's saw Cristo one morning as they were both leaving their apartments. "Hey beautiful, where have you been? These arms are missing you," he yelled up.

146

She fibbed a little, "I've been so busy lately, but I do miss those big, strong arms of yours."

Cristo walked up to her. "Do you like Polish food? I'm a good cook, learned at the knee of my grandmother back in Camden, New Jersey."

"Wow, an artist, and he cooks too! How did I get so lucky?" Patsy said, laughing out loud. "I've never had Polish food, but I'm game if someday you let me make you my family's specialty, corned beef and cabbage."

"It's a date. I'll see you Sunday at 3, your place." Patsy didn't get a chance to answer back before he turned and took off, pulling his rubber band out of his ponytail and tossing his shiny hair back and forth as he flexed his perfect biceps. Patsy's laugh echoed as she watched him disappear. He knew exactly how to turn a girl on.

Patsy woke early Sunday and spent some time fantasizing about her coming tryst with Cristo. She went out to buy wine to go with dinner, but was still ready by noon. In her lacy orchid thong and matching silk bra, she slid into an off-the-shoulder bolero top and tight hip-hugger jeans. She spritzed on Opium perfume and painted her lips the same color as her top. She thought she looked just right, her hair loose, but not too sexy—until the moment when she'd strip down to her lingerie.

At 3 p.m. sharp, there came a knock on her door. "Hope you're hungry. I will create a meal fit for a goddess!" Cristo called out as he entered her apartment and went straight to her tiny kitchen.

As she watched him pull down mixing bowls and go through her kitchenette drawers for wooden spoons, Patsy thought her only appetite was for that perfect body, but she smiled as she watched him unpack two large shopping bags filled with all sorts of ingredients onto the counter, including two chefs' caps. With great flair, he placed one on Patsy's head and one on his own.

147

"I am making my Babcia's famous Polish golumpki and pierogis. She was famous in our neighborhood, and I have her secret recipe that is only served to special people like you, you little Irish gem. When you taste these culinary delights, you'll want to change your country of origin, I assure you."

Patsy laughed, "Well, you can try, but I was born and raised on Irish lamb stew." She inhaled deeply. "This does smell scrumptious. I can't wait to taste all these new dishes."

He was very exacting in his measuring and chopping and stirring all the while singing arias, "*Figaro, Figaro, Fi-ga-ro….*"

Patsy dubbed him "The Singing Gourmet." She poured herself a glass of wine. "You apply the same concentration to your cooking as you do your art."

"I seek perfection in all my creations!"

Cristo continued like a mad scientist and said he needed to get more comfortable, so off came his shirt and then his cutoff jeans, and he stood boldly in black silk briefs and, of course, his chef's cap, along with a colorful scarf around his neck.

"Two can play at that game!" Patsy laughed as she removed her clothes and stood only in her lingerie.

The kitchen was a mess by then. Cristo turned down the sauces and turned off the oven. "Could you just for a minute stand there and twirl for me?" he asked politely.

Patsy said shyly, "Of course," knowing she looked stunning in her lacy undergarments. She twirled and looked seductively over her shoulder, crooking her finger in a come-hither gesture. She took him to the bedroom, and Patsy's dream of the two of them christening those black silk sheets came true. They made love tenderly and softly as their bodies melted into each other.

After, Cristo spoke first, "Sorry, I just couldn't wait. I had to have dessert first."

"Me either, but now I'm starved!"

148

They stuffed their bellies with golumpki and heavy pierogis that Cristo called "sinkers" and finished off with a dessert of sugary kruschiki.

After dinner, Patsy invited Cristo to her sweet Salon de Bain for a romantic bubble bath in her clawfoot tub. They got a little playful splashing around, nearly flooding the small room with water.

Wrapped in thick terry towels, they retreated to the silk sheets with scented candles waiting in the bedroom and experienced delicious sex once again. Finally, they fell exhausted into a blissful nap, still holding each other until the twilight crept through the windowpane—a perfect ending to a perfect afternoon.

A few days later, Patsy went to her mailbox and found a note that read, "My heart bleeds for you," and under it was a painted red heart. Patsy was sure it was from Cristo. She would have to thank him properly, but for now she was heading to the city to meet Mr. S for a show rehearsal and a lunch date. Patsy held the note close to her before carefully putting it in her handbag. Then, smiling, she started down the street.

***

He'd been at her place for days, just waiting, from early morning, watching for what seemed like hours each day, until she finally appeared. His heart beat out of his chest as he watched her lift the note from the mailbox. He was elated as she smiled and held it close to her bosom. He snapped a photo of her, then another as she walked down to the subway, her lovely hips sashaying in time to his breathless heart pulsations.

On the train, she pulled out the note. He knew now that she loved him as much as he loved her. He snapped another shot at just the right angle to catch her beautiful lips and the curve of her breast clutching his Valentine. Crowds got in front of him and blocked his view. He pushed an older woman and kicked her grocery cart in anger. She screamed. He didn't care. His beloved was getting away. He was furious as he ran, but he lost

149

her somewhere between the turnstile and the steps. He was getting confused now, causing the CLICK, CLICK, CLICK to return to his brain.

He couldn't wait any longer. He ran home to develop the photos as he stripped naked, waiting for her beautiful face to emerge from the solution in the developing pan. With prongs, he picked up the picture, oh so carefully, and hung her lovely image to dry. It was the one of her clutching his note to her heart. When it developed completely, he grabbed his cock, imagining she was holding it, squeezing it, and even kissing it. He was sure now that she was dreaming of him as he moaned in ecstasy. It was the best day of his life. She was finally returning his affection. He stayed in the darkroom for hours reeling in passion. He had her. She was his and his alone.

CHAPTER 23
Confidential

Patsy grew bored and longed to return to her craft as the days went on, but Mr. S could not come up with any work. Yoga, crossword puzzles, and tea weren't stimulating enough. She was able to keep busy on the weekends, but she dreaded the weekdays. No one was around, and she didn't want to bother Cristo, knowing he was working on his next art show. Madge visited now twice a week, but when she left, Patsy felt the jitters settling in again.

Early one Monday, much to her surprise, Patsy heard a male voice. "Knock, knock, it's me, Cristo, please let me in, oh beautiful one."

"Give me a minute, kind sir, as I'm not decent!"

"Oh, but I love an indecent woman, don't you know. Take your time, good woman, and this mere serf will await you within the royal hallway."

Patsy laughed loud enough for him to hear and instantly tore off her robe, kicked her bunny slippers across the room, and ran to her bedroom. She slid into her favorite jeans and a pink silk blouse. She put a little deodorant under each arm, a splash of perfume and a quick brush of both teeth and hair, and she was ready. On her way to the door, she applied lipstick, smacking her lips as she made a kissing sound and giggled to herself.

"Oh, please, Entrée Vous," she said with a slight bow of her head. "Dreadfully sorry to keep you waiting."

Cristo replied, "You are more than worth waiting for, and it took you mere seconds to look dazzling."

"Just for you," she said, feeling a little embarrassed at the compliment, but also proud of her appearance. Even if it was just flattery, she took it.

"I was wondering if you would like to take a walk with me?" Cristo asked.

151

Patsy was a little surprised, but also delighted. "I'd love to." She was pleased that Cristo wasn't interested in her just for sex, and she liked the sweet idea of taking a walk with him on a beautiful day.

They even held hands, which made her heart melt. "Coffee?" she asked as they approached Java Joe's.

"My thoughts exactly," he answered.

The intoxicating aroma of freshly roasted coffee beans met them as they opened the door to the café. Most tables were filled with creative types—some scribbling in notebooks or on sketchpads, others deeply immersed in books. Cristo and Patsy grabbed a booth by the back window.

They were preoccupied stealing kisses when a hippy-looking waitress donning a Java Joe's cap approached them. "What can I get for you two lovebirds this morning, or shall I come back later?"

Cristo asked for two lattes and two bear claws. The waitress pulled a pencil from behind her ear and drew a big heart on her ordering pad, showing it to them as she smiled. "Coming right up. Now carry on you two!"

Cristo reached across the table and gently stroked Patsy's hand. His touch immediately sent a surge of passion through her body. She spoke quickly so as not to get too lost in his touch, "So, what a surprise it was to see you today. To what do I owe the pleasure?"

"I just thought it would be nice to get to know each other a little better. I don't typically like to get too personally involved with my subjects, but Patsy, there's just something about you that draws me to you…a feeling of familiar comfort." Cristo leaned in closer.

"I feel the same way about you," she blurted out, not meaning to, but caught up in the moment.

They gazed into each other's eyes as Cristo continued to stroke Pasty's hands. "To get to know me, I feel you need to know where I came from. My neighborhood in Camden was mostly Polish and Catholic, and it was awesome. I was a happy kid, even though my dad passed away when I was only seven. My grandmother, my Babcia, was my best friend and always encouraged me to continue with my art. My mother had to work long hours, so most days were spent just Babcia and me." His eyes turned solemn when he spoke of his grandmother.

He raised his shirt to show Patsy the tattoo on his chest of a heart with *Babcia* in cursive right in the middle. She recalled seeing the tattoo when they'd made love and was so relieved to know it was for his grandma, not another woman. Patsy was so taken with Cristo at that moment she couldn't help reaching across the table to touch the pretty heart.

Cristo smiled and lowered his shirt. "One spring day in junior high, I rushed home to show Babcia a painting I did for her. I got to our porch and called out her name, but she didn't answer. Inside, the priest had his arm around my mother, who was crying. 'Babcia, Babcia, where are you?' I called.

"The priest explained that my dear Babcia had a heart attack in her little garden. I hated him and the words coming out of his mouth. I almost hit him, screaming, 'No, you're lying, shut up!' I was so overcome with grief. When he put his arm around me, I pushed him away, not believing it could be true, and my life felt ruined in one awful day. Everyone tried to console me, but I hated them and only wished they were all dead, and only me and Babcia were alive in this cruel world.

"The next time I saw Babcia was when she was laid out in her casket. After her funeral, I dug up her garden down on my hands and knees, scratching the earth until my fingers began to go numb. I cried out, 'Why God? Why?' Her beautiful garden was now evil, the garden of death, the garden that took her. I wanted to bury myself in it. I lost my best friend." Cristo's voice lowered to a whisper.

"I'm so sorry," Patsy said as she reached over to Cristo's cheek and softly wiped away a tear.

With a heavy sigh, Cristo continued, "My mother couldn't manage the house by herself, so we moved up to Passaic in North Jersey to live with her sister, my Aunt Dot, and my nasty Uncle Joe. My two cousins shunned me. They were short and fat and were on the high school wrestling team. Uncle Joe was around 300 pounds and thought that anyone into art was gay, and he wasn't afraid to say it. He always made fun of me. I was miserable in the new neighborhood and a new school with no friends. I cried into my pillow every night. I kept all Babcia's babushkas, and to this day I wear a different one every day.

"I finally started hanging with these cool guys who went into the city a lot—musicians, artists, and free-thinking types. They were my friends, and I'd scheme every day about escaping to New York forever. I saved all the money I made from entering my artwork in different competitions and from gifts I received for my graduation. When high school was over, I wrote a goodbye letter to my mom and Aunt Dot and headed to the bus station. I grabbed my art supplies, my French beret, all Babcia's babushkas, and the book I cherished from Babcia, *The Count of Monte Cristo,* and I took off to the city. My friends were waiting with open arms, and I went from being Ralph Sokolewski of Camden, New Jersey, to 'Cristo' of New York City!" Cristo paused and waved his napkin like a flag in celebration.

Patsy laughed, "Cristo, the Great!"

She was excited her miserable childhood matched Cristo's, and they both ended up in New York City. "My story is so similar. I too escaped my mundane life in Yonkers and came to the city to pursue acting and dancing. I moved in with two friends that I'm still close to—friends like I never had before. We call ourselves *The Three Amigos.*"

"I wish I could say that about my so-called friends, but it just ain't so," Cristo explained, "Listen to this: I moved into a rundown building in Hell's Kitchen with my pals Rico, Boomer, and Johnny D. They were great at first and only charged me fifty dollars a week that we kept in an old cookie jar. We operated on the honor system. I set up my easel in a different spot by the Port Authority every day and was doing surprisingly well sketching tourists. One day my friend Stash, the pretzel vendor, said he could get me a spot right outside Central Park and it was terrific. Some days I made $100 and had lines of people waiting to be sketched. Life was good. My roommates were gone all night, and I was gone all day. It was going well until all hell broke loose!" Cristo raised his voice and slapped both hands on the wooden table.

He leaned towards Patsy, "I decided to stop home since I already made ninety bucks, and it wasn't even noon. I stopped for a six-pack, thinking I could finally catch the guys for a change. Running up the steps, I heard a racket in the hall. People were standing around, and our apartment door was open. I saw the cookie jar in pieces on the floor but no money around it."

Patsy saw distress in Cristo's face, "There was trash strewn all over the floor. In the hallway, I overheard a young boy say to his grandmother that three guys living in the apartment were busted for dealing drugs and hauled off to the police station. The kid said they were dealing coke, pot, and Kellogg's cereal. I knew right away the boy meant the drug "Special K," and I held back a laugh, but this was not funny. It wasn't funny at all.

"That's when I panicked and thought I might get arrested if they found me there. I grabbed my clothes and art supplies and hurried down to the local café where I hung out. My friend Maurice lived with his drag queen partner Black Cherry in a third-floor walkup on the side of the cafe, so I decided to go upstairs to see Maurice and plead for refuge. At that point, I didn't know what else to do.

"Maurice listened to my tale of woe, but he was just as upset for himself because he used to score drugs from my roommates, and he was losing his connection. Luckily though, he saw my sadness and said, 'Sure, Man, mi casa, su casa. The couch is yours!' Just then, in a burst of explosive color and song,

155

Black Cherry sauntered into the room. He was dressed in full drag and singing at the top of his lungs that Queen song, *"We are the Champions, my friends...."*

Patsy stifled a laugh at the name Black Cherry, almost spraying her drink across the table as Cristo continued, "Black Cherry said, 'Let this sweetie boy stay as long as he wants, Mauri, he's sooo pretty!' Maurice shooed him away as I tentatively handed him the crumbled ninety dollars, the only money I had at the time. But Maurice refused my money and told me I was their guest. I felt so lost, like when Babcia died, and we were forced to move."

Patsy could tell Cristo was drifting back to that time as he looked up and stared out the window. Finally, she broke in, saying, "Cristo, I know that feeling so well. It has happened to me so many times."

Cristo took a deep breath and continued. "All I could think of in every waking hour were the horrible days when I lived with Big Joe and the two trolls. It was helplessness, hopelessness, with no answers in sight. I knew I had to stick it out with Maurice and his crazy drag queen partner. No way was I going back to Jersey."

Patsy was fascinated with Cristo's honesty and splashes of humor. He was vulnerable yet strong. She felt very connected to him at that moment. Despite his hardships, his sense of determination prevailed.

Two hours flew by, and Patsy changed to tea while Cristo continued drinking espresso. "Now comes the fun part. It's funny now, but I was shaking in my boots at the time. Black Cherry liked me, and he was at least six feet tall and very provocative, if you know what I mean. I distinctly remember the day when he yelled out, 'Hey, Mr. Artiste, do you like these yellow shorts with these spiked heels?' He stood right in front of me and blew kisses in my face. Then he made this bending over pose, hand on hip, seductively turning to show off his tight derriere with his ass cheeks peeking through."

Patsy laughed so hard when Cristo said the words ass cheeks, "Only in New York. There's every imaginable type of person in this city. I love it!"

"I put up with his antics and shot back, 'Yes, I do. They are so YOU!' Maurice, being a little saner, often shooed Black Cherry away as an annoyance saying, 'Leave our sweet Jersey boy alone, you washed up drag queen.'

"The finale came one night when Black Cherry was determined to impress me. So, HE magically turned into SHE and appeared in full drag. She had on a long red wig with blonde highlights, her lips were bright red, her cheeks rosy gold against her dark skin. She wore bright blue eye shadow and must have had three pairs of eyelashes on. She wore a sequined, silver dress, and huge boobs proudly bounced with glitter in her cleavage. Patsy, they looked so real as she shook them, and glitter scattered all over me. I even had some in my nose. She pranced up and down a fictitious catwalk at least ten times."

"Oh, my Lord, that's incredible," Patsy said.

"My creative side saw the beauty in this sweet soul, and I made a promise to paint her someday. She went along, pretending she was a model on the Paris catwalk as I yelled out, 'Work it, Girl! Strut your stuff. Girl, you are a star.' I was mesmerized by the exquisite image of this big feminine creature. Black Cherry taught me a lesson in civility that day. She also emboldened me as an artist. No more prejudice or petty opinions for me."

"Cristo, that's touching. You gave her hope and inspiration."

"Well, not so fast. The next few days with Maurice and Black Cherry and their constant lines of coke on the coffee table, and outrageous antics, made me realize I had to bolt just to keep my sanity. The clincher came when I woke up one day with my usual morning wood, and Black Cherry was staring down at me. He said, 'What do we have here Crissy? Hmm, must be dreaming of Black Cherry.'

157

Maurice knew it was the last straw by the look on my face. I said a quick, 'Later friends, thanks for letting me crash here,' then I ran like twenty blocks to the YMCA, art supplies and all.

"On the way, I thought in colors, as often do. I decided my life had become a sad canvas of white powder and Black Cherry. I clutched Babcia's scarf tight in my fist as the wind blew across my cheek. I remember it like it was yesterday. I felt she was telling me to reach out to my mom, and so I called and we talked for a while. I asked her for a small loan just until I could get back on my feet. She said she was so delighted to hear my voice and offered to wire me money right away. I only asked for two hundred dollars, but she offered to send money every week if I promised to call her.

"I gratefully agreed and made the promise with one stipulation: she'd have to call me Cristo and not Ralph. I explained that Babcia gave me *The Count of Monte Cristo* to read when I was twelve years old so I took the name from that story as a tribute to her. Any mention of her mother always made her happy and she agreed."

Patsy took Cristo's hand again and promised, "I'll never call you Ralph."

"Things were beginning to turn around almost immediately, and I looked to heaven to thank my beloved Babcia. I received a small but nice sum from my mother that got me a room over a restaurant in Little Italy. I felt safe and inspired. The first full day there, I stepped out on the pavement in the morning sunshine to see the chubby Italian men rolling out their colorful awnings. Spotting the "Little Italy" sign halfway down the street, I remember so clearly yelling loudly to no one in particular, Buongiorno, buongiorno, my name is CRISTO!"

Patsy shouted out, "Bravo! Bravo!"

Cristo looked at his watch. "Unfortunately, I need to go now," he said as he kissed her wrist in a grand gesture. "I have an appointment with my mentor, the lady sponsoring me for my SoHo showcase, and I can't be late. But, let's plan to do this again soon. I'd love to learn more about *you*. It's been all me, me, me," Cristo said apologetically.

"Anytime," Patsy replied, flashing a big smile. Cristo touched his lips to hers and was gone.

Patsy lingered in the coffee shop for just a few minutes and thought of how similar their values were. They shared a similar upbringing in a close-knit town, and their desire to follow their dreams. She knew she couldn't tell him about the stalking incident just yet as she vowed confidentiality to Mr. S and Calgon, but it was so cathartic to listen to his story and learn about his struggles.

CHAPTER 24
Nude

Five days later, a familiar knock came on Patsy's door. Instinctively, she knew it was Cristo. He looked a bit apprehensive when he walked in. "Do you want to hear more of the Cristo saga? I really need your advice on something too, and it did me a world of good to talk to you last week. Hope you don't mind."

"Not at all. I've been wishing you would come by. It was so enlightening to hear everything about you. Do you want to come in or go out?"

"Java Joe's," he smiled sheepishly.

Again, they walked hand in hand to the cafe. Patsy felt the slight grip of reassurance from Cristo's hand. The gesture seemed as natural as breathing. Their palms pressed together which sent a slight chill up Patsy's arm that shot straight to her heart.

Cristo ordered an espresso, and Patsy ordered Earl Grey tea. Cristo looked worried, "Remember when I told you I was settled in Little Italy and feeling pretty confident? Well, I immediately started back to claim my favorite spot outside Central Park. I usually hopped on a bus or sometimes rode the subway carrying my fold-up chairs and easel in a large canvas sack. I was getting so used to it and even whistled a favorite song by the Rascals on my way." Cristo sang out loud, "*It's a beautiful morning. I feel like going outside for a while and just smile....*"

The folks in Java Joe's listened and applauded. Then, very impulsively, their waitress joined in with, "*Just take in some clean, fresh air, boy. Ain't no sense in stayin' inside. If the weather's fine an' you got the time. It's your chance to wake up and plan another brand-new day. Either way....*"

Now everyone in the place sang out, *"It's a beautiful mornin'...."* Laughter and applause filled the café. It was one

160

of those spontaneous moments Patsy was sure she would never forget.

When the excitement calmed down, Cristo continued, "Life was finally more stable, and I was away from the dangers of criminal drug dealers and pushy drag queens. That was a crazy ride, I must admit, and my somewhat sensitive nature couldn't take the drama."

"I feel ya," Patsy laughed.

"I set myself up on the outskirts of Central Park. The greenery was abundant, and the sky was shades of mauve and bright blue. To my amazement, a small crowd gathered around me. It was like they were expecting me. Previously, I charged fifteen dollars for a picture but decided with my new lease on life to make it twenty dollars now. On my homemade sign, which was titled, *Portraits by Cristo*, in parenthesis, I wrote, two for thirty dollars, in case there was a child and a dog or two people in the portrait."

"I wore a colorful bandana around my head and tied it off to one side. I had real long hair then and a full beard, and always wore tight shirts. I tried to show off my pecks and look as artsy and bohemian as I could. I worked hard at attracting the crowd and the curiosity of the bystanders too." Cristo gave a sly smile to Patsy, "I was going for the mysterious, other-worldly look, ha!"

Patsy rolled her eyes, "You are definitely out of this world, my friend."

"A little girl sitting upright on my stool was my first sketch. I moved her arms to strike a cute pose and placed her little hands folded on her lap. As I worked on the charcoal drawing of the young girl, people lingered and watched. I could hear their comments and the whispers—things like, 'Wow, that is sheer perfection. He has captured her essence.' I was elated and feeling in my element. Before the first stroke, I always glanced up to the sky in prayer, thanking Babcia for this good fortune. It was my new mantra. I believed she was looking down on me every minute.

"I turned with a little pride to show my audience the finished product. There it was an absolute image of the little girl. To my delight, people began to applaud. Comically I gave a slight bow and quickly moved on to my next subject. One drawing was of a boy with a cocker spaniel puppy, and next came a couple, obviously in love. I shouted out, teasing them, 'hey young lovers, save it for the bedroom. Look this way for at least two minutes.'

"I was becoming quite the comedian, and I loved it. Seeing the couple so happy, I wished for a split second that I was romantically involved. Oh sure, there were a few girls in the Italian neighborhood that wanted to take me home, but it would be for one-night stands and not the real thing. I just wasn't swept away, so my art had to be my love object. I feel now that it might be you, beautiful one."

Patsy blushed and squeezed Cristo's hand, giving him a little peck on his cheek. She was shocked Cristo made such a bold statement so nonchalantly.

"Anyway, this went on for weeks, and the crowds grew bigger and bigger. By this time, I made two hundred dollars on good days. I finally had some sort of a steady lifestyle and income, but most importantly I loved what I was doing. My mom was still sending checks, but I didn't need the extra bucks anymore." He sighed, sat back, and said, "OK, Patsy, I'm getting to the part where I might need some advice."

"I'm ready. Bring it on."

"As time went by, I noticed an extremely attractive woman, who came to observe me nearly every day. She watched me, but always from a distance. Being in a flirtatious mood one day, I stared back at her and said, 'Come closer, don't be shy, let me sketch you.' But she never moved to get in line. As I said, she was attractive, although much older, and she was dressed like a woman of means. I must admit, I was intrigued.

"One day, while I was packing up my easel and supplies, this stylish lady sauntered over to me. Holding out her hand, she said in clipped sentences, 'My name is Madeleine. I've been watching you. You are quite good.'

"Patsy, I didn't know what to say, but finally stammered out a complete sentence, 'Why not sit for me? I would love to sketch you.' She replied, 'Maybe another time. I'm an art enthusiast. Here's my card. Give me a call so we can perhaps get together to discuss your talents a little further.'

"Well, I took the card and watched her walk away, not believing what just happened. I felt so fortunate that she made the first move. All the way home to my tiny room, I thought about her and wondered where this woman came from. I took out her card and read the name, Madeleine Landsteller, Curator of Fine Arts, Metropolitan Art Museum. Yes, my luck was certainly changing. Again, I looked up to the heavens and thanked Babcia for my stroke of luck.

"I frantically went through all of my oil paintings, sketches, and watercolors and arranged them around my tiny room. I was euphoric as my head danced with thoughts of what might be coming my way. I just had a feeling Madeleine Landsteller was there at just the right time to make a few of my hopes and dreams a reality.

"The next day, I hurried to the park, and to my amazement, she appeared around an hour later. I motioned for her to sit down on the portable stool as I finished up the sketch of an elderly woman with a feathered hat on. 'You're next, Ms. Landsteller,' I said as she sat down with a big smile on her face.

"She replied, 'If you insist, Cristo, but please call me Madeleine.' My hands flew confidently over the canvas as I dramatically sketched Madeleine and exaggerated her full tresses and almond-shaped eyes. I was silently praying the sketch would be to her liking. To my delight, she smiled brightly when I tore the drawing off the sketch pad and showed her.

She showed the drawing to the audience that gathered around us. The crowd applauded as she pointed to me and stated, 'Here you have Cristo, sketch artist Magnifique!' I was flattered, but also a little embarrassed as people began to line up for their turn. Madeleine said, 'Please call me. We must talk.' She gave me a folded-up bill that I quickly shoved into the top pocket of my shirt, but a few minutes later, I looked down and saw it was a hundred-dollar bill.

Two hours later, from a payphone, I dialed the number on the card. When she picked up, I told her that she gave me too much and that I owed her eighty dollars. She said I owed her nothing. She wanted to meet me at a little coffee house on 57th and told me to be discreet, which of course, Patsy, you know I always am."

"Oh yes, you are…so I guess you met her?"

"Of course, I did! I gathered up my supplies and made my way to the coffee house as if I was walking on air. Outside the shop, I took Babcia's scarf off my arm and put it around my neck as I popped a tic-tac in my mouth and arranged my black beret on my head at a slight tilt. I figured I might as well look the part. I felt like I was going on my first real interview as an artist and maybe an entrance into their sacred artistic world in New York City.

"I saw her sitting by a window inside the coffee house and felt a surge of energy go through me. I propped my art supplies in a corner near her table and greeted her, tipping my beret, and giving a slight bow."

Patsy urged him for more, "Go on, go on, I can't wait to hear what's next."

Even more excited now, Cristo continued, "After we had coffee and chatted a while, she said she wanted to see more of my work. At first, I felt shy because everything I had was in my tiny apartment. But she insisted she needed to come to see them.

As soon as we walked in my place, she gasped and said, 'No, no, Cristo, an artist like you can't work in such a tiny space.' I didn't know what to say, so I just stood there while she walked about and looked at each drawing and painting. She even picked up one of my sketchbooks and carefully went through each page.

"Finally, she turned to me and said quite matter-of-factly. 'My husband, who is often away on business, owns properties in Tribeca.' She went on to say that she was sure her husband would give me a break on the rent of a great apartment if I did certain things for her—just art things, nothing else. She made it quite specific that she was interested in my style and talent. She could tell I was shocked. She got me this showing in SoHo almost immediately, and she even promised someday a chance to have a real gallery showing in Chelsea. Well, I said sure, Chelsea would be a dream come true. Before that happened, she said she had a special proposition for me. I wanted to appear sophisticated and take it all in stride, but honestly, it floored me."

"What, Cristo, what did she want? Is it YOU she wanted?" Patsy couldn't help feeling and sounding jealous.

"Oh no, it's not me, believe me. She wanted me to paint her in the nude as a gift for her husband's fiftieth birthday. She didn't wait for an answer. She just showed up one stormy morning at my door in a raincoat and six-inch hot pink stiletto heels wearing nothing but a string of pearls! She said, 'OK, I'm ready. Let's get started.' I stood there frozen."

"Oh my God!" Patsy screamed. "That's a riot. What did you do next?"

Cristo laughingly replied, "I pretended it was a natural occurrence and acted exceptionally smooth even though I was shocked. After my hands stopped shaking, I grabbed my sketch pad and got to work. Patsy, one time she even held her balance in stilettos in the yoga tree pose. How she ever kept from falling is a mystery to me. I never sketched so fast in my life and kept yelling out to her. 'I got it. You can relax now. I got

165

it!'"

Patsy nearly choked as drops of Earl Grey tea spewed out her mouth into her napkin.

"I just don't know if I can continue doing this. She wants a few more sessions so I can capture her many moods. She's even talking about bringing in props. I'm afraid to ask what they might be!"

Patsy thought how strange and different people are. For a brief second, she recalled her own stalking incident, but dismissed it, not wanting any negative thoughts to spoil this moment when Cristo opened up to her. Feeling relieved that Madeleine didn't proposition Cristo, Patsy replied in both a joking and matter-of-fact tone, "Well, why not I say. My only question is, how much is she gonna pay ya?"

"Hey, I'm a good Catholic boy, Patsy. What would my dear Babcia think?"

Patsy said with a bit of whimsy, "She's probably calling on the Holy Spirit right now to protect her beloved grandson from sin."

They both laughed as Cristo quickly blessed himself with the sign of the cross and said, "You got that right. Do I hear an Amen!"

CHAPTER 25
CLICK

Patsy was thrilled her relationship with Cristo was deepening. She woke every morning singing to herself *Good Day Sunshine*, one of her favorite Beatles' songs. Patsy knew Cristo was extremely hard at work painting and gearing up for an art show, so she busied herself around her house. She spent hours reading, especially *Variety* and the *Village Voice*, fashion, and decorating magazines, and even a few romantic novels. She wandered through the used book shops and lingered at the newsstands, but averted her eyes when she came upon a National Enquirer. It was still too raw and frightening.

Patsy called Madge and asked her over for coffee. When Madge arrived, Patsy was bustling around her tiny kitchen, "Madge, I have cinnamon raisin bagels and cream cheese just for you."

Madge grabbed half a bagel. She looked concerned but comical with cream cheese sticking on her bottom lip, "OK, *Schatzi*, tell old Madge what's on your mind. I know it's more than bagels."

"You know me so well. The truth is, I'm tired of my hiatus from Calgon. I'm yearning to be back working and performing again. Could you talk to Mr. S? I'll take any part no matter how small. I need to be active, or I'll go crazy. And I'm all yoga-ed out."

"I'm working on it, *Schatzi*. I'll give Mr. S a push to see if he can find you some fulfilling work until it's safe to return to Calgon. That *schmuck* peeping Tom screwed up everything. I'd like to cut his tiny dick off and stuff it up his nose."

Patsy laughed, "I know you'll come through. You're my fabulous Wonder Woman."

"And you're my *Shayna Punim*. But you gotta remember that Mr. S's priority was only to keep you safe. He's doing this for your protection. He knows best. So, stay put a little longer.

167

Ol' Madge will come through. I can handle Mr. S. He always gives in to me or he knows I'll smother him with these double D's, and Patsy Girl, he ducks when I come at him. These puppies are eye level with his face!"

Like magic, after only two days, Mr. S called Patsy and said cheerfully, "Hello Dearheart, to keep you happy, I'm arranging for you to do rehearsals in *Bright Lights*, a small off-Broadway musical I'm sponsoring. I feel sure you'll do well as a stand-in or understudy for the lead actress Kate Sweeney. Although it's doubtful you'll perform for a live audience, it looks good on your resume. I feel it is safe too for now," Mr. S said very hopefully. "It's a happy play, full of song and dance, and perfect for you to learn what a Broadway production is all about. I know you'll be thrilled working with Kate. She's a gem. It's due to go into production next week. This will be good practice for when you get your own show someday."

Patsy couldn't contain her excitement, "Mr. S, thank you so very much. You have no idea what this means to me. I could just kiss you!"

"Oh, I have a bit of an idea, and hold the kiss for the next time we meet. But Patsy, please remember you still need to be careful," Mr. S warned.

"I know, I know, and I will. Thank you Mr. S. You're the BEST!" Patsy was ecstatic.

Patsy's hands were sweating as she opened the heavy door to the theatre entrance. An older man was there and looked like a custodian. "Are you here for rehearsals or on the writing staff?"

With a shaky voice, Patsy answered, "Hello Sir, I'm Patsy Mahoney. Mr. S sent me."

From the middle of the theatre, Kate shouted out, "Welcome, Patsy, we heard a lot of good things about you!" Immediately, confidence came pouring back, and she was ready and eager. This was another big chance, and her heart exploded with joy.

Over the next few days, Patsy shadowed the lead actress diligently and was mesmerized by her talent. She couldn't believe she was experiencing this fantastic opportunity and was grateful to be around real show people. Being the understudy, Patsy practiced more hours than the rest of the cast and attended other rehearsals just to watch. She wanted her performances, even though unobserved by the public, to be perfect.

Opening night brought great reviews, and as the weeks went on, the audience grew. One day in rehearsal, Kate did a difficult sprint and leapt across the stage. Patsy practiced this same stunt dozens of times, so she was paying little attention to Kate. That is until she heard a boom, crash, and a shriek ring through the air. Kate screamed out in what sounded like excruciating pain. "Oh God, oh no! It's broken, I can't move!"

Patsy, ran to Kate, "Are you OK?"

Kate began to cry, "No, I'm not, I can't move. It's so painful. I can't believe this. My whole body is shaking. You might have to go on for me, Kid!"

An EMT arrived and told Kate, "Honey, I'm sorry, but that ankle looks bad. Let's get you to the hospital to get an x-ray. I think you might be out of commission for a while." Kate was loaded on a stretcher. An entourage of folks rode behind the ambulance—the director, writer, and leading man, as Patsy stood there shocked.

She overheard one of the cast members say, "Oh shit, I hope we don't have to close now."

Another voice chimed in, "No, Patsy will save our asses. She's ready. I know it. That girl is good."

Patsy never saw who said those words, but she heard them loud and clear. She knew they believed in her. Now she just needed to believe in herself. Like she heard so many times before, "The show must go on," and it would, yes it would. She felt it in her soul.

Patsy never dreamed she would step in, and she was sad Kate was hurt, but her heart was singing deep inside. Over the next few days, she rehearsed for hours and hours as the directors, producers, and Kate, whose leg was in a cumbersome boot, watched her every move. Finally, by the following weekend, Patsy was ready to go.

The play contained musical numbers and lots of tap-dancing routines. It told the story of a down-and-out waitress who sings for her supper until a Broadway producer falls for her and furthers her career. It was perfect for Patsy's dancing skills, especially tap. There was a theme song titled *Bright Lights* that Patsy rehearsed night and day. Patsy's backup was a chorus of seven cast members. Her only worry was the solo finale and holding that last long note. Other than that, she felt excited and ready to perform.

Patsy couldn't wait to tell her mom about the show. She was filled with excitement when she called, but thought to tease her mother a bit. "Mom, you won't believe this. When you visit, I'm taking you and Cathleen to a new Off-Broadway musical."

Bridget screamed into the phone and out to Cathleen, "Cathleen, did you hear that? Patsy's taking us to a Broadway show!"

Patsy replied, almost feeling herself well up with tears, "Oh, and Mom, guess who is in the show?" Before Bridget could answer, Patsy blurted out, "It's me, Mom! It's me!"

"Surely you are kidding me?"

Through tears, Patsy answered, "I can hardly believe it myself. The lead star sprained her ankle, so I'm going on. Those tap-dancing lessons from you paid off. I'm going on!"

Tears turned to laughter as Patsy heard Bridget say to Cathleen, "Pack your bags, Cathleen, your sister is a Broadway star, and we'll be sittin' right up front. Good God Almighty, my prayers are answered."

***

He couldn't't believe what he was reading in the Times Square flyer. She was playing Off-Broadway. He was lucky he spotted her name on her mailbox while he was spying on her. He missed her so much. As he walked past the photos that were strewn across his wall, he began to hear the noise. His cameras were clicking as if they created a life their own, and they were as excited as he was. They all vied for attention, each hoping they would be the one chosen for the new shoot.

The noise of CLICK, CLICK, CLICK sounded louder and louder in his head. He screamed, "Shut Up, Shut up!" as he put his hands over his ears to stifle the chaos in his brain. Finally, in desperation to make the sound disappear, he chose the German handheld camera as the winner. This camera was the one with the best zoom lens so he could catch her at just the right angle. Her performance would be for him and him alone.

He rushed off to buy his tickets for the Thursday night performance, two tickets on the aisle for the fourth-row orchestra. He was careful to buy the seat next to him, so he'd have no distractions and enough elbow room to work his magic. He didn't like people anyway—especially sitting close to him. They'd interfere with his primary purpose, and that attention belonged only to her. She would be the only one to touch him for the rest of his life.

She was his idol, his perfect girl. No one else mattered. The thought of her sent excitement that permeated to his loins, and he rushed home from buying the tickets, dreaming of his conquest. As his hand moved faster and faster, he let his images of her on the wall do the rest of the sexual pleasure. Proudly glancing down at his engorged erection, he let out an animal moan as semen squirted in the air. He cleaned it up quickly, careful not to get it on the precious tickets, and soon fell into an exhausted sleep.

He woke with a start when he realized he was still clutching the theatre tickets to his chest with one hand, and his other hand was on his now sore cock. The noise in his head began as soon as he got out of bed to get a cold beer. The CLICK, CLICK, CLICK grew louder and built in momentum. He downed two Vicodin and gulped the beer. He was sure she was waiting, yes, she was rehearsing right now, and her performance would be just for him.

***

Patsy was still an unknown in the Broadway acting circle, so she knew she needed to prove herself. She worked long hours and stayed after rehearsals. She was determined to impress the producer and other cast members. Over the next few days, she overheard the other cast members who seemed to have a sincere affection for her, and even invited her to their after-rehearsal gatherings. She never made it, she opted to work harder and longer than the professionals. They offered rides to the theatre and advised her to build up her muscle tone for her tap dancing and running lines to sharpen her acting skills. She heard the director say he couldn't believe she took no formal dance or theatre training. She was thrilled when she heard their remarks.

Even Kate, the lead actress sitting with her foot resting on a stool, shouted out from the empty theatre, "Girl, you are getting better than me. I know you will nail it come Thursday night!"

After a long ten-hour day, Patsy was usually exhausted. But today, she was wide awake and excited to go home. There were only a few minutes to quickly tidy up the apartment before her mom and Cathleen arrived. Once there, Cathleen jumped into Patsy's arms, shouting, "My sister the star, my sister the star!"

"Cathleen, you're getting so big. I wouldn't even recognize you. You're a lovely young lady and not the chubby little kid I remember."

"I cycle through Yonkers bike trail every day, and believe it or not, I've given up Little Debbie cupcakes. Instead, I want to end up looking like my big sis. Although I have a long way to go...."

"I think you are beautiful in every way, and you are uniquely sweet and wholesome too. You just have to be you." Patsy looked carefully at Cathleen and saw so much of Roney's looks in her sister. But she was nothing like Roney.

Patsy couldn't help but ask the dreaded question, "Do tell, how is Dad doing?" Thus began the stories that went on and on as Cathleen did the hilarious imitation of her dad as he wandered in the house every night 'drunk as a skunk,' as she put it. "Where's me dinner, woman?" Cathleen imitated Roney staggering across the room, then collapsed snoring in a chair.

Patsy chuckled. "You even sound like him and how well I remember."

Bridget's face turned sad. "Patsy, he's gotten so much worse and is drinking every minute of the day, plus the boys are following in his footsteps. We got him to go to an AA meeting after his brothers found him face down in the alley of Mahoney's one morning. They were disgusted and took him to a meeting the next day, but you know your father. No one tells him what to do. He ended up speaking at the AA meeting, and he did admit he was an alcoholic, then he proceeded to invite the whole meeting to Mahoney's bar for free drinks. He's never going to change."

Grabbing Bridget's hand, Patsy said, "I want to know how you are, only YOU and no one else."

Bridget sighed, "Well, there's good and bad, but that's how life is. First, let me say how I feel about you. You are a bright, beautiful, motivated young woman, and you have stuck to your hopes and dreams."

"Thank you, Mom. You're the one who inspired me to pursue my dreams, and if it weren't for your support, I'm not sure I would have made it. But, enough about me."

"Well, since your dear ol' dad is drunk every day, I just do my thing, but it hasn't been easy. Things haven't changed much since you were there except for the new stage, but the cash from the trifecta winnings is practically gone. I managed to stash some away, but that's for the kids and even sometimes to buy food. Things deteriorated, and the money we thought was such a blessing turned out to be a curse giving your father an excuse to drink and brag every day. There's truly little to celebrate now. But, I have something else to tell you, and I must swear you to secrecy because no one knows any of this," Bridget said with a slight smile.

Patsy leaned closer to Bridget. "Patsy, I met a man from my Monday night novena devotion, and one day he asked me to coffee afterward. He said he lost his wife to cancer a year before. His name is Tony DiPasquale, and he is so handsome Patsy, and he thinks I'm beautiful. It's been so long since someone thought that and even longer that I had a man, a SOBER man, to talk to!

"We've never become affectionate, but he did lean in to kiss me goodnight two weeks ago, and Patsy, I can't get it out of my mind. I wanted to kiss him back. It's been nine weeks now, and he is kind and respectful and sympathetic and knows how your dad ignores and mistreats me. He never asks anything of me, but if he did, I might say 'YES,' God forgive me, I'm a sinner for sure."

"Oh, Mom, you're not a sinner. You are a beautiful, alive woman, and I am so happy for you."

"Your father and I haven't had sex for years. He never asks where I am since going to novena is something I've been doing for a long time. Patsy, I don't feel guilty. Living with your father now is so horrible. I hope you don't think less of me. Do you?"

Patsy could see in Bridget's eyes the deep internal struggle her mom was faced with. She kissed her on the cheek, "Mom, you have to believe me. I'm so happy for you finding

174

some joy with this wonderful man. I think it's awesome. I consider him a blessing, and it's meant to be that you found each other."

Bridget's face softened, and she grabbed Patsy for a long hug.

The next day Patsy took her mom and Cathleen shopping to buy outfits for the show. It seemed like old times, the three of them together. Cathleen must have tried on five different outfits and was having a blast. "Wow, there's so much to choose from. This sure ain't Yonkers!"

Bridget emerged from the dressing room in a silk, beige dress with a V-neck trimmed in rhinestones. Patsy walked up to her mom as she stood in front of the full-length mirror and whispered, "You look gorgeous! I'll bet Tony would want more than a kiss if he saw you in that number."

Bridget whispered back, "Hey if ya got it, flaunt it!" They both laughed as Patsy and her mom winked at each other with their shared secret.

Patsy yelled to the salesgirl, "Wrap it up, this is on me!"

Patsy woke the following day amazed she finally fell asleep the night before. All she could think about was her upcoming Broadway debut. When Patsy left for the theatre, she left a note on the kitchen counter reminding Bridget there were two orchestra tickets for them at the box office. She told them to come early and ask for Archie, the head usher, and he would direct them backstage to Patsy's dressing room. She was nervous and excited at the thought of her family seeing her perform.

It was a hectic time, but Patsy was ready for her debut and could feel the anticipation in the air. Everyone was in their own zone. The prop guys and grips took orders from a loud stage director swinging a clipboard and hammered last-minute scenery. The orchestra was tuning up, sounding like all instruments were playing at once to different tunes. The cast did a quick rehearsal of the big tap number along with stretching motions to limber up. Patsy practiced her lead song, *Bright Lights,* and reached the high note at the end flawlessly. The crew stopped and clapped for her.

Returning to her dressing room, doing some deep breathing exercises, and sipping hot lemon water, a soft tap came on her door. "Knock, knock, your biggest fans are here," Cathleen giggled.

Patsy let her mom and sister in, putting a finger to her lips to make sure they knew to be quiet. "I was going to take you on a tour backstage, but I got the jitters so that will have to wait. It's time for me to pretend I'm back on the rickety little stage at Mahoney's. I do that sometimes to calm me down."

Bridget smiled, "You are going to be great, Patsy. Remember the Yankee Doodle Dandies and how you got the kids ready. This is the big time Patsy—you have arrived!"

"You're right…I am so glad you're here." She hugged them both. "Come on, let's get you two beauties settled in your seats." Patsy rushed Bridget and Cathleen off stage and pointed them to their seats.

"Break a leg, Sis!" Cathleen burst out with pride.

Forty minutes later, Patsy took the stage. Her mind was sharp, bright, and right on point. She didn't miss a step in the opening dance routine. Her feet were flying a mile a minute as she tapped across the stage, arms waving in perfect timing.

***

He arrived at the theatre early and was one of the first in the building. He took his seat and placed his camera in his jacket pocket, and then a second camera under his shirt. The zoom lens was ready to go. Knowing he may get caught and asked to leave, he prepared a dupe camera ready to go. It was a cheap Kodak, and his German camera was the best money could buy. He would outsmart them with his genius plan, knowing he thought of everything. His heart raced with anticipation.

176

When the lights went out, the curtain rose, and there she was facing him, speaking directly to him. His body trembled, causing a familiar stirring in his pants. *Settle down*, he told himself. He squirmed in his seat to begin his task at hand— plenty of time for sexual fantasies later in his darkroom.

He said to himself, *Ready, set, go!* And instantly it began the CLICK, CLICK, CLICK, FLASH, FLASH, FLASH, and then again CLICK, CLICK, CLICK, zoom in on her face, then her breasts, then her hips, as his mouth watered and breathing came fast. Finally, the money shot of her lovely crotch in a scantily clad outfit that longed for him. That was the ultimate. Half hard now, he craved her and nearly forgot where he was as he finished with the last CLICK, CLICK, CLICK.

Sounds of rumbling footsteps running down the aisle startled him. There was no time to react as two security guards rushed him, grabbed him out of his seat, and straight into the back lobby. He couldn't believe how quickly and quietly they did their job, so he needed to think fast before the knuckleheads started to frisk him. He pulled the Kodak out of his pocket and said in his most apologetic voice, "Sorry fellows, no sweat, here's the camera. Really sorry, it won't happen again."

The one guard said, "No, it won't, asshole 'cause if I catch you here again, the police will deal with you."

He smiled, realizing he fooled the bastards. Exhilarated, he hurried home to develop the photos of his beloved one and looked forward to bringing himself to quick satisfaction. He would do it two or three times he decided, panting heavily at the thought.

***

At the finale, the announcer called Patsy's name. The crowd clapped, whistled, and applauded as she took a bow, her heart swelling with pride and pounding out of her chest. Bridget and Cathleen were clapping and cheering the loudest, calling out her name. Pasty blew kisses to them, and she pointed in their direction. Then, she took three steps back, held hands with the

177

cast, took another bow, and a second and third curtain call. She thought to herself, *this is what true happiness feels like: to make others join in the fun is the greatest gift of all.*

When Patsy returned to her dressing room, roses were everywhere: red, white, pink roses, even a rare purple rose. She could hardly get into the tiny room. One card read, *To My Special Girl with Love, Mr. S* She started to cry. He never came backstage, but Patsy knew he was out there watching her.

After the show, she spotted Mr. S talking to the director offstage when the crowd filed out. She ran downstage to him and directly into his arms. She asked, "So, how did I do?"

"You were fabulous, Dearheart, totally fabulous!"

Bridget prepared Patsy's favorite meal of corned beef and cabbage when they returned to her apartment, even though it was close to midnight. The Mahoney girls once again shared stories and dreams way into the night.

Cathleen was again the first to go to bed. When she left the room, Patsy said, "Mom, I saved a little money, and rent here is cheap, so let me lend you a few hundred. To tell you the truth, I never spent the money you gave me when I first moved here."

Bridget put her head down, "Thank you, Patsy, thank you so much."

Patsy gave her a stack of bills with a twenty-dollar bill on top. She carefully disguised ten one-hundred-dollar bills under the twenty. Returning all the money her mother gave her made Patsy so happy.

On Friday morning, Bridget and Cathleen packed up and said goodbye. They must return for the weekend to help at Mahoney's bar. They all promised they would see each other more often. As Patsy watched her mother and sister walk away, a part of her longed to go with them. But she knew deep down that any return home would not be pleasant, especially with Roney reverting to his old ways. Besides, it was only Bridget and Cathleen she missed, no one or nothing else.

In her heart of hearts, Patsy knew she belonged in New York City—the dazzling lights, the excitement, and the specialness that only the Big Apple could provide. This was her home now. She rushed off to prepare for Friday's show. She was a part of it now. Gathering her leotard and tap shoes, she hurried to hail a cab.

CHAPTER 26
Bonjour

Early one morning, Patsy received a call from Mr. S. "Hi Dearheart, want to check out my newest song and dance investment, *Brazilian Holiday*? I'll get you front row seats."

"Of course," Patsy replied. She knew she must do anything Mr. S said, not because he was so powerful, but Patsy never wanted to hurt his feelings or disappoint him, especially since he confided in her. She knew how vulnerable and sensitive he was.

Also, she finished with her three weeks doing the Off-Broadway show. Kate was back and in perfect form. Patsy was feeling a little bored and let down and welcomed the invitation.

When she arrived at the theatre, the ticket was waiting for her at Will Call. The usher escorted her to the best orchestra seat. The seat next to her remained empty until the show started, and Mr. S slipped in and sat beside her. He gave her a quick peck on the cheek and grabbed her hand.

As soon as the first act began, Patsy saw a sight on stage that her eyes could not believe. It was the dancer at the end of the first row of the routine. *Oh my God, could it be?* She thought to herself. Then it registered, and emotion came pouring out of her. Her heart raced furiously, and she started to tremble. In a stupor, she jumped out of her seat and started toward the stage. Mr. S tried to grab her, but she kept walking. Without thinking, she yelled, "Henry, Henry, is that you? Is that really you?"

An usher gently touched her arm and whispered, "Please return to your seat, ma'am."

His touch and words broke her trancelike state. Embarrassed, Patsy responded, "I'm so sorry," and she quickly returned to her seat.

Mr. S whispered, "Patsy, what's wrong?"

"Please, I must go to the back and see Henry. It's my Henry," she said urgently.

180

"*Your* Henry?" Mr. S questioned.

"From high school. Remember how I told you we were in love, or at least I was, and he moved to New York City to be on Broadway?"

"Yes, I do. We must go see him then as soon as the show ends, I'll take you right to the back."

Patsy paid no attention to the show. Instead, her eyes stayed on Henry. His every move made her heart pound. Even during the scenes he wasn't in, she stared at the side stage curtains waiting for his return. The moment came when Henry spotted her and shot her a beaming smile from the stage. During the final curtain call, he mouthed, "Bonjour, bonjour, mon ami!" as he blew her several kisses.

As the last curtain closed, Mr. S grabbed Patsy's hand and led her through the backstage doors amidst the sea of the scurrying actors and actresses. Patsy spotted Henry with his back towards her. She yelled, "Henry!"

He turned around and yelled back, "Patsy!"

They ran towards each other and embraced tightly, not letting go of one another for a long time. Patsy was crying, and she thought he was too. It was almost impossible to believe. Patsy Mahoney was with Henry Johnson, her first love. And just like that, Fred and Ginger were reunited.

When they finally let go of one another, they continued to hold hands and stare into each other's eyes. Patsy felt there was something different about Henry. Of course, he wore thick make-up, and yes, they were both older, but Henry didn't quite look like himself. He didn't look well. His skin was sallow, and his ocean blue eyes weren't twinkling. Of course, Patsy didn't know anything about Henry's life since the last time she saw him at the train station in Yonkers. He could have lived a troubled life, but she always thought that he'd be living large, going on dates every night, or at least he'd have a steady, gorgeous girlfriend.

Mr. S smiled at them and said, "What a reunion! You two must have so much to catch up on!"

Patsy turned around to face Mr. S. She almost forgot he was there. "Yes, yes we do, and all thanks to you," Patsy said gratefully.

"Thank you, Mr. S!" Henry said enthusiastically as they shook hands.

"It wasn't my doing. We just all happened to be at the same place at the same time. It was meant to be." Mr. S graciously bid them both goodbye.

"So, where do we start?" Patsy asked. "I have a million questions for you. Am I going to wake up in the morning and realize this is all a dream?"

"I know how you feel, but it's so real and meant to be. I'm so delighted you are finally here, mon ami, but how did you get here, and what are you doing with one of the biggest producers on Broadway?"

Patsy dismissed his comment, "Can we meet tomorrow, maybe, and talk?"

"Of course, we can. I'm too tired to catch up tonight anyway. Let's meet at Central Park. There's a little bench right by the entrance on East 72nd. Want to meet there around 10 a.m.?"

"Of course!"

Henry kissed her cheek, "Are you OK to get home?"

"Sure thing, I'm a city girl now," she winked.

"See you tomorrow, mon ami."

The next morning, when Patsy approached Central Park, Henry was waiting with Patsy's large hot tea. Henry kissed her cheek and handed her the tea. "That is so sweet of you to remember that I love tea."

"I know you, no matter what time of day, you love your tea. I got you Earl Grey with honey."

Patsy couldn't wait any longer to ask Henry about a girlfriend. She was so nervous to ask him, but she wasn't sure why. Was it that she didn't want to know he was madly in love with another woman or that he had so many lovers, he turned out to be a womanizer? Something told Patsy neither of these scenarios was the case.

Finally, she blurted out, "Are you seeing anyone? Do you have a girlfriend?"

Henry seemed taken aback, but he answered quite matter-of-factly, "No, I had a boyfriend, his name was Marco, but he just passed away." Patsy gasped and nearly spilled her tea all over herself. Henry looked at her with a confused and angry look on his face, "There, I said it. Do you hate me now?"

Patsy wasn't sure if she was more shocked that Henry was dating a man or that Henry's boyfriend just passed away. Instantly negative thoughts about the rumors from high school returned. She couldn't let him think she hated him. She profusely apologized to Henry and expressed her sympathies. "Oh, my dear, sweet Henry, I'm so very sorry," Patsy replied with reverence.

It was then Henry fell apart. He put his head in his hands, and his body was racked with giant sobs. Patsy reached for him, and he burrowed his head in her shoulder. "It's going to be all right. I'm here for you now."

Finally, between sobs, Henry's voice cracked, "No, it's not Patsy, I'm HIV positive."

Patsy Mahoney and Henry Johnson cried in each other's arms on a lonely park bench on the outskirts of Central Park. His shoulders moved frantically up and down as she tried to comfort his shaking frame that now felt so bony and frail. "Henry, I'm here, and I'll never leave you. We'll fight this thing together." Thoughts filled her head, and sheer panic took over. *How could she find him, after all this time, only to lose him once again?* Sobs took over her body, matching his as they held each other close.

It was a week later when Patsy walked into Henry's tiny flat in Washington Heights. She could sense Marco's presence all over the little space. There was even a lingering scent that wasn't Henry's cologne. Instead, it was a strong odor of cumin mixed with a leathery smell that she imagined was Marco's. Pictures showed he was extremely handsome. His dark skin and dark hair showed he was of Hispanic descent. He was also quite muscular. Patsy could see his muscles protruding through his shirt.

Picture after picture of Henry and Marco were placed perfectly all over on the walls and on the coffee table. Images of Henry and Marco smiling, arms around each other's waists, holding hands, toasting glasses, even in one picture sharing a kiss. For a moment, Patsy felt a tinge of jealousy creep into her thoughts. At one time, she'd wanted that same closeness and romance from Henry, but that was then, and this is now, so she let the envy go and scolded herself for thinking of it in the first place.

"Henry, I can feel Marco's manifestation here, and I know he is smiling down on you—actually, it's a beautiful feeling." Patsy said this, knowing it was something Henry needed to hear.

"Marco believed in that connection too. He always said he would send little reminders of our love and told me to look for them. I have so much to tell you about his deep spirituality. He made me a better person. Marco and I watched so many of our friends die of this horrible disease, one after another— vibrant men in their twenties. Before Marco got extremely sick, we volunteered for God's Love We Deliver to make sure AIDS patients had healthy meals.

"Not only would Marco bring them meals but he would sit with these men on their final days and tell them to 'let go,' and he'd give them hope of a better life in heaven.

"It's so hard for many of us to have faith while watching too many good, young people die so suddenly. But not Marco, he always kept his faith. When it was Marco's turn to go, I sat with him day and night. But most of the time, it was him comforting me, telling me it was going to be all right." Henry began to fill up with tears again as Patsy held him close.

"So many of them were all alone because their families disowned them once they found out they were gay. Our community only has each other plus a few other caring souls like you and Mr. S," Henry said, wiping away the tears and looking up at Patsy lovingly.

Patsy wiped the remaining tears off Henry's face. "How did you and Mr. S meet?"

"Once Marco died, I was devastated. It wasn't long after one of my fellow dancers told me how involved Mr. S is in AIDS-related charities. Mr. S was producing one of the shows I was dancing in. I didn't know him well, but one day I saw him at a rehearsal and asked him to help me get involved. From then on, I pretty much threw myself into ACT UP, attending protests and rallies. It was all I could do. All we could do. We couldn't just sit back and keep watching so many of our friends die. Unfortunately, I don't have the energy anymore to attend the protests. But Mr. S has been so great, not just to me, but to all of us. If we need a day off, we just let him know, as he always says, 'we are all in this together.'"

Patsy agreed, "Mr. S is wonderful. He's like an angel. I'd love to hear more, but it's time for you to rest now." Patsy kissed Henry on the cheek and watched his eyes start to close as he slid down on the chaise lounge. For a split second, she felt Marco was there, bringing the two of them together.

Patsy didn't know much about the AIDS epidemic. Still, once she took on "Project Henry," she delved into finding out all she could about experimental drugs, clinics, doctors, and dietary demands. Patsy went to the New York Public Library and scanned through the latest info and breakthrough news on the autoimmune system. She read periodicals and journals and heavy medical books until her eyes ached. She then decided to ask Mr. S what he knew since he was involved with many AIDS charities.

Mr. S began timidly at first, "Patsy, I never wanted to bring the subject up with you so as not to upset you with such things, but it is a thorn in my side and has been for quite a while. I have seen such heartache, and it disturbs me deeply. To be gay is so difficult. Of course, there is the suffering of the disease itself, but there are also the taboos placed on the epidemic's origins. It is referred to by many as the "Gay Man's Disease" since the plague hit the gay community the hardest. It makes these poor kids feel twice as bad as if they are not in enough pain.

"Today, everyone fears HIV and AIDS, and life is less of an adventurous romp than the '80s was known for. HIV is especially rampant in the Broadway community, where many talented dancers, singers, and actors work and thrive with their beautiful and creative talents and their openness with their sexuality. That is why I began to get involved. I've seen young man after young man die. There was one show I was producing in 1987 where I lost half of the male dancers in a matter of months."

"Why isn't anyone doing anything about this?" Patsy asked.

Mr. S paused thoughtfully before answering, "Many don't want to acknowledge what's really going on. There are those out there who have no pity on these poor sick people. Gay men everywhere are being shunned and treated like lepers by the ignorant public." He shook his head with disgust and sadness.

"There is research being done, and some great doctors are trying their best to understand the disease better. But research takes money and support. California is a bit more advanced with its funding, but New York is lax with medical treatments and breakthroughs, and funding is minimal. New York hospitals are not financially equipped to deal with the overwhelming health threat. What research that does happen here, happens very slowly," Mr. S said sadly.

Patsy saw the anguish in his face. She realized how close Mr. S was to what was happening to so many in the business. "There are good people out there who are trying to raise money for AIDS research. That's why I started to get involved in these groups, like Gay Men's Health Crisis and ACT UP, AIDS Coalition to Unleash Power. We are trying to raise money and awareness."

Patsy interjected, "Oh, wait, I've heard and read about some of those groups. I never knew you did so much good, Mr. S. You are so wonderful and kind." With this, Patsy broke down and began to cry. "I'm so terrified Henry is going to die, and there's nothing I can do about it. Please help us through this. We need your strength."

"Patsy, I understand what you're going through, believe me," Mr. S said forlornly. "I've lost dancers, actors, musicians, some who would be incredibly famous today if it wasn't for that horrible scourge. They possessed the most beautiful attitudes even up to the very end when suffering was paramount," Mr. S declared with desperation in his voice as he spoke, "But Patsy, none were as close to me as Henry is to you. I want you to know, I'm here for both of you. I'll help in every way possible. I like Henry, and I'll keep him in the show if he wants to stay. Whatever accommodations he needs, it's no problem. Of course, whatever support either of you need, just know I'm always here. Let's fight this thing together!"

"Yes, we'll fight this thing together," Patsy repeated determinedly.

Patsy observed Henry's physical appearance changing rapidly, as well as his energy level, but his dancing skills were still excellent. As weeks turned into months, Henry became weaker and weaker. There were still giddy times between them though, when they recalled all the happiness they shared as teens at Patsy's house and Susan's house on those endless Fridays.

"Boy, you could chug a beer for a girl!" Henry laughed.

"Well, I had a lot of practice sneaking them. It comes naturally for Irish girls."

It was bittersweet for both, but they took it one day at a time and made the most of precious moments together. They rehearsed every day for four hours but took many breaks in between. At first, a choreographer was sent in, but Patsy was even better than the professional instructor.

One day Mr. S stopped by to say hello, "You two are quite the pair. You complement each other with your dance moves."

"Thank you, Mr. S, thank you for everything," Henry replied gratefully.

One night Henry confessed to Patsy as they cuddled on Henry's plush sofa, "When I fell into a depression after Marco's death, I could hardly function. I was even suicidal at times, especially when I found out I was infected with HIV. The sadness almost did me in," he said softly, lowering his head.

Then he perked up, "I was so grateful to get to know Mr. S and become so involved in ACT UP. It was truly a blessing, and it kept me going and gave me a purpose. Then you came along like a gift from God. You appeared and gave me a brand-new outlook. Patsy, you are my angel and saving grace. I think Marco sent you." He stared at her with sad eyes.

"Oh, Henry, that's so sweet of you. I'm just so grateful to be reunited with you." She kissed his pale, cold cheek.

Patsy spent hours with Henry in his tiny apartment in Washington Heights. First, she learned about the best foods to eat to fight the disease. Then, when Henry napped, she whipped up the most recent concoction.

When he awoke, she was there. "Have a good nap?" she asked, "I have a wonderful energy-filled shake for you," offering it to him. He made a face of displeasure. "Henry, you must drink this vegetable shake. It builds red blood cells. It's the latest recipe and touted by doctors from Johns Hopkins."

"I would love to drink it if it wasn't so green. It's just so damn green—anything but putrid green, Patsy."

Patsy laughed and added blue food coloring, declaring, "Well, I hope you're happy now. I made it aqua, which I know is your favorite color. Now drink up, man." It was laughter that kept them sane during scary times.

Trying to feel normal, Patsy and Henry often sat on the stoop with Henry's neighbors. Patsy met all of Henry and Marco's neighborhood friends. They all noted how much they loved Marco and Henry.

One evening, Javier, a charming and engaging boy who was always singing Spanish songs, joined his friends on the stoop. He explained to Patsy, "We cherish the memory of Mr. Marco as he brought 'the joyful' to all who knew him. He was so handsome and so talented, and we call him Marco Angelica because he is our blessed angel friend. He would sing with us in Spanish, and then he would grab da hand of Mr. Henry, and they would do da sexy samba, and everyone would clap hands and beg for more. Julio Iglesias was Marco and Henry's favorite. Julio my favorite too. We loved Marco," Javier said as he unashamedly started to cry.

Patsy held his hand, "I understand."

Patsy was a welcomed new friend. They warmed up to her immediately. She and Henry decided they'd continue doing what he and Marco used to do. Patsy put on a mixed tape they made that blared on a boom box heard down the block. A crowd gathered, urging them to continue as they shouted. "Go, Henry, Go, Henry, Go, Henry!"

Henry yelled back, using a homemade megaphone, "Let's give the people what they want, Ginger."

Patsy grabbed his extended hand, "I'm ready, Freddie. Go, Man, Go!"

They started with a waltz that took them halfway down the block and did a fancy Cha-Cha on the way back. They finished off with a sexy Tango, where Henry dipped her deep as she kicked her leg high in the air. There were whistles heard everywhere! More friends and neighbors came out as they clapped and cheered them on.

Mrs. Ramirez brought out trays of tacos and beer for the adults, along with cookies and lemonade for the kids. Their little shows soon turned into block parties each week, and everyone was dancing, eating, drinking, and enjoying life. The partygoers soon saw the addition of horns and bongos as Patsy and Henry did their thing, ending up with a soft shoe tap dance. Then, on a whim, Patsy called Mr. S and blurted out, "Come join the fun! Henry and I have a new gig that ended up in a real authentic block party in Washington Heights. You must see the crowd that gathers. Please come next Sunday at 4 p.m. to Henry's and party on the stoop with us. Please, Mr. S?"

"I'll be there," he replied. "What should I wear for this shindig?"

"Well," Patsy slyly stated with a sparkle in her voice, "I'd say you have to dress with a Latin flair. It is Washington Heights, after all."

Mr. S showed up that next week dressed in a ruffled shirt and wearing snake skinned high heeled boots too, and he was shaking a pair of maracas as he sang "*La La La La LaBamba.*" Patsy never saw him so animated. Henry rushed over to join in with a tambourine, and Patsy did an elaborate flamenco dance with Spanish castanets. The folks on the street whistled as they joined in stomping their feet and clapping their hands over their head.

Unexpectedly, an Action News truck crew pulled up, who filmed them for a segment of 6 p.m. Neighborhood News. It was one of the best days of their life together. For a few hours, they didn't have a care in the world. Instead, they were doing what they were meant to do—entertain.

190

CHAPTER 27
Tenderness

When she wasn't doing small walk-on parts or helping Mr. S assist talented newcomers with dancing auditions, Patsy's days were spent with Henry. Late one Friday afternoon, the long-awaited phone call came. "Shatzi, I'm in the Calgon office with your director, and they want you to return next week," Madge spoke breathlessly into the phone.

Patsy yelled out a big, "YIPPEE!" not knowing she was on speakerphone.

She heard a roar of laughter from the other people in the background and shouts of "Welcome Back, Bubbles!" Finally, she would be allowed back to her friends and co-workers to shoot the commercial after many worrisome months off.

The return to Calgon filled her days with photo shoots for the upcoming commercials, and she even joined their marketing meetings. She was elated to be back in the groove and around people who made her feel vital and welcomed. She shined with the advertising execs, wrote a few jingles, and helped with the set designs. She was in her glory calling on her *Bubbles Lamour* persona, who always provided good material—outrageous with a little sexy thrown in for good measure. A bit reticent from the Peeping Tom episode, Madge insisted on being on-set for the first few photoshoots.

Patsy still spent her nights and weekends with her beloved Henry. She urged him to tell her everything about his hopes and dreams, especially about all the exotic places he wished to travel. She sat with *Fodor's* travel books sprawled all over the floor as Henry explained in detail his desire to visit Africa, Greece, Argentina, and other intriguing places. Patsy scanned through the travel books and read to Henry all the best attractions at each destination. Together they created a journal of each country and the places they'd visit.

"Did you and Marco ever travel?" Patsy asked.

"No, Marco was content staying close to home. He didn't even like to leave the city very often. Going out to Fire Island to spend the weekend with friends at the beach was a huge ordeal. He'd pack up bags and bags of his stuff as if we were going away for a month. He liked all his own stuff and his own bed," Henry said, with a flicker of happiness in his eyes. "It was OK though, my years with Marco were some of the best years I've had."

"You must have felt a little bad that you couldn't visit all of these wonderful places together?"

"Yes, I guess I always thought we'd have time for that. Who knew a disease would come and destroy us, and so quickly. What I've learned from all of this is never wait to fulfill your dreams," Henry's voice cracked.

"Enough sadness for now." Patsy jumped up off the floor and kissed Henry's cheek, "I'm going to make us some delicious smoothies." She made them both fruit smoothies as Henry continued mapping out his itineraries in elaborate detail.

"These are my imagined expeditions," Henry explained, as he handed Patsy a list. It begins with Argentina and the Patagonia Mountains, and then Egypt and the Nile River. He put a question mark next to Greece. "I always pictured myself at these exotic places. I used to study history and cultures, and they fascinated me. I'm just not exactly sure the best place to end up."

Patsy knew he was too weak to make any journey, but she took notes of all his thoughts in their travel journal. She brought him books, pictures, and articles. There was something so special between them. It felt like they were transported back to the innocence they experienced in their youth together.

On one visit, Patsy gave Henry a homemade gift, "Look what I made for us, Henry. They're our special passports."

Henry laughed with excitement as Patsy presented him with two homemade passports, and the photos on the fake passports were of Ginger Rogers and Fred Astaire! "Now, all we need is a steamer trunk, your high heels and my top hat, and we're off!" Henry exclaimed. Patsy smiled wistfully. It was as if they were teenagers once again, Fred and Ginger, together in Bridget's secret hat stash.

One evening, Patsy decided to call her mother to let her know about Henry. "Hi, Patsy! So good to hear from you. It's been a while. How are things in the big city?" Bridget was always excited to hear from Patsy.

"I'm sorry I haven't called lately. I've been so busy. You're never going to believe who I saw in New York, and now we're such close friends again—Henry! Remember Henry from High School?"

"Oh yes, Henry Johnson. He went to New York to study dance senior year. His sister was the famous ballerina."

"Yes, that Henry!"

"You were so very sad when he left," Bridget recalled. "You never said much, but I could tell you were hurting."

"Yes, well, he was such a good friend. Actually more than a friend. I really thought I loved him. I did love him. I still love him!" Patsy confessed. "It was so amazing to see him again. But…it's the saddest thing. He has HIV. Do you know what that is?"

"Yes, I've heard of that. Isn't that the disease gay men get?"

"Yes, it is more prevalent in gay men, but it's not just gay men who get it," Patsy replied.

"Oh, I see. I don't know much about it."

"Well, Mom, you'd be so proud of me. I've become involved in this charity called ACT UP," Patsy explained. "I'm helping to fight the disease."

"Good for you," Bridget said lovingly.

"Even though it doesn't only affect gay men, Henry does happen to be gay, and his boyfriend just died of the disease. I'm trying to help in any way I can so he can beat this disease."

"You can't catch it, can you?" Bridget blurted out.

Patsy couldn't hide her annoyance. "No Mom, it's a sexually transmitted disease."

"I'm sorry, I worry that's all. But I can see how this is so important to you. And the Lord works in mysterious ways, so maybe this reunion was meant to be. I'll pray for him," promised Bridget.

Patsy knew her mother would understand when she swore her to secrecy. They both agreed Roney could never find out. He was closed-minded and bigoted, and right now, Patsy didn't need the extra negativity. She asked for Bridget's prayers and nothing else. And despite everything, she felt her sadness lift after she hung up with her mother. Her spirit was renewed for the moment.

While Patsy's life was busy with Henry and Calgon, she maintained her relationship with Mr. S, which often gave her time to regroup. One Saturday night, Mr. S planned a night on the town for just the two of them. He sent a driver to pick Patsy up and bring her to his penthouse, where their evening would begin.

"Hello, Miss Patrice, I'm here to escort you to Mr. S's penthouse. I'm Blu, and I'll be driving you tonight. So pleased to make your acquaintance."

Patsy responded, "Happy to meet you, Mr. Blu. I've noticed you in the theatre and around Mr. S quite a bit. Do you work for him?"

"Just Blu, no mister, and yes, Mr. S is my employer and my friend. We go back many years. So, let's say we saved each other many times, and I'm sure he'll tell you the story of how we met, so I'll leave it to him to fill you in."

"I can't wait. I'll bet it will be an interesting tale if I know Mr. S."

"Oh yeah, you will love how he tells it."

After greeting Mr. S with a giant hug, Patsy asked him quietly, "You must fill me in on Blu. He claims you two have an interesting history."

Mr. S chuckled, "Oh yes, that's my lifesaver Blu. He's been with me for ten years. I don't know what I would do without him. Blu is my bodyguard and my friend, and he can do anything. Blu—come here and sit with Patsy and me." Patsy saw that special gleam in Mr. S's eye and knew he was getting ready to tell a story, something he enjoyed doing. Patsy moved closer.

Mr. S became animated, "One day, when my career was starting to skyrocket, I was in a rush to get to a new set design meeting for my latest Off-Broadway production. As I went running down the street to the theatre, I was shocked by the puff of steam that rushed from the sidewalk grate. Startled by the noise and the smoke, I stumbled and fell, and went down with a thud, losing one of my loafers that was now stuck in the grate, leaving me unable to get up or move at all. Plus, I watched my foot swell up before my eyes.

"Just then, a small crowd gathered around me, offering to call 911, or take me to the hospital. But, as an immensely proud and stubborn man, which I was even back then, I shooed them away and said I was fine. I tried to get up, but I just couldn't. My foot hurt so badly. The whole time I was cursing in Yiddish, so people were now afraid to go near me. They all thought I was a crazy person."

Patsy burst out laughing.

"Hey, stop laughing. When I'm in pain, I curse in Yiddish!" He winked at her and continued, "So anyway, from out of nowhere, a homeless guy flew by the grate, stole my shoe, and tore the other one from my foot. I yelled out in horror, 'Stop, you dirty bastard—they're my Manolo's.' As quickly as I uttered the swear words, I saw a large black man chase the thief down the block. The huge man tackled the homeless guy, grabbed the shoes, and returned them to me."

195

Blu was laughing at this point like he'd heard this story a thousand times and jumped in. "So, Mr. S here, thanks me and asks how he can repay me. Which kinda hit me as strange cause all I did was save his shoes."

"My Manolo's," Mr. S reminded him.

"Yeah, right, Manolo's. Like I had any idea what that meant. Anyway, then he says to me in this real gentleman-like voice. 'Thanks, my man. You did me a favor. How can I repay you for your brave rescue? Kindly tell me your name and let me compensate, please?'"

At this point, Mr. S took over the storytelling again. "Blu told me his name was Horacio Blutone, but everyone called him *Blu Steel* because of his reputation of bending steel with his bare hands." Blu held out his hands then and flexed them. They did look enormously powerful. "So, I introduced myself and tried hard to stand, but my feet wouldn't work, and I reached for Blu's hand. I proceeded to tell him how I was stuck, but before I even got the words out, Blu unstuck me, scooped me up in his arms and carried me—this little Jewish guy—two blocks to the theatre. We laughed and chatted the whole way and waved to the people passing by who saw a huge six-foot, six-inch, strong dark man carrying a skinny little pasty, white guy holding on tight to his patent leather Manolo's. I tell ya, we could have been a comedy act!"

Patsy could hardly contain her laughter. Mr. S went on, "Blu explained to me that he had a nursing degree, worked as a stevedore on the docks, and was a bouncer at the High-Hat Club in Harlem. He told me he grew up in East Harlem, was raised by his four-foot, eleven-inch grandmother and was six-feet-tall at the tender age of twelve. He had a tough life, but he studied hard and did well in school, eventually earning a degree on his own. Some kids his age were scared of him because of his large frame, but those who took the time to know him found out he had a kind and gentle heart. He loves to help people, especially those who are smaller and weaker than himself. I remember his exact words, 'My mighty strength is never used to intimidate, only to defend and protect.' A regular Superman, I told him. And we both had a good laugh over that!

"Anyway, after hearing all of this, I was so impressed I offered him a full-time job, right there on the spot. I told him I could use his skills for several duties such as security, hauling set designs, personal bodyguard, and even part-time nurse. I stated a salary that no man would ever turn down and offered him a fine place to live. From that day on, we became friends and formed a type of partnership that bonds us together in complete trust. Since then, Blu has lived in the apartment below my penthouse. So…that's how I met Blu, and we've been together ever since. Losing those shoes was the best streak of luck I ever had."

Like a flash, Blu lifted Mr. S up and down like doing arm curls and counting one, two, three, four, five. "And this is how I do my daily workout routine every morning. I gotta keep in shape just in case I have to do a rescue mission again!"

They all laughed together, sharing the hilarious scene until Mr. S cried out, "You can put me down now, you big show-off. We get it. You're strong."

It was a special night to remember with a dear friend, and Patsy felt sure she just made another friend in Blu.

197

CHAPTER 28
Wow

Patsy woke up with only one thought—seeing her handsome artist. With both their hectic schedules, they hadn't seen each other for a while. Today though, she needed him and was going to get him. She showered, sprayed on her best perfume, and slipped on a lace teddy. She grabbed a thin raincoat and started toward her door.

She was ready to run down to his studio when someone knocked on her door. "Who is it?" she cried out, feeling slightly annoyed.

"It is I, Cristo, Artiste Extraordinaire. I'm here to see my muse, my sexy wench, my favorite subject de art." Patsy quickly swung open the door.

Patsy couldn't move fast enough, losing the raincoat, grabbing Cristo by his shirt, and leading him straight to her bedroom. "You read my mind. Come here, handsome, and see what I got for you."

"Oh, you look luscious and oh so beautiful. Let me ravage that gorgeous body of yours!" Falling in bed, Patsy wrapped her legs around him as he moved down inch by inch with his tongue, slowly concentrating on every part of her body, whispering, "You are delicious, my darling, so very succulent."

Patsy giggled as he lifted her legs straight up in the air and mounted her, pushing himself inside. He closed his eyes, "I can't look at you. You are just too exquisite." Her heart soared as he turned her over, facing away from him. Then, he pulled her up on all fours and entered her from behind. He began pounding her now and crying out, "Oh God, I'm close, I'm close!"

He was moaning so loud she thought he would orgasm before her, so Patsy took control, eager for her own satisfaction. She collapsed herself, turned over, and swiftly changed course. Patsy climbed on top of him, a position she loved. Throwing her hair back, she began moving slowly at first, and then she was riding him faster and faster with unbridled passion. Finally, she came to climax with a final crescendo shouting out, "Yes, yes, ooooh yes!" They both let go as Cristo's body shuddered with the last thrust of his warmth inside her as a long moan escaped his throat. Her hands squeezed tight, and the pleasure was magical.

She clung to him in the aftermath of their lovemaking. Their connection took on deeper intimacy, and they lay content with their bodies blissfully intertwined. "Wow," was all Cristo could muster.

"I think ya mean, Wow-Eeee!" Patsy laughed.

Later that evening after Cristo left, she recalled the beautiful card he gave her showing his affection through art that stated, *My heart bleeds for you.* It was so sweet and artistic, and it looked like actual droplets of blood. He was so talented. She pulled it out of her nightstand drawer to look at it again, noticing some of the brightness turned to a darker brownish red. She put it back in the envelope to preserve its beauty. She would thank him next time.

Several mornings later, Cristo returned bearing flowers and waving a card. "Special request for a special lady!" he exclaimed. He seemed thrilled as he showed Patsy the embossed invitation to his first private showing in Chelsea.

"Cristo, this is wonderful. I'm so thrilled for you!" She flung her arms around his neck and gave him a big hug.

Cristo smiled from ear to ear, "Patsy, would you mind helping me pick the best pieces to display? Of course, the gallery owner and operator will have the final say, but I'd appreciate your opinion."

"Of course, I'd love to help," Patsy said without hesitation. She wondered if he'd include his painting of her.

"Also, would you like to attend as my special guest?"

Patsy teased, "I'd be honored to see you honored."

"Thank you! I feel so proud, but also nervous. It's a dream come true. And to think, I'm just a poor kid from

Camden, New Jersey, about to have my first real art showing in New York!"

Patsy thought how wonderful this would be if Mr. S and Henry could be there. Without going into detail, she asked a bit hesitantly, "Is this an exclusive private showing, or is it open to the public?"

"It is a charity benefit show. Tickets cost $250 each, and proceeds go to the AIDS foundation."

Patsy could hardly believe her ears. "Oh Cristo, is it OK if I ask my employer, Mr. S, and dear friend Henry if they could buy tickets? They love art and support the AIDS charities."

"Of course, any friend of yours can always come."

The gallery showing took place on a beautiful sunny afternoon in Chelsea. The weather was perfect, with cool breezes, but not too cold, even as the event stretched into the evening hours. "Oh my," Patsy said as she entered the small but elegant room. "Cristo, this is lovely."

There was classical music playing, champagne chilling, and just the right degree of tinted lighting. Patsy wore silk harem pants that shimmered when she walked and a black blouse that was back-less. In addition, she wore a pink boa and a sequenced tiny purse over her shoulder. She was chic and refined at the same time.

Cristo kissed her hand and then spun her around to get the full view. "You are looking quite fetching tonight," he winked at her.

"You look handsome yourself." She scanned his puffy artist shirt and tight, black leather pants and of course, one of Babcia's brightest red-flowered scarves around his neck. His ponytail got a workout that night as he pulled the rubber band out of his hair and let it flow free, shaking his head dramatically, but then turned around and put it back in again in a nervous frenzy.

Cristo was beaming as he showed Patsy around and told her to note the 'sold signs' that were already under several paintings. He explained that the gallery price-marked all the pieces, and it was far beyond anything he'd expected. From his wide grin and sparkle in his eyes, Patsy could tell he was thrilled, and Patsy was equally excited for him.

As she was helping Cristo arrange the many sold signs, she glanced up when she heard a commotion in the crowd. She peered out the gallery window to see a long, white stretch limo pulled up to the curb. Emerging from the limo were Mr. S and Henry.

Mr. S was sporting an Armani Suit with a pastel pink shirt, floral tie, and pocket silk to match. Henry was fashionable in a black bow tie and white sports coat with black and white shiny spectator shoes. Both looked smashing and fit in perfectly with the art crowd. The curator rushed over to greet them.

Patsy grabbed Cristo's hand and guided him over to meet Mr. S and Henry. Cristo put out his hand, "Thank you both for coming. So, you're the wonderful Mr. S Patsy told me about. It's a pleasure to meet you for sure. And you must be Henry. Man, you are looking sharp in your black and whites, my friend."

Henry replied with a coy smile, "You're not so bad yourself."

Mr. S added, "I'm impressed with what I see so far. I heard much about your work from our girl, and she wasn't wrong."

Patsy was in her glory and proud of herself for bringing them together. She was experiencing a most nostalgic moment watching the three men. She continued by Cristo's side most of the time, laughing and helping him put up more sold signs. There was a crowd forming in line outside the tiny gallery. The place was jam-packed the whole time.

Cristo sold all but four of his paintings. He made $4,800 in one show. The ticket sales and over 60% of the profits would go to the AIDS foundation. Hopefully, Patsy thought Cristo would be a recognized artist now.

Patsy watched as she saw Cristo talking to the president of the AIDS foundation and a woman who must have been the same one Cristo spoke of as his benefactor and mentor. Hmm, she was incredibly attractive with lovely red hair. Patsy wondered if Cristo completed the painting of her in the nude. A bald man accompanied the redhead, and Patsy assumed he was the lucky recipient of his special birthday gift.

Patsy joined Mr. S, "How do you like the show so far?"

"Oh, Dearheart, it's lovely, and I did make a small purchase that I will cherish. They are wrapping it now. Your young artist friend is quite remarkable, and he captured you beautifully."

"You bought the painting of me? I'm so flattered. Thank you so much, and it's for such a worthy cause too." For a minute, Patsy thought of Mr. S and this woman who helped Cristo. They each saw something special in someone else and gave them their big break. Life was funny that way.

Henry wandered over, emerging from the men's room. He looked pale and a bit shaky. Patsy noticed beads of sweat on his upper lip. "Patsy, I think I'm fading a little, and it's time for me to end the day, but let me tell you a secret. Mr. S gave a separate donation of $1000 to the foundation. Isn't that wonderful?"

"I'm so grateful that you both came. I can see you're tired Henry, but it's a day for all of us to remember." Mr. S summoned Blu to pull up the car. Patsy felt sad as she saw Henry struggle to get into the limo. She ran over and gave him a final hug and promised to call him later. "I love you both so much. Thank you for honoring my friend."

With a twinkle in his eye, Mr. S replied, "Oh, sweet girl, I'm thrilled to have this painting of you. I'll cherish it."

"Me too," Henry added. "Thank you so much for thinking of me. Sorry, I had to punk out early. Love ya, girl!"

When Patsy returned to the gallery, Cristo ran up to her. "Come here, you!" he said, pulling her close. Then he kissed her in front of everyone. "Your friends were great, thanks for inviting them, and I want you to know, I think you're wonderful!" Patsy never saw him so happy. She felt closer to him than ever before. All those hours of sitting on the hard wooden stool in his flat paid off for him, and it was gratifying to be a part of his success.

She kissed Cristo's cheek and congratulated him, "It doesn't get any better than this."

That night, in those precious moments, Patrice Marie Mahoney from Yonkers loved three men, and they all loved her back. She felt like the luckiest girl in the world.

CHAPTER 29
Goodbye

Only a few days after Cristo's art show, Henry took a turn for the worse. Luckily, Patsy was with him fixing him the usual protein shake when she heard his desperate scream, "Patsy, the room is spinning. I can't breathe. Help me!"

"It's OK. Don't move. I'm calling 911," she comforted him.

The ambulance was at Henry's place in five minutes as they loaded him onto a stretcher. They sped through the neighborhood, sirens blasting into the city. Patsy's mind was racing. She held his hand tight as the medics administered oxygen. They were there in a matter of minutes, but the ride seemed endless as she begged God to please let him live.

Patsy helped check Henry into the hospital and stayed by his bedside in a special section for AIDS patients. Henry fell in and out of light sleep. He was shivering, although the temperature in the stark white room was warm and felt stuffy to her. She asked the nurse for another blanket and pulled them all up to his chin. Still, he was clearly uncomfortable.

Patsy kept looking at the clock on the wall. They were in the room for an hour and only one nurse came in and out with little to say. Henry sounded weak, "I'm OK…really."

"Well, I'm not," she said as she left the room for the closest medical station. "Excuse me," she said to a nurse whose eyes were staring at a computer screen. The nurse looked up, but seemed to Patsy she was looking right through her. "My friend Henry Johnson was brought in an hour ago and no doctor has seen him. He's in pain and dizzy, which is why we're here. When is the doctor coming?" she demanded, surprised by the authority in her voice. "He needs pain medication now!"

The nurse nodded, "You said Henry Johnson? Dr. Frankel should have seen him by now. I think he's caught in some emergency."

"This is an emergency, too. Mr. Johnson is in terrible pain. Something has to be done." The nurse picked up the phone, but turned away as she started in on a conversation. Patsy was feeling as angry as she'd ever felt. This was Henry—her Henry—and it was bad enough he was dying of AIDS. He didn't have to suffer. She wanted to scream this to the nurse. But instead, she impatiently tapped her fingers on the counter, both surprised and pleased with what Madge would surely call her newfound *hutzpah*.

The nurse turned back to her, "I'm sorry. Dr. Frankel can't come for a while. But Dr. Albertson is on his way."

"Thank you, Patsy," Henry said as the pain meds began to take hold. "I heard you fighting for me out there. You sounded pretty tough."

She took his hand, warmer now, and pressed it to her lips. "Anything for you, *mon ami*. You know that. Do you want to nap now?"

"No, I have a feeling I'm going to be in an endless sleep before too long. Can you sit with me? I want to tell you some things."

Henry never spoke much about his family, but that day he revealed so much to Patsy. He explained, timidly at first, "When I came to Manhattan, I came to grips with my newly admitted gayness. I felt free since there was no more walking on eggshells around closed-minded hypocrites. Every day I thanked God for this escape to New York and the total turnaround of my personality. But the scars of my family life took their toll. Believe me. It wasn't easy.

"This sinister bigotry applied mostly to my father as my mother usually took my side. In fact, so much so that it was the chief cause of their splitting up. At first I blamed myself, but later was glad my mom escaped the harshness of my father. He was toxic."

"Henry, I know exactly what you mean," Patsy said as she thought of her father and his destructive ways.

"I felt the bonds loosen and began to breathe again in my new lifestyle, and when I met Marco, I let it all go. When my parents divorced, I never heard from my dad again," Henry said with bitterness in his voice.

"I was still close to my sister Nancy, but when she was offered a place as a prima ballerina with the Paris Garnier Opera troop, we didn't speak as much. I understood though since her schedule was insane. I'm in awe of her and her courage to follow her dreams and talent. She doesn't know of my battle with AIDS—I just can't tell her," Henry broke down as Patsy quickly leaned forward and wiped tears from his eyes.

In between sobs, he confessed, "I'm sorry I hurt you when we were kids. I thought if you knew, you'd hate me. I'm so, so sorry…." His voice trailed off.

"Stop," Patsy whispered, "Stop, please." She held him gently, now feeling every bone through his tissue-thin skin.

That day in that hospital, Patsy knew the meaning of real love with another human being., beyond the so-called being in love with someone to a higher plane into a spiritual realm. She absolutely loved Henry Johnson with all her heart.

One afternoon, while Henry was napping in his hospital bed, Patsy flipped through a box of his belongings she brought to help pass the time, and found his address book. She found his sister's phone number and called her to let her know Henry was dying of AIDS. Nancy was distraught to learn about Henry's condition, but said because of her schedule she couldn't make it back to the states.

Hearing what Patsy did, Henry was annoyed. "I'm not surprised my sister can't make the trip, she's very busy and I don't want to ruin her career. Please don't contact my mother. I don't want her upset. She has respiratory problems and is in a weakened state," said Henry in a shaky voice. "I don't want her to go through any more pain. She's been through hell as it is."

He began to cry, "That woman was always on my side and loved me unconditionally. I want her to remember me healthy, not with sores and bruises and looking like a skeleton. Our phone calls are enough. I don't want visitors except for you."

Patsy apologized, feeling embarrassed, and promised she'd always consult with him first concerning his family and even his friends and neighbors. She could only imagine how awful he felt about his appearance. Changing the tone of the conversation, she said, "Well, don't think you're getting rid of me anytime soon. I'm here to stay whether you want me or not."

Henry laughed and did a pinky swear, calling out, "Friends 'til the end!" as Patsy curled her gloved little finger around his.

Patsy removed some travel brochures from the box, "In Argentina, I'm buying myself a pair of alpargatas just like the gauchos did long ago, walking on foot and riding on horseback, always wearing alpargatas to keep their feet warm and comfortable. What color should I buy? You pick. I know you love blue. Maybe I'll buy blue."

"Red, I think, because you like to stand out," Henry replied with a smile, "or how about plaid or polka dot, or even fuchsia with yellow lace-ups?" These conversations continued for hours as Patsy just tried to keep Henry laughing, engaged, and not thinking about his bleak future.

During Henry's last days, Patsy rarely left his side and continued reading to him as long as he was lucid. She searched for his smile every time she read a passage of their travelogue, but more and more, she felt him slipping mentally, or caught him staring straight ahead. He usually smiled when she sang and danced, so she brought her tap shoes to the hospital and clicked her heels around the room, crooning, *"I'm singin' in the rain, just singin' in the rain...."*

Henry laughed so hard his laughter turned to a coughing fit. Finally, he got control and shouted out, "Brava, Brava!" He clapped and blew kisses her way while she took a series of bows. As she turned around to do an encore, she noticed him beginning to wilt and finally close his eyes.

Patsy fought a lump in her throat, "Go and sleep now, Sweet Prince, we'll rehearse more tomorrow. The crowds will love us. We'll have at least six curtain calls."

As the days wore on, she donned a plastic gown and gloves since he developed pneumonia. Henry's entire head and upper body were placed in an oxygen tent to deliver high oxygen levels. The doctors were skeptical that the oxygen tent would do much at this point, however Patsy knew early studies showed high oxygen levels could boost T-cell counts in HIV patients. She was determined to try absolutely anything to keep Henry alive.

Increasingly though, she wasn't getting any response from Henry when she sang or danced or even when she asked him to squeeze her hand. The sores in and around his mouth became so red and raw even drinking water through a straw looked painful. In contrast, his skin was an awful yellow, signifying the disease was attacking his liver and vital organs. He was so thin his bones protruded from his skin and there were times when his image terrified her. Intravenous needles caused large bruises which covered the entire length of his inner arm to his elbow. It was getting harder to look at him, but Patsy never let it show. She remained upbeat even though her beautiful Henry was being eaten from the inside out from this horrid disease.

At times of silence, Patsy sat in a depressed state. She cursed the "powers that be," wondering why this was happening to this lovely man who did nothing but bring joy to others. Finally, when a priest came in to give Henry the last rites, Patsy shouted to him, "How could God be so cruel? How can He be so cruel?"

The priest was calm, "We cannot always understand God's way, but He's always here for us."

Patsy started sobbing, "I'm so sorry. I didn't mean to yell at you."

The priest answered kindly, "Forgive yourself, my child. This pain you feel only God can relieve. I will pray for you, but know Henry is on his way to heaven where there is no pain and suffering."

The next day, she found the rosary her great Aunt Bea gave her for her First Holy Communion. She brought it with her to visit Henry. Feeling more peaceful, she found solace in believing that he was getting ready to enter heaven. Her prayers came true when several doctors assured her Henry was no longer in pain and was in a peaceful coma. She prayed again, "Dear God, just give me another day—another hour."

Patsy was feeling drained after the morning of sitting and praying. Henry lay so still, with so many tubes attaching him to machines. A nurse came in the room, "You need to take a break, dear. I'll keep a close watch on your friend."

"You're right, I'll be back as soon as I can…." Patsy voice trailed off.

When she arrived home, she slipped into a warm bubble bath. She stepped out from the bathroom in a terry robe and thought of making a cup of tea when Cristo knocked on her door. "I miss you," he said, "I just wanted to make sure you are OK."

"Oh, Cristo, that's so sweet of you. I miss you too. I'm so sorry I haven't been around. I've been helping a sick friend. You remember Henry, he came to your art exhibit, and he raved about it for weeks after," Patsy said with a slightly forced smile.

"Yes, such a nice guy. I'm so sorry. Please remember I'm here for you. I hope you know that." He placed a tender kiss on her lips. About an hour later, a big bouquet of autumn wildflowers arrived with a sweet note that read, *Call Chef Cristo when you are ready. We'll cook together again, my sweet!* For a moment, it made her smile, and she needed that.

Later that afternoon, a call came from the hospital asking Patsy to come in and say a final goodbye to Henry. "It's time," the nurse said.

It's time. *What a ridiculous statement,* she thought. *Time for what? Time to say a final farewell when she knew she could not? Time to watch her world collapse? Time to admit failure after days, weeks, months of fighting to keep him alive? Yes, it was time—time to have her heart ripped out.* For months, Patsy devoted her life to Henry. She felt afraid and empty, wondering what she would do without him.

As she entered his room for what she knew would be the last time, she took Aunt Bea's rosary and held the beads clutched in her hand, not ready to recite the Hail Mary prayer yet. Nurses and an attending physician were waiting. The monitor showed he was still breathing, but it was nearly flat lined. She thought desperately of trying to save him. *Just give me one last chance to save him, please God.*

The nurse spoke softly, "It won't be long now. Maybe you would like to share a final thought or prayer."

"I was just wondering if you contacted his mother."

"Yes, we called her right after we called you, but the poor woman was unable to talk much because of her breathing problems."

Patsy called Henry's mother from the room to make sure she knew Patsy was there and thinking of her. By the sound of Barbara's weak voice, Patsy realized this loving woman couldn't take much more sadness as she broke down, repeating over and over, "My sweet boy, my dear Henry, may God now be with you in heaven." She thanked Patsy over and over, and they cried together.

"Mrs. Johnson, Henry always said to me how much he loved you and that you were always on his side."

Barbara cried, "I feel I'll see him someday soon."

Patsy broke down too, "I can't imagine life without him. I really can't."

"Thank you for caring for my son. God Bless you."

As Patsy waited for the last breath, she looked around, and there was an aura of peacefulness in the typically depressing hospital room. A single ray of light shone through the window that fell on Henry and brightened his sallow skin. She sat down close beside him holding his cold hand, and close to his ear, she spoke to him softly, "Henry, mon ami, I think it's time for you to be with Marco again dancing together. I will make sure I visit all the places we mapped out together. You will come with me in spirit. Je t'aime, mon ami." Patsy saw her precious Henry take his last breath. The machines next to him flatlined, and the nurse removed the oxygen. "Je t'aime, mon ami. Now you are resting with the angels."

Patsy heard the squeak of the wheels as they rolled a gurney into the hospital room. It reverberated in her ears. The nurses and one intern were there disconnecting the tubes and apparatus from his thin and fragile body.

Patsy yelled out, "Be careful. Don't hurt him!"

The nurse gingerly replied, "Henry's at peace now."

"How do you know?" she cried out with real screams that tore from her heart.

In a moment of clarity, she felt suddenly alert and began to plan her suicide. For some reason, it was a thought that brought some comfort and solace. She didn't like it here in this unfair world anyway without Henry. *So why not? Why not let me come too, God?*

All she really knew was it would be swift. No suffering day after day, week after week, month after month like Henry. Death lurked all around the room, slowly stealing each breath and knowing it would be triumphant. That was Henry's fate to suffer. It wouldn't be hers. She would control her demise.

She recalled that summer when he left her as a teen, and she tried without success to do the same thing. She stabbed her

211

thigh with the steel file, drawing blood. She never went through with it. Now, she would try anything so the pain on the inside would be less than any pain she could endure on the outside.

All Patsy knew was she wanted to follow him into oblivion to stop the pain and escape this horrible life. Henry was gone, rolled out of the room to the squeak, squeak of the wheels carrying him so limp and lifeless. Just when she got him back, she thought, he was viciously ripped away again with the most wicked suffering. Once again, she faced a world without Henry as she began to shake and sob uncontrollably.

Patsy looked around the empty room and cursed a God who demonstrated nothing but cruelty to her. She tried to get out of the chair, but her knees were weak, and the room was spinning.

"Is there someone I can call to take you home?" the nurse asked.

"Mr. S," Patsy answered. "Here's his card. Call the emergency number, please."

Once home, Patsy could barely get out of her bed for the next three days. She got calls from Cristo and Madge who wanted to visit, but she didn't have the energy to see anyone. Instead, she was spiraling through a myriad of emotions: sad, angry, frustrated, and finally the realization that there were only two roads she could take—either fall into a deep depression or be grateful for the time she spent with Henry.

Depression felt unworthy of the fun and joy she and Henry shared, and she found herself going to the unique "Henry place" in her brain that took her back to when they were kids, and she was so in love. He filled her every thought with romance and bliss during those marvelous times. It was then she knew what she needed to do. Henry's prophetic words of wisdom rang true to Patsy just like he was right there with her, and she could hear him, "The path you choose to walk down is what creates your destiny."

Then, almost like a bolt of energy from above, she realized she was starving. She ate nearly a whole box of double fudge cookies, two bananas and drank three cups of tea. Next, she took a bath, dressed in black gaucho pants, long black boots, and a tweed jacket topped off with a bright scarf of autumn colors. She even put on a fragrance, one that Henry loved, called *Toujours Moi*. The words fittingly meant "Always Me," and that symbolized their forever devotion to each other. Spraying the fragrance, she felt strength drift through the air and envelop her senses.

She practically flew over to see Mr. S, decided to pick up Henry's ashes, and shared a plan with Mr. S for Henry's last wishes. Determination took the place of the heaviness that occupied her heart. "It's time to embark on the journey that would make Henry's dreams come true. I'll be carrying what's left of his physical being with me, but he'll be watching me from heaven. Henry spoke at length of going on trips to Argentina and the Patagonia Mountains and a fabulous Nile cruise. It made him so happy. I need to do this for him."

"I don't know, I think it's too soon. I don't think you are ready for this yet."

Patsy was determined, "I am ready. I must go now. Henry is waiting. Please Mr. S, I feel I must go now." Patsy didn't necessarily need Mr. S's permission, but she preferred his approval, and she knew she couldn't afford it on her own.

"Mr. S, I'll pay you back every cent, and I promise I'll travel on a budget. I just want to fulfill Henry's wishes."

Mr. S's eyes showed deep compassion, "Dearheart, you don't have to even think about money at a time like this. Don't you know you are loved, and I'll always help in any way I can?" Mr. S took her hands in his, "We will all miss Henry, and now we have to take care of you. You mean the world to me. Are you sure this is what you want?"

Patsy replied immediately, "Yes, I feel I must—and I need your blessing."

Mr. S stared at her for what seemed forever, but finally agreed, "Ok, but under one condition: Blu Steel will accompany you as your bodyguard. In addition to providing the best companion in the world, I will also see to it that you two have the best accommodations."

"Deal!" Patsy uttered and was ecstatic she would have a companion.

Mr. S called Blu and explained the assignment. "Ok, Blu is on board. Let me have the travelogue, and Blu will start studying it. He will take care of you every step of the way."

"You are the best!" Patsy exclaimed as she gave him a big hug. "You are the most wonderful man I know, and I can never repay you, but please know I love you with all my heart."

Mr. S said, "I love you too Dearheart, and I knew it the day you fell into my arms at the Calgon meeting. You're my girl, and I gotta take care of my girl."

When Patsy woke up the morning she was set to leave for Argentina, for a minute, she didn't remember Henry's passing. Often Patsy woke up and couldn't remember if her dream was just a dream or reality. Reality quickly set in though as she sat up in her bed, looked toward her night table, and saw the Pewter Grecian style urn with big, bold letters engraved, "Henry Johnson," and right under his name the dates of his short life. Henry was gone. Then, she recalled her dream even though it was in bits and pieces and very cryptic and baffling to discern.

Alone in a cold, stark white room, there's a bed with a man's lifeless body, covered to his chin in a white sheet. There is stillness. The thick stagnant air doesn't circulate. It's suffocating. She cracks a window, then sits in a chair, her head cupped in her hands and her blond hair falling around her face.

Suddenly she feels a cool breeze and turns towards the small window next to her. The breeze begins to circulate the air. In with the breeze comes sunlight. The ominous room is now illuminated with brightness. She sees the sallow skin of the man in the bed turn a baby pink color as the sides of his mouth curve upwards. She gravitates towards the body. Her warm lips touch his stone-cold lips. Suddenly she feels an unexpected release of tension when she stands upright.

She follows the breeze to the window and then closes the window. With her palm pressed to her heart and feeling exhaustion overtake her, she lets out a deep breath and flops back into the chair. As sadness dissipates from the room, relief envelopes her and floods through her being. The heavy dread is finally lifted, but still she cannot determine if the man is dead or alive. She wants to help him, but cannot seem to move any part of her body except for her eyes as they are drawn mystically to the one beautiful streak of light that remains. She inhales its glowing radiance seeking comfort.

She tried to cry, but there were no tears left. Henry didn't want sadness. He was all about happiness. He spent his life performing to bring others joy. Not only did he spend his life making others smile, but he also believed everyone was accountable for their own happiness. It amazed Patsy how much wisdom Henry possessed for living such a short life.

She looked at her watch—still a few hours before Blu would pick her up for the airport. After she dressed and made sure she packed everything she needed, she decided to say goodbye to Cristo. She held back tears as she told him a condensed version of her journey, "I don't know how long I'll be away, but I won't be alone. Mr. S's bodyguard is traveling with me."

"I'm glad you'll have protection. I'll miss you. You know that."

"I'll miss you, too. I haven't been much of a friend or lover to you lately."

"We'll make up for that when you get back," he said with a twinkle in his eyes. He took her in his arms and a hug soon turned into a soulful kiss. "That's so you won't forget me."

"Not a chance," Patsy quipped.

PART THREE
CHAPTER 30
Argentina

***

He knew now she loved him just from the valentine she clutched to her chest that day on the train. His heart was full. He tracked her for weeks now, calculating her every move. He watched her for many days going in and out of a hospital looking worried. Wanting nothing to do with her sadness—he felt no pity, just impatience for her to get back to fulfilling his lustful desires. He followed her through the hospital halls and noticed the rooms were private and quarantined. He despised the patient who was swallowing her time. His mind screamed, *die already. I want my beloved back, and I want her sexy and longing for me, not visiting some zombie in the hospital.*

He hired an old employee of his notorious father to pose as a telephone repairman so he could trace her phone calls. The guy would do anything for money. He paid him a thousand dollars and promised more if he'd bug her apartment. After the jerk in the hospital became a corpse, her phone calls were then all about an upcoming trip. She was coming back to him now and not sharing her time with another. She would soon be all his. *Welcome back to your real man Valentine.*

He now knew all the details of her trip. She was off to Argentina, a place surrounding the Patagonia Mountains. The gods were indeed on his side when he heard her confirming her flight reservation date, time, flight number, and even her seat number. Immediately, he booked a seat on the same flight and then looked up information about the Patagonia Mountains. They were beautiful, and he knew for sure this was the place high on a mountaintop where he'd have sex with her for the first time.

He calculated his moves. He still had his credentials and press pass from his National Enquirer days. When he got to

LaGuardia airport, he flashed his badge, stating his reason for the trip. He declared confidently to airport officials that he was filming a documentary on the natural habitat of wildlife in Argentina. They quickly let him through along with all his expensive cameras and equipment. They seemed impressed with his assignment and began asking questions. He annoyingly waved them off. "It's classified," he told them.

"You can tune into the Discovery channel next month for a sneak peek." They treated him like a celebrity and he knew once more fate was on his side. His plans were falling perfectly into place.

***

After a travel day with connecting flights through Buenos Aires, Patsy and Blu finally landed in El Calafate. Out the window, Patsy saw the glorious snowcapped Andes Mountains. She held Henry's ashes close to her chest as they slowly came in for a landing. She was infused with a renewed energy and strength that she hadn't felt in months.

"Hey Blu, we finally made it."

"Yes we did, and you caught a nice nap on the flight too. It was good to see you sleep so peacefully."

***

At the luggage claim area, he saw the annoying Hulk-like ogre was still by her side. He was irritated by this guy's presence, but patiently watched as they gathered their bags and headed out of the airport to a waiting cab. *If you were with me Valentine, you wouldn't have to wait at all.*

There was a crushing crowd around the line of cabs, so he forcefully pushed himself through the commotion. He was careful not to lose track of her as he hoisted his duffel bag with the camera equipment over his head, rushing to the taxi behind theirs. *Damn.* He didn't hear what the massive giant said to the driver about their destination. He figured the Goliath must be a trip guide or something. It reminded him of a story he read as a child where a behemoth was the villain. He decided to call him

218

'the behemoth'. He felt instant hatred for him for even being near his beautiful beloved one.

"Follow that taxi. I'm with that party. I'm shooting a documentary!" He promptly handed the driver a hundred-dollar bill. Then he added harshly, "And don't lose them!"
"Yes sir. Whatever you say, sir," the cabbie replied as he grabbed the C-note and sped off.

When Patsy and Blu pulled up to the hotel in El Calafate, she admired the beautiful views of the snowcapped mountains. She hung back as Blu helped the driver with their bags at the quaint inn. Patsy could feel Henry observing the splendor from his vantage point in the heavenly host of clouds overhead.

The hotel was picturesque and inviting. The lobby had red walls with dark mahogany wood beams, along with red accents—red pillows and red rugs. The hotel was a combination of a rustic country inn and a charming ski lodge. There were multiple fireplaces all around and vases of red roses placed perfectly around the lobby.

"Mr. S didn't want us in a big hotel. He thought you needed a smaller space with not too many people around, and this is the best and quietest hotel in the area."

"It's wonderful," Patsy smiled.

"Let's settle into our rooms, and then we can decide when to head to the mountains."

"As soon as possible, I want to go as soon as possible," Patsy pleaded.

About an hour later, Blu knocked on Patsy's door, "Miss Patrice, it's me."

"I'm ready to go," Patsy said, all freshened up and in her hiking outfit.

***

He sat in the lobby and watched them intently. He heard the man behind the desk say to them, "You will be in rooms 214 and 216. Enjoy your stay, and please let us know if we can do anything to accommodate you." *Only I will accommodate my*

219

beloved, he smiled. He was relieved they had separate rooms, but wondered if they were adjoining. He would get a room close by, maybe even a suite.

He just completed his reservation when Blu and Patsy returned to the lobby. For a moment, he thought he should follow them, but then had a better idea. He quickly went to his room on the third floor, dumped his bags and equipment, and slithered down to the second floor. He wasn't sure how he'd get into their rooms, but he knew whatever he found inside would give him clues to their whereabouts and the identity of the behemoth with her.

He spotted a maid with a stack of towels headed for their door. He ran up to her, putting on his best acting skills. He began fumbling in his pockets feigning lost keys. In a whisper, he spoke provocatively, "Por favor, my beautiful senorita, can you help me? You see, I have lost the key to my room."

She blushed and reluctantly stated in broken English, "It is against rules, but senor can go to front desk for help."

"Oh, Bella," he smiled, "your English is as beautiful as you! But you see, it is an urgent matter. I am filming a documentary, and I would love for you to be in it. Could we meet later?"

She perked up when he slipped her a hundred-dollar bill and immediately opened the door. She giggled, "My shift over at 5 p.m., senor. Where shall we meet?"

"I will find you. I'll bring champagne."

He entered the room, but quickly realized it wasn't her room when he noticed huge boots in the corner. It was the behemoth's room. *Damn!*

Poking around, he saw what looked like an itinerary, brochures, and their whole trip with every location, excursion, and airline reservation mapped out for them. He found the motherlode right there in plain sight.

He wrote down every detail on the back of an old menu. He tried the door of the adjoining room, but it was locked. *Damn*

220

again. He would have loved to steal a pair of her panties. He grew hard at the thought. He scurried back to his own room, anxious to study the itineraries. He would be one step ahead of them now.

In his room, his thoughts returned to the giant traveling with his love. He began seething with anger. Thoughts of the behemoth with his size 15 boots screwing her consumed him. He could see him stripping her naked and taking her fast, his big body smothering her and roaring like a wild animal. *Don't touch her, you massive behemoth,* the voice inside his brain cried out. It made him ache for her even more. Keep the door locked tight, my beloved. No one touches you except me. He must get rid of the behemoth, but how?

The torturous CLICK, CLICK, CLICK filled his head. He tried to fight against it by downing two little bottles of scotch whiskey from the minibar. The rage built as he paced the room. He planned a fatal accident for the massive hulk and laughed out loud as he pictured the fiend falling off a high Patagonia mountaintop and toppling to his death. The thought of it made him feel powerful, even horny in his triumph.

As desire stirred in his belly. He stripped naked, looked at his reflection in the mirror, and saw his chubby white body staring back. He was so much shorter than the behemoth, and his flabby belly protruded as he looked at a side view. He began to imagine the giant pumping his dick inside her as his own grew hard. He looked at his pathetic body, then stood up tall and sucked in his gut. He watched the rolls around his stomach contract then release. His dick wasn't tiny, but it wasn't huge like the behemoth's must be. Judging from his shoe size—at least ten inches.

He went soft now and began hammering himself over the head with a thick bible he found on his bed stand. His self-deprecating act continued as he thrashed and beat himself until his forehead began to bleed. Screaming out loud at each pounding of the book on his skull, he cried, "I know his cock is bigger than mine! *The creep is trying to fuck her right now. Giant monster with a huge cock inside my beloved raping her right now.* He threw the blood-stained bible across the room and drank the rest of the scotch in the mini bar, eventually crying himself to sleep.

In his dream, she was with him, alone on a summit, and when they couldn't wait any longer, they tore off their heavy clothing and lay carefully on the edge of the cliff. In her complete surrender to him, he released all his pent-up passion. He was instantly ready to explode inside of her as he mounted her, grabbing her firm ass. To his delight, he watched his dick glide in and out of her. It was slow at first, but as he thrust faster she pleaded for him to go deeper as she moaned with raw animal passion. Finally, she burst out in a primal howl of glorious rapture, wrapping her legs tight around him. Her screams echoed through the mountain range. That was the moment he knew she belonged only to him.

As he woke from this erotic dream, he felt sure of himself while he pondered his next move. *How do I get rid of the behemoth and make it look like an accident?*

*****

A van pulled up to the hotel, and out stepped a beautiful dark-haired, dark-skinned young man. "My name is Ramon, and I will be your tour guide today. Please be careful as you get onto the van," he stated in a Spanish accent and extended his hand to Patsy.

Patsy stepped onto the bus. Blu followed her but denied Ramon's hand. Patsy giggled and whispered to Blu, "What? Are you too masculine to touch another man's hand?"

"Yes, I am," Blu laughed.

Three older couples also boarded the van, probably retirees Patsy thought. Along the way, Ramon was lecturing about the history of the Argentine land, but Patsy tuned him out and just stared out the van window to admire the spectacular scenery.

Exiting the van, they all transferred to a boat which took them to the Perito Moreno Glacier. As the boat got closer, Patsy gazed at the electric blue face of the glaciers against the white tips. Patsy's focus though was to find the best place to spread Henry's ashes.

The glacier sat at sea level with the beauty of the Patagonia Mountains behind it. Even the thickening clouds couldn't hide the beautiful landscape. Patsy said to Blu, "This is the most breathtaking natural wonder I have ever seen. I've been to Niagara Falls and the Grand Canyon, but this is even more spectacular."

"It certainly is," Blu said as he marveled at the scenery.

"It's mystical—somewhere between reality and imagination. Henry was right," Patsy said sadly, "If only he could see it with his own eyes." The memory of the days of travelogues and maps with Henry was still fresh in Patsy's mind. She felt her eyes welling up again, but she pushed back the tears.

They departed the boat and stepped foot on the glacier. Ramon helped everyone put on their crampons. He attached the spiked iron plates onto the bottoms of their shoes to prevent them from slipping on the ice, and he explained how to use them. Ramon handed Patsy and Blu ice axes to help them trudge across the icy surface.

"Ramon do you mind if Blu and I start to trek up the glacier?" Patsy glanced over to their older travel mates to give Ramon a non-verbal clue that she didn't want to be stuck with them.

"Si, si, no problem, but make sure you stay on the trails."

"Of course. Thank you, Ramon," Pasty flashed him a big smile.

Through the light snow flurry, Patsy and Blu trekked up the Perito Moreno Glacier. Her feet ached, but she didn't complain. They scaled the mountain for an hour, walking primarily in silence side by side. Patsy wasn't sure when she would release the ashes. When they reached a platform at the top of the glacier, the warm sun peeked through. Patsy was sure this was Henry's way of telling her it was time.

Perito Moreno Patagonia Mountains

Patsy had divided the ashes into three little bags for the three locations they would visit. This was the first bag, and as Patsy opened the bag, there was a blasting sound like a gunshot.

224

She practically jumped into Blu's big arms. He held her tightly, shielding her, and immediately went into protection mode, scanning everywhere around them.

A couple hiking alongside them broke out in laughter and Ramon said, "Ah don't worry, ice fell from glacier."

Patsy and Blu laughed too. They were thrilled by the sight and the thunderous sound of the enormous pieces of ice split off the glacier and fall into the water. Patsy cried softly as she poured Henry's ashes down the mountain. Just then, a burst of wind caused some to whirl about and fly higher. She spotted a majestic Condor with a large wingspan and a beautiful ruff of white feathers around its neck as she looked up. This moment was Patsy's sign that Henry was there in spirit soaring above. "Mouche, mon ami, Mouche!"

As her eyes followed the ascending bird, she reached out and grabbed Blu's hand. "It's him," Patsy said, "it's Henry."

"Without a doubt."

Exhausted and overwhelmed, Patsy and Blu headed back to El Calafate, with Ramon in the lead. Patsy spent the next two days sleeping until noon, headed over to a small café to eat dulce de leche crepes with a few glasses of Argentine red wine, wandered in and out of shops, then went back to the inn around 3 p.m. for a siesta.

All the while, Blu was right beside her. Her emotions fluctuated—she was fine one minute, only to find herself sinking into feelings of loneliness and hopelessness the next. For the past year, "Project Henry" was her life. Now that Henry was gone, she wasn't sure her purpose. She knew she needed to choose a path for her life. She prayed for guidance, pleading, "Please God, send me a sign."

Most evenings, Patsy was exhausted both physically and emotionally by dinner time and would order room service and fall into a deep sleep. It was Blu who insisted on a dinner out for their final night in Argentina. They headed to a local pub to experience Argentine cuisine and nightlife. They feasted on

225

Argentine wine and braised lamb with roasted potatoes. As they ate and talked, she was grateful to Blu for insisting they dine out. Patsy shared stories of Henry, primarily stories of their teenage years—their Friday nights at Susan Klein's house, and their tap-dancing in Patsy's childhood home.

Blu was a great listener, and as she shared these stories, it was cathartic. To her delight, Salsa music began in the background, instantly lifting her spirits. "Would you like to dance?" Patsy asked Blu.

"Miss Patrice, you know I would do just about anything for you, but there is one thing I won't do…and that one thing is dance."

"Then I guess I'll just have to find another dance partner," she said brazenly. She stood up and walked towards a handsome stranger at the bar who she noticed eyeing her when she walked in. He was middle-aged, with tanned skin, and long, dark hair. By the shape of his body and the way he moved, she could tell he was a good dancer.

Patsy introduced herself and asked the man to dance just as Julio Iglesias' song *Besame' Mucho* came on. As Patsy and this dark, handsome stranger danced, she knew Henry and Marco were dancing together in heaven. She felt them looking down on her as the stranger dipped her when the song ended, and the nearby crowd of admirers applauded. Patsy curtsied and blew kisses to the small crowd. She thanked the dark stranger with a quick peck on the cheek and walked back to Blu.

"We can go now," Patsy smiled to Blu.

"Yes, Ma'am. That was quite a performance."

"I know, and you missed out," Patsy said playfully, grabbing his bicep as they left the restaurant arm in arm.

***

He watched her that evening with the big behemoth by her side. The hovering giant wouldn't leave her alone. Then he saw her jump to her feet and head over to some other guy. She whispered something, and then they were dancing. She was dancing with another man. What the fuck?

The man was tan and Latino-looking with long dark hair. He wished he had hair like that, but he was balding and had little hair anywhere on his soft, stubby body. He ached for her. She swayed back and forth to the music in front of everyone. He tried hard to memorize the steps the man took and just knew he could dance like that if he focused. It took everything in him to refrain from 'cutting in' on them. He dared not though, with the behemoth watching so closely.

It infuriated him that she was so seductive when she should belong only to him. He didn't even try to photograph her. He was so mad at her flirtation. Then he saw her happily leave with the hulk. *NO, STOP!* He fought the clicking sound invading his head! *Whore, Pig, Flirt, Harlot! Go then—go with your huge behemoth.*

He began to drink alone at the bar, bereft with sorrow and disappointment. Several minutes had passed when two prostitutes approached him. One giggled, "Don't be sad. Want to have a little fun?" She was thin with dark hair and very attractive. The other was Asian with beautiful blonde hair. That excited him because his beloved's hair was blonde. He decided—fuck it—two can play this game.

He gave the blonde a few crisp $100 bills as he wrote his hotel and room number on a coaster and practically spit out the words, "Come in fifteen minutes." Pushing her aside, he closed with, "Don't keep me waiting."

When his hired revenge arrived on schedule, he wasted no time ripping off her top and pushing her to her knees as he sat on the edge of the bed, exposing himself. "I'll call you Valenine," he told her. When she tried to reply, he cut her off, "Don't speak. Quiet!" He closed his eyes as she serviced him, running his hands through her blonde hair, imagining it was his beloved one, and calling out, "Valentine, my love, Valentine."

227

Growing hard, he moaned out in ecstasy. "Oh yeah, Valentine, I'm almost there, beautiful Valentine. I feel your luscious wet lips and tongue on my big throbbing cock, my beloved...ooh, sweet Valentine," he wailed. As he came close to climax, he pulled on her long blonde hair as blood rushed to his engorged hard-on. He yelled, "Valentine, beautiful Valentine— I'm coming. I'm coming!" He gave her hair one final yank.

Suddenly, the blonde hair came off the prostitute's head, right into his hands. He exploded in a fury as he held the limp tangled hair and stared down at his matching limp wrinkled dick. "It's a wig, you bitch, it's a wig!" he screamed. His knee shot up, hitting her chin with a thud and she cried out in pain. He threw the wig across the room. He watched as she swooped up the fake hair and her top, and ran away.

"Fraud, Phony, Cheap Bitch!" he screamed after her as she disappeared down the hallway. He knew there was only one true woman who could fulfill him, only one who would be his precious Valentine. He wanted her now more than ever.

He stared naked at his flaccid self in the full-length mirror, rubbing his penis wildly, trying to bring it alive again. As it began to grow hard again, he cried out, "Big behemoth, I'm just as big as you. You ugly, clumsy gargantuan. I can dance too. Just watch me!" Totally crazed, he snapped his fingers and danced around the room, imagining her in his arms. As he turned, he bellowed out, "One, two—cha cha cha, three, four— cha cha cha!"

CHAPTER 31
Nile

There were six more days with two more destinations ahead of them. The next stop the place Henry spoke of the most—the gorgeous Nile. Patsy recalled he said the only way to experience the Nile is on an exclusive Dahabiya cruise. She recalled Henry's excitement and his words, "These private boats were the way the elite of Europe toured the Nile."

***

He tried to get ahead of them at the airport so he could watch her from afar. He was baffled by this destination, but he would follow her to the ends of the earth if necessary.

He sat in first class, two rows behind and across the aisle from his beloved, with a perfect view of her luscious blonde hair. Feeling a tinge of shame, he winced at the thought of the whore whose hair came off in his hands in Argentina. His beloved was the real thing with stunning tresses, a perfect woman!

First Class was luxurious, and the hostess kept checking on him to make sure he was comfortable and happy. He was becoming impatient with this fawning. *Get out of the way, bitch! I can't see my beautiful one, and no, I don't want another glass of champagne unless it's toasting my one and only love. Leave me alone.*

Of course, he would never say these things out loud, but the clicking in his head reminded him of his stress. He carefully popped a valium to calm his nerves. Focusing back on his beloved, she rose from her seat and walked down the aisle. She was coming toward him. *Oh no…I'm not ready Valentine.* He began to shake uncontrollably as she took one step, then another, then another. *Oh my God, I'm seeing her up close, and the clicking won't stop.* His whole body was jerking. *No, not too near, I'm not prepared.* The CLICK, CLICK, CLICK in his head was deafening and distorting his vision as he succumbed to

229

the madness in his brain. Sweat broke out, and the astonishment of seeing her up close terrified him. He felt out of control, frozen and helpless. As he looked down now in disgust, he saw two droplets of urine leak out of his pants. She took two more steps, and it was over. She walked past him on her way to the bathroom. In disgrace and feeling exhausted with this unexpected shockwave, he popped another valium, and numbness took over his body. Finally, the noise in his brain subsided.

The rest of the flight was mostly calm, and even though he was quite groggy, he didn't take his eyes off her, until he drifted into a dreamless sleep. He awoke to the hostess shaking his shoulder, "We've arrived, Sir." He immediately recalled the awful incident of her walking past him while he wet his pants. Next time he would be ready for her and the rendezvous would be on his terms.

***

A limo took Blu and Patsy to their private Dahabiya from the airport. Its name was "Empress of the Nile," and it was quite fitting. Mr. S rented the private boat for three days to take Patsy and Blu from Luxor to Aswan. When Mr. S reviewed the itinerary with Patsy, she remembered him saying how the calmness of being on the water would be exactly what she needed after a physically exhausting trip in Argentina. Although typically, the Dahabiyas stop so passengers can explore temples, tombs, and local villages, Mr. S told Patsy he felt a relaxing trip with no sightseeing would be best for her. Patsy thought he was certainly right.

The beautiful long boat sparkled like gold, and two large masts blew in the wind. Patsy remembered how Henry explained that cruising on the Dahabiya was so tranquil because there were no engines, and the boat just glided down the river with the sound of the wind stroking the sails. It was a perfect mix of tradition and luxury.

230

She loved starting her day on the Dahabiya with mint tea on the half-shaded sun deck. She watched the egrets and herons as the sun rose. The river's edge was blooming with exotic flowers and lush green plant life. The sound of the river splashed against the side of the boat. Patsy closed her eyes to recall when she and Henry watched Agatha Christie's film *Death on the Nile*.

Thanks to Mr. S, wanting to give Henry some pleasure during his last days, Mr. S placed a VCR in Henry's hospital room. Mr. S knew watching movies was a boundless joy for Henry, and Patsy too. They shared many of those precious days watching films and escaping to a fantasy world. She even bought Henry a Panama hat so he could pretend to be Hercule Poirot, the Belgian detective investigating the murder on the riverboat. Henry sported a Belgian accent while discussing the clues one by one, trying to deduce who was the killer. No matter how many times they watched the movie, they conversed as if it were the first time.

Patsy missed those days with Henry, sitting next to him for hours, just the two of them. It seemed like time was standing still in those moments, but that was so far from the truth. Henry's time on earth was rapidly slipping away.

***

He was distracted when he heard the agent say, "Enjoy your trip." This would be tricky because his beloved and her behemoth were on a private vessel, and he would have to follow it somehow. He knew the boat's name, but also knew he couldn'tt be seen anywhere near them. It was too risky, so he checked into a nearby four-star hotel. The brochure for the cruise said it ends in Aswan so his destination would be Aswan. He gathered his thoughts and strategically planned his next move.

He rented a Jeep to follow the boat route on land. He brought his necessary zoom lenses and camera with him and left the larger equipment in the room. He would try to capture shots of her alone without the behemoth lurking. He salivated, thinking of his sneaky plot.

Two days later, he found out they were due at the dock in Aswan. It wasn't far from the hotel, but he followed along the river road, which took around forty minutes. The jeep handled great on sand and rocky roads, and he came to the edge of jungle full of flora and trees with large pummelo leaves. It was located right on the river's edge. It was perfect for his mission as he carefully parked the jeep back off a dirt road. He stationed himself deep in the underbrush and scurried through the foliage to set up his tripod. A thousand thoughts filled his head as he waited breathlessly to catch a first glimpse of his one and only Valentine.

He was all set, and the thought of her approaching made his dick start to move in his khaki pants. Maybe she'll be wearing short shorts or even a bikini. Excitement consumed him and made his member throb. His only problem was the behemoth. He thought of a million ways to kill him and rescue her from the giant, but when he saw the boat approach, she was laughing and having fun.

No, no, Valentine. You can only have fun and laugh with me! He saw her with the big creep, and they popped a bottle of champagne. His brain started to explode. *She should only want to be with me, her one and only ME!* He nearly cried as the clicking invaded his aching head. Once again, the longing in his groin started to erupt like an earthquake.

He was desperate for her, yet feeling anger toward her too. He knew he needed to punish her. Maybe he would teach her a lesson and spank her for betraying him. The thought of spanking her bare bottom excited him, but also made rage rush as he tasted bitter bile in his throat. He would beat her, but only after he killed the behemoth. Yes, that was his new plan. She would pay for her dalliance, but only when he became her master, and she would do what he commanded. He wondered what kind of whip he would use. *Would it be velvet or leather? Or both.*

***

On the final day of the trip, Patsy decided it was time to spread Henry's ashes. She wanted it to be special and ceremonial. She looked around at the bright sun and blue sky and thought the front of the vessel would be the right place. Lovely pummelo trees were lining both sides of the river. It was a perfect setting. Henry would approve.

"Blu, can you please help me get to the front of the boat. I'm afraid I might lose my balance, and it's pretty windy," Patsy asked.

Blu held tightly onto Patsy's hand and walked with her to the head of the boat. She steadied herself, stood at the edge of the deck, looked up in the heavens, and said as a prayer, "Here's to you, my dear Henry. I know you're up there dancing in the clouds, and I do love you!"

She thought she heard Henry's laugh for a split second and swore she heard his voice say, "Back at ya, Ginger." It was so clear it almost frightened her.

As she started to scatter the second bag of ashes, a blast of wind sprayed water. The ashes came back into their faces and hit Blu in his vast chest. They both began laughing as they stared into each other's grey, ashen-covered faces. Patsy instinctively hugged Blu as her laughter turned to tears while she remained in his arms. She didn't know if she was laughing or crying, or if she was sad or happy.

To lighten the mood, Blu said, "Sure glad Ms. Patrice that I didn't have my mouth open."

Patsy shot back, removing ashes from her tongue, "Wish I could say the same! This calls for champagne."

"Coming right up," Blu said, popping the bottle and filling their glasses with bubbly.

***

233

Waiting patiently on the jungle floor, he spotted them at the front of the riverboat as he crouched behind some large pummelo trees. Bulky nearby bushes gave him a perfect view with lots of cover. He saw the behemoth embrace her as she threw something off the starboard side of the boat. He wished he possessed a gun or at least a poison dart to get rid of him. He thought he saw his beloved crying and for a minute, even imagined that she was being held captive by the ogre. Yes, that was it—she was held against her will. She must be nice to him. She was longing for her true love, her ideal lover, and was anxious to escape the lair of the behemoth. *I'm here, beloved, I'll save you, I promise.*

As he positioned himself to take another close-up shot, a large bird flew by, causing him to lose his balance and fall in the wild underbrush. "Fuck!" he cried out loud.

***

Blu's eyes darted back and forth, looking to see what was making the commotion in the bushes. "There!" Patsy pointed to a man struggling to stand. He seemed to be holding out a camera on a tripod, as if to protect it. "Do you see him?"

"Yes!" Blu shouted. "Go back to the cabin," he ordered as he jumped into the water. The boat was so close to shore, he swam only a few yards to reach land. Patsy couldn't move as she watched Blu swimming his way to the shore.

***

The behemoth was coming for him. He sprinted through the thick, wet underbrush even though his ankle hurt. He ran, dropping his one camera still attached to the tripod. He didn't care. The photos would be marred by behemoth's massive image anyway, so he didn't need them. But that was his good camera with several other photos on it. *Damn that monster to hell!*

***

Patsy watched as Blu disappeared in the underbrush and then came out holding a camera over his head. She was relieved

234

to see him unharmed, but flabbergasted at the crazy scene. *What in God's name was going on?*

***

He ran faster and faster, finally reaching a dirt road as the CLICK, CLICK, CLICK exploded in his head. He was exhausted. His legs felt like cracking glass and his ankle throbbed. He needed to stop, turn around, and see if the behemoth was still following him. *God, what if he was? The giant fiend would beat him to a pulp.*

Finally, he collapsed on the side of the heavily wooded road. He could hardly catch his breath. He couldn't move. He heard only silence. No car, no sounds of pounding feet. He waited until his heaving body began to calm. Then he pushed himself up and looked around. The road was empty. *Holy God, at least he was safe.* And he knew what to do. Somehow, someway find a means to exterminate him and rescue her. He needed to make a new plan and do it fast. His need for her made his groin ache with desire as he hobbled lamely down the road.

***

Blu climbed back into the boat, "Dammit, I wasn't fast enough. The bastard got away, but I did get his camera."

"What do you think is on the film?" Patsy asked, unsure why Blu went off in such a rush. They were in Egypt, on the Nile. Why would this guy have anything to do with them? She didn't speak up because Blu looked so furious, and it frightened her. He was such a controlled man. She never saw him rattled before.

"I couldn't get a look at the guy, but he was white. I don't like it, not at all." He removed the camera from the tripod and handed it to the First Mate, "How fast do you think you can get the film developed?"

"We'll be docking in less than an hour. It shouldn't take long, Sir. Do you want me to report what happened?"

"No, not until we see the photos. I could use something to drink, though. After I change into dry clothes."

235

He started to leave, but Patsy reached for his arm. "Why did you do that? You frightened me. What's going on now?"

"Sorry, but I have a job to protect you," Blu replied, "and that's what I intend to do on this trip." He spoke in a no-nonsense tone and was very sure of himself.

"Should I be worried? You would tell me, wouldn't you?"

In a soothing voice, Blu comforted her, "I sure would. We have no secrets. I'll always protect you. That's what I do best, and besides, Mr. S would have me tarred and feathered if anything happened to you."

Blu takes chase rushing off the Dahabiya

***

He walked for what seemed like forever before he stumbled upon a crude marketplace. The people behind the stands were dirty and scary looking. It was a seedier part of town and they were undoubtedly nefarious types. Still, for some reason, he was drawn in. He perused the tables strewn with

236

watches, fancy knives, copper pitchers, and even one filled with what looked like antique weapons.

A vendor presenting his wares approached him, showing off a curved sickle with an ivory handle. He could picture himself severing the behemoth's head with it. "You buy? Just one hundred American dollars," the dealer said in broken English.

He felt like shoving the skinny, slimy-looking vendor and running away, but he was trapped. Other dark-skinned Egyptians were closing in, looking at him with evil stares, holding up machetes, hatchets, and one was wielding a sword. All of them were talking at him, screaming, threatening. The CLICK, CLICK, CLICK vibrated through his skull. He must get away— just throw money at them and run.

Suddenly a tall Egyptian in a hood and a long white gown approached him. The others retreated in fear. He spoke perfect English, "What is it you are looking for, my friend?"

Feeling a bit settled now, he replied, "I am looking for a firearm, a small pistol perhaps. Can you help me? He flashed the man a few hundred-dollar bills to show his sincerity."

The hooded man motioned him to a secluded location. He led him to what looked like an army tent and proceeded to unzip the low doorway. They both ducked to get inside. "Come Sir, for your eyes only. The best selection for many miles around. Pull off the cover and feast your eyes."

Intrigued, he ripped off the tarp and laid eyes on several firearms under the canvas. There were rifles, 357 magnums, and several pistols. His heart skipped a beat as he chose a small 45 pistol, like the one he learned to shoot with on his father's ranch when he was just a boy. "How much?"

"Only five hundred American dollars and for you, free ammo." The mysterious hooded man then passed him a box of ammunition as he smiled, showing a gold tooth to accompany his grin.

Being no fool, he gave the man four one-hundred-dollar bills, knowing that was more than enough. As they made the exchange, the dark man said, "Ah, you got a special bargain, my friend." Then the tall Egyptian carefully escorted him out of the tent and guided him safely to the main road.

After a few yards he spotted his abandoned jeep over the hill. Again, fate was on his side. Two teenagers were hanging around the auto as he boldly wielded the gun and yelled out, "Beat it, or I'll blow your legs off!"

The cold steel in his hands created a combination of power and euphoria. He wasn't fucking around anymore. He carefully placed the gun in his empty camera case to disguise it, packed up his equipment bag, and was ready to rescue his beloved. *I'll save her and annihilate that behemoth. She's waiting for her hero, her lover, her real man.* Confidence flooded his body as he set off to slay the dragon.

***

CHAPTER 32
Gotcha

Patsy looked back on the trip and relaxed on the headrest. Closing her eyes, she reminisced about Henry and their times on the stoop, dancing and singing. Patsy was sure Henry was pleased with her tribute to him. She was full of gratitude that she could do this beautiful thing for him, but also for herself. Everything worked out perfectly.

Her heart was bursting as she anticipated Greece. Mr. S said there was a major surprise waiting for them. She thought about what a wonderful trip it has been, as she heard the plane engine purr, and she slid into a peaceful sleep.

Patsy and Blu arrived at Athens International airport after a ten-hour flight, then it would be another two-and-a-half-hour journey to Delphi. Luckily when they reached the airport, they knew Mr. S would have a private driver waiting to whisk them to their hotel and their next destination.

***

He flashed his National Enquirer badge at the airport, lied, and said he was photographing untamed animals for his assignment, and therefore possessed a license to carry a gun. There was a brief holdup, but he managed to get on their flight, however he couldn't get his usual first-class ticket. His gun was confiscated, and he was told it would be returned to him at Customs in Athens. There was no time to argue, so he reluctantly handed over the gun and ammo.

He felt the CLICK, CLICK, CLICK begin in his aching head. He took his seat in coach next to a fat Greek woman who reeked of garlic. He immediately asked for a drink from the hostess and stared at the disgusting woman. "Make it a double!" he insisted. His blood boiled knowing his beloved was in first class and he was stuck next to this fat slob in coach. He quickly downed the drink, asked for another, and then dozed off with the help of valium. He was awakened by the announcement they

239

were about to land shortly. He was greeted by the acrid smell of garlic and a toothless smile from his Greek neighbor.

Once on the ground, he ran to Customs and picked up the gun with little trouble. The idiots didn't even ask for his credentials. *Hurry, hurry,* his clicking brain repeated as he was practically sprinting now—he needed to follow the behemoth to their hotel. He was relieved when he spied the giant in the distance. He saw him grab her bags off the turnstile.

He followed them outside as they stepped into a car. He jumped into the next taxi. He yelled to the driver, "Follow that car and don't lose them," as he handed the driver a crisp hundred-dollar bill. He was on a mission, excited now, as he pulled the gun from his bag, taking it out of its case, and stroking it. He dreamed of his love as he caressed the gun tenderly. He gripped it tighter. He was on a quest with a job to do—spraying the enemy's body full of bullets!

***

Patsy and Blu arrived at their quaint hotel bordered by the Parnassus Mountains and the Gulf of Corinth. Olive groves and countryside surrounded the massive mountains. Patsy and Blu stood outside the hotel to admire the scenery.

"Blu," Patsy said in a whiny voice, "I know I should be enthralled by the stunning mountains and the sparkling water, but I'm exhausted and run down from all the traveling."

"I feel your pain, Ms. Patrice. I'm starting to fade a little too. We covered quite some territory though, didn't we?"

"Goodness, yes," exclaimed Patsy. "You are the best guide ever, and you took such loving care of me. Thank you, kind sir!"

"It is my pleasure," replied Blu flashing his pearly white smile.

It suddenly dawned on Patsy that she didn't know much about Blu besides how he and Mr. S met. They traveled together all this time, and Patsy realized she was so selfish, always talking about herself. She never once asked him anything about

240

himself. She wondered, "Does he have children? Where did he grow up? What's his favorite food?"

Patsy was on a quest to find out more about her mysterious traveling companion. This new mission gave her a jolt of energy. Patsy turned to Blu and asked, "Do you want to get something to eat? I'm starving!"

Blu looked at her, "I thought you were exhausted. I was hoping to take a nap."

Patsy chuckled, "We can always sleep, and suddenly I am famished. Please can we grab a bite to eat? Then we can rest. I promise."

Blu shook his head, "How can I resist an invitation from a beautiful lady like you?"

When they sat down in the cafe inside the hotel, she started carefully, feeling out this big, handsome, generous man. She said coyly, "Tell me a secret about you. It can be anything at any time, but it has to be a secret."

"Very well, but you cannot divulge my secret, ok?"

"I promise."

Blu cupped his hand and whispered in her ear, "I'm deathly afraid of spiders. I was bitten once, and my arm swelled up, and I thought I was gonna die. I cried when they gave me the tetanus shot. I thought I was a goner."

"Oh no, when did it happen?" Patsy asked, hardly believing this huge man would ever cry over anything.

"When I was five," Blu laughed out loud.

"Well of course, you were only a little boy. That's not fair. That's not a good secret."

"Well, I'm way over six feet now, and I still run like heck when I see a spider web. I would say it's pretty embarrassing."

"OK, then tell me about your childhood, that is, if you want to. I picture you a sweet and kind little boy," said Patsy very softly.

"Ms. Patrice, I was never *little*."

Patsy burst out laughing.

241

Blu continued, "My early years were spent with my grandmother, who raised me. I never knew my father, and no one ever mentioned him to me. My mother died of an overdose when I was six, so I barely remember her. I worked hard on my studies throughout school and went on to get a nursing degree. To pay for my education, I went to school at night and worked in construction during the day. I did well in construction, being in demand as a 'Man of Steel.'" Blu smiled with pride when he mentioned his nickname, "That's when folks began to call me Blu Steel."

Blu stopped after that. Patsy didn't push and figured he would tell her another time. That was enough for now. She knew he was exhausted, and she was too, as she felt the sleepiness creep back.

The next morning, Patsy and Blu set out to spread Henry's ashes at the site of the Delphi Oracle. Patsy wanted to go to the top of the Delphi Theatre, which looked above the Temple of Apollo. When she and Henry talked about the Delphi Theatre, she knew at the time that this landmark was the perfect place for Henry to visit, whether his physical being could be there or not, since Henry spent most of his life preparing for or performing in the theatre.

Patsy and Blu hiked up the mountain until they reached the immense theatre with a spectacular view of the entire sanctuary below and the valley beyond. The stadium looked as if it could accommodate thousands of spectators. Patsy sat on the cool limestone bench. She closed her eyes and imagined she was in a world long ago observing ancient Roman plays. When she opened her eyes, Patsy felt she was ready to release the ashes. She poured her third bag of ashes down to the round stage below. "Break a leg, Henry!" Pasty shouted.

Delphi Oracle

Patsy suddenly realized this was the final resting place of Henry, all the bags of ashes were now empty, and Patsy possessed no more physical evidence of Henry's being. Tears streamed down her face as she held the empty bag tight. Blu put his arms around her as she buried her head in his chest. She wondered how someone so young and so alive could have their life suddenly taken from them. There was so much Henry still needed to experience, so much joy he could still bring to the world, and now it was just darkness—a shining light switched off prematurely.

After Patsy couldn't shed another tear, she lifted her head from Blu's chest, "Let's go down to the Temple."

"Are you sure you don't want to rest here for a little longer?" asked Blu.

"No…as Henry would say, 'the show must go on!'" Patsy declared, raising her arms in the air.

Patsy and Blu hiked down to see the Temple of Apollo. Inscribed at the entry of the temple was the phrase *Know Yourself,* written in Greek. She remembered how Henry knew how to pronounce it in Greek. She prayed someday soon she would gain full knowledge of herself.

243

As they left Delphi, Blu confided that Mr. S arranged for a private yacht tour on the Aegean Sea. It was to be the culmination of their trip.

***

When he awoke in the hotel, every bone in his body ached. He was rubbed raw from the constant masturbating. He saw on the stolen itinerary that they were going to the Delphi Oracle, but he could not move, and he still smelled of garlic from the nasty Greek woman in coach class. He decided to wait until their next destination to continue his pursuit. He read the words carefully—a yacht docked off the Aegean in the Port of Piraeus.

This time he would be smart. This time he would be prepared. The day of reckoning was here. He would be waiting for them at their next destination, and he would destroy the behemoth forever. He packed only underwear, a small camera, binoculars, and, of course the gun in a small knapsack. He caressed the weapon. Suddenly, his cock came to life again at the thought of destroying the gargantuan. Adrenalin pumped through his veins at the final glory of the kill.

He continued to follow them, this time to the yacht docked off the Aegean Sea. He watched like a hawk through binoculars, marking their every move. He kept track of them carefully as they boarded the craft named *Showtime*, a shining white vessel gleaming in the harbor. He thought it would be an excellent place for a honeymoon after capturing his beloved Valentine and destroying his nemesis. He would throw the monster's body overboard and let the sharks devour him.

He imagined the wind whipping in his beloved's hair and the swaying of the ocean as she lay naked on the starboard deck, her lovely skin glistening in the sun. He would take her right there, her moans drowning out the roar of the ship's engine.

He watched the monster as they boarded the yacht in the busy port. Hatred consumed his body as his mind raced. He needed to devise a scheme to get on that ship. He noticed a few sailors who looked like part of the crew hurry off the plank and run into a seaside watering hole. He surmised they were getting one last drink before sailing. Instantly a scheme came to mind. He walked into the tiny bar crowded with sailors and locals and cautiously asked the bartender when the *Showtime* would set sail. Then, he casually put down a hundred-dollar bill and ordered a quart of their best whiskey.

The bartender replied, "It's due to take off in thirty minutes, but you should ask the fellow over there for sure. I believe he is one of the deck crew."

In the corner, sitting alone, he spotted the downtrodden deckhand and walked over. By way of introduction, he began a conversation offering him an entire bottle of whiskey as they sat and drank. "Hey my friend, the whiskey is on me."

The Greek sailor perked up with the mention of whiskey.

"When do you shove off on your excursion? Do you speak English? Do you understand me?"

"Soon, my friend. Thanks for drink."

"Take the bottle. I'm sure they don't pay you enough for all the work you do."

"You are so right," the sailor shrugged. "You see I must feed my wife and kids. But I no be picked this time. Private sailing crew, and they no want me. I no good 'cause English broken."

This couldn't be more perfect, he thought. His plan was just growing more brilliant by the moment. It didn't take much convincing, and in no time, the man was giving him his uniform jacket, badge, and the name of the steward so he could slip on board unnoticed. Money talks, and in return for only three hundred dollars and the remains of the bottle of whiskey, his plan was complete. Again, fate was on his side.

Quickly he was off with ten minutes to spare. He followed the crew in line to get on board and find his beloved. There was only one small camera in his bag. Hidden in the bag wrapped in his underwear was the gun he would use to kill the behemoth so he could sweep his one and only away with him, at last!

***

Patsy never saw a boat so big except in the movies. She was in awe of what money could buy and yelled out before she stepped aboard, "God bless Mr. S!"

The ship seemed equipped with every convenience and luxury. Looking around, Patsy only saw crew members and a few sailors, along with the captain. Other than that, it was for her and Blu alone. She heard lovely music sung in Greek, but with a Latin beat. She smelled the delicious aroma of rich coffee as a high-ranking crew member with medals and epaulets on his white and gold jacket escorted her to the massive top deck. She recognized him as the captain.

A horn signaled that they were soon ready to set sail down the Aegean. Patsy was thrilled to be on board. She didn't care where they were going. Patsy was content to be waited on and pampered, especially after the treks in jungles, up mountainsides, and down pebbled paths. Patsy felt self-satisfied that it was over, and she accomplished what she set out to do. As she peered over the railing, she could feel Henry smiling down on her.

***

It was surprisingly easy to get on board. He felt it was a good omen. He spotted them from the lower deck. The behemoth talked to the captain as his beloved gazed over the railing. He knew she was dreaming of him, and he was so close now to making her his woman and wipe out the hulk-like being for all eternity. He knew he'd be victorious. Adrenaline flowed through his veins as he confidently walked to the main deck, ready to destroy the enemy. He was suspicious as two men in plainclothes approached him, but relieved as they smiled. Idiots fooled again.

He grabbed a tray and a few champagne flutes to make it look like he was busy getting things ready to set sail. Protected

246

from view behind the ship's bar, he quickly put the tray down and unzipped his bag. He carefully pulled out the revolver wrapped in the underwear and stashed the whole package in his belt, feeling it against his bare skin. He arranged his white cotton shorts to look like a waiter's napkin. He admired his brilliance. Again, he thought of everything.

The whole scenario was surreal, guided by a stronger force. It was all so simple now. She would soon be released from the bondage of the swine holding her against her will, and he would be her new master. In fact, she would call him 'Master' when he firmly flogged her before sex.

***

Patsy gazed as the sunset luminated over the deep blue Aegean Sea. The air smelled sweet as the breeze blew her hair into her eyes. She felt the sting of saltwater as she naturally took Blu's hand in hers. "Thank you, my sweet friend, for keeping me safe and taking such precious care of me. You are so wonderful and so dear to me."

The ship's captain approached them, but this time he pulled Blu aside in a confidential conversation. Patsy eavesdropped as the captain spoke softly to Blu, "The photos you asked to be developed are of your companion. From them, we see that the perpetrator has been following her since you left New York."

Then the captain and Blu stepped further away, and Patsy could hear only a few words like fingerprints, camera, passport, mugshot, but she couldn't make out the whole conversation. In a louder voice, the captain said, "Perhaps we should get your protégé below deck in a private cabin while we work. We can't be too careful."

"No," Blu replied, "let's catch this bastard in the act so we can snag him. I want to get my hands on him."

The captain handed Blu a phone, "That is not wise, good sir. It is our jurisdiction. You cannot take matters into your own hands."

Patsy was annoyed at being left out and disappointed in being treated like a helpless woman. She hated when men did that. "Blu, tell me what's going on!"

Blu said softly, "Be quiet, Ms. Patrice. Will you kindly let me handle this?" Patsy felt anger rush to the surface as she walked away in a huff. "Stop!" demanded Blu, "Do not leave my side. I'll explain later. Stay here." Patsy sensed the danger emanating from this typically calm and collected man and felt frightened now, so she obeyed.

He turned his back to her and, putting the ship's phone to his ear, said, "Sir, she is fine. The captain has assured me his crew has eyes on him." There was silence, and finally, Blu said in a strong but concerned voice, "I understand, I'll put her right on, Sir." Blu handed the phone to Patsy, "Mr. S needs to talk to you. It's particularly important, so I need you to listen carefully."

Patsy practically grabbed the phone out of Blu's hand. "Dearheart," Mr. S began, "I'll get right to the point. We are planning a sting on the stalker who we believe to be the same as the Calgon Peeping Tom who photographed you."

Patsy gasped, "Oh no, what are you saying? You mean here…on this ship, now? How can that be?"

Mr. S shushed her and continued, "First, listen carefully. It's important that you do what we say. We are asking you to act naturally to avoid suspicion.

"The River Police on the Nile had the photos developed, and they are harmless. They are now collaborating with the Greek authorities, but we must have evidence against this sicko. Nothing criminal has happened yet, and we want to hold him on criminal charges, so he won't bother you anymore.

"Please stay close and stay calm. You are protected with Blu. Please do what you're told, and we'll get him. And do not worry. As I said, he is harmless so far. We think he is just a crazy admirer—not violent, but we cannot take chances. Do you

248

understand?" Mr. S asked. Then he repeated firmly, "Do you understand?"

"Yes," Patsy answered with a cracking voice, then said, "I want to come home, Mr. S."

"I'm working on that as we speak. Sit tight, and do what I told you. And remember, you're my girl. No one hurts my girl," Mr. S said softly.

Patsy began to shake, "I was so confident that the Calgon incident was buried in the past. How could this be? All this time he's been following me?"

Mr. S paused, then added, "We have detectives here in New York searching his apartment just to get a profile on the loser. That's all I can say for now. Nothing found by my private investigator turned up anything like that photo. I want you to be brave. Stick close to Blu and do what he says. Let the professionals do their job. We have to nab this guy."

Patsy felt her stomach turn and her throat heave as the taste of vomit rushed up without warning. At that, she ran to the edge of the ship and threw up. She felt that same uncontrollable doom she felt as a child, and now she couldn't run, couldn't cover it up with some fake excuse when the panic set in. She was trapped.

Blu picked her up and carried her to her cabin where a nurse and doctor waited. "I don't need a doctor. I just want to go home," she sobbed.

The doctor handed her two small yellow pills. "These shall help calm you."

In twenty minutes, calm from the meds, Patsy heard the commotion of running footsteps above as loud sirens went off and shadows of red lights flashed.

Patsy pleaded, "Blu, please tell me what's happening. What is that noise?"

Blu sat down on the bed next to her and took her hands tenderly in his. "I cannot tell you more than I know. I must let the Greek authorities handle this. We're in their country and must cooperate. You are safe, and we are going home. A helicopter is on its way."

***

Suddenly two men grabbed his arm. The clicking in his head began as one said in a Greek accent, "You have the right to remain silento. Anything you say…." After that, all he heard was the wretched, loud clicking sound. CLICK, CLICK, CLICK. He quickly broke free and attempted to reach for the gun buried in his pants, but the men tackled him as sirens went off around the ship.

BLEEP, BLEEP, BLEEP—the sounds were deafening in his ears. Then bright red lights flashed in his eyes as he cried out to drown the CLICK, CLICK, CLICK in his exploding head. He screamed. "I tried to rescue you, Valentine, my beloved Valentine. Remember how my heart bleeds for you. Remember my card that you loved so much. I'll return for you, Valentine, I promise!" He felt sure she heard him and knew she loved him too. They were holding her against her will, trying to ruin their perfect love.

They finally got him off deck and into a motorboat with huge letters ASTYNOMIA on the side. He laughed, thinking they were a bunch of clowns who could never hold him for anything. He committed no crime. Being in love is no crime.

His laughter became hysterical as the one guard who spoke broken English told him to shut up, or he would shut him up. He yelled out again, "I'll be back, Valentine!" As the motorboat sped off, he promised himself he would return. He knew now more than ever he would never abandon her. "Just wait a little longer, my darling. I'm coming for you," he cried.

The boat raced away as the water splashed up, hitting his face. Already he knew he would hire the best lawyer money could buy. He did nothing wrong. Nothing except love his beautiful one. He knew his conquest wasn't over as the cold ocean splashed his face again. He felt sure now, sure he would have her—at any price. His laughter continued to the police

250

station, but then faded as the CLICK, CLICK, CLICK returned to occupy his tortured brain.

***

CHAPTER 33
Pissed

Patsy and Blu flew home, and Mr. S scheduled a limousine to pick them up at the airport and drive them straight to his penthouse. She looked around at the bustling city she cherished and was relieved to be back.

Patsy was eager to see Mr. S. She jumped out of the limo and sprinted to the penthouse entrance. Patsy threw her arms around Mr. S and held him tightly. She longed to embrace his comfortable stature and smell his fresh, clean scent. "Now this is a welcome!" he laughed. "Maybe I should send women across the world more often so when they come home, I get this grandiose return."

"Ha ha," said Patsy, "As happy as I am to see you, I am also furious about all that you and Blu hid from me. I'm a big girl, and I want the facts about what you know about this stalker. I'm not taking any more bull about me being too frail and too weak to handle it."

"I guess the travel brought out the feisty woman in you," Blu laughed.

Mr. S walked away for a minute as Patsy collapsed on the couch. Blu followed. She could see the dark circles under Blu's eyes. He indeed looked exhausted. For a minute, she felt terrible about being so mad. Mr. S returned with a manila envelope. Patsy emptied the envelope and photos scattered all over. Patsy gasped in horror. The pictures were all of her. There were pictures of her on the subway, at her mailbox, at the theatre, and even going into the hospital to visit Henry.

As she sat staring at the photos in disbelief, anger welled up inside of her like a volcano spewing lava. How could they keep such a personal secret from her? She felt betrayed. Were they her friends, or were they controlling her, working behind her back? Did they think she was a helpless female who couldn't

252

take the world's strife? She shook all over at first, but then adrenaline rushed through her veins.

"How dare you!" Patsy shouted, "You need to tell me right now about this sick guy who was following me for over a year. Look at all these pictures. They are all of me—ME. I need to know the whole story. Right now, goddammit!"

"Are you sure you are up to it right now?" Mr. S tried to calm her. "You and Blu must be exhausted."

"I need to know right now," Pasty said sternly.

Mr. S began nervously, "You should know we were going to tell you, once the asshole was arraigned, sentenced, and hopefully permanently behind bars."

Patsy noticed Blu sat quietly and let Mr. S do all the talking.

Mr. S began slowly, "Patsy, it is crucial that this is kept confidential and must stay that way. We want to put this guy away for a long time."

Mr. S spoke carefully, "When Blu found the camera, he sent it to me, and I got the camera swiped for fingerprints by my buddy in the FBI. When my friend identified the guy, we tracked his passport and found that he was in Argentina and then traveled to the Nile. We assumed he was following you and would end up in Greece.

"Fortunately, my FBI friend had a good buddy in the American Embassy in Greece and connected with the Greek EYP, their intelligence agency, to set up a sting operation to catch the culprit. At the same time, the FBI was conducting their own operation in the States. They were checking this guy's background and his apartment along with any other criminal records he might have. New York police records showed the guy had a restraining order against him years ago and other priors for bothering an underage girl. His rich father tried to get the record expunged, and that's when we found out through his passport photo and an old mug shot that he previously worked at the

253

National Enquirer. All of this information was relayed to Blu, who had to play it close to the vest until we could get ample evidence.

"We had to be extremely careful after that because the sicko was now in a foreign country, and their international legal system is a little different from ours. You see, we do not have a reciprocal agreement with Egypt. So, it was evident we really couldn't hold him for anything. That's when I called my FBI friend in on the case."

Patsy looked stunned, but continued to listen intently. "The Greek officials were wonderful to work with, but it was their turf. So, we had him followed to the yacht to set up the sting. It had to be perfect timing, and we needed to follow their lead. It was their jurisdiction.

"With my influence with the NYPD, we also managed to get the super of his building to let us in without a search warrant just to look around his place. That's where we discovered the photos of you, and we made copies. He has been following you since the Calgon debacle, and he never stopped. The final piece to the puzzle was the gun he got a hold of in Egypt. That was the icing on the cake. We knew then he could be held on charges."

"Oh my God, was he going to kill me…or take me at gunpoint?"

"Oh, I'm sure not. He was obsessed with you. But, he may have taken a shot at Blu."

Patsy gasped, "Oh, my God, how horrible!"

"Remember the dunk I took in the Nile and you were questioning why?" Blu chimed in, "Well, that was the sicko. Believe me, nothing would happen to you on my watch. I've been through much worse."

Mr. S continued, "Our problem comes because he has powerful lawyers, and he is worth millions. To get him sentenced will be difficult because he didn't commit a crime—a real crime. He could be back in New York and out on the street in 48 hours. We don't have much on him, except for the gun he was packing after the incident on the Nile. However, police did confiscate a torn notebook from his last hotel room wastebasket. It had love yearnings of you and death threats towards Blu, whom he referred to as 'the behemoth' 'cause Blu is so petite, I guess." They all chuckled.

"For that reason, we might be able to get him on attempted murder. Also, the police advise you to avoid the city—for now. We cannot know if he will be back and get off free of all charges.

"We only ask now that you do not discuss this with anyone while the case is pending. He is being held without bail right now, but that could change. We want to put this sicko away for many years. We could not tell you everything at the time. Now do you understand why?" Mr. S finished speaking.

After some silence, Mr. S added cautiously, "OK, Dearheart, let's hear the questions, but don't attack us, please. You are safe now and he is behind bars."

"Well," Patsy started, "I want to see that notebook and talk to the cops and be kept up to date from now on. It's my case and I demand to be kept informed. When can I meet with the police?"

"The lead detective is in Greece on the case right now, but we will arrange a meeting, and from now on, you will know everything that's going on. This I promise. Remember, everything we did, we did for your safety."

There were tears in Patsy's eyes, but she was laughing as she hugged them both. "You two wonderful men saved me, and I can't ever repay you for taking such loving care of me. You are my two best friends on earth, and I know Henry is sending protection too from heaven. I am so blessed, so blessed."

Just as she thought she couldn't feel any more love, Patsy was stunned and delighted at what Mr. S said next, "Dearheart, I have a wonderful surprise for you. I've been waiting for the right time to tell you. You can recover in luxury and get away from the rat race and problems in the city, and you can do it in style. It

255

is somewhere I reserve only for my very favorite people. You need sun, relaxation, and to get out of the city. I have just the spot."

Mr. S chuckled now and sounded like a host on a TV show as he bragged, "You will relax for as long as you like on my private, exotic island in magnificent Indonesia! I have a full staff waiting to pamper you in a secluded beach cottage with all the amenities and comforts a girl could want."

Patsy embraced Mr. S again and held onto him for a few minutes. She was so grateful as she sincerely stated, "You are so very kind to me. I don't know how I can ever repay you."

Later that evening, Patsy returned home. It felt eerily quiet and lonely. When she walked into the bathroom, a chill traveled up her spine as she glanced at the little window. It conjured up thoughts of the stalker and the emotional journey she just went through. Her mind started wandering as her heart began to race, but she knew she needed to focus on packing for Indonesia. She took a few calming breaths—in through her nose and out through her mouth—and smiled as thoughts of Madge and Yogi Shantar popped into her head. She laid down and closed her eyes just for a minute but soon drifted off....

She saw a door opening, it was blurry at first, but it became clearer and clearer. It looked like a monster. She ran towards the door to try and close it before the monster could come in, but something was stopping her. She couldn't get close enough to the door, and the monster kept coming closer and closer. She struggled to break through the invisible barrier, but she couldn't move any nearer. Finally, she could faintly hear a woman's voice saying, "Please give him another chance." She tried to yell no, but the words didn't come out as the grotesque monster moved closer and closer.

Patsy jolted awake. She glanced around to see if anyone was there. Realizing it was just a dream, she took a deep breath.

256

She suddenly felt the need to call her mother. She began the conversation about her tiring trip and her journey to spread Henry's ashes. She said nothing about the stalker as requested by Mr. S, but expressed the need to relax, and told her mother she was going to a tropical island. "The city was just too much to handle," she explained, then added, "there is something I need to understand from you. How can you spend so many years with a monster?"

"What do you mean, monster? Your father is not a monster. He might have some problems, but he's not a monster!" By the tone of her mother's voice, Patsy could tell she was angry.

Patsy did not want to go hundreds of miles away from her mother having a strained relationship. "I'm sorry, I know, I know he was a wonderful man when you met. Forget I ever said anything." There was silence on the other end of the phone. "I love you Mom, so very much," Patsy said, her voice trembling.

Bridget's voice softened and said, "I love you too. Please be safe, and send me a postcard."

Patsy also wanted to say goodbye to Cristo with a sweet note tucked under his door. After she wrote the message, she walked to his apartment, slid it halfway under his door, but quickly retrieved it. She thought of his beautiful ways and his gorgeous body, and without hesitation, she knocked on his door.

Cristo didn't give her a chance to say anything as he immediately swept her up in his arms and led them to his leather sofa. Patsy melted as she tried to explain her journey, but Cristo put his finger to her lips to quiet her. "There will be time for that later," he whispered. Cristo ripped off his clothes and undressed her. She didn't know whose clothes came off the quickest. Clothes flew all over the floor, and Patsy's zipper to her jeans ripped apart with a grand two-handed gesture.

"I missed you," Cristo admitted. They devoured each other in kisses and caresses and deep probing tongues licking and sucking every part of each other's bodies. It was so longed-for, so appreciated, so beautiful.

After, Patsy told Cristo about her journey to spread Henry's ashes. She cried, but it was a good cry, releasing all the pent-up sorrow she kept buried. Cristo held her for several minutes until she felt peaceful again.

She carefully told Cristo of her arranged getaway for mental and physical health reasons, and he understood, saying he would always be here waiting for her. "This is not really goodbye," Patsy said as she left, "it's only Au Revoir for now."

Patsy was at peace and experienced a sweet lucidness as she walked outside to wait for the car that would take her to her flight. Strength and determination rushed through her body, and she wasn't afraid anymore. She was safe now and leaving the city's chill, grateful to be headed to the warm sunshine of Indonesia.

PART FOUR
CHAPTER 34
Utopia

Blu accompanied Patsy on the flight to Indonesia. Arriving at the airport, there was a dark-haired, swarthy man with a beaming smile waiting for them and holding up a sign which read *Patsy and Blu*. "Hello, my name is Darma and I am here to take you to Paradise," he stated.

He was a very slim, tidy man. He wore a cravat and spectacles and was formal and polite. Patsy instantly admired his demeanor. "Nice to meet you," she laughed, "I sure can use some Paradise right now."

Blu chimed in, "You sure can!"

"Follow me," Darma said as he whisked them away to a water taxi docked right outside the airport.

Onboard, Patsy felt a warm breeze and the spray of the ocean on her face. As the water taxi moved faster, there was a sudden jolt. Patsy grabbed Blu's muscular arm to steady herself.

"It's all right," Blu assured her. "Nobody's stalking you anymore. Remember, he's locked up tight in jail or a loony bin, right where he belongs." Patsy knew Blu sensed her uneasiness when he started telling her a story to distract her, "When your funny friend Madge heard about the trip, she begged Mr. S to let her chaperone. 'Not a chance Madge, now get those double D's outta my face right now!' he told her." Patsy laughed as she clung to Blu. Deep inside, she dreaded their parting. He was more than a chaperone. He was her friend, protector, and confidante.

After the water taxi arrived onshore, while looking around, it felt a little lonely at first, but Patsy did see some activity on the dock, which made her feel less apprehensive. A jeep was waiting to take Patsy to Mr. S's estate. Patsy turned to Blu and squeezed his hand, "So I guess this is it?"

"I'm afraid so, Ms. Patrice. You see, I'm off to Thailand to work a new deal for Mr. S for a movie contract, so I must be about my business. No rest for the weary…although I do have a special friend I may visit, if you know what I mean."

"Oooh you lucky man, another secret, well enjoy, you deserve it,"

"Thank you, Ms. Patrice. I will surely miss you though."

She grabbed him for a long embrace. "Blu, you are my best friend next to Mr. S, and there is nothing in the world that will ever make me forget you and your kindness to me. I feel very sure when I say I love you, and I always will."

Patsy saw tears in Blu's eyes as he whispered, "I love you too, Ms. Patrice." She watched him lumber off with his head down, leaving Patsy quite alone.

As she climbed into the waiting jeep, she wondered when she would see him again. She waved until he disappeared. She turned and saw acres of plush meadow and rows of flowers everywhere. She smelled a fragrance in the air that made her giddy. "This is so amazing," she said.

"Welcome to Paradise, Ms. Patrice. I know you will love it as we all do."

Patsy viewed the main estate. It was a lovely homestead with gardens like those in many period films she watched with her mother. Another building that looked like it could contain suites or apartments sat off to the right, and another one in the distance, further back, could be stables of some sort. Everywhere she looked were pink and blue skies, floribunda, birds chirping, and sounds of the sea carried on calming ocean breezes.

An older woman greeted her at the front door. She led Patsy into the main mansion to a hallway to meet the staff who welcomed her with polite nods. She immediately felt their warmth.

The older woman looked like she oversaw the group. In line were three men who gave her big smiles and bowed their heads. Two were dressed in chefs' caps and aprons and one looked like a butler dressed in a neat Nehru shirt and loose casual trousers. Patsy was surprised by the cutest curtsy that a tiny younger girl executed at the end of the line. She had beautiful jet-black hair and bright green eyes looking so lovely in a sarong of bright orange draped on her waif-like body. "My name is Amira, and I will always be here to help, mademoiselle," she spoke in a quaint yet undetectable accent.

Patsy shook the girl's tiny hand and asked her politely, "What is your country-of-origin Amira? What accent do I hear?"

Amira giggled, "Well, Ms. Patrice, it could be Irish, or it could be Asian. My mother was from County Cork, Ireland, and she brought me here as a young girl. My dad was from Bali. I have a bit of both of them in me, I'm sure." Her voice turned proud, "Though right now, my heart is truly here in Indonesia. I never want to leave."

Patsy perked up at the mention of Amira's Irish roots. "I am 100% Irish through and through," she announced. It was amazing to Patsy how quickly she and Amira connected. A shared kinship drew her to the girl immediately. "Whatever you are, you sure turned out beautiful."

Amira blushed as Patsy gave her a wink. Patsy was so happy she found an acquaintance to chat with casually. It would be delightful. This would fill the void of Blu being gone after so much time together. "Mr. S told us of your arrival, and I'm so pleased to be of help for anything you might need. There is a phone line that goes directly to the main house from your cottage. Don't hesitate to call anytime for anything."

"Thank you," Patsy said and politely smiled at the entire staff.

"Now please, Ms. Patrice, let me show you to your lovely abode. You will be very much pleased with the cottage, I'm sure. It is heavenly," Amira said with a twinkle in her eye.

As Patsy followed in anticipation, they walked a short way down the hill to a winding path along the pearly, white beach. In the distance, Patsy gazed upon the most wondrous little cottage she ever saw. It sat secluded on a higher plain like a singular jewel sparkling in the sun.

The dwelling had white shutters flapping in the breeze and there was a hammock on the wraparound porch. On the other side was a glider, with bright, fuchsia-colored cushions. Patsy took a quick ride on the glider laughing to herself all the while. Tucked in the corner near the entrance was a rolled yoga mat and several fancy parasols stuck inside an umbrella holder. A wreath of real flowers and island greenery in the shape of a heart adorned the front door.

Surrounding the sweet cottage, everywhere she looked were pink roses, jasmine, and moon orchids. Patsy stood in awe as she heard the wind chimes hanging at the edge of the porch roof that swayed to their own tingling tune. "I feel so blessed," she beamed.

Amira laughed, saying, "Just wait till we step inside— you are in for a treat."

The minute Patsy stepped foot in the sweet little cottage, she knew in her heart if there was one dream of sheer happiness, contentment, and beauty, it would be the moment she was feeling right now.

The first little room was a sitting area. It held a matching flowered sofa and an easy chair. Patsy sat on each one—they were luxurious looking and comfy too. Against one wall, she saw bookshelves filled with what looked like first edition books and heavy leather-bound classics like *War and Peace, Huckleberry Finn*, and *Dr. Zhivago*.

To her surprise, hanging on a hook in the corner of the shelves was a pair of bright red tap shoes. A note was attached, *Here are your ruby slippers to dance on the hardwood floors at your new residence. Hope you find peace 'over the rainbow!* It was signed, *Love, Mr. S.*

"I'm astounded when I think that Mr. S did all this for me. It's like he read my mind and fulfilled my every desire."

"Miss Patrice, we couldn't wait to meet you. It's so wonderful to have you here. We have orders from Mr. S to make you as comfortable and happy as possible. Come, there's more to see," Amira led her to the kitchen, where copper fixtures hung everywhere and an impressive antique stove with a copper tea kettle proudly resting there. Patsy looked to see at least twenty-five assorted flavors of tea nestled on the shelf below.

Finally Patsy cried out, "Oh my Lord, Mr. S knows I love tea. I'm so overwhelmed." She looked up to see the prettiest little bird sitting outside on the windowsill. "Hello there," She said aloud to the chirping bird, "I'm going to call you Henry, OK?"

Amira said, "Ahhh, the Bird of Paradise is welcoming you to your new home."

"I know exactly who he is too."

They continued through a narrow hallway where there was a small, but elegant bath with a large round tub that took up much of the space. It was lovely and feminine, and she couldn't wait to soak in hot, bubbly water and cuddle up in the plush terry robe she saw hanging on the back of the door. She would then sip a cup of ginger-mint tea, of course.

The bedroom was at the end of the cottage hall. She ran and fell on the canopied bed as she laughed in absolute delight.

"There's even more, Miss Patrice. Mr. S said you were quite fond of music and very musically inclined. Come, let me show you my favorite room."

Patsy caught her breath, "I cannot believe there is even more."

Amira tiptoed to a tiny room that was adjoining the back of the bedroom. Patsy opened the door and her eyes went immediately to the center, which hosted a full set of drums and a small piano keyboard. Leaning in the corner against the back wall was a Fender guitar.

"Wow!" Patsy gasped, as she played her favorite chords on the Fender. She only knew a few by heart. In the other corner

263

was an old RCA Victrola, and next to it was a hook-up for a microphone and tape recorder. Along the back wall were shelves with at least fifty albums. They included greats like Billie Holiday and Benny Goodman on 78 records. A giant g-cleft sign was painted on the wall for just the right touch.

Patsy was familiar with the music in the albums, as her mom often played these same artists. Positioned out in front of the many records was an album of song and dance music from Fred Astaire and Ginger Rogers from the movie *Top Hat*.

Patsy was sure Mr. S did this for her and Henry. Patsy kissed the photo on the album and began to dance as she grabbed Amira and led her in a fun waltz, singing out, *"Heaven...I'm in heaven, and my heart beats so that I can hardly speak...."* Amira laughed and went right along with Patsy as they danced and swayed together.

Patsy also noticed a triangle on the other side of a mantle hanging on a hook, just like Patsy played in grade school. It was perfection. She wondered, did God's favorite angel Henry order all this just for her? Then quickly she remembered it was her Earth Angel, Mr. S.

Amira left, allowing Patsy to breathe in all the incredible beauty. She returned later after Patsy soaked in a soothing bath. She was asleep on the porch glider in her plush terry robe when Amira awoke her with a scrumptious-looking tray of goodies. "Here we have delicious island desserts, Durian cream crepes, bolu kukus, and Bika Ambon."

"It is much too pretty to eat, but I will try—oh yes—I will try. But Amira, please stay and share the food and tea with me as thanks for everything you did for me today. And, I have one more request." Amira looked curiously at Patsy, as Patsy stated quite emphatically, "Please do not call me 'Ms. Patrice.' I would like you to call me Patsy. I will remain Ms. Patrice to all the others, but I consider you a friend now."

"I would be honored Ms. Patrice — I mean Patsy."

As the days passed, Patsy felt peace like she hadn't known before. It permeated her being and renewed itself with each breath she took. Patsy Mahoney from Yonkers was in Indonesia, or was she really in Paradise? Right then, at that moment, she couldn't tell which. She only knew serenity was hers as she tried on her red tap shoes and shouted out to the Bird of Paradise perched on her windowpane, "Look Henry, an exact fit!" Patsy laughed as she remembered Henry stuffing his feet into her mom's tap shoes. She was sure he was laughing too.

Every morning, a covered pitcher of juice appeared on her tiny porch table. It was a different one every day and, along with the colorful juice was a note that explained its nutrients, origin, and healing powers.

Methodically, she rang the triangle three times and then zoned into a meditation state as she chanted OOHMM and set her intention for the day. Then came her yoga routine for thirty minutes on the straw mat she found rolled up in the umbrella stand on the porch. She liked the feel of the course straw next to her skin much better than the rubberized, cushy mats she was used to at home.

Her yoga routine included multiple sun salutations and all three warrior poses. There were also some balance poses, and her favorite—the dancer's pose, which she proudly held for a full sixty seconds. She ended with a shoulder stand and even a five-minute savasana, during which Patsy laid flat on her back with her heels spread as wide as the yoga mat and arms at the sides of her body, palms facing up. She said her "Namaste" to no one there, but to everyone in general. She felt like the world was hers.

Next would always be a call from the main house asking her what she preferred for breakfast. Sometimes it was just Croissant Bali, and sometimes it was a full breakfast like Bubur Ayam—rice topped with shredded chicken, eggs, soybeans, and shrimp crackers. There were so many choices. She was exposing her tastebuds to this new healthy and delicious cuisine.

265

Amira visited with her as much as she could, but she was extremely busy in the main house, so she could never stay too long. One morning, Patsy asked her, "When Mr. S visits, who are usually his guests? Are they men? Women? Indonesians? Americans?"

Patsy noticed almost immediately Amira was uncomfortable with these questions. It looked to Patsy as though she was weighing her words carefully when she finally replied, "Mr. S has owned this island for many years. He also has an interest in an Indonesian export business, which he has local businesspeople handle for him. He also employs so many of us on his island, keeping up his property, even though he isn't here often."

Patsy realized Amira was avoiding her question. But she did learn that Mr. S was not only her savior, but these less fortunate people of Indonesia were also grateful to him for their employment. "Does he actually own this whole island?"

Again, Amira replied carefully, "Most of his resort properties and businesses are within a five-mile radius, but yes, he does own the whole island." She quickly finished, "That's all I really know, Patsy. I'm sure you know by now Mr. S is a very private man. Even when he visited last, he feigned off the spying eyes of anyone who may have traced his whereabouts. He likes to remain anonymous and doesn't let too many people in."

Patsy replied, "He is exactly that way back in the states. We are so lucky to know and love him, aren't we?"

"Yes we are Ms. Patrice. I mean, yes we are Patsy," Amira quickly corrected herself.

A few days later, Patsy walked along the beach for miles and spotted a few tiny huts and outside stands, but the beachfront itself was secluded, except for the roar of the ocean and sound of the seagulls overhead. She gave a silent prayer to Mr. S for making this island such a beautiful place for so many.

This walk became Patsy's daily routine. One late afternoon though, she continued further and what she heard startled her. Music played in the distance, and as she edged closer to the direction of the drumbeats over a tiny hill, she saw people dancing both outside and at the entrance of the hut-like structure. There was laughter and the sound of bongos, and it looked like the island folks were surely having fun. A huge sign hung over the roof that read in big red letters: *The Tiki*. Patsy was curious, but leery to go investigate further. Not yet she thought—but soon. Suddenly though, she felt like dancing.

She hurried back to the cottage to call Amira. If anyone knew about this place, it most certainly would be Amira. She dialed the direct line and spoke into the antique French phone, "Hello Amira, could you stop over, please? I have a question for you and would like to chat with you in person, if possible."

"I would be happy to stop by after my chores at the main house are done."

When Amira arrived, Patsy ran to meet her and blurted out excitedly, "Amira, I came upon this tiny bar about a mile from our stretch of beach called *The Tiki*, and it sure looked like people were having a great time there. The music was drawing me in." Feeling a little naughty, she continued, "I was wondering what you knew about it?"

Amira hesitated, took a deep breath, and when she spoke, it was in measured clips, "Yes, Patsy, I know of the place, but I do not frequent it. Been there for a burger once or twice, but that's all. I do not think it is the place for you right now, if you want my sage advice."

"Well, it made me feel like dancing again, and perhaps you and I could go there sometime just for a bite to eat and so I can feel out the musical vibes?"

"Oh no, I don't think that would be desirable just yet. Mr. S gave strict orders to keep you as calm and serene as possible. Further on in your stay, but not quite yet," Amira smiled but stated her words most emphatically.

Patsy reluctantly nodded, "I understand, and Mr. S knows best. I do need more time to decompress I suppose. It has only been a few days. Thanks for your input. We'll talk more about it later." Amira nodded as she hurriedly left the cottage, almost tripping as she ran out.

Strangely enough, that evening dinner was served by the older woman saying Amira was too busy to make the trip back so soon. The woman said she would be back to pick up the tray and turn down Patsy's bed.

Respectfully, Patsy said, "Thank you, but that won't be necessary, it can wait till morning. I can clean the dishes myself."

Once alone, she contemplated the mysterious scene that took place that day. She was sure Amira was shielding a secret or knew much more than she was saying. Patsy was determined to go back to *The Tiki* and find out for herself what kind of a place it was and what exactly went on there. Still in a dancing mood, she put on an album by the Baja Marimba band and began doing the Samba as she spied the Bird of Paradise on the kitchen sill. She sang loudly, "Dance with me Henry."

"Ok, mon ami," she was sure she heard him say back. She danced until her legs began to ache, she wasn't sure from the walk or the dancing. She was exhausted and climbed carefully into her porch hammock. It was indeed a strenuous day. She felt the cool breeze caress her skin as the hammock swayed back and forth in a motion that rocked her like a baby and sent her into a peaceful nap.

As she drifted off, she saw the sign for The Tiki, and inside The Tiki were many happy people urging her to enter. She felt the pull of the crowd motioning her to come in. She found herself walking through a large blue cloud and was instantly enveloped in a cool breeze. The cloud suddenly changed, and a sparkling sunlit warmth broke through as she passed the doorway and toward the tiny dance floor. She spied several people dressed in bright colors as they danced, sang, and laughed.

They were imploring her to join them so she moved closer. It was as if she was carried by the warmth toward the welcoming crowd. Off in the distance, she saw the most handsome man she ever laid eyes on. She gravitated in his direction, immediately taken by his beautiful demeanor. With the most natural inclination, she stepped toward him with a tender yearning that consumed her. The man spoke softly, saying, "Bonjour, Ms. Marie, I've been waiting for you...."

She woke hours later when she heard rain pelting the porch roof. Running inside, Patsy climbed into her comfortable bed, and as her head hit the pillow, she slept until the first-morning sun and the sound of Henry on her windowsill welcoming a brand new day.

She went outside to stretch her arms high into the bright blue sky, and spied the lovely pitcher of juice on her tiny table. Patsy smiled as she read the note—it was papaya and full of vitamin C, potassium, and more antioxidants than any other fruit. Patsy drank her juice, unrolled her yoga mat, sat cross-legged gently, touching her thumb and forefingers together as she set her intention for the day.

She felt so wonderful and stared at herself in the full-length mirror in her bedroom. She was amazed that her color was coming back after so many weeks of crying over Henry, along with the stress of her physical and emotional breakdown. It was almost magical how this island made her feel. She looked at her body totally nude. It was fit and trim, and the Oscar De La Renta bikini she slipped into made her smile at her reflection with a secret pride at her shapely figure. Feeling erotic, she immediately thought of the sensual times with Cristo in her feather bed, or even their paint-stained bodies on his artist table.

She quickly dismissed the thought of Cristo and decided to take a walk along the secluded beach. She wore a bikini of muted leopard tones and tied a dark gold silk sarong around her hips to walk on the wet sand close to the ocean.

Patsy glanced up several times at the tropical sky as the clouds moved along, gliding in and out, gesturing her to move on. In the distance, a faint echo of music blended in with the murmur of warm breezes and the ocean surf. *Come closer, come closer* it spoke to her in a spiritual beckoning. Her body seemed to glide weightlessly with no effort. She stopped to look around and for a minute thought this must be what heaven looks like. She felt a force pulling her towards the beat of a bongo drum as the pungent aromas of coffee, oranges, and a hint of pineapple invaded her senses.

The Tiki sat by itself back off the beach on a slight incline nestled under a group of palm trees. She inched up carefully and nervously peeked in. Suddenly, a short jolly gent appeared, taking her hand and guiding her in with the help of several others. It was as natural as breathing.

"Ahhh," he said, "we've been waiting for you. We heard from the Cloud Gods that a beautiful enigma would appear, and here you are." The jolly little man then whispered, "My name is Banyu. Come, come and dance with me please. We have been longing for you to dance for us."

Patsy laughed, "My name is Patrice Marie, and I would love to dance with you Banyu." She perused the room filled with wooden tiki statues on shelves everywhere. She instantly felt at home as she spotted the dance floor in the middle.

Laughter filled the room as Patsy formally took Banyu's hand even though she was a head taller than him. The crowd applauded, and Patsy felt the pure pleasure of dancing once again. Her body moved around the tiny floor just as naturally as breathing.

Even though it was still morning, the bongos played, and now a piano was blending in as all the people sang, "*Day-O...Day-O, Daylight come, and me wanna go home.*" Everyone was smiling and singing, and now they were clapping too. It was as if they expected her, and she was now one of them.

Finally, she told Banyu she needed to sit down. He led her to the little booth in the corner, bowed, and started back to the dance floor. She realized she was famished and turned to see if she could order some food, but before she could even motion for the waiter, coffee, eggs, and fresh papaya appeared before her. She devoured the food, not believing her voracious appetite. This island enhanced all her senses and magnified them a hundred times over.

Patsy decided it was time to return to her cottage. She waved goodbye to Banyu and threw him a kiss.

"Come back soon, Patrice," Banyu urged her.

"I sure will," Patsy shouted back.

Again, she felt this mystical aura taking over her being. It was exhilarating, but it also felt as if her whole body exuded a feeling of euphoria. The island had a hold on her, and the people there knew she was a dancer, and even knew she was hungry before she said or did anything. It was a captivating feeling that encompassed her mind and body. Whatever was happening, she embraced the enchantment with full abandon.

Patsy knew now she would visit *The Tiki* every day. In this brief time, a meaningful catharsis began to take shape. When she smiled, she really meant it. It wasn't her Broadway forced smile. It was what Patsy called her *soul-filled* smile. She was coming back to herself after being lost for so long in the tensions that occupied her thoughts day and night. Her feelings reminded her of more innocent times when her endless dream state fueled excitement and anticipation.

As the days passed, she began writing, dancing, and singing again. Only now, it was because she wanted to do these creative things, not because someone else wanted her to enact them. Every afternoon, Patsy walked on her personal journey to *The Tiki*. It was Patsy's new, secret obsession.

One afternoon, as Patsy was leaving *The Tiki*, she looked out to the sparkling sand. She saw the most beautiful man emerge carrying several heavy cartons. His muscles glistened with beads of sweat. His beautiful face and tanned body left her dizzy. There he was, before her, this perfect man.

She shook herself, wondering if it was a vision. However, the exact same man who she dreamed about was now standing before her, and he was flesh and real. Could this be true? *It's the island,* she said to herself, *I am a part of it now, and I belong to its enigma.* She thought of her feelings when she fell in love with New York City. This was the same kind of intensity, but unlike the city, the island enfolded her and loved her back.

CHAPTER 35
Florencio

Patsy arrived at *The Tiki* in the early afternoon most days and stayed until late afternoon, but she didn't see the mysterious stranger who appeared in her dreamscape. She loved being there. There was always something going on: shuffleboard, card games, dancing and singing, or just enjoying life. The place had regulars on staff, but the clientele frequently changed as the patrons had different working hours.

Every afternoon, as soon as Patsy set foot in the place, several people approached her. The usual greetings were, "Gracious Good Morning, Ms. Marie," or "Here she is, our lovely Patrice Marie" or "Save a cha-cha for me, Ms. Marie!" And, the proprietor Banju always rushed to kiss her hand and do her bidding.

Patsy basked in the glow of the beautiful people and felt such warmth emanate from them. This place became her sanctuary, but she couldn't deny the real reason she came daily now —to see a particular man. She could not stop thinking of him. He crowded her thoughts and stirred her desires to such a point, it became an obsession.

One lucky day while sitting at her usual table, she looked up to see a vision. It was the Adonis, the one from her dream. He emerged as if by some mystical pull. Just as she pictured him, he appeared before her. "Bonjour," she whispered without thinking. The word just came out of nowhere.

He turned and so naturally said to her with a beautiful smile, "Ah, Bonjour, you must be the famous Ms. Marie I have heard about. So honored to meet you." He extended his hand. She felt a lightning bolt of stimulating energy at his touch that made her entire body quiver. "Let me bring you a coffee. It's café au lait that you prefer, am I correct?"

"How did you know?" Patsy stumbled over her words.
"Just a feeling."

On his return, Patsy was less nervous. "Please, won't you come and sit with me for a little while so we can talk? I would like to know you," she said, shocked that these brazen words were coming out of her mouth.

"Of course," he said, "My name is Florencio, but everyone calls me Ren. I am so incredibly pleased to talk with you, mon ami."

Patsy was elated as she thought of Henry and how he always referred to her as *mon ami* and thought he sent this beautiful man to her. "You called me mon ami. What made you say that?"

"I often speak French you see, for it is one of my favorite languages."

"I love that you said that," Patsy murmured, "Merci beaucoup. What other languages do you speak?"

Ren looked down timidly and began, "I speak fluent Spanish, Portuguese, French, German, and as you can see, I struggle just a little bit with English."

"I'm impressed. Please tell me more," Patsy urged him on.

"I just came back from a semester abroad at the University of Paris, Sorbonne. I am about to finish my studies at Gadjah Mada University, but I love this island. I missed it so much that I wanted to delay my studies for a while and come back to my roots."

"You see," he said shyly, "I am grateful for my life. I am one of the fortunate ones on this island. My father runs a highly successful export business. I have received the best of everything in life. My job here is only for my own pleasure. Plus, I love helping others who may not be as fortunate as I have been."

She observed him intently, noticing he was soft-spoken but confident. He was so polite, yet she observed distinct intellectual qualities for someone so young. She wondered how old he was, but she didn't care right then—he was so damn beautiful.

Florencio had short jet-black hair, beautiful hazel eyes, full lips, and his skin had an olive tint. He wore dark jeans which hung slightly below his waistline and a loose white button-down short-sleeve shirt, with a few buttons open at the top and one button open at the bottom. She caught only a glimpse of his well-defined abs and chest. From the few glances of his body, Patsy could tell he was strong and muscular. But, she knew his muscles didn't come from working out at the gym like American men. They were natural muscles from arduous work and active life in Indonesia. Also, a soft fragrance arose from his being like a mixture of gardenia, patchouli, and pineapple. It drove her wild when she inhaled his essence.

Their easy conversation was as natural as breathing, and Patsy hoped he sensed it too. She leaned in closer to him, feeling the intimacy between them. She touched his arm with her fingertips as electric chills swept over her. "Tell me more about your father," Patsy inquired.

"Well, my father is Indonesian. He is from a family that legend says goes back generations consisting of Indian gods. I, of course, don't really believe that."

"Oh my, what sacred gods are these?" She thought he indeed looked like a god so handsome and regal in every way. At that point, Patsy pictured him as an Indian god, and she is feeding him grapes and dancing for him. The image made her smile.

"They say God Vishnu, preserver and protector. My mother says she knew that and cast a spell on my father on their first meeting. It's quite the story, actually. My father travels a lot. One day I will join him in his export business. But right now, I am content and love my life working at *The Tiki*."

"Do you have any siblings?"

"I am an only child."

275

"Tell me about your mother, where is she? Does she live on the island too?" Patsy continued, feeling wonderfully comfortable now.

Ren hesitated, "We'll save that for another time if you please, Ms. Marie. It's back to work now. These cartons will not move themselves."

A little disappointed, Patsy bid him farewell, "*Au Revoir,* Ren, I hope we can continue our conversation soon."

"Ah...that would be *tres bien,* Ms. Marie. I bid you *Adieu* till then."

She watched his backside as he walked away and spotted an expensive-looking Harley Davidson motorcycle parked outside. She thought it must be Ren's and instantly imagined herself on the back with her legs apart and close to his hips, all while hugging him as they sped along the tiny narrow streets. They would end up in his bed or her bed, or even naked on the beach—she didn't care where. She only cared about when. She shouldn't, but she just had to. She wanted to make the dream of him real. It was a force beyond her power, pulling her, and just like the island, it simply would not let her go.

Patsy floated back to her cottage like she was on a cloud. She pictured this elegant man and conjured up his image as she practically danced along the sand. By the time she reached her island home, it was almost dusk. She sang a Sade song she heard earlier that day, *"You give me the sweetest taboo...."* She was ready to plunge, head over heels into the sweetest forbidden fruit.

As Patsy continued her daily visits to *The Tiki,* she was keenly aware and even encouraged by the peace she found with the locals, and anxious to continue her budding friendship with Ren. Unfortunately, for the next few days, she didn't see him at all. She was disappointed and growing impatient to be with him again. One afternoon on her way there, she spotted the Harley and was overjoyed, but then so quickly he emerged from the back and left before she could get there.

That afternoon, Patsy walked slowly back along the stretch of beach. She had his image on her mind and thought how exquisite it would be to have him, or for him to have her. Arriving home, Patsy decided to celebrate by herself with a glass of champagne, but one led to another, then another, and another. She scolded herself for drinking too much too fast, but her mind quickly drifted back to the tall, tan body of the young man called Ren.

There were rumblings of thunder she could hardly hear, but could feel the disturbance. As the sun slowly disappeared behind the deep blue clouds, she fell onto her hammock for a muddled, half-drunken sleep.

She walked down a long corridor into the dreary, dark bar and ordered a scotch and soda. She drank the first one in a few gulps. "Run me a tab," she told the bartender. She robotically consumed drink after drink. She sat on the barstool, but now her legs felt numb, and her vision was foggy.

Three guys, probably in their twenties she surmised, approached her. By the few words she caught and their empty-headed laughs, it seemed as though they were waging bets on who would get to take her home, but she quickly turned her back to them and looked the other way. She wanted to feel the numbness permeate her whole body to get rid of this deep sadness that consumed her. She didn't want to talk to anyone.

The bartender came over and asked her politely, "Miss, how about I call you a taxi so you can go home and get some rest."

She raised her voice and blurted out, "No, just pour me another scotch and mind your own business." The bartender shook his head and walked to the other side of the bar.

She needed to use the restroom, but didn't want to walk past the twenty-somethings who were still eyeing her. She managed to stagger to the small ladies' room and was disgusted by the filthy wads of toilet paper strewn on the cracked tile floor. She laughed when she saw the pathetic, dead daisy in a tiny vase on the rusty sink.

She wanted to get out of the dilapidated bar, but her need for a drink was more consuming than her need to flee. She went back to her stool, but the bartender denied her. "Sorry, Miss, I cannot serve you any more drinks, but my offer is still good to call you a cab."

From across the room, a man with a bottle of scotch in his hand said, "Over here, Honey, I got what you want right over here." Through blurry vision, she started over across the room and tried to focus her eyes to see the man's face.

The man crept slowly towards her with an unsteady gate. She could smell his odor of cigarettes and scotch which disgusted her, but she knew he held what she needed in the bottle he was gripping. His ghoulish face was unshaven and beads of sweat showed under his greasy black hair. He was ugly to her, and for a minute she thought of turning away, but he beckoned to her, "C'mon, girlie, you're almost here, c'mon little girlie," he said, waving the bottle. He had a nasty smile that seemed filled with disdain as he finally spoke with slurred speech, laughing like a hyena. He took a bow and announced proudly, "Allow me to introduce me-self, me name is Roney...." Through the nightmare, she screamed in horror, but no sound came out.

The nightmare jolted her back to reality, and she was so grateful when she woke from the morbid dream. Her heart was beating so hard, and she was tightly clutching the champagne bottle. She whispered her gratitude to the heavens that it was just a dream. She crawled into bed, feeling embarrassed, even though she was entirely alone.

She longed to see Ren again and the wholesomeness she felt with him. He was just what she needed now to erase the ugliness from her past.

278

The next day welcomed a gorgeous morning and Patsy arrived much earlier than her regular time at *The Tiki*. She longed to see Ren and was so excited when she spotted him loading cases of water in what looked like an assembly line of the patrons. Men were passing cases and stacking them down a hatch that led to what looked like a tiny room under the floor.

Before Ren approached, Patsy heard Banju frantically yell out to her, "Ms. Patrice, you should not have come today. We are expecting the blackness. Blackness is coming."

Patsy laughed as she saw the sky was perfectly pink and blue. A vibrating sound then swept over the little bar. In less than three minutes, a blackness spread over the eastern sky, then just as quickly it disappeared. It was quite entrancing to Patsy as one side of the sky was pink and blue, and the other was pitch black. It was like the island was split in two. Patsy saw the regulars scurrying all over. Banyu told Ren to secure everything quickly, as the storm was moving in fast. The rumbling sound grew louder, and the wind whipped several chairs outside in a circle where the men nearly had to catch them twirling in mid-air.

Banju yelled out, "Ms. Patrice, you must hurry home before time runs out. The tempest is wicked."

Banju ordered Ren to go with Patsy to her home as they all prepared to go underground to a safe place below. "Ren will protect you. He knows what to do. Our safety hatch is no place for a beautiful woman like you. It smells of bananas and stale beer." Banju laughed, but Patsy understood the concern in his voice.

"It would be my pleasure to escort you home, Ms. Marie, Ren said to Patsy, then leaned in to whisper, "I'll take excellent care of you, I promise." He crossed his heart.

Patsy melted at the sensuality in his voice, and even though the sun was still shining bright in half the sky, she happily accepted his offer. As they walked quickly along, a vast

279

black cloud followed close overhead, pressing them to move faster and faster. Ren now grabbed her hand, and they began a soft jog down the sand as the wind picked up and the blackness came closer and closer. Patsy didn't have time to think, so instead she followed him like an obedient child.

Patsy looked over at him. His body was that of a Greek God with well defined, protruding muscles and large, shapely calves. They sprinted as the wind picked up. Patsy's sarong blew open. They ran in perfect unison, like a beautiful ballet performance. For a split second, Patsy thought of Henry and how they always moved in seamless timing when they danced. She never thought she would feel that way again—that is, until now with Ren.

CHAPTER 36
Tempest

Suddenly, the beautiful ballet was interrupted with a crash like no other Patsy ever heard as everything around her turned dark. A streak of lightning lit the sky, and then BOOM, BOOM, BANG—everything turned pitch black.

Patsy screamed. Ren picked her up and carried her a quarter mile down the beach. She held on tight, her arms around his neck, her legs wrapped around his waist, and her head buried in his shoulder. "God, help us!" Patsy cried out, holding tightly on to Ren.

" I will protect you, Ms. Marie," Ren comforted her.

A massive zagged bolt of lightning lit up the sky, as a clash of turbulent thunder struck again. Patsy screamed aloud, and Ren lost his footing and fell directly on top of her. He did a one-armed push-up at the last second to avoid crushing her fragile body with his. "I'm sorry, Ms. Marie, are you alright?"

Lying now in the sand, Patsy said, "You barely touched me." Then she said as they lay face to face on the beach, his gorgeous body over hers, "Please, Ren, please do touch me— now." She arched her body up to his pulling him down to her with all her might.

Ren kissed her as lightning burst through the sky in crashing bolts, causing the beach to reverberate beneath them. It was as if the pulsating island could sense their passion. Not caring if the lightning strike that followed would hit them, each booming blast made them long for each other even more. Fiery streaks lit up their faces but only for a split second, and then they once again plunged into pitch darkness. Patsy felt wild exhilaration as the deafening storm surge rippled from his hands through to every cell of her body.

A final thunder burst brought rain cascading all around, pelting them in coolness, so they only felt the heat that lingered on their hungry lips. The torrent of the gushing rain made them sink deeper into their passion. Patsy held on tightly to Ren as they lay drenched in the wet deluge.

Ren was suddenly embarrassed by his brash action. "I'm so sorry, Ms. Marie, I could not help myself, you are so beautiful to me…," his voice began to crack.

"Please just kiss me. I've been craving you since I laid eyes on you, don't you know that?"

"*Je te veux tellement, ma magnifique*, Ms. Marie."

Patsy pulled him back to her, enjoying the French words whispered in her ear, and they stayed there for a full minute devouring each other with their mouths and tongues as the torrent of teaming rain pounded down on them without mercy. Finally, the thunder subsided, but their yearning could not wait. They sprinted toward the cottage soaking wet, but now laughing the rest of the way. Their haste was fed with their uncontrollable need to make love to each other.

Once they were safe inside the cottage, Patsy pulled off Ren's sleeveless shirt and marveled at his muscular, clean, smooth chest. His bronze skin glowed, showing off his bulging pectoral and bicep muscles. His tropical scent was intoxicating.

They kissed for a while slipping and sliding on each other's wet skin as Ren carefully unhooked her bathing suit top while kissing her neck, throat, and breasts. Tenderly at first, then moaning and devouring uncontrollably.

Patsy was about to explode, longing to be caressed further. She realized as sexy as he was, he was young and not very experienced. She rubbed his hardness through his cutoff jeans, and he hastily unzipped his pants.

She stroked her nails up and down his back. Finally, she couldn't wait any longer and placed his hand down her rain-drenched bathing suit bottoms. He stroked her softly at first, but Patsy didn't waste another second as she tore the bottoms off herself, falling back onto her soft bed.

Patsy smiled as Ren eagerly ripped off his cutoff jeans. Looking at his naked body, she wondered how could any man be so gorgeous? His bare body glistened with tiny droplets of rain still clinging to it. She felt as if she was witness to absolute perfection. She stared. She couldn't help it. "Is everything all right?" Ren asked.

"Spectacular!" she gleefully replied.

Patsy pulled him onto the bed, spread her legs, and guided him into her. He moved rhythmically inside of her, along with the low boom of the thunder still vibrating outside as they made love. It seemed like fifteen minutes lasted for an eternity. Patsy gave in to her orgasm, moaning with delight. With Ren's final thrust deep into her, he whispered, "My beautiful Ms. Marie." They collapsed in breathless silence.

"What just happened?" Patsy finally spoke first.

"The most wonderful thing in the world, Ms. Marie."

Patsy agreed, "Yes, it was wonderful, and Ren, but you can drop the Ms. now, just Marie will do."

"Thank you so much," replied Ren, "Marie just happens to be my favorite name in the entire world."

"Oh, really," Patsy laughed, "now, isn't that a coincidence."

A sudden brrr-ring on the French phone shocked them from their ecstasy. She wasn't used to the phone's sound since she always was the one who did the calling. But, because of the weather, she knew she had to answer it.

The call was from Amira checking on Patsy's safety and offering to send others to fetch her to come to the main house for dinner. Patsy said she was fine and there was plenty of food, so not to bother. She assured them all was well.

Patsy was very adamant when she turned back to Ren, "We must keep this to ourselves for now. I am here for a respite and not to have an affair."

"It is our secret, and I will do whatever you want. I must go now and let everyone know you are safely home. And I promise what is ours will remain between us. But Marie, I will dream of you tonight."

"Oooh, and I cannot wait to dream of you, mon ami!"

Patsy watched as Ren moved left to return to *The Tiki*, "I must help them deal with the damages, but my mind will be only on you."

Patsy danced around the small cottage, singing, and twirling and settling into her little music room to compose a love song that she was holding in her heart for Ren. Words and melody instantly poured out of her, and it was just the right time to stir up all those creative juices. It was as if she was young again and living through her imagination in a childlike, furtive fantasy. Like the time she first fell for Henry. It felt just like Ren was Henry, but with the bonus of sexual fulfillment. She didn't know why, but knew the first blush of youth and passion mixed with uncontrollable desire had something to do with it.

She found a blank musical book of chart paper for notes and a lined pad for words. She was so grateful now Richie helped her learn how to play some guitar chords, and she took classes with Mandi at NYU on music composition. It only lasted until the Calgon commercial came through, but now there was plenty of time to learn more.

She penned a beautiful song for Ren, pouring out her feelings in sensual lyrics and strumming out a tune to match the guitar. She was impressed with herself as she tried all the chords she knew. It was a delightful private time. She went back to it, often delighting in the progress. She longed for Ren physically, but knew she had to be discreet—it just felt wrong to share what they felt with anyone else. Also, she thought of Mr. S and his generosity and realized she couldn't do anything to disrespect him when he sent her to the beautiful island to refresh and recover. Her relationship with Ren, Patsy decided, would have to be secret and indulged in with the utmost caution.

On her next visit to *The Tiki*, Patsy asked Banju if someone could replace some shingles that flew off her roof in the storm.

"Oh, I have just the man who can help you tomorrow, Ms. Patrice, or I could send Ren today if you want."

Patsy very craftily said, "Thank you, Banju, anytime is good."

Ren interrupted, "I'm off in a few hours. I would be happy to help."

"Great," Patsy replied, "I'll see you later."

Patsy ran home, relishing this crafty plan. She balanced herself on her glider and using all of her might she tore four shingles off her porch roof to make it look more authentic. She soaked in her bubble-filled round tub and waited for her new repairman to drop by.

Patsy then changed into something quite easy to get out of and called the main house to cancel dinner, explaining she had eaten earlier. Then she got out her guitar and practiced the song she wrote just for Ren to make the time pass more quickly, which seemed so long, even though it was only an hour. She would not play it for him though until it was finished.

Ren arrived, carrying a toolbox, and looking so sexy as Patsy opened the cottage door. "Now, this is what I call a hot handyman."

Ren bowed, "At your service Ma'am, what can I do for you today?"

Patsy laughed as she pulled him inside by his shirt, saying, "You can drop the toolbox and get handy all over my body."

"Yes, Ma'am, it will be my pleasure." Patsy squealed with delight as Ren threw her gently on the bed and kissed her all over, and for her, the world went away. It was just the two of them feeling healthy and beautiful and wanting nothing except to please each other.

Now that they were lovers, Patsy devised times and places to meet and make love. It was exciting and clandestine. Ren raced her around on his Harley scanning the island he knew like the back of his hand. They had various places for their excursions, including a secluded rocky terrain, an empty hidden stretch of beach, and the end of an isolated street. One secluded destination was a cave on the side of a hill where they would arrive separately, meeting up in each other's arms.

On one cloudy and balmy afternoon, Patsy and Ren sat huddled in their cave. As they joined together in an embrace, Patsy revealed her secret song to him. She sang and played the guitar, and to her, it was everything she was living for at that time. The music, love, and connection were so strong that a part of her never wanted to leave this island, and it seemed to her that Ren felt the same way.

Each time they visited their cave, Patsy sang to Ren and played her guitar. Later Ren joined the song, and they sang to each other in harmony. It was one of the most romantic times of her life.

287

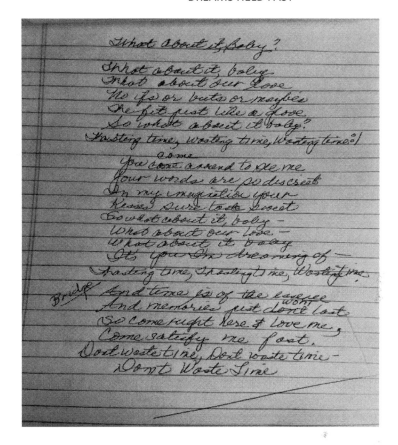

Patsy sang to him all the love songs she ever memorized from her younger days and Broadway shows. They walked a secluded beach on the island's far side, singing, laughing, and loving. Ren, in turn, sang to her in French and Spanish, and sometimes Italian. They let their guard down and revealed their true selves.

They indulged themselves for days on end, doing nothing except eating, making love, and falling asleep in each other's arms. They were naked a good deal of the time and loved each other's bodies, which were tan, smooth, and beautiful.

288

This affair mostly took place at Patsy's cottage. Occasionally, Ren would return to *The Tiki* to help. There was so much storm damage from the monsoon, it was rarely open, so their days were mostly free to bask in the enchantment of their passion.

One afternoon, Patsy asked, "Ren, may I see your home? I want to see how you live."

Patsy saw Ren turn very somber as he spoke, "I feel embarrassed as to how you will perceive it. My mother decorated it, and I was too afraid to criticize her, so I let her have her way. Marie, it is hideous." He paused, then hesitantly said, "Also, I have something to tell you about my mother. It's very painful for me to talk about, but I feel you must know from me and not another."

"Ren, nothing about you could ever make me stop caring for you, please tell me. I'm ready to know you and everything about you."

Patsy saw Ren put his head down and say in an extremely faint voice, "Marie, my mother believes she is a sorcerer and is rumored as being a witch. I was sent to the island by my father for my safety. It's a long story, but she loves me above all things, and I feel sorry for her. Marie, you could be in danger if she finds out about us."

Patsy laughed at the ridiculous story he was telling, thinking he was playing a joke on her, but she changed her tone when she saw Ren look heartbroken as he jumped to his feet and darted off.

CHAPTER 37
Batshit

Patsy was so distraught, she ran shouting, "Ren, please stop…I'm sorry, please stop!"

He didn't answer her.

She lost her footing and fell on the uneven rocks. Ren turned around when she yelled out, "Help me! I'm stuck. My foot is wedged in this crater."

Ren came back to rescue her, removing her sandal from the deep wedge and caressing her foot tenderly. Instinctively they embraced and kissed, and Patsy said softly, "I'm so sorry, please tell me what you want to about your mother. I didn't mean to hurt your feelings."

Ren replied with his head hanging down, "It is hard for me to talk about, and I hesitate to upset you with this, but you're right. I shouldn't have run off like I did. I feel it is time you know the truth."

Patsy spoke up, "Nothing you say will upset me. I want to know everything about you, no matter how disturbing it might be. Believe me, I can take it."

They sat on the rocks holding each other tightly. Patsy watched Ren as he spoke painstakingly of his mother, "My mother is an attractive beauty, especially when she was young. She always said that was a big reason my father married her. She was younger than he, but was also a woman of culture and great intellect. Along with that though was the other side of her that was vengeful and jealous, and consumed with the belief that she was descended from witches."

"Oh my!" Patsy exclaimed in disbelief.

"She did possess some unusual hot-tempered Portuguese ancestry that went back many generations to a coven of witches in sixteenth-century Portugal. She prayed to a great, great, great grandmother by the name of Cintia who she claimed sent her visions. She was always chanting, "Cintia, Cintia, come into my soul and direct me." Then she would spread her arms out wide to invite all the spirits of her deceased ancestors in to feel the glow of their powers wash throughout her being…or at least that is what she told me.

"Marie, she was totally insane when in the clutches of these so-called visions and spells. It was scary for me as a young child. She reiterated to me over and over stories of when she was a girl in Portugal. Her mother and grandmother told her exciting and fascinating stories of her ancestors that she loved to hear and thought I would also love. As a child, I was too afraid to object. She felt as though she had gifts of strong and powerful women, handed down to her from generations. She constantly said she would pass the spells onto me someday. She always made potions of herbs, leaves, and flower petals, and God knows if they were poisonous. She believed they gave her powers of casting demonic spells and healing.

"My mother told me proudly that people came from all over to see VoVo—grandmother Cintia and her ritualistic spells, and partake in her potent mixtures. She claimed she had bewitchments that could either seduce lovers or harm wretched husbands. Cintia's magical elixirs were known all throughout Spain and Portugal. However, her poor ancient ancestor succumbed to a brutal death when the authorities deemed her a purveyor of evil incantations and witchcraft. I think it was her stories of sleeping with all eight demon kings and bragging that they were much better sexually than any mortal men. That legend really did her in. These stories upset me as a young teen, but truthfully, Marie, they fascinated me also…."

Patsy leaned closer to Ren with her eyes wide with anticipation, "Tell me more, this is fascinating!"

Ren continued, "Before her great-great grandmother's demise however, her coveted recipes and potions were passed down through the generations, but only to special and selected females and only to be kept in the family. Rosalita was now the lucky one that held the spellbinding family secrets. I remember vividly my mother staring for many minutes into the stained black mirror mounted in her herb cellar, beckoning the spirit of Cintia, chanting, "Come from beyond, enter my body and soul to fill me with the power of your darkest strength."

"Then she would dance in circles and honestly believe the image of her ancient relative came through the mirror. She continued spinning and twirling until she dropped helpless and exhausted, believing the spirit's rush entered her body and soul. I would watch her and see the whole thing taking place before my eyes. I would see her body tremble. She really believed that her body was being taken over by this ritual. She did have a gift of preserving eternal youth and believe me, being very vain, Rosalita revered her ties to this sorcery that she adamantly believed kept her young, vibrant, and beautiful. She needed to be beautiful to herself and never allow old age to decay her body. She drank the sweet tea brew, flavoring it with just a touch of succulent tupelo honey she extracted from her beehives. She wanted me to taste it too, but I never would.

"The town's people dubbed her Crazy Mamacita Rosalita as they witnessed her throwing knives of all shapes and sizes against the trees that abundantly grew on our vast plantation. My father was quick to dispel these outrageous fables and brush them off. He constantly berated her for influencing me with what he referred to as 'macabre bunk.' However, as time went on, her tales of spells and potions and visions became increasingly insane and even at times, dangerous. Our home was filled with darkness and enveloped with many huge volumes about sorcery and witchcraft, and my mother was obsessed with her relatives whose photos I stared at constantly. Funny, they looked just like her, but dressed in dark robes and hooded cloaks of those primordial times. I could never bring school friends home, so for years she was my only friend."

"How sad," Patsy replied, listening intently.

Ren went on, "When I was a young boy, my father was away on business a great deal of the time. It was just the two of

292

us, and she was especially kind to me, and she taught me the ways of birds and animals on our vast acreage as well as magical potions from flowers and herbs. I pretended to be interested, and she had beautiful, intriguing stories, and I loved her if only because she was my mother and the only one around. She seemed totally devoted to me. I soon realized her attentions were obsessive.

"All her love was focused on me, and that may sound good, but it was a heavy burden to bear for a child. The kids at school began to make fun of her, and it hurt me to the core, but I yearned for friends my own age, and she just wouldn't allow it. I immersed myself in my studies and made them a priority."

"Finally, when my father saw the strain I was under, he sent me to expensive boarding schools abroad, insisting that it was the best thing for me. They fought over this. Even though a relief, I felt very sad to abandon her. The time off from school was spent here on the island, and although she would visit, it was evident that my father did have my best interest at heart when he sent me here. You see Marie, my mother was becoming consumed with me and wanted no one else in my life but her."

"Because my Papa was gone for extended periods, I do believe my mother was lonely, and her loneliness drove her to a lot of foolish things. When they were together, there were fights and accusations of others he was with. She accused him of cheating and said she saw visions of the other women in what she called '*fleshly hauntings.*' That's when the real trouble began."

Patsy listened intently, feeling sure this was an embellished story, but she was so intrigued and curious, she couldn't wait to hear more. "Tell me everything, Ren. I'm beginning to understand her hold on you."

As words poured out, Ren seemed to be unleashing pent-up emotion. Patsy held his hands in hers and urged him to continue, "My mother could wield a machete with the skill of a Samurai warrior and incidentally was quite skilled at throwing knives and daggers with expert precision. There was always a knife or two stuck in our trees on the estate."

"That's scary. Did she ever hurt anyone?" Patsy asked.

"There was one time that stays in my memory which occurred before I was to leave for school abroad. One night, as we all sat in our gazebo after dinner and one of the few times we were all together, in walked our faithful servant girl Maya. She was innocently bringing more wine for my father. My father looked up, smiled, and said, 'Thank you.' That's all he said, and like a blast of wind, a butcher knife flew through the air, whisking by my head on its path. It stuck in the gazebo wall, almost cutting off the poor girl's left cheek. Everyone screamed in horror—everyone except Rosalita. My mother shouted out to my father, 'Why are you making eyes at this young girl? She is only a servant, I'll rip her face off, and she will never be attractive to you again.' Then my mother laughed hysterically and said, 'Next time it will be in her heart, and I won't miss!'"

"How horrible!" Patsy exclaimed.

"The poor Indonesian girl fled, screaming all the way, and holding her bloody cheek. I tried to run after to help her, but she was gone. All I remember is my mother's hideous laughter as my father tried to subdue her. Then he lashed out at me and said I should never speak of this horrific incident again because it would ruin his reputation in the business world.

"Things calmed down for a while and to my knowledge, my father never looked at another woman after that. The poor servant girl ran away to Northern Thailand and we never heard from her again, although her story made its way back to our mainland, and the rumors flew. After that, everyone feared the wrath of Mamacita Rosalita. Word spread all over that Rosalita would stab or maim anyone who stood in the way of her marriage or who touched her precious and beloved son. I was dubbed a 'Mama's Boy' or 'Mama's Flower' or 'Witch Boy' after that and humiliated all over our town." Ren lowered his head, "I knew I could never return to live on the plantation or among the naysayers."

Patsy was mesmerized, "So, what happened after that?"

"My mother remained on the plantation, still living with my father, but he managed to be away for longer and longer periods. My mother grew worse and worse and was drinking her potions concocted from the homegrown herbs and now adding tiny doses of belladonna from her gardens. While I was here on the island, she did continue to visit me once a month as she blew onto the island on a hydrofoil to check up on me. One of the things I hate most is that she named me Florencio. I despise that I was named after the Portuguese flowery equivalent. So, I secretly changed my name to Ren."

Patsy laughed and gently teased him, "I promise I will never call you Flower Boy or even Florencio."

Ren replied more seriously, "Marie, please, let's keep our secret safe to us. I would die if anything bad happened to you."

They kissed tenderly, but Ren had even more to share. He confessed shyly, "While away at school and even here on the island, many women would gladly offer themselves to me in a sexual way. I must tell you, my heart has never felt the way it does with you, and I would not want you to be in any danger, so it's best we keep what we have private for both our sakes. I have always dreamed of a love that would be divine and meant just for me, and then like magic, you appeared and you have become so precious and special."

Patsy kissed Ren as they tenderly made love outside the cave on the smooth rocks and fell off to sleep in each other's arms. Once awake, Patsy begged Ren to please take her to his home so she could know him a little better. After much pleading, Ren finally gave in. "Don't forget that my mother decorated my place, not me."

Patsy smiled and assured him, "I promise. Your place can't be that bad."

Ren blurted out, "Oh, Marie, let me assure you, you are about to enter a dwelling that is something between the Addams family and Young Frankenstein, but don't say I didn't warn you."

CHAPTER 38
Daggers

Patsy hopped on the back of the big Harley and they rode for about ten minutes. When they reached the front of the house, Ren said jokingly, "Welcome to Casa Rosalita."

"It doesn't look bad at all," Patsy said as she approached the small stucco structure Ren called home.

From the outside, it was quite charming, except for the broom that hung on the door. It was made of bristles and twigs, willow wood and feathers, and had a circle in the middle with ribbons and flowers that looked black or nearly dead. There was a hex shape in the middle of the circle. It smelled a blend of sage and patchouli with a strange redolence of garlic that stung her nose when she inhaled. What she saw next though would stay with her for a long, long time. Ren was correct when he called it Casa Rosalita—the House of Gloom and Doom.

Inside it was a monstrosity of primarily brown, black, and purple colors. There were wooden beads used in the doorway as a room separator and papier-mâché blackbirds and bats hanging from the ceiling. It was ghastly to Patsy and clearly the design of a crazy person, however she didn't say a word, not wanting to upset Ren. After all, she did beg him to invite her. She turned to him and forced the happiest smile she could manage, but Ren shook his head and mumbled, "I told you, it's my mother who is responsible for the décor."

Patsy felt dreadful for Ren. A sense of evil hung in the air. She felt compelled to save Ren from this horror show he called home. "I have a plan," she announced, "I'm going to Feng Shui your home and give my beautiful man an equally beautiful space to live and breathe in."

"Why can't I say no to you, Marie?"

Patsy laughed as she walked around the structure, shouting out ideas and saying, "Oh no, this definitely has to go," as she threw a half-melted candle in the trash. "Let's find a new

297

home for this hideous ceramic cat. Say…the closet? Oh, my Lord, everything in here is so dark. Is that a real rat in the corner?"

"No," Ren laughed, "It is taxidermy."

A ring of the phone disturbed their playfulness. Patsy surmised Ren was talking to his mother when he said, "Please, Mama, let me know when you are coming next so I can take you out to dinner this time." He then spoke in Portuguese, and sounded as though he was almost pleading to make his mother understand.

Patsy walked outside to give him privacy and happily began her purge on the renovation. She took the crazy twigs and herbs off the front door.

"That was my mother," Ren explained as he joined her outside.

Patsy nodded. "I thought so. Is everything OK?"

Ren hesitated, "Yes…it's fine. She won't be coming soon. I talked her out of it. I told her the storm made it unsafe." He sighed in relief and laughed, "My mother said she felt through Cintia that I was in danger. I am in danger—of being madly in love with you."

"Well, that's spooky. Her calling the first time I'm in your house."

He raised his eyebrows, "I told you. She's psychic. But don't worry, I'll always protect you. No one will harm you."

Patsy felt a chill run down her spine. But quickly changed the subject.

"Good—then let's get started. First, we'll go to the hardware store and get some paint." They jumped on his Harley and zoomed away. They returned with sea-green paint for his front door.

Patsy continued to re-style Ren's home, pausing only to eat and occasionally make love, even with paint spatters on their tanned bodies. They were having so much fun together. "Hey Ren, you missed a spot on that brown wall," Patsy teased. Ren smiled and put a spot of beige paint on her nose as he grabbed her tight, stopping to steal kisses in between coats of paint.

Patsy painted the door and arranged a little frog water fountain near the entrance with a lovely plant off to the side. She placed a welcome mat at the door entrance and established just the right amount of good "chi."

Patsy spent three days re-arranging and de-cluttering the tiny home, running back and forth to her cottage to avoid any suspicion. She brought her own touches of shabby chic and minimalist fashion to the place. She moved furniture and took away all the rococo and garish artifacts, ridiculous knick-knacks, and disturbing artwork. She did notice some of the 'objects de art' were very expensive and made of rare materials, so she packed them away instead of throwing them out. Some things though just had to go.

She felt she should relieve him of the clutter in his life and even the bad juju his mother subjected him to. Patsy set out to make him as tranquil as she was.

As she walked through the renovated dwelling, Patsy asked, "Does your mother think she's a witch or does she just have a yen for the macabre?" He didn't answer. He looked worried now, so Patsy thought she said too much. She felt a little guilty being so bold and critical when she saw his sad face. "When do you think she will visit next?" Patsy tried a different question, which drew him back in.

"Transportation to the island has been suspended indefinitely because of the storms, so she would have to swim here," he laughed. "I think we are safe, for now." Ren sounded happy about that. "This place looks and smells so good. We should add a few of Rosalita's pieces so as not to wipe her style out completely. I do believe she means well, but I must say I'm thrilled with all your changes and hard work. Thank you so much."

"Thanks, but I'm not digging out the stuffed rat. That's a definite!"

"Deal. The rat stays hidden."

When Patsy's project was nearly complete, she wrapped her arms around Ren, "Thank you so much for letting me continue my quest and not stopping me. This must have been difficult for you."

"I am so in love with you. I couldn't bear to stop you. I must put my mother's taste and domineering ways out of my life anyway. It's time for a change," he squeezed her even tighter, "I actually love how the house smells and how very bright and airy it feels!"

Relaxing in Ren's bedroom, Patsy opened an end table drawer and dug beneath the surplus of condoms for an envelope which held a few photos of Ren. The first one was Ren as a child. He looked so adorable to her, but he was dressed in all black and wearing a cape. "You were such a sweet-looking boy, but why are you wearing a cape?"

"Why do you think? My mother said I should be dressed as royalty because I was a descendant of kings."

Patsy burst out laughing, "Well, at least you're handsome in your cape, that's for sure. May I have this photo, please?"

"Of course."

Patsy found another picture of Ren on his Harley and said, "Oh, I need to have this one too. You look hot."

"Be my guest. Those pictures have been there for years. That one was the day I got my bike. An extremely happy day for me, but hey, you owe me a photo of you some time too."

Patsy felt a spark of apprehension at the request, recalling the pictures the stalker took of her, but quickly pushed it out of her mind. She only wanted happiness to prevail right here and right now with Ren. "Deal."

As Patsy put the finishing touches in Ren's living room, she came upon a garnet encrusted frame face down in a desk drawer. She was stunned by the picture of a dark, sultry beauty. She was in awe, "Is this your mother? Oh my God, how old is she?"

"She is 38 in March or, at least, that's what she tells me."

Clumsily, Patsy dropped the frame to the floor and broke the glass. A garnet flew across the room and landed on a windowsill right next to a baby spider. Patsy was upset at the spider and the broken frame, but mostly that Rosalita was only nine years older, or so she said.

She stared at the picture. She was captivated by this beautiful woman in the photo but alarmed by the piercing stare. Patsy couldn't get those dark, glaring eyes from the photo out of her mind. Rosalita looked crazed.

She was distracted and hardly heard Ren speak, "Marie, didn't you hear me?"

"Yes…I'm sorry," as she attempted to retrieve the broken frame from the floor.

"Leave it. I'll deal with it later. Now it's important that I kiss you all over, my beautiful interior decorator." Patsy felt calmed by Ren's words. "We can now enjoy our new love nest." He popped the cork off a bottle of champagne and toasted their successful hard work, after which they made sweet love and slept blissfully.

The next morning, Ren had another bottle of champagne and strawberries waiting as Patsy emerged from the tiny bathroom into the now lovely "feng shui" bedroom. The whole house smelled of lemon and lavender. It was bright and beautiful.

Patsy noticed Ren didn't pick up the picture frame holding the photo of his mother that dropped on the floor the day before. Before she could bend down to retrieve it, Ren grabbed her up from behind and carried her swiftly back into the bedroom. "I cannot tell you how grateful I am for your redecorating, so please let me show you," he said sweetly.

Patsy tried to relax her body and let him lift her onto the bed where crisp, clean sheets and a soft plush coverlet awaited them, but the broken picture nagged at her, "Ren, let me get the broken glass and frame off the floor."

Ren ignored her with a whisper in her ear, "Later Baby, I have something else for you to think about now," as he held her hips in his strong hands, kissing her bare stomach.

Patsy giggled, "Carry on if you must." Ren kissed Patsy tenderly and they made love in the fragrant room that was now so cheery. Afterward, they fell asleep exhausted and wrapped in each other's arms.

Patsy woke from her peaceful sleep when she heard cursing in a foreign language, and a big crash which sounded like it was coming from outside the front door.

She heard a voice scream out, banging on the tiny window, "Let me in, let me in!" Startled and still naked, Patsy shook Ren awake with a nudge to his shoulder. Now they both heard a loud bang on the door and a screeching, high-pitched voice saying over and over, "Florencio, Florencio."

It wasn't a human voice, Patsy thought. It was more like the squeal of a creature. It sounded like foreign tongues mixed, but more like a fit of revolting torturous rage that ended in a moaning howl.

Patsy jumped up, "Ren, My God, who's that making all that racket? It's coming from the front of the house. I heard loud crashes, too!"

Again, the screeching voice cried out, "Florencio, Florencio. I'm here to save you. I'm here. Let me in!"

"Oh my God—it's my mother!" Ren yelled, and quickly put on his shorts while nearly dragging Patsy out of bed to shove her into the bathroom. He quickly tossed her clothes in with her. Very low and slow, he pleaded, "Do not move, stay quiet, and lock the door."

Patsy was shocked and a bit annoyed at this treatment, though she understood Ren's mother instilled fear in him. He was almost shaking as he bolted toward the front door.

Patsy tried to listen and was confused, but she did what Ren asked and waited in the bathroom. She knew it was not the right time to meet Ren's mother, but the hiding made her

302

uncomfortable. She called out to Ren, "What in God's name is going on? Why is she screaming? Don't leave me here alone, please."

Ren turned in the hall, "Quiet please, she's having one of her fits. Stay in the bathroom and keep the door locked."

Patsy remembered his story about his mother's erratic temper and jealousy during the incident with the servant girl when she fought with Ren's father.

Patsy heard Rosalita ranting and raging, half in Portuguese, half in English. Ren spoke back to her in a pleading voice as she went on and on, accusing him of being possessed by an "evil one."

Patsy was rattled as she listened to Rosalita ask over and over, "Where is she? Where is she? She took away my beautiful things. Why did you allow it? What has she done to you?" Patsy heard her jump up and down, and it sounded like she was pounding her fists against the walls.

Patsy unlocked the bathroom door and peeked out of the bedroom through a tiny crack. She noticed Rosalita spotted the broken frame and shattered glass with her picture inside. Patsy regretted not putting the picture away and cleaning up the mess. It sounded like Rosalita was having a seizure when she gazed at it.

Patsy put on her shorts and top, ready to confront Rosalita, even though she was scared. Gathering strength, she was ready to walk down the hallway when what sounded like a wounded animal shrieking out stopped her, "Cintia, Cintia, come from beyond and destroy her. Let me find her, Cintia." She threw some sort of oil from a decanter into the air and yelled out again, "Cintia find the She-Devil." Patsy peeping into the room could scarcely believe it as she watched Rosalita dancing in a wild circle, around and around, calling out for Cintia to find the She-Devil.

Patsy couldn't fathom why this crazy lunatic was calling her a She-Devil. Rosalita stopped dancing and fell to her knees

303

as she begged the "High Priestess Cintia" once more for help, "Oh, Grand High Enchantress, Cintia, she pierces my eyes with this brightness. Bring back the dark protection to my Florencio, take away her light. Help me, Cintia!" She moaned as she pushed herself up and began stomping her feet as she chanted in what sounded like gibberish.

Patsy could only see part of Ren's face, but he looked terrified as he tried to subdue his mother. He was shaking her now and saying, "Mother, why are you here? Why are you doing this? Please stop. Stop!"

Rosalita was too far gone. She yelled again, "You have betrayed me! Where is she? Where is she? I'll kill her. I'll kill her!"

Patsy felt panic consume her whole body and her legs went weak as she felt bitter bile rush to her throat. She heard Rosalita screaming like she was spouting off incantations.

Patsy prayed to God, "Please, dear Lord, please help me."

Based on what Ren shared with her about his mother, Patsy knew Rosalita must be unstable, however she never imagined it would be to this degree. Patsy tried not to make a sound, fearing for her life. She was trapped in the hallway, not knowing whether to rush back to the bathroom or try to escape out the tiny window. She strained to hear over the clamoring of the stomping and squealing coming from the living room.

Patsy heard Ren beseech his mother once again, "Mama, please stop." It looked as though he was trying to pet her and even comfort her. She wondered why Ren wasn't angrier with his mother. Could he be scared to death of this woman and what she would do next?

Patsy peeked as Rosalita continued throwing things against the walls now and breaking things right in front of Ren who couldn't seem to stop her. Patsy saw plates flying like saucers and paintings torn off the wall. She dominated him completely. Patsy could see Ren cowering. She gasped, but the sound stuck in her throat.

Patsy crept back to the bathroom for shelter, realizing she may be facing her demise. Again, she prayed a simple prayer, "God, if you are there, please help me." A warm sense of calm washed over her, and she felt her strength return.

Patsy decided this was enough. She moved toward the hallway once again. She was going out to help Ren. With renewed courage, Patsy called out to him, "Ren!" With that, she heard a guttural moan escape Rosalita's throat.

Rosalita began to scream again, "What did she say? Where is she? She even changed your name, Florencio. She changed your beautiful name!"

Patsy now saw that Ren was restraining his mother with his own body, but Rosalita pushed away and rushed brusquely past her son. She picked up her leather satchel and pulled out the longest dagger as she crept down the small hallway towards the bedroom like a cougar seeking out her prey.

Frantic now, Patsy saw Ren lunge down the hallway toward her, barricading his mother against a wall. He now had his mother trapped as he ordered Patsy in a low whisper, "Quick, run out the back kitchen door, I'll handle her."

Patsy ran swiftly past Rosalita, turning her head so as not to look at this insane woman. As Patsy passed, she heard a hissing sound—the kind a poisonous rattlesnake makes.

Unfortunately, Rosalita broke loose. She laughed and shouted out, "You cannot win, you cannot win Whore, Cintia is inside me now, and I will destroy you!" She sprung like a viper down the hallway.

Patsy tried to head out the back door, but just as swiftly as she moved, Rosalita threw the sharp pearl-handled stiletto towards her intended victim. Ren yelled, "Oh no, not the dagger, please!" and instinctively jumped in front of Patsy to shield her.

Rosalita yelled out like a wild banshee, "Die, Evil One, release my Florencio, Die, Bitch, Die!"

Ren leaped in front of Patsy, helping to defer the dagger as it sped through the air, but instead, it hit his arm and ricocheted to Patsy cutting her leg. Blood squirted out immediately from Ren's arm.

Patsy screamed, "Stop her, Ren, she has another one." Rosalita already reached for the second dagger in her leather scabbard.

By this time, Ren and Patsy were both bleeding. Ren was hurt more than Patsy. The chaos continued as Rosalita screamed and convulsed as a final wail escaped from her throat. Ren sprung up and tackled his mother before she could throw the second knife. Patsy was crying now, and frozen in panic. Ren signaled her by moving his head, "Just go home."

"No, I'm not leaving you."

Patsy started toward him, but Ren held up his hand commandingly, "Go now. Everything is ruined, go please." Patsy knew it wasn't a request.

Rosalita spat at Patsy as she walked by and murmured in a low, vicious voice, "Go, She-Devil, go." Patsy felt her temper explode as the hot saliva hit her shoulder. Rosalita wasn't done, "I win, Bitch. He is mine now. You can never possess him!"

Ren was so upset, he put his hand over his mother's mouth, "Enough!" He seemed utterly mortified at what just took place in his home and so humiliated that Patsy had to be involved. Patsy now felt helpless and defeated.

Ren looked down at his mother, cradling her in his arms. Even with all that just happened, Patsy couldn't believe that Ren still showed his mother sympathy. At that moment, she felt sympathy too, but it was for herself. She felt only hatred for Rosalita and resentment towards Ren for taking his mother's side and ordering Patsy to get out. Rosalita reached for Ren's face and said very satisfied, "You are safe with me, my son, safe with me." She twitched and passed out.

Ren sat next to his mother, still lying on the floor. He put his head in his hands and sobbed. Patsy wasn't sure if he was crying for his loss of her or the sheer humiliation of his evil mother. She thought of going to him but was repulsed at the same time. This crying man became a helpless little boy right before her eyes. She was spurned by his weakness, but at least he stepped in to save her. She realized she could have been killed.

Patsy saw Ren's chest heave uncontrollably as complete grief consumed him. Ren spoke again to Patsy very quietly, "Please Marie, please just go. I cannot speak. Please just go." Ren was choosing his mother over her. Grabbing her bag, she ran out the door and cried, stumbling to the beach. He didn't even say he was sorry.

She realized she was still bleeding, and it was running down to her ankle as she started toward the edge of the sand. She soaked her leg in the warm salt water. She still couldn't process what just happened. As she watched the tiny wave wash over the stinging gash, an immense sadness consumed her. A beautiful day was ruined, and it could have cost Patsy her life. She knew this tragedy could never be undone.

Limping home, she looked up to the azure sky and breathed in the beauty of this mystical island that so quickly enfolded her in romance and passion. She knew its radiance would soon be replaced by the horrific memory of a bloody stab wound, but for now, in a moment of clarity the island and the shoreline soothed her aching heart.

CHAPTER 39
Epiphany

Patsy went for a week without a word from Ren. She wasn't sure how she felt about anything. She only knew she was sad and feeling alone. It was a feeling she knew well and would have to get used to once again. She wished she could talk to Henry one last time, but that wasn't possible. She prayed for peace of mind as she walked alone for what seemed like miles up and down the beautiful stretches of the beach until complete exhaustion set in.

Patsy felt deep-rooted feelings of hurt and helplessness trying to creep back in, but she knew she had to fight those negative thoughts. She was stronger now and realized taking care of herself took precedence over everything else. Even though Ren was a most wondrous diversion, upon reflection, she realized their relationship could never have been long term. Nothing would ever be like Henry. Once again, she longed for him as she spread out a large beach towel and drifted off to a much-needed nap. A vivid dream took over her psyche as she fell from conscience to semi-conscience to oblivion.

Along a secluded beach, and although clouds were hovering, there was a touch of the lovely, pink sky that her eyes kept following. Her legs and feet were tired, but she trudged on. Her sarong blew open with the gentle breeze as she stepped closer to the shoreline for relief in the cool water.

Off in the distance, she saw an image of a short female wearing a bright red skirt with garish tassels hanging from it. Around the woman's waist was a leather belt that reminded her of the kind that a gunslinger would wear. However, it held a pearl-handled, stiletto knife instead of a gun. The woman whose back was to her was laughing. She pivoted, carefully avoiding the woman, but at the same time, she braced herself if an attack

became imminent. She continued walking. Her feet closer to the
wet sand on the ocean floor in case she needed to flee.

She began to follow the thin pink cloud and became
enamored with its glow as she watched it open. Steadfast now on
her journey, she advanced in that direction. She let its beautiful
formation overtake her as she tiptoed in the wet sand.

She was distracted and annoyed when she heard the
woman in the tasseled skirt scream. She looked over to see that a
flock of black crows was pecking at the woman's black hair.
Their squawking was mixed with her screams and cries for help.

She felt no desire to help the woman—no pity whatsoever.
The birds bit at the woman's head until she fell face down in the
white sand. The sand began to turn red under the woman's head
and her dark hair became entangled with the blackbirds who
continued loudly squawking and pecking away. The birds were
trapped, now tangled in the woman's thick hair.

She wished the noise would stop so she could get back to
her pretty "pink cloud journey." She regained focus as she
continued down the beach, enthralled by the beautiful billowing
shapes like powder puffs in the sky.

Off in the distance, a young man appeared. He was so
appealing, with a blond curl poking out of the front of a top hat.
He was wearing a tux and tap shoes. She thought it rather
comical since they were on a beach. Just then, the sweet man
reached out his hand and said, "Let's hit it, Ginger."

Without hesitation, she quickly turned, reached for his
hand, and began a familiar dance routine. It was so natural
since she did it a hundred times before and memorized it by
heart. Her sarong whipped around her as she did a pirouette
and several twirls with grace and elegance. Her feet now felt
lighter and she glided through the air with ease. She looked
down at the sand below and realized she was dancing on air.

The dapper gentleman then began singing a favorite Fred
Astaire tune. She joined him as they sang and twirled together,
"Gray skies are gonna clear up, put on a Happy Face...." Then,

309

they did a delightful two-step moving down the beach in unison under the glowing pink sky.
They then disappeared, hand in hand, running straight into the awaiting cloud. Their feet, high off the ground now, sent them up into the stratosphere as the man broke into a new tune,
"Heaven, I'm in heaven, and my heart beats so that I can hardly speak...."

When Patsy woke, the sun was half hidden, sinking into the horizon. She tried to process the dream and wished she could go back to sleep and continue the feeling of joy it brought her. But instead, reality came rushing in as she remembered the tragic scene at Ren's house, her mind fuzzy with fright recalling the details of the ordeal. Ren saved her life, and was such a sweet boy, but Patsy realized his sweetness also showed her his complete immaturity and decision to send her away and stay with his deranged mother. She knew that was his choice to make. She recalled what he said about the others calling him "Witch Boy" and realized sadly he would always be under his mother's spell.

Still, she was grateful to God. The ordeal could have been so tragic, but she was saved, and for that alone she was thankful. Even so, there were many questions she asked herself—most importantly, "Who am I?"

Her identity was enmeshed in the dreams she kept for herself and brought to every aspect of her life. She needed and depended on them for sustenance. But who was she really, the girl who tried to make fantasies come true or the girl who ran to the safety of them and away from reality?

The week went by, and some sort of sanity resumed. Patsy returned to the routine that gave her happiness when she first arrived on the island: sleep, yoga, fresh fruit, healing teas, and long walks on the beach. The only thing she didn't do was return to *The Tiki*. Instead, she forced herself to let her mind go blank as she meditated and prayed for peace each day. The island was magical, but it may have been just a dream of what she wanted it to be. The beauty of this place enchanted her whole being, and the thought of New York caused tension and a dichotomy. She would like to return home, but did she really want the harshness of the city? She would like to stay enveloped in the enchantment of the island…but could she?

When Patsy was a little more lucid and out of the daze that shrouded her, she found beautiful stationery she brought with her that her mother gave her as a gift when she left to live in New York. She was grateful to have it now as she planned her exit from the island.

She wrote one letter every hour. The first to her mother, the second to Mr. S, then one to Cristo, to Ren, and the last to Henry. Each letter was filled with love and gratitude, but she poured her heart out to her mother. She felt so much appreciation for the one person who never let her down and was always on her side.

> *Dear Mom,*
> *I cannot tell you how much you*
> *mean to me. You are so important in*
> *my life, and I feel I don't tell you*
> *enough how much I love you. Your*
> *life has been selfless, and you always*
> *encouraged me and gave me*
> *confidence even when I didn't have it*
> *myself. I have learned a lot about*
> *myself in this past year, and*
> *although the island respite has*
> *taught me even more about facing*
> *my fears, I realize that you were*
> *always there in the back of my mind*
> *urging me on and giving me*
> *strength. I feel across the miles your*
> *everlasting love that keeps me going*

through trials and happy times too. I
pray we can be together and meet in
some special place, just the two of
us, to catch up on life. It's time for
us to laugh and dance and sing
again. Thank you for always being
there, and if I could choose anyone
at all to be with in this lifetime, it
would most certainly be you, my
lovely mother.
All my love, Patsy.

She addressed all the letters and walked them up to the
main house for mailing, except the letter to Henry which she
would keep forever. She asked the security guard if the one for
Ren could be delivered to *The Tiki*. She thanked all the staff at
the house for their kindness. There were many hugs and a few
tears. Patsy didn't know them well, but she knew how kind they
were to her. She found Amira, who stood with her back turned
away from the others and lingering alone. Patsy saw she was
crying, and she hugged her for a few seconds more than the
others as she whispered, "I'll miss you most of all."

Amira broke down, "Please come back someday. I'll miss
you, and our private talks too."

"I promise I will, sweet girl."

When Patsy returned to the cottage, she walked around
one last time. She sat on the glider on the veranda and felt a deep
calm wash over her. She held Henry's letter over her heart.

She went into the bedroom to pack her small suitcase and
tote bag. She spotted one of Ren's headbands as she pulled the
colorful quilt up from the bed. A chill ran down her spine, but
she would not allow herself any more sadness. No matter how
badly it ended, she and Ren experienced a pure and beautiful
love affair.

312

She thought to herself how extraordinary things somehow must come to an end. "I loved you, Ren. I hope you can hear me," she said aloud as she picked up a pillow, savoring his scent that still lingered there. She was grateful for their short time together. As she packed her last bag, she came upon the two photos of Ren and carefully tucked them away along with the music and lyrics she wrote for him. Her throat ached as she prepared for a huge cry, but instead bit her lip and thought, *there is no time for tears.*

Finally, Patsy gathered all her power for tranquility. She placed a call to Mr. S and very cheerily said, "My dearest Mr. S, I cannot thank you enough for my hiatus. It has been glorious here on this enchanted island. I have a special request if I might be so bold."

She could no longer stop the tears. "I love you so much," she cried, "and want you to know that. I could never be what I am today if it hadn't been for your kindness. You saved my life, and I am beholden to you forever. I love you with the purest love."

"In many ways Dearheart, you saved me too. You gave me someone to care for and to be devoted to. You are my gift. And yes, we have a pure love between us. It was written in the stars. As for your request, what can I do for you?"

"Well…I was wondering if I might take a short detour before I make any big decisions about my future. I still must contemplate where my life is headed. The island offered healing, but there is still something that remains unfinished in my mind. Do you understand what I'm trying to say? I'm just not sure I can return quite yet or even if I want to."

"Where would you like to go?"

"I'm not sure, but I will let you know when I get to the plane," Patsy promised.

"I promised I would take care of you, and that's what I will do. I must say, you sound like you're almost back to yourself, so I'm happy to grant you your wish before you resume the hustle-bustle of the New York lifestyle."

Patsy replied without thinking, "Especially if it's not the right city." When she said those words, she realized she just made a subconscious decision. It was as if Henry was there convincing her, *you know where we would go together. You know, Patsy, you know.*

Excited now, she told Mr. S, and instantly he sounded equally pleased at her choice. "Why Dearheart, I have a friend there who finances my Off-Broadway productions. This is wonderful! I'll contact Pierre LaMeir, and he will get you set up in his exclusive hotel chain. Pierre is a fabulous friend from my pre-Broadway days. He will meet you at De Gaulle Airport. All I want is for my girl to be happy again."

Patsy choked back more tears, "I love you so, Mr. S. I feel like I'm beginning again and doing it as an independent woman. I'm not afraid anymore." Her voice cracked as she repeated, "Please know, I love you."

"And I you, Dearheart, and I you!"

Her belief made her feel free and confident about her decision. She loved Audrey Hepburn and remembered watching the movie *Sabrina* and the quotes from the film, *"Never run away from life,"* so she decided she would run toward life this time.

As the plane left the runway, Patsy looked down on the island. She then looked up to the sky and prayed for Henry. She knew he would always guide her to the right places at the right time, so, she closed her eyes and pretended he was sitting next to her.

Patsy dozed off with the memory of Henry in his tap shoes and fedora. As they were flying over Thailand, Patsy woke up queasy and nauseous. She was feeling this way off and on the past few days. She hoped it would pass as soon as she left all her negative thoughts behind. Patsy forced herself to think

314

only of the beauty and serenity that the island brought to her during the month of solitude.

She felt free, unafraid of what lay ahead. She was her own person, off to Paris and liking herself, and ready to take Henry with her. She was making her own decisions, hopefully soon making her own money, and her escape would be one of mystery and adventure.

"Merci, Henri!" she said aloud to herself.

She lived on dreams and fantasies, and they never let her down. At times, they were not exactly as she envisioned them, but there would be new ones coming soon, and she was never going to give up the delight they brought to her.

She took out the pretty card from Henry's desk she found when she sorted through his things. She carried it with her always and used it now to help guide her in the right direction. She felt his love consume her and knew she was doing the right thing for herself and her only real true love. She turned the card over and wrote the phrase in French on the back, *Paris est toujours une bonne idee.*

She was manifesting her new dreams on her new journey. Yes, Patsy was off to Paris as she recalled her childhood fantasies and all those old *Dreams Held Fast.* She was sure now of where she was going, as she repeated the quote to herself again, "Paris est toujours une bonne idee." She would indeed make all future dreams come true, and the City of Lights was the perfect place to start.

Patsy held Henry's letter close to her heart once more and whispered to the clouds, "Bonsoir, mon ami," as she drifted off to a tranquil sleep.

The End

Made in the USA
Monee, IL
16 March 2024

edc2e4fa-5c59-4d45-9224-e9f1e08baccdR02